NORA ROBERTS

"Her stories have fueled the dreams
of twenty-five million readers."
—*Entertainment Weekly*

"Roberts is indeed a word artist, painting her story
and her characters with vitality and verve."
—*Los Angeles Daily News*

"Nora Roberts just keeps
getting better and better."
—*Milwaukee Journal Sentinel*

"Roberts creates exceptional characters who...
live on in the reader's imagination and heart."
—*Publishers Weekly*

"Roberts has a warm feel for her characters
and an eye for the evocative detail."
—*Chicago Tribune*

"Roberts...is at the top of her game."
—*People* magazine

"Roberts' bestselling novels are
some of the best in the romance genre."
—*USA TODAY*

"...an author of extraordinary power."
—*Rave Reviews*

"Nora Roberts' gift...is her ability to pull the reader
into the lives of her characters—we live, love,
anguish and triumph with them."
—*Rendezvous*

"Everything Nora Roberts writes turns to gold."
—*Romantic Times*

NORA ROBERTS

#1 *New York Times* bestselling author Nora Roberts
is "a word artist, painting her story and characters with
vitality and verve," according to the *Los Angeles Daily
News.* She has published over a hundred novels, and her
work has been optioned and made into films, excerpted
in *Good Housekeeping,* and has been translated into over
twenty-five different languages and published all over the
world.

In addition to her amazing success in mainstream, Nora
has a large and loyal category romance audience, which
took her to their hearts in 1981 with her very first book,
a Harlequin Romance novel.

With over 200 million copies of her books in print
worldwide and a total of eighty-seven *New York Times*
bestsellers, twenty-two of them reaching #1, she is truly
a publishing phenomenon.

Nora Roberts

Into The Unknown

Mills & Boon™

First Published 1999
Third Australian Paperback Edition 2010
ISBN 978 1 742 55563 8

First Published 1983
Third Australian Paperback Edition 2010
ISBN 978 1 742 55563 8

INTO THE UNKNOWN © 2010 by Harlequin Books S.A.

THE PERFECT NEIGHBOR
© 1999 by Nora Roberts
Philippine Copyright 1999
Australian Copyright 1999
New Zealand Copyright 1999

UNTAMED
© 1983 by Nora Roberts
Philippine Copyright 1983
Australian Copyright 1983
New Zealand Copyright 1983

Published by
Harlequin Mills & Boon®
Level 5
15 Help Street
CHATSWOOD NSW 2067
AUSTRALIA

Printed and bound in Australia by
McPherson's Printing Group

CONTENTS

The Perfect Neighbour

THE MACGREGORS

For all my cyberpals
who've touched my heart with so many smiles

Chapter 1

"So…have you talked to him yet?"

"Hmm?" Cybil Campbell continued to work at her drawing board, diligently sectioning off the paper with the skill of long habit. "Who am I talking to?"

There was a long and gusty sigh—one that had Cybil fighting to keep her lips from twitching. She knew her first-floor neighbor Jody Myers well—and understood exactly what *him* she was referring to.

"The gorgeous Mr. Mysterious in 3B, Cyb. Come on, he moved in a week ago and hasn't said a word to anyone. But you're right across the hall. We need some details here."

"I've been pretty busy." Cybil flicked a glance up, watching Jody, with her expressive brown eyes and mop of dusky-blond hair, energetically pace around the studio. "Hardly noticed him."

Jody's first response was a snort. "Get real. You notice everything."

Jody wandered to the drawing board, hung over Cybil's

shoulder, then wrinkled her nose. Nothing much interesting about a bunch of blue lines. She liked it better when Cybil started sketching in the sections.

"He doesn't even have a name on the mailbox yet. And nobody ever sees him leave the building during the day. Not even Mrs. Wolinsky, and nobody gets by her."

"Maybe he's a vampire."

"Wow." Intrigued with the idea, Jody pursed her pretty lips. "Would that be cool or what?"

"Too cool," Cybil agreed, and continued to prep her drawing, as Jody danced around the studio and chattered like a magpie.

It never bothered Cybil to have company while she worked. The fact was, she enjoyed it. She'd never been one for isolation and quiet. It was the reason she was happy living in New York, happy to be settled into a small building with a handful of unapologetically nosy neighbors.

Such things not only satisfied her on a personal level, they were grist for her professional mill.

And of all the occupants of the old, converted warehouse, Jody Myers was Cybil's favorite. Three years earlier when Cybil had moved in, Jody had been an energetic newlywed who fervently believed that everyone should be as blissfully happy as she herself was.

Meaning, Cybil mused, married.

Now the mother of the seriously adorable eight-month-old Charlie, Jody was only more committed to her cause. And Cybil knew she herself was Jody's primary objective.

"Haven't you even run into him in the hall?" Jody wanted to know.

"Not yet." Idly, Cybil picked up a pencil, tapped it against her full-to-pouty bottom lip. Her long-lidded eyes were the green of a clear sea at twilight, and might have been exotic or sultry if they weren't almost always shimmering with humor.

"Actually, Mrs. Wolinsky's losing her touch. I have seen him leave the building during the day—which rules out vampire status."

"You have?" Instantly caught, Jody dragged a rolling stool over to the drawing board. "When? Where? How?"

"When—dawn. Where? Heading east on Grand. How? Insomnia." Getting into the spirit, Cybil swiveled on her stool. Her eyes danced with amusement. "Woke up early, and I kept thinking about the brownies left over from the party the other night."

"Atomic brownies," Jody agreed.

"Yeah, so I couldn't get back to sleep until I ate one. Since I was up anyhow, I came in here to work awhile and ended up just standing at the window. I saw him go out. You can't miss him. He must be six-four. And those shoulders…"

Both women rolled their eyes in appreciation.

"Anyway, he was carrying a gym bag and wearing black jeans and a black sweatshirt, so my deduction was he was heading to the gym to work out. You don't get those shoulders by lying around eating chips and drinking beer all day."

"Aha!" Jody speared a finger in the air. "You *are* interested."

"I'm not dead, Jody. The man is dangerously gorgeous, and you add that air of mystery along with a tight butt…" Her hands, rarely still, spread wide. "What's a girl to do but wonder?"

"Why wonder? Why don't you go knock on his door, take him some cookies or something. Welcome him to the neighborhood. Then you can find out what he does in there all day, if he's single, what he does for a living. If he's single. What—" She broke off, head lifting in alert. "That's Charlie waking up."

"I didn't hear a thing." Cybil turned her head, aiming an ear toward the doorway, listened, shrugged. "I swear, Jody, since you gave birth you have ears like a bat."

"I'm going to change him and take him for a walk. Want to come?"

"No, can't. I've got to work."

"I'll see you tonight, then. Dinner's at seven."

"Right." Cybil managed to smile as Jody dashed off to retrieve Charlie from the bedroom where she'd put him down for a nap.

Dinner at seven. With Jody's tedious and annoying cousin Frank. When, Cybil asked herself, was she going to develop a backbone and tell Jody to stop trying to fix her up?

Probably, she decided, about the same time she told Mrs. Wolinsky the same thing. And Mr. Peebles on the first floor, and her dry cleaner. What was this obsession with the people in her life to find her a man?

She was twenty-four, single and happy. Not that she didn't want a family one day. And maybe a nice house out in the burbs somewhere with a yard for the kids. And the dog. There'd have to be a dog. But that was for some time or other. She liked her life right now very much, thanks.

Resting her elbows on her drawing board, she propped her chin on her fists and gave in enough to stare out the window and allow herself to daydream. Must be spring, she mused, that was making her feel so restless and full of nervous energy.

She reconsidered going for that walk with Jody and Charlie after all but then heard her friend call out a goodbye and slam the door behind her.

So much for that.

Work, she reminded herself, and swiveled back to begin sketching in the first section of her comic strip, "Friends and Neighbors."

She had a steady and clever hand for drawing and had come by it naturally. Her mother was a successful, internationally respected artist; her father, the reclusive genius behind the long-running "Macintosh" comic strip. Together, they had given her and her siblings a love of art, a sense of the ridiculous and a solid foundation.

Cybil had known, even when she'd left the security of their home in Maine, she'd be welcomed back if New York rejected her.

But it hadn't.

For over three years now her strip had grown in popularity. She was proud of it, proud of the simplicity, warmth and humor she was able to create with everyday characters in everyday situations. She didn't attempt to mimic her father's irony or his often sharp political satires. For her, it was life that made her laugh. Being stuck in line at the movies, finding the right pair of shoes, surviving yet another blind date.

While many saw her Emily as autobiographical, Cybil saw her as a marvelous well of ideas but never recognized the reflection. After all, Emily was a statuesque blonde who had miserable luck holding a job and worse luck with men.

Cybil herself was a brunette of average height with a successful career. As for men, well, they weren't enough of a priority for her to worry about luck one way or the other.

A scowl marred her expression, narrowing her light-green eyes as she caught herself tapping her pencil rather than using it. She just couldn't seem to concentrate. She scooped her fingers through her short cap of brandy-brown hair, pursed her softly sculpted mouth and shrugged. Maybe what she needed was a short break, a snack. Perhaps a little chocolate would get the juices flowing.

She pushed back, tucking her pencil behind her ear in an

absentminded habit she'd been trying to break since childhood, left the sun-drenched studio and headed downstairs.

Her apartment was wonderfully open; aside from the
studio space, that had been the main reason she'd snapped
it up so quickly. A long service bar separated the kitchen
from the living area, leaving the lower level all one area. Tall
windows let in light and the street noises that had kept her
awake and thrilled for weeks after her arrival in the city.

She moved well, another trait inherited from her mother.
What her father called the Grandeau Grace. She had long
limbs that had been suited to the ballet lessons she'd begged
for as a child—then grown tired of. Barefoot, she padded
into the kitchen, opened the refrigerator and considered.

She could whip something interesting up, she mused.
She'd had cooking lessons, too—and hadn't become bored
with them until she'd outdistanced her instructor in crea-
tivity.

Then she heard it and sighed. The music carried through
the old walls, across the short hallway outside her door. Sad
and sexy, she mused, the quiet sob of the alto sax. Mr. Mysterious in 3B didn't play every day, but she'd come to wish he
would.

It always stirred her, those long liquid notes and the swirl
of emotion behind them.

A struggling musician? she wondered. Hoping to find his
break in New York. Brokenhearted, no doubt, she continued,
weaving one of her scenarios for him as she began to take
out ingredients. A woman behind it, of course. Some cold-
blooded redhead who'd caught him under her spell, stripped
his soul, then crushed his still-throbbing heart under her
four-inch Italian heel.

A few days before, she'd invented a different lifestyle for
him, one where he'd run away from his filthy rich and

abusive family as a boy of sixteen. Had survived on the streets by playing on street corners in New Orleans—one of her favorite cities—then had worked his way north as that same vicious family—headed by an insane uncle—scoured the country for him.

She hadn't quite worked out why they were scouring, but it wasn't really important. He was on the run and comforted only by his music.

Or he was a government agent working undercover.

An international jewel thief, hiding from a government agent.

A serial killer trolling for his next victim.

She laughed at herself, then looked down at the ingredients she'd lined up without thinking. Whatever he was, she realized with another laugh, apparently it looked like she was making him those cookies.

His name was Preston McQuinn. He wouldn't have considered himself particularly mysterious. Just private. It was that ingrained need for privacy that had plopped him down in the heart of one of the world's busiest cities.

Temporarily, he mused, as he slipped his sax back into its case. Just temporarily. In another couple of months, the rehab would be completed on his house on Connecticut's rocky coast. Some called it his fortress, and that was fine with him. A man could be blissfully alone for weeks at a time in a fortress. And no one got in unless the gates were lifted.

He started back upstairs, leaving behind the nearly empty living room. He only used it to play—the acoustics were dandy—or to work out if he didn't feel like going to the gym a couple of blocks away.

The second floor was where he lived—temporarily, he

thought again. And all he needed in this way station was a bed, a dresser, the right lighting and a desk sturdy enough to hold his laptop, monitor and the paperwork that they often generated.

He wouldn't have had a phone, but his agent had forced a cell phone on him and had pleaded with him to keep it on.

He did—unless he didn't feel like it.

Preston sat at the desk, pleased that the little turn with his sax had cleared out the cobwebs. Mandy, his agent, was busy chewing on her inch-long nails over the progress of his latest play. He could have told her to spare the enamel. It would be done when it was done, and not a minute before.

The trouble with success, he thought, was that it became its own entity. Once you did something people liked, they wanted you to do it again—only faster and bigger. Preston didn't give a damn about what people wanted. They could break down the doors of the theater to see his next play, give him another Pulitzer, toss him another Tony and bring him money by the truckloads. Or they could stay away in droves, critically bomb the work and demand their money back.

It was the work that mattered. And it only had to matter to him.

Financially, he was secure, always had been. Mandy said that was part of his problem. Without the need or desire for money to keep him hungry, he was arrogant and aloof from his audience. Then again, she also said that was what made him a genius. Because he simply didn't give a damn.

He sat in the big room, a tall, muscular man with disordered hair the color of a well-fed mink's pelt. Eyes of cool blue scanned the words already typed. His mouth was firm and unsmiling, his face narrow, rawboned and carelessly handsome.

He tuned out the street sounds that seemed to batter

against the windows day and night, and let himself slip back into the soul of the man he'd created inside the clever little computer. A man struggling desperately to survive his own desires.

The harsh sound of his buzzer made him swear as he felt himself sucked back into that empty room. He considered snarling and waiting it out, then weighed in human nature and decided the intruder would probably keep coming back until he dispatched them once and for all.

Probably the eagle-eyed old woman from the ground floor, Preston decided as he started down. She'd already tried to snag him twice when he'd headed out to the club in the evening. He was good at evading, but it was becoming a nuisance. Smarter to hit her face-on with a few rude remarks and let her huff away to gossip about him.

But when he checked the peephole, he didn't see the tidy woman with her bright bird's eyes, but a pretty brunette with hair short as a boy's and big green eyes.

From across the hall, he realized, and wondered what the hell she could want. He'd figured since she'd left him alone for nearly a week, she intended to keep right on doing so. Which made her, in his mind, the perfect neighbor.

Annoyed that she'd spoiled it, he opened the door, leaned against it. "Yeah?"

"Hi." Oh, yes, indeed, Cybil thought, he was even better when you got a good close-up look at the face. "I'm Cybil Campbell. 3A?" She offered a bright, friendly smile and gestured to her own door.

He only lifted an intriguingly winged eyebrow. "Yeah?"

A man of few words, she decided and continued to smile—though she wished his eyes would flicker away just long enough for her to crane her neck and see beyond him into the apartment. She couldn't very well try it when he was focused on her, without appearing to be prying. Which, of course, she wasn't. Really.

"I heard you playing a while ago. I work at home and sound travels."

If she was here to bitch about the noise, she was out of luck, Preston mused. He played when he felt like playing. He continued to study her coolly—the pert, slightly turned-up nose; the sensuously ripe mouth; the long narrow feet with sassily painted pink toes.

"I usually forget to turn the stereo on while I'm working," she went on cheerfully, making him notice a tiny dimple that winked off and on beside her mouth. "So it's nice to hear you play. Ralph and Sissy were into Vivaldi big-time. Which is fine, really, but monotonous when that's all you hear. They used to live in your place, Ralph and Sissy," she explained, waving a hand toward his apartment. "They moved to White Plains after Ralph had an affair with a clerk at Saks. Well, he didn't really have an affair, but he was thinking about it, and Sissy said it was move out of the city or she'd scalp him in a divorce. Mrs. Wolinsky gives them six months, but I don't know, I think they might make it. Anyway…"

She held out the pretty yellow plate with a small mountain of chocolate-chip cookies heaped on it, covered by clear pink plastic wrap. "I brought you some cookies."

He glanced down at them, giving her a very brief window of opportunity to sneak a peek around him and see his empty living room.

The poor guy couldn't even afford a couch, she thought. Then his unsmiling blue eyes flicked back to hers.

"Why?"

"Why what?"

"Why did you bring me cookies?"

"Oh, well, I was baking them. Sometimes I cook to clear out my head when I can't seem to concentrate on work. Most often it's baking that does it for me. And if I keep them all, I'll just eat them all and hate myself." The dimple kept fluttering. "Don't you like cookies?"

"I've got nothing against them."

"Well then, enjoy." She pushed them into his hands. "And welcome to the building. If you need anything I'm usually around." Again she gestured vaguely with pretty, slim-fingered hands. "And if you want to find out who's who around here, I can fill you in. I've lived here a few years now, and I know everybody."

"I won't." He stepped back and shut the door in her face.

Cybil stood where she was a moment, stunned speechless by the abrupt dismissal. She was fairly certain that she'd lived for twenty-four years without ever having had a door shut in her face, and now that she'd had the experience, she decided she didn't care for it.

She caught herself before she could pound on his door and demand her cookies back. She wouldn't sink that low, she told herself, turning sharply on her heel and marching back to her own door.

Now she knew the mysterious Mr. Mysterious was insanely attractive, built like a god and as rude as a cranky two-year-old who needed a swat on the butt and a nap. Well, that was fine, just fine. She could stay out of his way.

She didn't slam her door—figuring he'd hear it and smirk with that go-to-hell mouth of his. But when she was safely inside, she turned to the door and indulged in a juvenile exhibition of making faces, sticking out her tongue and wagging her fingers from her ears.

It made her feel marginally better.

But the bottom line was the man had her cookies, her

favorite dessert plate, her very rare animosity. And she still didn't know his name.

Preston didn't regret his actions. Not for a minute. He calculated his studied rudeness would keep his terminally pert neighbor with the turned-up nose and sexy pink toenails out of his hair during his stay across the hall. The last thing he needed was the local welcoming committee rolling up at his door, especially when it was led by a bubbly motormouth brunette with eyes like a fairy.

Damn it, in New York, people were supposed to ignore their neighbors. He was pretty sure it was a city ordinance, and if not, it should be.

Just his luck, he thought, that she was single—he had no doubt that if she'd had a husband she'd have poured out all his virtues and delights. That she worked at home and would therefore be easy to trip over whenever he headed out was just another black mark.

And that she made, hands-down, the best chocolate-chip cookies in the known universe was close to unforgivable.

He'd managed to ignore them while he worked. Preston McQuinn could ignore a nuclear holocaust if the words were pumping. But when he surfaced, he started to think about them lying in his kitchen on their chirpy yellow plate.

He thought about them while he showered, while he dressed, while he eased out the kinks brought on by hours sitting in one spot with posture his third-grade teacher, Sister Mary Joseph, had termed deplorable.

So when he went down for what he considered a well-earned beer, he eyed the plate on the counter. He'd popped the top, took a thoughtful drink. So what if he had a couple? he mused. Tossing them in the trash wasn't necessary—he'd given perky Cybil the heave-ho.

She was going to want her party plate back, he imagined. He might as well sample the wares before he dumped the plate outside her door.

So he ate one. Grunted in approval. Ate a second and blew out a breath of pure appreciation.

And when he'd consumed nearly two dozen, he cursed.

Like a damn drug, he thought, feeling slightly ill and definitely sluggish. He stared at the near-empty plate with a combination of self-disgust and greed. With what scraps of willpower he had left, he dumped the remaining cookies in a plastic bowl, then crossed the room to get his sax.

He was going to walk around the block a few times before he headed to the club.

When he opened the door he heard her stomping up the stairs. Wincing, he drew back, leaving his door open only a crack. He could hear that mile-a-minute voice of hers going, which had him lifting a brow when he saw she was alone.

"Never again," she muttered. "I don't care if she sticks bamboo shoots under my nails, holds a hot poker to my eye. I will never, ever, go through that torture again in this lifetime. That's it. Over, done."

She'd changed her clothes, Preston noted, and was wearing snug black pants with a tailored black blazer, offsetting them with a shirt the color of ripe strawberries and long dangles at her ears.

She kept talking to herself as she opened a purse the size of a postage stamp. "Life's too short to be bored witless for two precious hours of it. She will not do this to me again. I know how to say no. I just have to practice, that's all. Where the bloody hell are my keys?"

The sound of the door opening behind her made her jump, spin around. Preston noted that the dangles in her ears didn't match and wondered if it was a fashion statement or carelessness. Since she apparently couldn't find her keys in a bag smaller than the palm of his hand, he opted for the latter.

She looked flushed, flustered and fresh. And smelled even better than her cookies. And because he noticed, she only irritated him more.

"Hold on," he said simply, then turned back into his apartment to get her plate.

Cybil had no intention of holding on, and finally found her key where it had decided to hide in the narrow inner pocket of the bag—where she'd put it so she'd know just where it was when she needed it.

But he beat her. He strode out of his apartment, letting the door slam at his back. He carried his saxophone case in one hand and her plate in the other.

"Here." He wasn't going to ask her what had put that sulky look on her sea-fairy face. He had no doubt that she'd tell him, for the next half hour.

"You're welcome," she snapped, snatching it from him. Because her head was throbbing after two hours of listening to Jody's cousin Frank's monotone account of the vagaries of the stock market, she decided she'd give Mr. Mysterious a piece of her mind while the mood was on her.

"Look, buddy, you don't want to be friends, that's just fine. I don't need any more friends," she said, swinging the plate for emphasis. "I have so many now I can't take another on until one moves out of the country. But there's no excuse for behaving like a snot, either. All I did was introduce myself and give you some damn cookies."

His lips wanted to twitch, but he controlled it. "Damn good cookies," he said before he could stop himself, then immediately regretted it as the temper in her eyes switched to amusement.

"Oh, really?"

"Yeah." He walked away, leaving her reluctantly intrigued and completely baffled.

So she followed impulse, one of her favorite hobbies. After unlocking her door quickly, she stuck the plate on the table inside, locked up again, then, trying to keep her footsteps muffled, set off to follow him.

It would be a great strip gag for Emily, she thought, and handled right could play out for weeks.

Of course she'd have to make Emily wild about the guy, Cybil decided as she tried to tiptoe and race down the steps at the same time. It wouldn't just be normal, perfectly acceptable curiosity but dreamy-eyed obsession.

Breathless with the excitement of the chase, her mind whirling with possibilities, Cybil rushed out the front door, looked quickly right and left.

He was already halfway down the block. Long stride, she thought, and, grinning, started after him.

Emily, of course, would be sort of skulking, then jumping behind lampposts; or flattening herself against walls in case he turned around and—

Nearly yelping, Cybil jumped behind a lamppost as the object of the chase sent an absent glance over his shoulder. With a hand over her heart, Cybil dared a peek and watched him turn the corner.

Annoyed that she'd worn heels instead of flats to dinner, she sucked in a breath and made the dash to the corner.

He walked for twenty minutes, until her feet were screaming and her initial rush of excitement was draining fast. Did the man just wander the streets with his saxophone every night? she wondered.

Maybe he wasn't just rude. Maybe he was crazy. He'd been recently released from the asylum—that's why he didn't know how to relate to people in the normal way.

His filthy rich and abusive family had caught him, locked him up so that he couldn't claim his rightful inheritance from his beloved grandmother—who had died under suspicious circumstances and had left him her entire fortune. And all those years of being imprisoned by the corrupt psychiatrist had warped his mind.

Yes, that would be exactly what Emily would cook up in her head—and she'd be certain her tender care, her unqualified love, would cure him. Then all the friends and neighbors would try to talk her out of it—even as she dragged them into her schemes.

And before it was over Mr. Mysterious would—

She pulled up short as he walked into a small, dingy club called Delta's.

Finally, she thought, and skimmed back her hair. Now all she had to do was slip inside, find a dark corner and see what happened next.

Chapter 2

The place smelled of whiskey and smoke. Not really offen-
sive, Cybil thought. More…atmospheric. It was dimly lit,
with a pale-blue light illuminating a stingy stage. Round tables
hardly bigger than pie plates were crammed together, and
though most of them were occupied, the noise level was
muted.

She decided people talked in whispers in such places,
planning liaisons, affairs, or enjoying those already made.

At a thick wooden bar on the side wall, patrons loitered
on stools and huddled over their drinks as if protecting the
contents from invaders.

It was, she decided, the kind of club that belonged in a
black-and-white movie from the forties. The kind where
the heroine wore long, slinky dresses, dark-red lipstick
with a sweep of her platinum hair falling sulkily over her
left eye as she stood on the stage under a single key light,
torching her way through songs about the men who'd done
her wrong.

And while she did, the man who wanted her, and had done her wrong, brooded into his whiskey with his world-weary eyes shadowed by the brim of his fedora.

In other words, she thought with a smile, it was perfect.

Hoping to go unnoticed, she scooted along the rear wall and found a table and, sitting, watched him through a haze of smoke and whiskey fumes.

He wore black. Jeans with a T-shirt tucked into the waistband. He'd already taken off the leather jacket he'd put on against the evening chill. The woman he was speaking with was gorgeous, black and outfitted in a hot red jumpsuit that hugged every curvaceous inch. She had to be six feet tall, Cybil mused, and when she threw back her beautiful head and laughed, the full rich sound rocked through the room.

For the first time Cybil saw him smile. No, not just smile, she thought, transfixed by the lightning transformation of that stern and handsome face. That hot punch of grin, the hammer-blow power of it, couldn't be called anything as tame as a smile.

It was full of fun and affection and sly humor. It made her rest her chin on her fisted hands and grin in response.

She imagined he and the beautiful Amazon were lovers, was certain of it when the woman grabbed his face in her hands and kissed him lavishly. Of course, Cybil thought, a man like that—with all those secrets and heartaches—would have an exotic lover, and they would meet in a dim, smoky bar where the music was dreamy and sad.

Finding it wonderfully romantic, she sighed.

Onstage, Delta gave Preston's cheeks an affectionate pinch. "So now you got women following you, sugar lips?"

"She's a lunatic."

"You want me to bounce her out?"

"No." He didn't glance back but could feel those big green eyes on him. "I'm pretty sure she's a harmless lunatic."

Delta's tawny eyes glittered with amusement. "Then I'll just check her out. Woman starts stalking my sugar lips, I gotta see what's she made of, right, André?"

The skinny black man at the piano stopped noodling keys long enough to smile up at her out of a face as battered and worn as the old spinet he played. "That you do, Delta. Don't hurt her, now—she's just a little thing. You ready to blow?" he asked Preston.

"You start. I'll catch up."

As Delta glided offstage, André's long, narrow fingers began to make magic. Preston let the mood of it slide into him; then, closing his eyes, let the music come.

It took him away. It cleared his head of the words and the people and the scenes that often crowded his head. When he played like this, there was nothing but the music, and the aching pleasure of making it.

He'd once told Delta it was like sex. It dragged something out of you, put something back. And when it was over, it was always too soon.

In the back, Cybil drifted into it, slid down into those low, bluesy notes, rose up with the sudden wailing sobs. It was different, she thought, watching him play than just hearing it through the walls. Watching him, there was more power, more heartbreak, more of that subtle sexual pull.

It was music to weep by. To make love to. To dream on.

It caught her, focused her on the stage so she didn't see Delta moving toward her table.

"What's your pleasure, little sister?"

"Hmm." Distracted, Cybil glanced up, smiled vaguely. "It's wonderful. The music. It makes my heart hurt."

Delta lifted a brow. The girl had a bright and pretty face,

she mused. Didn't look much like a lunatic with that tipped nose and those long-lidded eyes. "You drinking or just taking up space?"

"Oh." Of course, Cybil realized, a place like this needed to sell drinks. "It's whiskey music," she said with another smile. "I'll have a whiskey."

Delta's brow only arched higher. "You don't look old enough to be ordering whiskey, little sister."

Cybil didn't bother to sigh. It was an opinion she heard constantly. She flipped open her purse, pulled out her driver's license.

Delta took it, studied it. "All right, Cybil Angela Campbell, I'll get your whiskey."

"Thanks." Content, Cybil rested her chin on her fists again and just listened. It surprised her when Delta came back not with one glass of whiskey but two, then folded that glamorous body into the chair next to her.

"So, what are you doing in a place like this, young Cybil? You got a Rainbow Room face."

Cybil opened her mouth, then realized she could hardly say she'd followed her mysterious neighbor all over Soho. "I don't live far from here. I suppose I just followed an impulse." She lifted the whiskey, gestured with it to the stage. "I'm glad I did," she said, then drank.

Delta's lips pursed. The girl might look like a varsity cheerleader, but she drank her whiskey like a man. "You go wandering around the streets alone at night, somebody's going to eat you up, little sister."

Cybil's eyes gleamed over the rim of her glass. "Oh, I don't think so. Big sister."

Considering, Delta nodded. "Maybe, maybe not. Delta Pardue." She touched her glass to Cybil's. "This is my place."

"I like your place, Delta."

"Maybe, maybe not." Delta let loose that rich laugh again. "But you sure like my man there. You've had your pretty cat's-eyes on him since you came in."

Thoughtfully, Cybil swirled her whiskey while she debated how to play it. Though she had no doubt she could handle herself on the streets—or anywhere else, for that matter—Delta outweighed her by at least thirty pounds. And as she'd said, it was her place. Her man. No point in making a potential new friend want to rip out her lungs at their first meeting.

"He's very attractive," Cybil said casually. "It's hard not to look. So I'll keep looking if it's all the same to you. I doubt his eyes are going to wander when he's got someone like you in focus."

Delta's teeth flashed in a brilliant grin. "Maybe you can take care of yourself after all. You're a smart girl, aren't you?"

Cybil chuckled into her whiskey. "Oh, yeah. I am. And I do like your place. I like it a lot. How long have you owned it, Delta?"

"This? Two years here."

"And before? It's New Orleans I'm hearing in your voice, isn't it?"

Delta inclined her head. "You got good ears."

"I do, actually, for dialects, but yours is one I couldn't miss. I have family in New Orleans. My mother grew up there."

"I don't know any Campbells—what's your mama's maiden name?"

"Grandeau."

Delta eased back. "I know Grandeaus, many Grandeaus. Are you kin to Miss Adelaide?"

"Great-aunt."

"Grand lady."

Cybil snorted, drank. "Stuffy, irritating and cold as winter. The twins and I—my brother and sister—used to think she was a witch of the wicked sort."

"She has power, but it only comes from money and a name. Grandeau, eh? Who's your mama?"

"Genviève Grandeau Campbell, the artist."

"Miss Gennie." Delta set her whiskey down so that she could rear back and thump a hand to her heart as she rocked with laughter. "Miss Gennie's little girl comes into my place. Oh, the world is a wonderful thing."

"You know my mother?"

"My mama cleaned house for your *grandmère,* little sister."

"Mazie? You're Mazie's daughter? Oh." Instantly bonded, Cybil grabbed Delta's hand. "My mother talked about Mazie all the time. We visited her once when I was a little girl. She gave us beignets, fresh and wonderful. We sat on the front porch and had lemonade, and my father did a sketch of her."

"She put it in her parlor and was very proud. I was in the city when your family came. I was working. My mama, she talked of that visit for weeks after. She had a place deep in her heart for Miss Gennie."

"Wait until I tell them I met you. How is your mother, Delta?"

"She died last year."

"Oh." Cybil laid her other hand over Delta's, cupping it warmly. "I'm so sorry."

"She lived a good life, died sleeping, so died a good death. Your mama and your daddy, they came to the funeral. They sat in the church. They stood at the grave. You come from good people, young Cybil."

"Yes, I do. So do you."

* * *

Preston didn't know how to figure it. There was Delta, a woman he considered the most sane of anyone he knew, huddled together with the pretty crazy woman, apparently already the fastest of friends. Sharing whiskey, laughs. Holding hands the way women do.

For more than an hour they sat together in the back of the room. Now and then, Cybil would begin what could only have been one of her chattering monologues, her hands gesturing, her face mobile. Delta would lean back and laugh, or lean forward, shaking her head in amazement.

"Look at that, André." Preston leaned on the piano.

André wiggled his fingers loose, then lit a cigarette. "Like a couple of hens in the coop. That's a pretty girl there, my man. Got sparkle to her."

"I hate sparkle," Preston muttered, and no longer in the mood to play, tucked his sax in the case. "Catch you next time."

"I'll be here."

He thought he should just walk out, but he was just a little irritated to have his good friend getting chummy with his lunatic. Besides, it would give him some satisfaction to let his nosy neighbor know he was onto her.

But when he stopped by the table, Cybil only glanced up and smiled at him. "Hi. Aren't you going to play anymore? It was wonderful."

"You followed me."

"I know. It was rude. But I'm so glad I did. I loved listening, and I might never have met Delta otherwise. We were just—"

"Don't do it again," he said shortly, and stalked to the door.

"Ooooh, he's plenty pissed off," Delta said with a chuckle. "Got that ice in his eyes, chills down to bone."

"I should apologize," Cybil said as she bolted to her feet. "I don't want him angry with you."

"Me? He's—"

"I'll come back soon." She dropped a kiss on Delta's cheek, making the woman blink in surprise. "Don't worry, I'll smooth things over."

When she dashed out, Delta simply stared after her, then let out one of her long laughs. "Little sister, you got no idea what you're in for. Then again," she mused, "neither does sugar lips."

Outside, Cybil dashed down the sidewalk. "Hey!" she shouted at his retreating back, then cursed herself for not having the sense to ask Delta what the man's name was. "Hey!" Risking a twisted ankle, she switched from jog to run and managed to catch up.

"I'm sorry," she began, tugging on the sleeve of his jacket. "Really. It's completely my fault."

"Who said it wasn't?"

"I shouldn't have followed you. It was impulse. I have such a problem resisting impulse—always have—and I was irritated because of that idiot Frank and...well, that doesn't matter. I only wanted to—could you slow down a little?"

"No."

Cybil rolled her eyes. "All right, all right, you wish I'd get run over by a truck, but there's no need to be upset with Delta. We just started talking and we found out that her mother used to work for my grandmother, and she—Delta, I mean—knows my parents and some of my Grandeau cousins, so we hit it off."

He did stop now, to simply stare at her. "Of all the gin joints in all the towns in all the world," he muttered, and made her laugh.

"I had to follow you into that one and make pals with your girlfriend. Sorry."

"My girlfriend? Delta?"

And to Cybil's amazement, the man could laugh. Really laugh, with a wonderful baritone rumble that melted all the ice and made her sigh in delight.

"Does Delta look like anyone's *girl*friend? Man, you are from Mars."

"It's just an expression. I didn't want to be presumptive and call her your lover."

His eyes were still warm with amusement as he stared down at her. "That's a happy thought, kid, but the guy I was just jamming with happens to be her husband, and a friend of mine."

"The skinny man at the piano? Really?" Pursing her lips, Cybil thought about it, found it charming and romantic. "Isn't that lovely?"

Preston only shook his head and started walking again.

"What I meant was," Cybil continued—he'd just known she couldn't possibly be finished—as she hurried along beside him, "I'm sure she came back to check me out, you know? To make sure I wasn't going to hassle you, and then, well, one thing led to another. I don't want you to be annoyed with her."

"I'm not annoyed with her. You, on the other hand, have gone so far beyond being an annoyance I can't find the word."

Her mouth fell into a pout. "Well, I'm sorry, and I'll certainly make it a point to leave you alone, since that's apparently what you like best."

Her perky nose went up in the air, and she sailed across the street in the opposite direction from their building.

Preston stood there a moment, watching her scissor those very pretty legs down the opposite sidewalk. Then, with a shrug, he turned the corner, telling himself he was glad to be rid of her. It wasn't his concern if she wandered around alone at night. She wouldn't have been out walking around on those silly, skinny heels if she hadn't followed him in the first place.

He wasn't going to worry about it.

And swearing, he turned around, headed back. He was going to make sure she got home, that was all. Back inside, where he could wash any responsibility for her welfare off his hands and forget her.

He was still the best part of a crosstown block away when he saw it happen. The man slid out of the shadows, made his grab and had Cybil letting out an ear-piercing scream as she struggled. Preston dumped his case, sprinted forward with his fists already clenched.

Then skidded to an amazed halt as Cybil not only broke free but doubled her attacker over with a hard knee to the groin, knocked him flat with a perfect uppercut.

"I only had ten lousy dollars in here. Ten lousy dollars, you jerk!" She was shouting by the time Preston gathered his wits and rushed up beside her. "If you'd needed money, why didn't you just ask!"

"You hurt?"

"Yes, damn it. And it's your fault. I wouldn't have hit him so hard if I hadn't been mad at you."

Noting that she was nursing the knuckles on her right hand, Preston grabbed it by the wrist. "Let's see. Wiggle your fingers."

"Go away."

"Come on, wiggle."

"Hey!" The shout came from a woman hanging out an open window across the street. "You want I should call the cops?"

"Yes." Cybil snapped the word back as she wiggled her fingers and Preston probed, then blew out a steadying breath. "Yes, please. Thanks."

"Polite little victim, aren't you?" Preston muttered. "Nothing's broken. You might want to get it x-rayed anyway."

"Thanks so much, Dr. Doom." She jerked a hand away, kept her chin lifted and gestured with her uninjured hand in what Preston thought of as a grandly regal gesture. "You can go. I'm just fine."

As the man sprawled on the sidewalk began to moan and stir, Preston set a foot on his throat. "I think I'll just stick around. Why don't you go get my sax for me. I dropped it back there when I still believed the Big Bad Wolf ate Red Riding Hood."

She nearly told him to go get it himself, then decided if she had to hit the jerk on the sidewalk again, she'd hurt herself as much as him. With stiff dignity, she walked down the block, picked up the case and carried it back.

"Thank you," she said.

"For what?"

"For the thought."

"Don't mention it." Preston added a bit more weight when the man on the ground began to curse.

When the squad car pulled up ten minutes later, he stepped back. Cybil wasn't having any trouble giving the cops the details, and Preston harbored the hope that he could just slide away and stay out of it. The hope died as one of the uniforms turned to him.

"Did you see what happened here?"

Preston sighed. "Yeah."

And that was why it was nearly 2 a.m. before he trooped up the steps with Cybil toward their respective apartments. He still had the unappealing taste of police station coffee in his mouth and a low-grade headache on the brew.

"It was kind of exciting, wasn't it? All those cops and bad guys. It was hard to tell one from the other in the detective bureau. Well, you could because the detectives have to wear ties. I wonder why. It was nice of them to show me around. You should have come. The interrogation rooms look just the way you imagine they would. Dark and creepy."

He was certain she had to be the only person on the planet who could find a sunny side to being mugged.

"I'm wired," she announced. "Aren't you wired? Want some cookies? I still have plenty."

He nearly ignored her as he dug out his keys, then his stomach reminded him he hadn't eaten anything for the past eight hours. And her cookies were a minor miracle.

"Maybe."

"Great." She unlocked her door, left it open, stepping out of her shoes as she walked to the kitchen. "You can come in," she called out. "I'll put them on a plate for you so you can take them back and eat them in your own den, but there's no point in waiting in the hall."

He stepped in, leaving the door open behind him. He should have known her place would be bright and cheerful, full of cute and classy little accents. With his hands in his pockets, he wandered around, tuning out her bubbling chatter while she transferred cookies from a canister in the shape of a manically grinning cow to the same bright-yellow plate she'd used before.

"You talk too much."

"I know." She skimmed a hand over her spiky bangs. "Especially when I'm nervous or wired up."

"Are you ever otherwise?"

"Now and then."

He noted a scatter of framed photos, several pairs of earrings, another shoe, a romance novel and the scent of apple blossoms. Each suited her, he thought, as perfectly as the next. Then he paused in front of a framed copy of a comic strip on the wall.

"Friends and Neighbors," he mused, then studied the signature under the last section. It read simply, Cybil. "This you?"

She glanced over. "Yes. That's my strip. I don't imagine you spend much time reading the comics, do you?"

Knowing a dig when he heard one, he looked back over his shoulder. It must have been the late hour, he decided, after a long day that made her look so fresh and pretty and appealing. "Grant Campbell—'Macintosh'—that your old man?"

"He's not old, but yes, he's my father."

The Campbells, Preston mused, meant the MacGregors. And wasn't that a coincidence? He moved over to stand on the opposite side of the counter and help himself to the cookies she was arranging in a stylish circular pattern.

"I like the edge to his work."

"I'm sure he'll appreciate that." Because he was reaching for another cookie, Cybil smiled. "Want some milk?"

"No. Got a beer?"

"With cookies?" She grimaced but turned to her refrigerator. Preston had a chance to see it was well stocked as she bent down—which gave him a chance to appreciate just what snug black slacks could do for a perky woman's excellent butt—and retrieved a bottle of Beck's Dark.

"This do? It's what Chuck likes."

"Chuck has good taste. Boyfriend?"

She smirked, getting out a pilsner glass before he could tell her he'd just take the bottle. "I suppose that indicates that I'm the type to have *boy*friends, but no. He's Jody's husband. Jody and Chuck Myers, just below you in 2B. I was out to dinner with them tonight, and Jody's excessively boring cousin Frank."

"Is that what you were muttering about when you came home?"

"Was I muttering?" She frowned, then leaned on the counter and ate one of his cookies. Muttering was another habit she kept trying to break. "Probably. It's the third time Jody's roped me into a date with Frank. He's a stockbroker. Thirty-five, single, handsome if you like that lantern-jawed, chiseled-brow sort. He drives a BMW coupe, has an apartment on the Upper East Side, a summer place in the Hamptons, wears Armani suits, enjoys French-provincial cuisine and has perfect teeth."

Amused despite himself, Preston washed down cookies with cold beer. "So why aren't you married and looking for a nice split-level in Westchester?"

"Ah, you've just voiced my friend Jody's dream. And I'll tell you why." She wagged a cookie, then bit in. "One, I don't want to get married or move to Westchester. Two, and really more to the point, I would rather be strapped to an anthill than strapped to Frank."

"What's wrong with him?"

"He bores me," she said, then winced. "That's so unkind."

"Why? Sounds honest to me."

"It is honest." She picked up another cookie, ate it with only a little guilt. "He's really a very nice man, but I don't think he's read a book in the last five years or seen a movie. A few selected films, perhaps, but not a movie. Then he critiques them."

"I don't even know him, and I'm already bored."

That made her laugh and reach for another cookie. "He's been known to check out his grooming in the back of his spoon at the dinner table—just to make sure he's still perfect—and he can spend the rest of his life, and yours, talking about annuities and stock futures. And all that aside, he kisses like a fish."

"Really." He forgot he'd wanted to grab a handful of cookies and get out. "And how is that exactly?"

"You know." She made an *O* with her mouth, then laughed. "You can imagine how a fish kisses, which I suppose they don't, but if they did. I nearly escaped without having the experience tonight, then Jody got in the way."

"And it doesn't occur to you to say no?"

"Of course it occurs to me." Her grin was quick and completely self-deprecating. "I just can't seem to get it out in time. Jody loves me, and for reasons that continue to elude me, she loves Frank. She's sure we'd make a wonderful couple. You know how it is when someone you care about puts that kind of benign pressure on you."

"No. I don't."

She tilted her head. Remembering his empty living room. No furniture, and now no family. "That's too bad. As inconvenient as it may be from time to time, I wouldn't trade it for anything."

"How's the hand?" he asked when he saw her rubbing her knuckles.

"Oh. A little sore still. It'll probably give me some trouble working tomorrow. But I should be able to turn the experience into a good strip."

"I can't see Emily laying a mugger out on his ass."

Cybil's face glowed on a grin. "You *do* read it."

"Now and again." She was entirely too pretty, he thought suddenly. Entirely too bright. And it was abruptly too tempting to find out if she tasted the same way.

That's what happened, Preston supposed, when you hung around eating homemade cookies in the middle of the night with a woman who made her living looking at the light side of life.

"You don't have your father's edge or your mother's artistic genius, but you have a nice little talent for the absurd."

She let out a half laugh. "Well, thank you so much for that unsolicited critique."

"No problem." He picked up the plate. "Thanks for the cookies."

She narrowed her eyes as he headed for the door. Well, he was going to see just how much of a talent she had for the absurd in some upcoming strips, she decided.

"Hey."

He paused, glanced back. "Hey, what?"

"You got a name, apartment 3B?"

"Yeah, I've got a name, 3A. It's McQuinn." He balanced his beer and his plate, and shut the door between them.

Chapter 3

When scenes and people filled her head, Cybil could work until her fingers cramped and refused to hold pencil or brush.

She spent the next day fueled on cookies and the diet soft drinks she liked to pretend balanced out the cookie calories. On paper, section by section, Emily and her friend Cari—who over the last couple of years had taken on several Jody-like attributes—plotted and planned on how to discover the secrets of the Mr. Mysterious.

She was going to call him "Quinn," but not for several installments.

For three days she rarely left her drawing board. Jody had a key, so it wasn't necessary to run down and let her in every time she dropped over for a visit. And Jody was always happy enough to dash down to open the door for Mrs. Wolinsky or one of the other neighbors who stopped by.

At one point on the third evening, enough people were in the apartment to have put together a small, informal party while Cybil remained coloring in her big Sunday strip.

Someone had turned on the stereo. Music blared, but it didn't distract her. Laughter and conversation rose up the stairs, and there was a shout of greeting as someone else dropped in.

She smelled popcorn, and wondered idly if anyone would bring her some.

Leaning back, she studied her work. No, she didn't have her father's edge, she acknowledged, or her mother's genius. But all in all, she did indeed have a "nice little talent."

She had a quick and clever hand at drawing. She could paint—quite well, really, she mused—if the mood was right. The strip gave her an arena for her own brand of social commentary.

Perhaps she didn't dig into sore spots or turn a sarcastic pencil toward politics, but her work made people laugh. It gave them company in the morning over their hurried cup of coffee or along with a lazy Sunday breakfast.

More than anything, she thought as she signed her name, it made her happy.

If McQuinn in 3B thought his careless comment insulted her, he was wrong. She was more than content with her nice little talent.

Flushed with the success of three days' intense work, she picked up the phone as it rang and all but sang into it. "Hello?"

"Well, well, there's a cheery lass."

"Grandpa!" Cybil leaned back in her chair and stretched cramped muscles. "Yes, I'm a cheery lass, and there's no one I'd rather talk to than you."

Technically, Daniel MacGregor wasn't her grandfather, but that had never stopped either of them from thinking of him as such. Love ignored technicalities.

"Is that so? Then why haven't you called me or your grandmother? You know how she worries about you down there in that big city all alone."

"Alone?" Amused, she held out the phone so the sounds of the party downstairs would travel through the receiver to Hyannis Port. "It doesn't feel as if I'm ever alone."

"You've got the place full of people again?"

"So it seems. How are you? How is everyone? Tell me everything."

She settled back, happy to chat with him about family, her aunts and uncles, her cousins, the babies.

She listened and laughed, added her own comments, and was pleased when he told her there was a family gathering in the works for the summer.

"Wonderful. I can't wait to see everyone again. It's been too long since Ian and Naomi's wedding last fall. I miss you."

"Well then, why do you have to wait until summer? We're right here, after all."

"Maybe I'll surprise you."

"I called with one for you. I'll wager you haven't heard as yet that little Naomi's expecting. We'll have another bairn under the Christmas tree this year."

"Oh, Grandpa, that's wonderful. I'll call them tonight. And with Darcy and Mac ready to have theirs any day, we'll have lots of babies to cuddle this Christmas."

"For a young woman so fond of babes, you ought to be busy making your own."

It was an old theme and made her grin. "But my cousins are doing such a fine job of it."

"Hah! That they are, but that doesn't mean you can shirk your duty, little girl. You may be a Campbell by birth, but you've got some MacGregor in your heart."

"Well, I could always give in and marry Frank."

"The one with the fish mouth?"

"No, he just kisses like a fish. Then again…yeah, the one with the fish mouth. We could make you some guppies."

"Bah. You need a man, not a trout in an Italian suit. A man with more on his mind than dollars and cents, with an understanding of art, with enough of a serious nature to keep you out of trouble."

"I keep myself out of trouble," she reminded him, but decided it was best not to mention the mugging incident. "Besides, Grandma won't let me have you, so I'll just have to pine away here in the big, bad city."

He let out a bark of a laugh. "All the men in that city, you ought to be able to find one to suit you. You get out and about, don't you? You're not sitting there all day writing your funny papers."

"Just lately, but I hit a hot streak here and needed to run with it. There's this new guy across the hall. Kind of surly and standoffish. No, actually, let's just say it straight. He's rude and abrupt. I think he's out of work, except he plays the sax sometimes in this little club a few blocks from here. He's just the perfect new neighbor for Emily."

"Is that so?"

"He stays inside his apartment all day, doesn't talk to anyone. His name's McQuinn."

"If he doesn't talk to anyone, how do you know his name?"

"Grandpa." She allowed herself a smug smile. "Have you ever known me to fail getting anyone to talk to me if I put my mind to it? Not that he's the chatty sort even when you prime his pump with cookies, but I wheedled his name out of him."

"And how does he look to you, little girl?"

"He looks good, very, very good. He's going to drive Emily crazy."

"Is he, now?" Daniel said, and laughed with delight.

When he'd gotten all that he needed to know out of his

honorary granddaughter, Daniel made his next call. He hummed to himself, examined his nails, buffed them on his shirt, then grinned fiercely when Preston answered the phone with an impatient, "Yeah, what?"

"Ah, you've such a sweet nature to you, McQuinn. It warms my heart."

"Mr. MacGregor." There was no mistaking that booming Scottish burr. In an abrupt shift of mood, Preston smiled warmly and pushed away from his computer.

"Right you are. And how are you settling in to the apartment there?"

"Well enough. I have to thank you again for letting me use it while my house is a construction zone. I'd never have been able to work with all those people around." He scowled at the wall as the noise from across the hall battered against it. "Not that it's much better here tonight. My neighbor seems to be celebrating something."

"Cybil? She's my granddaughter, you know. Sociable child."

"You're telling me. I didn't realize she was your granddaughter."

"Well, in a roundabout way. You ought to shake yourself loose, boy, and join the party."

"No, thanks." He'd rather drink drain cleaner. "I think half the population of Soho's crammed in there. This building of yours, Mr. MacGregor, is full of people who'd rather talk than eat. Your granddaughter appears to be the leader."

"Friendly girl. It comforts me to know you're across the hall for a bit. You're a sensible sort, McQuinn. I don't mind imposing by asking you to keep an eye on her. She can be naïve, if you get my meaning. I worry about her."

Preston had the image of her flattening a mugger with the speed and precision of a lightweight boxer and smiled to himself. "I wouldn't worry."

"Well, I won't knowing you're close by. Pretty young thing like Cybil…she is a pretty thing, isn't she?"

"Cute as a button."

"Smart, too. And responsible, for all it seems like she's fluttering through life. You can't be a dim-witted flutterer and produce a popular comic strip day after day, now can you? Got to be creative, artistic and practical enough to meet deadlines. But you know about that sort of business, don't you? Writing plays isn't an easy business."

"No." Preston rubbed his eyes, gritty from fighting with work that refused to run smooth. "It's not."

"But you've a gift, McQuinn, a rare one. I admire that."

"It's been feeling like a curse lately. But I appreciate it."

"You should get yourself out, take your mind off it. Kiss a pretty girl. Not that I know much about writing—though I've two grandchildren who make their living from it, and damn well, too. You should make the most of being right there in the city before you take yourself back and lock the doors on your house."

"Maybe I will."

"Oh, and McQuinn, you'll do me the favor of not mentioning to Cybil that I asked you to mind her a bit? She'd get huffy over it. But her grandmother worries herself sick over that girl."

"She won't hear it from me," Preston promised.

Since the noise was going to drive him crazy, Preston took himself off. He played at the club but found it didn't quite get him past the thoughts that jangled in his brain.

It was too easy to imagine Cybil sitting at the table in the back, her chin on her fists, her lips curved, her eyes dreamy.

She'd invaded one of his more well-guarded vaults, and he resented it bitterly.

Delta's was one of his escapes. There were times he'd

drive into the city from Connecticut just to slip onto the stage with André and play until all the tension of the day dissolved into, then out of, the music.

He could drive home again or, if the hour grew too late, just drop down on the cot in Delta's back room and sleep until morning.

No one bothered him at the club or expected more than he wanted to give.

But now that Cybil had been here, he'd started to look at that back table, and wondered if she'd slip in again. To watch him with those big green eyes.

"My man," André said as he stopped to take a long drink from the water glass he kept on his beloved piano. "You ain't just playing the blues tonight. You got 'em."

"Yeah. Looks like."

"Usually a woman tangled up there when a man's got that look about him."

Preston shook his head, scowling as he lifted the sax to his lips. "No. No woman. It's work."

André merely pursed his lips as Preston sent out music that throbbed like a pulse. "You say so, brother. If you say so."

He got home at three, prepared to beat on Cybil's door and demand quiet. It was a letdown to arrive and discover the party was over. There wasn't a sound coming from her apartment.

He let himself in, locked up, then told himself he'd take advantage of the peace. After brewing a pot of coffee strong enough to dance on, he settled back at his machine, back into his play, back into the minds of characters who were destroying their lives because they couldn't reach their own hearts.

The sun was up when he stopped, when the sudden rush

of energy that had flooded him drained out again. He decided it was the first solid work he'd managed in nearly a week, and celebrated by falling facedown and fully dressed into bed.

And there he dreamed.

Of a pretty face framed by a fringe of glossy brown hair, offset by long-lidded and enormous eyes the color of willow fronds. Of a voice that bubbled like a brook.

Why does everything have to be so serious? she asked him, laughing as she slid her arms up his chest, linked them around his neck.

Because life's a serious business.

That's only one-half of one of the coins. There are lots and lots of coins. Aren't you going to dance with me?

He already was. They were in Delta's, and though it was empty, the music was playing, low and sultry.

I'm not going to keep my eye on you. I can't afford it.

But you already are.

The top of her head reached his chin. When she tilted her head back, flicked her tongue lazily over his jaw, he felt the rush of his own blood.

That's not all you want to keep on me, is it?

I don't want you.

There was that laugh, light as air, frothy as champagne. *What's the point of lying,* she asked him, *in your own dreams? You can do anything you want to me in dreams. It won't matter.*

I don't want you, he said again, even as he pulled her to the floor.

He awoke, sweating, tangled in sheets, appalled, amazed, and finally when his head started to clear, amused.

The woman was a menace, he decided, and the only thing that had reflected any sort of reality in the painfully erotic dream was that he didn't want her.

He rubbed his hands over his face, glanced at the watch still on his wrist. Since it was after four in the afternoon, he judged he'd gotten the first decent eight hours of sleep he'd had in nearly a week. So what if it was at the wrong end of the time scale?

He trooped down to the kitchen, drank the dregs of the coffee and rooted out the only bagel that still looked edible. He was going to have to break down and buy some food.

He spent an hour working out, mechanically lifting weights, reminding his body it wasn't built to simply sit at a keyboard. Pleased that the sweat he'd worked up this time had nothing to do with sexual fantasies, he spent another twenty minutes indulging in a hot shower, and shaved for the first time in three—or maybe it was four—days.

He thought he might take himself out for a decent meal—which would be a nice change of pace. Then he'd face the tedium and low-grade horror of going to the market. Dressed and feeling remarkably clearheaded and cheerful, he opened his door.

Cybil dropped the hand she'd lifted to ring his buzzer. "Thank God you're home."

His mood wavered as his thought zoomed right back to the dream, and the barroom floor. "What?"

"You have to do me a favor."

"No, I don't."

"It's an emergency." She grabbed his arm before he could walk by. "It's life and death. My life and very possibly Mrs. Wolinsky's nephew Johnny's death. Because one of us is going to die if I have to go out with him, which is why I told her I had a date tonight."

"And you think this interests me because…"

"Oh, don't be surly now, McQuinn, I'm a desperate woman. Look, she didn't give me time to think. I'm a terrible liar. I mean, I just don't lie very often, so I'm bad at it. She kept asking who I was going out with, and I couldn't think of anybody, so I said you."

Because she'd meant it when she'd told him she was desperate, she darted in front of him to block his path.

"Kid, let me point out one simple fact. This isn't my problem."

"No, it's mine, I know it, and I would have made something better up if she hadn't caught me when I was working and thinking of something else." She lifted her hands, pushed them through her hair and had it standing in spikes. "She's going to be watching, don't you see? She's going to know if we don't go out of here together."

She whirled away to pace and rap her knuckles against her temples as if to stimulate thought. "Look, all you have to do is walk out of here with me, give an appearance of a nice, casual date. We'll go have a cup of coffee or something, spend a couple of hours, then come back—because she'll know if we don't come back together, too. She knows everything. I'll give you a hundred dollars."

That stopped him. The basic absurdity of it pulled him up short at the head of the stairs. "You'll pay me to go out with you?"

"It's not exactly like that—but close enough. I know you can use the money, and it's only fair to compensate you for your time. A hundred dollars, McQuinn, for a couple hours, and I'll buy the coffee."

He leaned back against the wall, studying her. It was just ridiculous enough to appeal to a sense of the absurd he'd all but forgotten he had. "No pie?"

Her laugh erupted on a gush of relief. "Pie? You want pie? You got pie."

"Where's the C note?"

"The…oh, the money. Hold on."

She dashed back into her apartment. He could hear her running up the steps, slamming around.

"Just let me fix myself up a little," she called out.

"Meter's running, kid."

"Okay, okay. Where the hell is my…ah! Two minutes, two minutes. I don't want her to tell me I'd hold on to a man if I'd just put on lipstick."

He had to give her credit. When she said two minutes, she meant it. She ran back out, her feet in another pair of those skinny heels, her lips slicked with deep pink and earrings dangling. Mismatched again he noted as she handed him a crisp hundred-dollar bill.

"I really appreciate this. I know how foolish it must seem. I can't stand to hurt her feelings, that's all."

"Her feelings are worth a hundred bucks to you, it's your business." Entertained, he stuffed the bill in his back pocket. "Let's go. I'm hungry."

"Oh, do you want dinner? I can spring for a meal. There's a diner just down the street. Good pasta. Okay, now. Pretend you don't know she's keeping her eye out for us," she murmured as they walked to the entrance. "Just look natural. Hold my hand, will you?"

"Why?"

"Oh, for heaven's sake." She snatched his hand, linked her fingers firmly with his, then shot him a bright smile. "We're going on a date, our first. Try to look like we're enjoying ourselves."

"You only gave me a hundred," he reminded her, surprised when she laughed.

"God, you're a hard man, 3B. A really hard man. Let's get you a hot meal and see if it improves your mood."

It did. But it would have taken a stronger man than he to

hold out against an enormous, family-style bowl of spaghetti and meatballs and Cybil's sunny disposition.

"It's great, isn't it?" She watched him plow through the food with pleasure. Poor man, she thought, probably hasn't had a decent meal in weeks. "I always eat too much when I come here. They give you enough for six starving teenagers with each serving. Then I end up taking home the rest and eating too much the next day. You can save me from that and take mine home with you."

"Fine." He topped off their glasses of Chianti.

"You know, I bet there are dozens of clubs downtown that would be thrilled to hire you to play."

"Huh?"

"Your sax."

She smiled at him, luring him to look at her mouth, that flickering dimple, and wonder again.

"You're so good. I can't imagine you won't find steady work really soon."

Amused, he lifted his wine. She thought he was an out-of-work musician. Fine, then. Why not? "Gigs come and they go."

"Do you work private parties?" Inspired, she leaned on the table. "I know a lot of people—someone's always having a party."

"I bet they are, in your little world."

"I could give your name out if you like. Do you mind traveling?"

"Where am I going?"

"Some of my relatives own hotels. Atlantic City's not far. I don't suppose you have a car."

He had a snazzy new Porsche stored in a downtown garage. "Not on me."

She laughed, nibbled on bread. "Well, it's not difficult to get from New York to Atlantic City."

As entertaining as it was, he thought it wise to steer off awhile. "Cybil, I don't need anyone to manage my life."

"Terrible habit of mine." Unoffended, she broke the bread in half and offered him part. "I get involved. Then I'm annoyed when other people do the same to me. Like Mrs. Wolinsky, the current president of Let's Find Cybil a Nice Young Man Club. It drives me crazy."

"Because you don't want a nice young man."

"Oh, I suppose I will, eventually. Coming from a big family sort of predisposes you—or me, anyway—into wanting one of your own. But there's lots of time for that. I like living in the city, doing what I want when I want. I'd hate to keep regular hours, which is why nothing ever stuck before cartooning. Not that it isn't work or doesn't take discipline, but it's my work and my time. Like your music, I guess."

"I guess." His work was very rarely a pleasure—as hers seemed to be. But his music was.

"McQuinn." Smiling, she nudged her bowl to the side, thinking it would make him a very nice meal later in the week. "How often do you really rip loose and come up with more than, oh, say, three declarative sentences in a row during a conversation?"

He ate the last half of his last meatball, studied her. "I like November. I talk a lot in November. It's the kind of transitory month that makes me feel philosophical."

"Three on the button, and clever, too." She laughed at him. "You have a sly sense of humor in there, don't you?" Sitting back, she sighed lustily. "Want dessert?"

"Damn right."

"Okay, but don't order the tiramisu, because then I'd be forced to beg you for a bite, then two, then I'd end up stealing half of it and go into a coma."

Keeping his eyes on hers, he signaled for the waitress with the casual authority of a man used to giving orders. It made Cybil's brow crease.

"Tiramisu," he told the waitress. "Two forks," and made Cybil weak with laughter. "I want to see if putting you into a coma actually shuts you up."

"Won't." She patted her chest as the last laugh bubbled out. "I even talk in my sleep. My sister used to threaten to put a pillow over my head."

"I think I'd like your sister."

"Adria's gorgeous—probably just your type, too. Cool and sophisticated and brilliant. She runs an art gallery in Portsmith."

Preston decided they might as well finish off the wine. It was a very nice Chianti, he mused, which probably explained why he was feeling more relaxed than he had in weeks. Months, he corrected. Maybe years. "So, are you going to fix me up with her?"

"She might go for you," Cybil considered, eyeing him over her glass and enjoying the happy little buzz the wine had given her. "You're great-looking in a sort of rough, I-don't-give-a-damn way. You play a musical instrument, which would appeal to her love and appreciation of the arts. And you're too nasty to treat her like royalty. Too many men do."

"Do they?" he murmured, realizing that his talkative dinner companion was well on her way to being plowed.

"She's so beautiful. They can't help it. Worse, she's irritated when they're dazzled by the way she looks, so she ends up tossing them back. She'd probably end up breaking your heart," she added, gesturing with her glass. "But it might be good for you."

"I don't have a heart," he said when the waitress brought their dessert. "I thought you'd figured that out."

"Sure you do." With a sigh of surrender, Cybil picked up her fork, scooped up the first bite and tasted with a long moan of pleasure. "You've just got it wrapped in armor so nobody can bayonet it again. God, isn't this wonderful? Don't let me eat any more than this one bite, okay?"

But he was staring at her, amazed that the little lunatic across the hall had zeroed in on him so accurately, so casually, when those who claimed to love him had never come close.

"Why do you say that?"

"Say what? Didn't I tell you not to let me eat any more of this. Are you a sadist?"

"Never mind." Deciding to let it go, he yanked the plate out of her reach. "Mine," he said simply. And proceeded to eat the rest.

He only had to poke her once with his fork to hold her off.

"Well, I had fun." Cybil tucked her arm through his as they walked back toward their building. "Really. That was so much more entertaining than an evening trying to keep Johnny from sliding his hand up my skirt."

For some reason, the image irritated him, but Preston merely glanced down. "You're not wearing a skirt."

"I know. I wasn't sure I could get out of the date, and this was my automatic defense system."

The breezy saffron-colored slacks struck him abruptly as more sexy than defensive. "So why don't you just break Johnny's face like you did the mugger's the other night?"

"Because Mrs. Wolinsky adores him, and I'd never be able to tell her that the apple of her eye has hands like an ape."

"I think that's a mixed metaphor, but I get the picture. You're a pushover."

"Am not."

"Are so," he said before he caught himself and fell too deeply into the childish game. "You let your friend Joanie—"

"Jody."

"Right, push her cousin on you, and the old lady downstairs sticks you with her nephew with the fast hands, and God knows how many other friends you have dumping their cast-off relatives in your lap. All because you can't just say butt out."

"They mean well."

"They're meddling with your life. It doesn't matter what they mean."

"Oh, I don't know." She blew out a breath and smiled at a young couple strolling on the opposite side of the street. "Take my grandfather. Well, he's not really my grandfather if you get picky, which we don't. He's my dad's sister Shelby's father-in-law. And on my mother's side, she's cousin to the spouses of his other two children. It's a little complicated, if you get picky."

"Which you don't."

"Exactly. There's all this convoluted family connection between Daniel and Anna MacGregor and my parents, so why niggle? My aunt Shelby married their son Alan Mac-Gregor—you might have heard of him. He used to live in the White House."

"The name rings a distant bell."

"And my mother, the former Genviève Grandeau, is a cousin of Justin and Diana Blade—siblings—who married, respectively, Daniel and Anna's other two children, Serena and Caine MacGregor. So Daniel and Anna are Grandpa and Grandma. Is that clear?"

"Yes, I can follow that, but I've forgotten the entire point of the exercise."

"Me, too." She laughed in delight, then had to tighten her grip before she overbalanced. "A little too much wine," she explained. "Anyway, let me think... Yes, I have it. Meddling. We were talking about meddling, which my grandfather—who would be Daniel MacGregor—is the uncontested world champ at. When it comes to matchmaking, he knows no peer. I'm telling you, McQuinn, the man is a wizard. I have..."

She had to stop, use her fingers to count. "Um, I think it's seven cousins so far he's managed to match up, marry off. He's terrifying."

"What do you mean 'match up'?"

"He just sort of finds the right person for them—don't ask me how—then he works out a way to put them together, let nature take its course, and before you know it, you've got wedding bells and bassinets. He just told me my cousin Ian and his wife are expecting their first. They were married last fall. The man's batting a thousand."

"Does anyone tell him to butt out?"

"Oh, constantly." She tipped up her head and grinned. "He just doesn't pay attention. I figure he's going to work on Adria or Mel next—give my brother, Matthew, time to season."

"What about you?"

"Oh, I'm too slick for him. I know his canny tricks, and I'm not going to fall in love for years. What about you? Ever been there?"

"Where would that be?"

"Love, McQuinn, don't be dense."

"It's not a place—it's a situation. And there's nothing there."

"Oh, I think there will be," she said dreamily. "Eventually."

For the second time, she pulled up short. "Oh, damn. That's Johnny's car. He's come in from New Jersey after all. Damn, damn, damn. Okay, here's the plan."

She whirled around, shook her head clear when it spun. "I should never have had that last glass of wine, but I'm still master of my fate."

"You bet you are, kid."

"Enough to know you call me 'kid' so you can feel superior and aloof, but that's beside the point. We're just going to stroll on down a few more feet until we're right in front of her window. Very natural, okay?"

"That's a tough one, but I'll see what I can do."

"I just love that nasty streak of sarcasm. Okay, this is fine, this is good. Now, we're going to stand right here, because she's watching, I promise. Any minute you'll see her curtains twitch. Look for it."

Because it seemed harmless, and he was starting to enjoy the way she held on to him, he flicked a glance over her head. "Right on cue. So?"

"You're going to have to kiss me."

His gaze shot back to hers. "Am I?"

"And you're going to have to make it look good. If you do it right, she'll figure Johnny's a lost cause—for a while, anyway. And I'll give you another fifty."

He ran his tongue around his teeth. She had her face tipped back and looked as appealing as a single rosebud in a garden of thorns. "You're going to pay me fifty bucks to kiss you."

"Like a bonus. This could send Johnny back to Jersey for good. Just think of it as being onstage. Doesn't have to mean anything. Is she still watching?"

"Yeah." But he wasn't looking at the window now, and didn't have a clue.

"Great. Good. Make it count, okay. Romantic. Just slide your arms around me, then lean down and—"

"I know how to kiss a woman, Cybil."

"Of course you do. No offense meant whatsoever. But this should be choreographed so that—"

He decided the only way to shut her up was to get on with it, and to get on with it his way. He didn't slide his arms around her—he yanked her against him, and nearly off her feet. He had one glimpse of those big green eyes widening in shock, before his mouth crushed down on hers and sent the next babbling words sliding down her throat.

He was right. That was her last dizzy thought. He was absolutely right. He did know how to kiss a woman.

She had to grab on to his shoulders. Had to rise up to her toes.

She had to moan.

Her head was spinning in fast, giddy circles. Her heart had flipped straight into her throat to block any chance of air. It made her feel helpless, lost, shaky as his mouth pumped heat like a furnace into her body.

And his mouth was so hard, so hard, and stunningly hungry. What else could she do but let him feed?

It was like the dream, he thought. Only better. Much, much better. Her taste hadn't been so unique in his imagination. Her body hadn't trembled with quick, hard little shock waves. Her hands hadn't clawed their way up into his hair to fist while she moaned pure pleasure into his mouth.

He yanked her back, but only to see if her eyes had gone dark, if heat had climbed into her cheeks the way he felt it climb through his system. She only stared at him, her breath coming short and fast through parted lips, her hands still clutched in his hair.

"Next one's on me," he murmured, and took her under again.

A horn blasted. Someone cursed. There was a rush of displaced air from a passing car. Someone shoved an apartment window open and let out a stream of blistering rock music and the acrid smell of burned dinner.

She might have been on a deserted island with crystal-blue waves crashing at her feet.

When he drew her away the second time, he did so slowly, with his hands skimming down from her shoulders to her elbows, then back in a gesture that stopped only a hint short of a caress. It gave her enough time to feel her head revolve once, like a slow-motion merry-go-round, before it settled weakly on her shoulders.

He wanted to lap her up on the spot, every inch of that flushed, lovely skin. To devour her innate—and, to him, misplaced—cheerfulness that shone out of her like sunlight. He wanted all that impossible, unflagging energy under him, over him, open to him.

And he had no doubt that once he had, he'd leave them both bitter.

Now the hands that lingered on her shoulders eased her back off her toes. Steadied her. Released her. "I think that ought to do it."

"Do it?" she echoed, staring up at him.

"Satisfy Mrs. Wolinsky."

"Mrs. Wolinsky?" Absolutely blank, she shook her head. "Oh. Oh, yeah." She blew out a long breath and decided her system might settle sometime before the end of the next decade. "If it doesn't it's hopeless. You're awfully good at it, McQuinn."

A reluctant smile flitted around his mouth. The woman was damn near irresistible, he thought, and, taking her arm, turned her toward the front of the building. "You're not half-bad at it yourself, kid."

Chapter 4

Cybil sang as she worked, belting out a duet with Aretha Franklin. Behind her, the open window welcomed the cool April breeze and the amazing noise that was the downtown streets in brilliant sunshine.

The stream of light was no sunnier than her mood.

Turning to the mirror on the wall beside her, she tried to work her face into a state of shock to help her with a character expression. But all she could do was grin.

She'd been kissed before. She'd been held by and against a man before. As far as she was concerned comparing all her other experiences to that stunning sidewalk embrace with the man across the hall was like pitting a firecracker against a nuclear attack.

One hissed, popped and was momentarily entertaining. The other detonated and changed the landscape for centuries.

It had left her marvelously dizzy for hours.

She loved the sensation, adored every moment of that

giddy, slack-muscled, purely feminine rush. Could there be anything more wonderful than feeling weak and strong, foolish and wise, confused and aware all at the same time?

And all she had to do was close her eyes, let her mind wander back, to feel it all over again.

She wondered what he was thinking, what he was feeling. No one could be unaffected by an experience of that…magnitude. And after all, he'd been right there with her at ground zero. A man couldn't kiss a woman like that and not suffer some potent residual effects.

Suffering, Cybil decided, as her body tingled, was highly underrated.

She chuckled; she sighed; then, bending over her work, sang with Aretha about the joys of feeling like a natural woman.

"God, Cyb, it's freezing in here!"

Cybil looked up, beamed. "Hi, Jody. Hi, sweet Charlie."

The baby gave her a sleepy-eyed smile as Jody strode to the window with him cocked on her hip. "You're sitting in front of an open window. It can't be more than sixty degrees out there." With a little grunt, Jody shoved the window closed.

"I was feeling kind of warm." Cybil set her pencil aside to stroke Charlie's pudgy cheek. "It's miraculous, isn't it, that men start out this way? As pretty little babies? Then they…wow, boy do they grow up into something else."

"Yeah." Puzzled, Jody frowned, examined her friend's somewhat glassy eyes. "You look funny. Are you okay?" Jody laid a maternal hand on Cybil's forehead. "No fever. Stick out your tongue."

Cybil obeyed, crossing her eyes as she did and making Charlie bubble with laughter. "I'm not sick. I'm fabulous. I feel like a million after taxes."

"Hmm." Unconvinced, Jody pursed her lips. "I'm going to put Charlie down for his morning nap. He's zonked. Then I'll get us some coffee and you can tell me what's going on."

"Sure. Um-hmm." Dreaming again, Cybil picked up a red pen and began to doodle pretty little hearts on scrap paper.

Since that was fun, she drew larger ones, sketching Preston's face inside one.

He had a great one, she mused. Hard mouth, cool eyes, very strong features set off by that thick, dark hair. But that mouth softened a bit when he smiled. And his eyes weren't cool when he laughed.

She loved making him laugh. He always sounded just a little out of practice. She could help him with that, she mused, drawing his face again with the warmth of laughter added. After all, one of her nice little talents was making people laugh.

And after she'd helped him find some steady work, he wouldn't have so much to worry about.

She'd get him some work, make certain that he ate regular meals—she was always cooking too much for one person anyway—and she was sure she could find someone who had a secondhand sofa they were willing to part with on the cheap.

She knew enough people to start the ball rolling here and there for him. He'd feel better, wouldn't he, once he was more settled in, more secure? It wouldn't be like meddling. That was her grandfather's territory. She would just be helping out a neighbor.

A gorgeous, sexy neighbor who could kiss a woman straight into the paradise of delirium.

Of course that wouldn't be why she was doing it. Cybil shook herself, turned the scraps of paper over a little guiltily. She'd helped Mr. Peebles find a good podiatrist, hadn't she?

And nobody would consider him a cool-eyed Adonis with great hands, would they?

Of course not.

She was just being a good neighbor. And if there were any other…benefits, well, so what?

Satisfied with her plans, she folded her legs under her and got back to work.

Jody settled the baby, thinking as she always did when she tucked him in that he was the most beautiful child ever to grace the planet. When his heavy eyes shut, his blanket was smoothed and his favorite teddy bear left on guard, she trotted downstairs to turn down the music.

As at home in Cybil's kitchen as her own, she poured morning coffee into two thick yellow mugs, sniffed out a couple of cranberry muffins, then loaded up a tray.

The midmorning ritual was one of her favorite parts of the day.

In the past few years, Cybil had become as close as a sister to her. Closer, Jody thought, wrinkling her nose. Her own sisters were always bragging about their husbands, their kids, their houses—when anyone could see her Chuck and her Charlie were miles superior. But Cybil listened. Cybil had held her hand through the difficult decision to quit her job and stay home with the baby full-time. It had been Cybil who'd stood by during those early days when she and Chuck had been panicked over every burp and sniffle Charlie had made.

There was no better friend in the world. Which was why Jody was determined to see Cybil blissfully happy.

She carried the tray up, set it on the table, then handed Cybil her mug.

"Thanks, Jody."

"Great strip this morning. I can't believe Emily decking herself out in a trench coat and fedora and tailing Mr. Mysterious all over Soho. Where does she get this stuff?"

"She's a creature of impulse and drama." Cybil broke off a piece of a muffin. It was usual for them to discuss Emily and the other characters as separate people. "And she's nosy. She just has to know."

"What about you? Did you find out anything yet about our Mr. Mysterious?"

"Yeah." Cybil said it on a sigh. "His name's McQuinn."

"I heard that." Instantly alert, Jody jabbed out a finger. "You sighed."

"No, I was just breathing."

"Uh-uh, you sighed. What gives?"

"Well, actually…" She was dying to talk about it. "We sort of went out last night."

"Went out? Like a date?" Quickly, Jody pulled over a chair, sat, leaned close. "Where, how, when? Details, Cyb."

"Okay. So." Cybil swiveled so they were face to face. "You know how Mrs. Wolinsky's always trying to fix me up with her nephew?"

"Not again?" Jody rolled her dark eyes. "Why can't she see you two are totally wrong for each other?"

Vast affection prevented Cybil from mentioning that it might be the same selective blindness that prevented Jody from seeing the flaws in the Cybil-Frank match.

"She just loves him. But anyway, she'd cooked up another date for me for last night, and I just couldn't face it. You have to swear you won't tell her—or anyone."

"Except Chuck."

"Husbands are excluded from the vow of silence in this case. I told her I already had a date—with McQuinn."

"You had a date with 3B?"

"No, I just told her I did because I was flustered. You know how I start babbling when I lie."

"You should practice." Nodding, Jody bit into a muffin. "You'd get better at it."

"Maybe. So after I tell her, I realize she's going to be looking for us to leave together, and I have to cut some kind of deal with McQuinn to go along with it. I gave him a hundred and bought him dinner."

"You paid him." Jody's eyes widened, then narrowed in speculation. "That's brilliant. The whole time I was dating— especially during that drought period I told you about my sophomore year in college? I never thought about just offering a guy some money to have dinner with me. How'd you settle on the hundred? Do you think that's, like, the going rate?"

"It seemed right. He's not working regularly, you know. And I figured he could use the money and a hot meal. We had a good time," she added with a new smile. "Really good. Just spaghetti and conversation. Well, mostly one-sided conversation, as McQuinn doesn't say a lot."

"McQuinn." Jody let the name roll over her tongue. "Still sounds mysterious. You don't know his first name."

"It never came up. Anyway, it gets better. We're walking back. I think I loosened him up, Jody. He really seemed relaxed, almost friendly. Then I see Johnny Wolinsky's car, and I panicked. I'm figuring she's not going to stop trying to shove him at me unless she thinks I've got a guy. So I cut another deal with McQuinn and offered him fifty bucks to kiss me."

Jody pursed her lips, then sipped coffee. "I think you should've said that was included in the hundred."

"No, we'd already defined terms, and there wasn't time to renegotiate. She was looking out the window. So he did, right there on the sidewalk."

"Wow." Jody grabbed the rest of her muffin. "What move did he use?"

"He just sort of *yanked* me against him."

"Oh, man. The yank. I really like the yank."

"Then I was plastered there, up on my toes because he's tall."

"Yeah." Jody chewed, licked crumbs off her lips. "He's tall. And built."

"Really built, Jody. I mean the man is like a rock."

"Oh, God." On the moan, Jody rubbed her stomach. "Wow. Okay, so you're plastered up there, on your toes. What next?"

"Then he just…swooped."

"Oh-oh, the yank and swoop." Crumbs scattered as Jody waved her hands. "It's a classic. Hardly any guy can really pull it off, though. Chuck did on date six. That's how we ended up back at my apartment, eating Chinese in bed."

"McQuinn pulled it off. He really, really pulled it off. Then, while my head was exploding, he yanked me back, just looked at me."

"Man. Man."

"Then he just…did it all again."

"A double." Near tears with vicarious excitement, Jody gripped Cybil's hand. "You got a double. There are women who go all their lives without a double. Dreaming of, yes, but never achieving the double yank and swoop."

"It was my first," Cybil confessed. "It…was…*great!*"

"Okay, okay, just the kiss part, okay? Just the lips and tongues and teeth thing. How was that?"

"It was very hot."

"Oh…I'm going to have to open the window. I'm starting to sweat."

She jumped up, shoved up the window and took a deep gulp of air. "So, it was hot. Very hot. Keep going."

"It was like being, well, devoured. When your system just goes…" At a loss, she lifted her hands, wiggled them wildly. "And your head's circling around about a foot above your shoulders, and…I don't know how to describe it."

"You've got to." Desperate, Jody squeezed Cybil's shoulders. "I'm on the edge here. Try this—on the one-to-ten scale, where did it hit?"

Cybil closed her eyes. "There is no scale."

"There's always a scale—you can say off the scale, but there's always a scale."

"No, Jody, there is no scale."

Eyeing Cybil, Jody stepped back. "The no scale is an urban myth."

"It exists," Cybil said soberly. "The no scale exists, my friend, and has now been documented."

"Sweet Lord. I have to sit down." She did so, her eyes never leaving Cybil's face. "You experienced a no scale. I believe you, Cyb. Thousands wouldn't. Millions would scoff, but I believe you."

"I knew I could count on you."

"You know what this means, don't you? He's ruined you for anything less. Even a ten won't satisfy you now. You'll always be looking for the next no scale."

"I've thought of that." Considering, Cybil picked up her pencil to tap. "I believe it's possible to live a full and happy life, hitting with some regularity between seven and ten, even after this experience. Man goes to the moon, Jody. Travels through space and time, finds himself on another world, but only briefly. He must come back to earth and live."

"That's so wise," Jody murmured, and had to dig a tissue out of her pocket. "So brave."

"Thank you. But in the meantime," Cybil added with a

grin, "there's no harm in knocking on the door across the hall from time to time."

Because she didn't want to appear overanxious, Cybil put in a full morning's work. She didn't break until after two, when she thought her neighbor might enjoy sharing a cup of coffee, maybe a nice walk in the April sunshine.

He really had to get out of that apartment more, she decided. Take advantage of all the city had to offer. She imagined him brooding behind his locked door, worried about his lack of employment, the bills.

She was certain she could help him with that. There was no reason she couldn't put a buzz in a few ears and get him a few gigs to tide him over.

She heard the sax begin to weep as she stood in her bedroom fussing with her makeup. It made her tingle again, the low, sexy throb of it.

He deserved a break, something to take that cynical gleam out of his eyes. Something that would prove to him life was full of surprises. She wanted to help him. There was a quality about him—an underlying unhappiness she was driven to smooth away.

After all, she'd made him laugh. She'd helped him relax. If she could do it once, she could do it again. She badly wanted to see him laugh again, to hear that sardonic edge to his voice when he made some pithy comment, to see that grin flash when she said or did something that got through his cynical shield.

And if they lit a few sexual sparks between them while she was at it, what was wrong with that?

She was on her way downstairs, and singing again, when the buzzer from the entrance door sounded on her intercom.

"Yes?"

"I'm looking for McQuinn. 3A?"

"No, he's 3B."

"Well, damn it. Why doesn't he answer?"

"Oh, he probably doesn't hear you. He's practicing."

"Buzz me in, will you, sweetie? I'm his agent and I'm running way behind."

"His agent." Cybil perked up. If he had an agent, Cybil wanted to meet her. She'd already thought of half a dozen names to pass on for possible jobs. "Sure. Come on up."

She released the door, then opened her own and waited.

The woman who stepped out of the little-used elevator looked very professional, very successful, Cybil noted with some surprise, in her snazzy power suit of drop-dead red. She was thin and wiry, with a sharp-featured face, dark-blue eyes that were snapping with annoyance and an incredibly fabulous mane of streaked blond hair.

She moved with the precision of a bullet and carried a leather briefcase that Cybil estimated cost the equivalent of a month's rent on a good uptown apartment.

So, she mused, why was her client scrambling for work if his agent could afford designer duds and pricey accessories?

"3A?"

"Yes, I'm Cybil."

"Amanda Dresher. Thanks, Cybil. Our boy here isn't answering his phone, and apparently forgot we had a one o'clock at the Four Seasons."

"The Four Seasons?" Baffled, Cybil stared. "On Park?"

"Is there another?" With a laugh, Mandy pressed the buzzer on 3B and—knowing her prey—held it down. "Our Preston's loaded with talent, but he's my biggest pain in the butt."

"Preston." It only took a minute for the confusion to form,

settle, then clear away. "Preston McQuinn." She let out a shaky breath that was equal parts betrayal and mortification. *"A Tangle of Souls."*

"That's our boy," Mandy said cheerfully. "Come on, come on, McQuinn, answer the damn door. I thought when he decided to stay in the city for a couple months I'd be able to keep better track of him. But it's still an obstacle course. Ah, here we go."

They both heard the bad-tempered snick of locks being turned. Then he yanked open the door. "What the hell do you…Mandy?"

"You missed lunch," she snapped. "You're not answering the phone."

"I forgot lunch. The phone didn't ring."

"Did you charge the battery?"

"Probably not." He stood where he was, staring across the hall to where Cybil watched him with wounded eyes in a pale face. "Come on in. Just give me a minute."

"I've already given you an hour." She tossed a glance over her shoulder as she walked inside. "Thanks for buzzing me up, sweetie."

"No problem. No problem at all." Then Cybil looked Preston dead in the eye. "You bastard," she said quietly, and closed her door.

"Don't you have any place to sit in here?" Mandy complained behind him.

"No. Yes. Upstairs. Damn it," he muttered, despising the slide of guilt. Doing his best to shrug it off, he closed his door. "I don't use the space down here much."

"No kidding. So who's the kid across the hall?" she asked as she set her briefcase on the kitchen counter.

"Nobody. Campbell, Cybil Campbell."

"I thought she looked familiar. 'Friends and Neighbors.'

I know her agent. He's crazy about her. Claims she's the only ego-proof, neurosis-free client he's ever had. Never whines, doesn't miss deadlines, never demands coddling, and is currently making him a fat pile of money on the sales of her trade books and calendars, plus the merchandising tie-ins."

She sent Preston a baleful look. "I wonder what it's like to have a neurosis-free client who remembers lunch dates and sends me gifts on my birthday."

"The neuroses are part of the package, but I'm sorry about lunch."

Annoyance faded into concern. "What's up, Preston? You look ragged out. Is the play stalled?"

"No, it's moving. Better than I expected. I just didn't get a lot of sleep."

"Out playing your horn till all hours again?"

"No." Thinking of the woman in 3A, he thought. Pacing the floor. Wanting the woman in 3A. The woman who now, undoubtedly, considered him a slightly lower life-form than slime.

"Just a bad night, Mandy."

"Okay." Because as irritated as he could make her, she cared about him. She crossed the room to give his tensed shoulders a brisk rub. "But you owe me lunch. How about some coffee?"

"There's some on the stove. It was fresh at six this morning."

"Let's start over, then. I'll make it." She moved behind the counter. After she had the coffee going, she poked into the cupboards. She considered Preston's welfare part of her job.

"God, McQuinn, are you on a hunger strike? There's nothing in here but potato-chip crumbs and what once might have been cracked-wheat bread and is now a science project."

"I didn't make it to the market yesterday." Again his

gaze flicked to the door and his mind to Cybil. "Mostly I call in dinner."

"On the phone you don't answer?"

"I'll recharge the battery, Mandy."

"See that you do. If you'd remembered sooner, we'd be sitting in the Four Seasons right now, drinking Cristal to celebrate." She grinned as she leaned on the counter toward him. "I closed the deal, Preston. *A Tangle of Souls* is going to be a major motion picture. You got the producers you wanted, the director you wanted and the option to do the screenplay yourself. All that plus a tidy little fee."

She gave him an amount in seven figures.

"I don't want them to screw it up," was Preston's first reaction.

"Leave it to you." Mandy sighed. "If there's a downside, you find it. So do the screenplay."

"No." He shook his head, walking to the window to try to absorb the news. A film would change the intimacy the play had achieved in the theater. But it would also take his work to millions. And the work mattered to him.

"I don't want to go back there, Mandy. Not that deep."

She poured two cups of coffee and joined him at the window. "Supervisory capacity. Consultant?"

"Yeah, that works for me. Fix it, will you?"

"I can do that. Now, if you'll stop turning cartwheels and dancing on the ceiling, we can talk about your work in progress."

Her dry tone got through, made his lips twitch. He set his coffee on the windowsill, turned and took her sharp-boned face in his hands. "You're the best, and certainly the most patient agent in the business."

"You're so right. I hope you're as proud of yourself as I am. Are you going to call your family?"

"Let me sit on it a couple days."

"It's going to hit the trades, Preston. You don't want them to hear about it that way."

"No, you're right. I'll call them." Finally, he smiled. "After I charge the phone. Why don't I clean up and take you out for that champagne."

"Why don't you. Oh, one more thing," she added as he started for the stairs. "Pretty Miss 3A? Are you going to tell me what's going on between you?"

"I'm not sure there's anything to tell," he murmured.

He still wasn't sure when he knocked on her door later that evening. But he knew he had to answer for that look he'd put in her eyes.

Not that it had been any of her business in the first place, he reminded himself. He hadn't asked her to come nosing around. In fact he'd done everything to discourage her.

Until last night, he thought, and hissed out a breath.

Bad judgment, he decided. It had just been bad judgment. He shouldn't have followed impulse and gone along with her. Shouldn't have compounded the mistake by enjoying himself.

Or by kissing her.

Which he wouldn't have done, his mind circled back, if she hadn't asked him to.

When she pulled open the door, he was ready with an apology. "Look, I'm sorry," he began, delivering it with an impatient edge of annoyance. "But it was none of your business anyway. Let's just straighten this out."

He started to step in, coming up short when she slapped a hand on his chest.

"I don't want you in here."

"For God's sake. You started it. Maybe I let it get out of hand, but—"

"Started what?"

"This," he snapped, furious at the sudden lack of words, hating the kicked-puppy look in her eyes.

"All right, I started it. I should never have brought you cookies. That was devious of me. I shouldn't have worried that you didn't have a job, shouldn't have bought you a decent meal because I thought you couldn't afford it on your own."

"Damn it, Cybil."

"You let me think that. You let me believe you were some poor, out-of-work musician, and I'm sure you had a few private laughs over it. The brilliant, award-winning playwright Preston McQuinn, author of the stunning, emotionally wrenching *A Tangle of Souls*. But I bet you're surprised I even know your work. A bubblehead like me."

She shoved him back a step. "What would a fluffy comic-strip writer know about real art, after all? About serious theater, about *literature?* Why shouldn't you have a few laughs at my expense? You narrow-minded, arrogant creep." Her voice broke when she'd promised herself she wouldn't let it. "I was only trying to help you."

"I didn't ask for your help. I didn't want it." He could see she was close to tears. The closer she got, the more furious he became. He knew how women used tears to destroy a man. He wouldn't let it happen. "My work's my own business."

"Your work's produced on Broadway. That makes it public business," she shot back. "And that has nothing to do with pretending to be a sax player."

"I play the damn sax because I like to play the damn sax. I didn't pretend to be anything. You assumed."

"You let me assume."

"What if I did? I moved in here for a little peace and quiet.

To be left alone. The next thing I know you're bringing me cookies, then you're following me and I'm spending half the night in the police station. Then you're asking me to go out so you can slip by a seventy-year-old woman because you don't have the guts to tell her to butt out of your personal life. And you top it off by offering me fifty dollars to kiss you."

Humiliation had the first tear spilling over, trailing slowly down her cheek and making his stomach clench. "Don't." The order whipped out of him. "Don't start that."

"Don't cry when you humiliate me? When you make me feel stupid and ridiculous and ashamed?" She didn't bother to dash the tears away but simply looked at him out of unapologetically drenched eyes. "Sorry, I don't work that way. I cry when someone hurts me."

"You brought it on yourself." He had to say it, was desperate to believe it. And escaped by stalking to his own door.

"You have the facts, Preston," she said quietly. "You have them all in an accurate row. But you've missed the feelings behind them. I brought you cookies because I thought you could use a friend. I've already apologized for following you, but I'll apologize again."

"I don't want—"

"I'm not finished," she said with such quiet dignity he felt one more wave of guilt. "I took you to dinner because I didn't want to hurt a very nice woman, and I thought you might be hungry. I enjoyed being with you, and I felt something when you kissed me. I thought you did, too. So you're right." She nodded coolly, even as another tear slid down her cheek. "I did bring it all on myself. I suppose you save all your emotions for your work, and can't find the way to let them into your life. I'm sorry for you. And I'm sorry I trod on your sacred ground. I won't do it again."

Before he could think of how to respond, she shut her door. He heard her locks slide into place with quick, deliberate clicks. Turning, he let himself in to his own apartment, followed her example by closing, then locking, the door behind him.

He had what he wanted, he told himself. Solitude. Quiet. She wouldn't come knocking on his door again to interrupt his thoughts, to distract him, to tangle him up in feelings and conversations he didn't want. In feelings he didn't know what to do with.

And he stood, exhausted by the storm and sick of himself, staring at an empty room.

Chapter 5

He couldn't sleep, except in patches. And the patches were riddled with dreams. In them he would find himself wrapped around Cybil. His back in a corner, up against a wall, at the edge of a cliff.

It always seemed as if she'd maneuvered him there, where there was nowhere to go but to her.

And when he did, the dreams became brutally erotic, so that when he managed to rip himself from them, he found himself aroused, furious and filled with the memory, the taste, of her in his mouth.

He couldn't eat, found himself picking at food when he bothered with it at all. Nothing satisfied him; everything reminded him of that simple meal they'd shared a few nights before.

He lived on coffee until his nerves jangled and his stomach burned in protest.

But he could work. It seemed he could always flow into a story, into his people, when his emotions were pumped. It was painful to tear those feelings out of his own heart and have the characters he created gobble them greedily up. But he relished the exchange, even fed on it.

He remembered what Cybil had said before she'd closed the door on him—that he used all his emotions in his work and didn't know how to let them into his life.

She was right, and it was better that way. There were, to his mind, very few people he could trust with feelings. His parents, his sister—though his need to fulfill their expectations of and for him was a double-edged sword.

Then Delta and André, those rare friends he allowed himself and who expected no more from him than what he wanted himself.

Mandy, who pushed him when he needed pushing, listened when he needed to unburden and somehow managed to care about him even when he didn't.

He didn't want a woman digging her way into his heart. Not again. He'd learned his lesson there, and had kept any and all applicants since Pamela out of that vulnerable territory.

She'd cured him, he thought, with lies, deceptions, betrayals. A man could learn a good deal at the tender age of twenty-five that held him in good stead for the duration. Since he'd stopped believing in love, he never wasted time looking for it.

But he couldn't stop thinking of Cybil.

He'd heard her go out several times in the last three days. He'd been distracted more than once by the laughter and voices and music from her apartment.

She wasn't suffering, he reminded himself. So why was he?

It was guilt, he decided. He'd hurt her and it had been neither necessary nor intentional. He'd been charmed by her;

reluctantly, but charmed nonetheless. He hadn't meant to make her feel foolish, to bruise her feelings. Tears could still rip at him, even knowing how false and sly they could be when they slid down a woman's cheek.

But they hadn't looked false or sly on Cybil, he remembered. They'd looked as natural as rain.

He wasn't going to resolve the problem—his problem, he thought—until he'd settled with her. He hadn't apologized well; he could admit that. So he'd apologize again now that she'd had some time to get those emotions of hers she was so free with under some control.

There was no reason for them to be enemies, after all. She was the granddaughter of a man he admired and respected. He doubted Daniel MacGregor would return the compliment if he learned that Preston McQuinn had made his little girl cry.

And, Preston realized, Daniel MacGregor's opinion mattered to him.

So, a little voice nagged at him, did Cybil's.

That was why he was pacing the living area of his apartment instead of working. He'd heard her go out, again, but hadn't been quite quick enough to get downstairs and into the hall before she'd gone.

He could wait her out, Preston thought. She had to come back sometime. And when she did, he'd head her off and offer her a very civilized apology. It was blatantly obvious the woman had a soft heart. She'd have to forgive him. Once she had, they could go back to being neighbors.

There was the matter of the hundred dollars, as well, which instead of amusing him as it had initially, now made him feel nasty.

He was sure she'd be ready to laugh the whole thing off now. How long could that kind of cheerful nature hold a grudge?

He would have been surprised to find out just how long, and how well, if he'd seen Cybil's face as she rode the elevator up to the third floor.

It annoyed her, outrageously, that she had to pass the man's door to get to her own. It infuriated her that doing so made her think of him, remember how stupid she'd been— and how much more stupid he'd made her feel.

She shifted the weight of the two bags of groceries she carried in either arm and tried to dig out her key so she wouldn't have to linger in the hallway a second longer than necessary.

The elevator gave its usual announcing thud when it reached her floor. She was still searching for the elusive key when she stepped off.

Her teeth set when she saw him, and her eyes went frosty.

"Cybil." He'd never seen her eyes cold, and the chill of them threw him off rhythm. "Ah, let me give you a hand with those."

"I don't need a hand, thank you." She could only pray to grow a third one, rapidly, that could find her bloody keys.

"Yes, you do, if you're going to keep rooting around in that purse."

He tried a smile, then scowled as they played tug-of-war with one of her bags. In the end he just wrenched it out of her grip. "Look, damn it, I said I was sorry. How many times do I have to say it before you get out of this snit you're in?"

"Go to hell," she shot back. "How many times do I have to say it before you start to feel the heat?"

She finally snagged the key, jabbed it into the lock. "Give me my groceries."

"I'll take them in for you."

"I said give me the damn bag." They were back to tugging, until she hissed out a breath. "Keep them, then."

She shoved open the door, but before she could slam it in his face, he'd shoved it open again and pushed his way inside. Their eyes met, both narrowed, and he thought he caught a glint of violence in hers.

"Don't even think about it," he warned her. "I'm not an underweight mugger."

She thought she could still do some damage but decided it would only make him seem more important than she'd determined he would be. Instead, she turned on the heel of her pink suede sneakers, dumped her bag on the counter. When he did the same, she nodded briskly.

"Thanks. Now you've delivered them. Want a tip?"

"Very funny. Let's just settle this first." He reached in his pocket, where he'd folded the hundred-dollar bill she'd given him. "Here."

She flicked the money a disinterested glance. "I'm not taking it back. You earned it."

"I'm not keeping your money over what turned out to be a bad joke."

"Bad joke!" The ice in her eyes turned to sharp green flames. "Is that what it was? Well, ha-ha. Now that you bring it up, I owe you another fifty, don't I?"

That hit the mark, had his jaw clenching as she grabbed up her purse. "Don't push it, Cybil. Take the money back."

"No."

"I said take the damn money." He grabbed her wrist, yanked her around and crumpled the bill into her palm. "Now…" Then watched in astonishment as she ripped a hundred dollars into confetti.

"There, problem solved."

"That," he said on what he hoped was a calming breath, "was amazingly stupid."

"Stupid? Well, why break pattern? You can go now," she said.

Her voice was so suddenly regal, so completely

princess to peon, he nearly blinked. "Very good, very effective," he murmured. "The lady-of-the-manor tone was so utterly unexpected."

Her next suggestion, delivered in the same haughty tone, was also utterly unexpected, to the point, and made him blink.

"That works, too," he acknowledged. "And I don't think you meant that in a romantic sense."

She simply turned, stalked around the counter and began to put away her groceries. If insults and swearing didn't work, perhaps ignoring him would.

It might have if he hadn't seen her fingers tremble as she pushed a box into the cupboard. And seeing it, he felt everything inside him fade but the guilt.

"Cybil, I'm sorry." He watched her hand hesitate, then grab a soup can and shove it away. "It took on a life of its own, and I didn't do anything to stop it. I should have."

"You didn't have to lie to me. I'd have left you alone."

"I didn't lie—or didn't start out to. But I let you assume something other than the truth. I want my privacy. I need it."

"You've got it. I'm not the one who just bullied his way into someone's apartment."

"No, you're not." He stuck his hands in his pockets, dragged them out again and laid them on the counter. "I hurt you, and I didn't have to. I'm sorry for it."

She closed her eyes as she felt the gate she'd sworn to keep locked on her heart creak open. "Why did you?"

"Because I thought it would keep you on your own side of the hall. Because you were a little too appealing for comfort. And because part of me got a kick out of you wanting to help me find work."

He saw her shoulders draw up at that and winced. "I didn't mean it that way. Cybil, how could I not be amused when you offered me a hundred dollars to have dinner with you? A hundred dollars so you could spare an old woman's feelings and get some out-of-work sax player a hot meal. It was…sweet. That's not a word that comes easy to me."

"It's humiliating," she muttered, and grabbed the second bag and began shoving produce into the fridge.

"Don't let it be." He took a chance and walked around the counter so they both stood in the kitchen. "It only backfired because the timing was off, and that's my fault. If I'd told you who I was over dinner, as I should have, you'd have laughed about it. Instead, I made you cry, and I can't stand knowing that."

She stood where she was, staring into the refrigerator. She hadn't expected him to care, for it to matter to him. But it did. She simply couldn't hold out against a caring heart.

Drawing a deep breath, she told herself they would start fresh. Try for casual friends. "Want a beer?"

Every knot in his shoulders loosened. "Oh, yeah."

"Figured." She reached in for a bottle, disposed of the top, reached for a glass. "I haven't heard you talk so much at one time since I met you." When she turned, offering the beer, her eyes were smiling. "You must be dry."

"Thanks."

Her dimple fluttered. "But I'm out of cookies."

"You could always make some more."

"Maybe." She turned away to deal with the groceries. "But I was thinking about baking a pie." Tossing a look over her shoulder, she lifted a brow. "We never did have that pie."

"No, we didn't."

Too appealing for comfort, he thought again. She was wearing an oversize cotton shirt, plain white. Leggings the color of summer skies, those silly shoes.

Since she'd been marketing, he doubted that the just-under-the-smoldering-point perfume had been dabbed on to please anyone but herself, and had no idea why she would wear two gold hoops in one ear and a single diamond stud in the other.

But it all combined into one fascinating package.

When she turned back to reach into the bag again, he took her wrist with his free hand. "Are we on level ground now?"

"Looks like."

"Then there's something else." He set the beer down. "I dream about you."

Now it was her mouth that went dry. And her stomach erupted with the crazed flapping of a hundred wings. "What?"

"I dream about you," he repeated, and stepped forward until her back was against the refrigerator. Her back against the wall this time, he thought. Not his. "About being with you, touching you." Watching her face, he skimmed his fingertips over the tops of her breasts. "And I wake up tasting you."

"Oh, God."

"You said you felt something when I kissed you, and thought I did, too." With his eyes still on hers, he ran his hands down her sides to her hips. "You were right."

Weak at the knees, she swallowed. Hard. "I was?"

"Yeah. And I want to feel it again."

She strained back as he leaned forward. "Wait!"

His mouth paused a breath from hers. "Why?"

And her mind went blank. "I don't know."

His lips curved in one of his rare smiles. "Stop me when you do," he suggested, then captured her.

It was the same. She was sure it wouldn't be, couldn't be the same fast, hot spin of heart and mind and body. But all those parts of her seemed to have been waiting, and poised to leap. Jody was right, she thought dimly. He'd ruined her.

Bright, fresh, soft as a sunbeam. She was all those things.

Warm, sweet, generous. All the things he'd forgotten to need were trembling in his arms.

And he wanted them, wanted her with a quick punch of greed he hadn't expected.

On an oath, he savaged her throat. "Here. Right here."

"No." It was the last thing she'd expected to hear come out of her own mouth when his hands were making her ache for more. Even as the need roared in her blood she said it again. "No. Wait."

He lifted his head, kept eyes that had gone the color of a storm at sea on hers. "Why?"

"Because I…" Her head fell back on a moan when his hands, slow and firm, stroked up her body, awakening every pore.

"I want you." His thumbs circled her breasts, over them. "You want me."

"Yes, but—" Her hands opened and closed on his shoulders as she fought off a new spurt of longing. "There are a few things I don't let myself do on impulse. I'm really sorry to say this is one of them."

She opened her eyes again, let out one more shaky breath. How closely he watched her, she realized. How sharply, even with desire clouding his mind. He could step back from it, look through it, and measure.

"It's not a game, Preston."

He lifted a brow, surprised that she'd understood his thoughts so clearly. "No? No," he decided, because he believed her. "You wouldn't be good at that kind of game, would you?"

Someone had been, she thought, and was suddenly, brutally sorry for him. "I don't know. I've never played it."

He stepped back, shrugged and seemed completely in control again while her system continued to jangle. Unconsciously, she lifted her fingertips to her throat where his mouth had aroused dozens of raw nerves.

"I need time before I share myself that way. Making love is a gift and shouldn't be given thoughtlessly."

Her words touched him and, for reasons he couldn't understand, settled him. "It often is."

"Not for me." She shook her head. "Not from me."

Because he had a sudden urge to stroke her cheek, he hooked his thumbs in his front pockets. Better not to touch again, he reasoned. Not quite yet. "And telling me that is supposed to make me content to step back?"

"Telling you that is supposed to make you understand why I said no, when I want to say yes. When we both know you could make me say yes."

Heat flicked into his eyes. "That's a dangerous kind of honesty you have there."

"You need the truth." She didn't believe she'd ever known anyone who needed it more. "And I don't lie to men I'm planning to be intimate with."

He stepped forward again, watched her lips tremble on a strangled breath. He could make her say yes…and the power of that was heady. Using it, he realized, would damage something he wasn't completely sure he believed existed.

"You need time," he said. "You got an estimate on that?"

Her breath shuddered out again. "Right now it feels like five minutes ago. But…" She managed a weak laugh when his lips curved. "I can't really say, except you'll be the first to know."

"Maybe we could shave a couple of days off it," he murmured, and indulged himself by leaning down to rub his lips over hers.

Hoping it would focus her, she kept her eyes open. But

her vision went blurry at the edges. "Um, yes, that's probably going to work."

"Let's shoot for a week," he murmured, deepening the kiss degree by degree until she went limp.

When he stepped back, she pressed a hand to her heart. "Fortnight. I've always liked that word, haven't you? We could try for a fortnight."

The last thing he'd expected to do when buffeted by desire was laugh. "I think we'll save that one for later."

"Right, good. Smart." She concentrated on breathing as he turned and picked up his beer. "Well, I have all this…" She gestured vaguely.

"Food?" he suggested. Delighted by her bewilderment.

"Food, yes. I have all this food. I thought I'd fix some…"

He waited a beat while she pressed her hand to her temple and frowned at the stove. "Dinner?"

"That's it. Ha. Dinner. Funny how words just skip out of reach sometimes. I'm going to fix dinner." She blew out a breath. "Would you like to stay for dinner?"

He sipped his beer, leaned back against the counter. "Can I watch you cook?"

"Sure. You can sit there and maybe slice vegetables or something."

"Okay." Because the idea had amazing appeal, he skirted the counter to sit on a stool. "You cook a lot?"

"Yes, I guess. I really like to cook. It's an adventurous process, all the ingredients, heat, timing, the mix of smells and textures and tastes."

"So…do you ever cook naked?"

She paused in the act of sniffing a glossy red pepper. Giggling, she set it on the counter between them. "McQuinn, you made a joke." She put a hand over his, squeezed. "I'm so proud."

"No, I didn't. That was a perfectly serious question."

When she laughed, leaned over to grab his face and kiss him noisily on the mouth, he wouldn't have recognized his own foolish grin. "So do you?"

"Never when I'm sautéing chicken. Which is what I'm about to do."

"That's all right. I have an excellent imagination."

She laughed again; then, catching the wicked gleam in his eyes, cleared her throat. "I think I want some wine. Do you want wine?" He only lifted his nearly full glass of beer. "Oh, yeah."

She took a bottle of white out of the refrigerator, then turned back, giggling again. "You're going to have to stop that."

"Stop what?"

"Stop making me think I'm naked. Go put on some music," she ordered, waving a hand toward the living area. "Maybe open a window, because it's really hot in here, and give me a minute to clear the lust out of my head so I can think of something else to talk about."

"You never have trouble talking."

"You consider that an insult," she said as he slid off the stool. "I don't. I'm a conversation connoisseur."

"Is that the current term for chatterbox?"

"Well, you're just full of wit and humor tonight, aren't you?" And nothing could have pleased her more.

"Must be the company," he murmured, then cocked a brow as he flipped through her CDs. "You have decent taste in music."

"You were expecting otherwise?"

"I wasn't expecting Fats Waller, Aretha, B.B. King. Of course, you've got plenty of chirpy stuff in here, too."

"What's wrong with chirpy music?"

In answer, he held up a CD of *The Partridge Family's Greatest Hits*. "I rest my case."

"Excuse me, but that was given to me by a very dear friend, and it happens to be a classic."

"A classic what?"

"Obviously, you have no appreciation for nostalgia and have failed to recognize the sly, underlying social commentary of David Cassidy's rendition of 'I Think I Love You,' or the desperate sexual motivation that permeates the mood of 'Doesn't Somebody Want To Be Wanted.' But I'd be happy to discuss them with you."

"I bet you actually know the lyrics."

She managed to swallow the chuckle and began to wash the vegetables. "Naturally. During a brief, shining period in my youth, *I* was in a band."

"Right." He settled on B.B.

"Lead vocals and rhythm guitar. The Turbos." She smiled as he walked back to the counter. "Jesse—lead guitar—was into cars."

"You play guitar."

"Yes. Well, I played the guitar. A hot red Fender, which I imagine my mother still has in my old room—along with my toe shoes, my chemistry set, the sketches I made when I was going to be a fashion designer and the books I collected on animal husbandry before I realized that if I became a vet, I'd have to euthanize animals as well as play with them."

She laid a cutting board on the counter, selected the proper knife from her block. "They were all quests."

Fascinating, he thought. The woman was absolutely fascinating. "Fender guitars and toe shoes were quests?"

"I couldn't make up my mind what I wanted to be. Everything I tried was so much fun at first, then it was just work. Do you know how to slice peppers?"

"No. Don't you consider what you do now work, of a sort?"

She sighed and began to slice the peppers herself. "Yes, and it's not of a sort, either. It's a lot of work, but it's still fun. Don't you enjoy writing?"

"Rarely."

She looked up again. "Then why do you do it?"

"It won't let me do anything else. It's my only quest."

She nodded, switching to fat, white mushrooms. "It's like that for my mother. She never wanted to do anything but paint. Sometimes, when I watch her working, I can see how painful it is for her to have a vision and to have to pull out all her skills to transfer what she wants to communicate to canvas. But when she's finished, when it's right, she glows. The satisfaction, maybe even the shock of seeing what she's capable of doing, I suppose. It would be like that for you."

She glanced up, saw him studying her speculatively. "It always surprises you when I understand something other than what's right on the surface, doesn't it?"

He grabbed her hand before she could turn away. "If it does, it only means I'm the one who doesn't understand you. I'm likely to keep offending you until I do."

"I'm ridiculously easy to understand."

"No, that's what I thought. I was wrong. You're a maze, Cybil. With dozens of twists and turns and unexpected angles."

Her smile bloomed slowly, beautifully. "That's the nicest thing you've ever said to me."

"I'm not a nice man. You'd be smart to boot me out, lock your door and keep it that way."

"Being smart, I've figured that out for myself already. However..." Gently, she laid a hand to his cheek. "You seem to be my new quest."

"Until it stops being fun and just becomes work?"

His eyes were so serious, she thought. And he was so ready to believe the worst. "McQuinn, you're already work, and you're still sitting in my kitchen." She smiled again. "Do you know how to slice carrots into pencil sticks?"

"I don't have a clue."

"Then watch and learn. Next time you're going to have to carry your weight." She peeled a carrot clean with a few quick, experienced strokes, then flicked a glance up at him. "Am I still naked?"

"Do you want to be?"

She laughed and picked up her neglected wine.

It took a long time to cook a simple meal when you were distracted by conversation, by lingering looks, by seductive touches.

It took a long time to eat a simple meal when you were sliding lazily into love with the man across from you.

She recognized the signs—the erratic beating of the heart, the bubbling in the blood that was desire. When those were tangled so silkily around dreamy smiles and soft sighs, love was definitely a short trip away.

She wondered what it would be like when she reached it.

It took a long time to say good-night when you were floating on deep, dark kisses in the doorway.

And longer still to sleep when your body ached and your mind was full of dreams.

When she heard the faint drift of his music, she smiled and let it lull her to sleep.

Chapter 6

With his hair still wet from his morning shower, Preston sat at his own kitchen counter on one of Cybil's stools she'd insisted he borrow. He scanned the paper as he ate cold cereal and bananas because Cybil had pushed both on him once she'd gotten a look at his cupboards.

Even a kitchen klutz—which apparently meant him—could manage to pour milk onto cold cereal and slice a banana, she'd told him.

He'd decided against taking offense, though he didn't think he was quite as clumsy in the kitchen as she did. He'd managed to put a salad together, hadn't he? While she'd done something incredible and marvelous to a couple of pork chops.

The woman was one hell of a cook, he mused, and was rapidly spoiling his appetite for the quick slap-together sandwiches he often lived on.

It didn't seem to bother her that they hadn't gone out to dinner since that first meal she'd cooked for him. He imagined she would, before much longer, tire of preparing the evening meal and demand a restaurant.

People generally got itchy for a change of pace when the novelty wore off and routines became ruts.

And he supposed they already had a kind of routine. They kept to their separate corners during the day. Well, except for the couple of times she'd dropped by and persuaded him to go out. To the market, just for a walk, to buy a lamp.

He glanced back toward his living room, frowning at the whimsical bronze frog holding up a triangular-shaped lamp shade. He still wasn't sure how she'd talked him into buying such a thing, or into paying Mrs. Wolinsky for a secondhand recliner she'd wanted to get rid of.

And rightfully so, he decided. Who the hell wanted a green-and-yellow plaid recliner in their living room?

But somehow he had one—which despite its hideous looks was amazingly comfortable.

Of course if you had a chair and a lamp you needed a table. His was a sturdy Chippendale in desperate need of re-finishing—and as Cybil had pointed out—a bargain because of it.

She just happened to have a friend who refinished furni-ture as a hobby, and would put him in touch.

She also just happened to have a friend who was a florist, which explained why there was a vase of cheerful yellow daisies on Preston's kitchen counter.

Another friend—of which Preston had decided she had a legion—painted New York street scenes and sold them on the sidewalk, and couldn't he use a couple of paintings to brighten up the walls?

He'd told her he didn't want to brighten anything, but there were now three very decent original watercolors on his wall.

She was already making noises about rugs.

He didn't know how she worked it, Preston thought, shaking his head as he went back to his breakfast. She just kept talking until you were pulling out your wallet or holding out your hand.

But they kept out of each other's way.

Well, there had been Saturday afternoon, when she'd invaded with buckets and mops and brooms and God knows what. If he was going to live in a place, she'd told him, at least it could be clean. And somehow he'd ended up spending three hours of a rainy afternoon when he should have been writing, scrubbing floors and chasing down dust.

Then again, he'd nearly gotten her into bed. Very nearly gotten her there, he remembered, when she'd stood in speechless shock at the state of his bedroom.

She'd gotten her voice back quickly enough and had launched into a lecture. He should have more respect for his workplace if not for his sleeping area, since they seemed to be one in the same. Why the hell did he keep the curtains drawn over the windows? Did he like caves? Did he have a religious objection to doing laundry?

He'd grabbed her out of self-defense and had stopped her mouth in the most satisfying of ways.

And if they hadn't tripped over a small mountain of laundry on the way to the bed, he doubted they'd have ended the afternoon with a trip to the cleaners.

Still, there were advantages, he thought. He appreciated a clean space, even though he rarely noticed a messy one. He liked tumbling into bed on freshly laundered sheets— though he would have preferred to tumble on them with Cybil. And it was hard to complain when you opened a cupboard and found actual food.

Even the sexual frustration was working for him. The

writing was pouring out of it, and out of him. Maybe the play had taken a turn on him, focusing now more on a female character, one with a shining naïveté and enthusiasm. A woman alive with energy and optimism. And one who'd be seduced by and damaged by a man who had none of those things inside him. A man who wouldn't be able to stop himself from taking them from her, then leaving her shattered.

He saw the parallels well enough between what he created and what was, but he refused to worry about it.

He sipped his coffee, reminding himself to ask Cybil why his always tasted faintly of swamp water, and turned to the comic section to see what she'd been up to.

He skimmed it, frowned, then went back to the first section and read it again.

She was already at work, her window open, because spring had decided to be kind. A lovely warm breeze wafted through along with the chaos of street noise.

After her sheet of paper was set and scaled, she set her T-square back in its place in the custom-built tool area she'd designed to suit herself. She tilted her head, facing the first blank section. It was double the size of what would appear in the dailies in a couple of weeks. She already had it in her mind—the setup, the situation and the punch line that would comprise those five windows and give the readership their morning chuckle over coffee.

The elusive Mr. Mysterious, now known as Quinn, huddled in his dim cave, writing the Great American Novel. Sexy, cranky, irresistible Quinn, so serious, so intense in his own little world he was completely unaware that Emily was crouched on his fire escape, peering through the narrow chink of his perpetually drawn curtains, struggling to read his work in progress through a pair of binoculars.

Amused at herself—because in her own way Cybil knew her subtle little probes and questions on how his play was going were the more civilized version of her counterpart's voyeurism, she settled down to lightly sketch her professional interpretation of the man across the hall.

She exaggerated ruthlessly, his good points and his bad. The tall, muscular body, the ruggedly chiseled looks, the cool eyes. His rudeness, his humor and his perpetual bafflement with the world Emily lived in.

Poor guy, she thought, he doesn't have a clue what to do with her.

When the buzzer sounded, she tucked her pencil behind her ear, thinking Jody had forgotten her key.

She stopped to top off her coffee cup on the way. "Just hang on. Coming."

Then she opened the door and experienced one more rapid meltdown. His hair was just a little damp and he wasn't wearing a shirt. Boy, oh, boy, just look at those pecs, she thought, and barely resisted licking her lips.

His jeans were faded, his feet bare, and his face—his face was so wonderfully serious and sober.

"Hi." She managed to make it sound bright and easy while she pictured herself biting him. "You run out of soap in the shower? Need to borrow some?"

"What? No." He'd forgotten he was only half-dressed. "I want to ask you about this," he continued, lifting the paper.

"Sure, come on in." It would be safe, she told herself. Jody would be there any minute and stop her from jumping Preston. "Why don't you get some coffee and come up? I'm working and it's rolling pretty well."

"I don't want to interrupt, but—"

"Not much does," she said cheerfully over her shoulder as she started up the stairs. "There's cinnamon bagels if you want one."

"No." Hell, he thought, and ended up pouring a cup of coffee and taking a bagel after all.

He hadn't been upstairs before, since he'd never come over when she was working. He tormented himself by glancing into her bedroom, studying the big bed with its bold blue cover and sumptuous mountain of jewel-toned pillows, the slim rods of the white iron headboard where he could imagine trapping her hands under his as he finally did everything he wanted with her. To her.

It smelled of her, fresh, female, with seductive undertones of vanilla.

She kept rose petals in a bowl, a book beside the bed and candles in the window.

"Find everything?" she called out.

He shook himself. "Yeah. Listen, Cybil…" He stepped into her studio. "God, how do you work with all that noise?"

She barely glanced up. "What noise? Oh, that." She continued to sketch, using a new pencil, as she'd forgotten the one behind her ear. "Sort of like background music. Half the time I don't hear it."

The room looked efficient and creative with its neat shelves holding both supplies and clever tchotchkes. He recognized the work of the sidewalk artist in one of the paintings on her wall, and the genius of her mother in two others.

There was a complex and fascinating metal sculpture in the corner, a little clutch of violets tucked into a glass inkwell and a cozy divan heaped with more pillows against the wall.

But she didn't look efficient, bent over the big slanted board with her legs folded up under her, the toenails of her bare feet painted pink, a pencil behind one ear and a gold hoop in the other.

She looked scattered, and sexy.

Curious, he walked around to peer over her shoulder. An act that, he admitted, had anyone dared to try on him would have earned the offender a quick and painful death.

"What are all the blue lines for?"

"Scaling, perspective. Takes a little math before you can get down to business. I work in five windows for the dailies," she continued, sketching easily. "I have to set them on paper like this, work out the theme, the gag, the hit, so that the strip can move from start to finish in five connected beats."

Satisfied, she moved to the next section. "I sketch it in first, just need to see how it hangs—you'd say a draft, where you get the story line down, then decide where it needs to be punched up. I'll give it more details, fiddle a bit before I switch to pen and ink."

He frowned, focusing on the first sketch. "Is that supposed to be me?"

"Hmm. Why don't you pull up a stool. You're blocking the light."

"What is she doing there?" Ignoring the suggestion, he tapped a finger on the second window. "Spying on me. You're spying on me?"

"Don't be ridiculous—you don't even have a fire escape outside your bedroom." She looked into her mirror, made several faces that left him staring at her, then started on the third section.

"What about this?" he demanded, rapping the paper on her shoulder.

"What about it? God, you smell fabulous." Pleasing herself, she turned and sniffed him. "What kind of soap is that?"

"Are you going to have this guy take a shower next?" When she pursed her lips in obvious consideration, Preston shook his head. "No. There has to be a line. I was oddly amused when you introduced this parody of me into the script, but—"

He broke off as he heard her front door open and slam shut. "Who's that?"

"That would be Jody and Charlie. So you've gotten a kick out of the new guy?" She stopped sketching and shifted to smile up at him. "I wondered, because you hadn't mentioned it before. You know, some people don't even recognize themselves. They just have no self-awareness, I suppose, but I thought you'd see it if you happened to read the strip. Hi, Jody. There's Charlie."

"Hi." It wasn't an easy matter, even for a happily married woman, to keep her tongue from falling out when she was so suddenly and unexpectedly faced with a well-muscled, naked male chest. "Uh, hi. Are we interrupting?"

"No, Preston just had some questions about the strip."

"I love the new guy. He's really got Emily in a spin. I can't wait to see what happens next." She broke into a wide grin as Charlie exploded out a "Da!" and reached for Preston.

"He calls every man he sees 'Da.' Chuck's a little put out by it, but Charlie's just a guy's guy, you know."

"Right." Absently, Preston ran a hand over Charlie's downy brown hair. "I just want to get something straight about how this thing is going," he began, turning back to Cybil.

"Da!" Charlie said again, arms extended hopefully, smile sleepy.

"Just how close to reality do you work?" Preston asked, automatically taking the baby and settling him on his shoulder.

Cybil's heart simply melted. "You like babies."

"No, I toss them out of third-story windows at every opportunity," he said impatiently, then shook his head when Jody squeaked. "Relax. He's fine. What I want to know is this business here." Shifting the baby, he dropped the comic section on her board.

"Oh, the 'no scale' bit. This is really part one. They'll run the second half of it tomorrow. I think it works."

"Chuck and I fell over laughing when we read it this morning," Jody put in, relaxed again as she watched Preston absently patting the now-sleeping baby.

"You've got these two women here—"

"Emily and Cari."

"I know who they are by now," Preston muttered, narrowing his eyes at both women. "They're discussing—they're rating, for God's sake—the way Quinn kissed Emily a couple days ago."

"Uh-huh. Chuck laughed?" Cybil wanted to know. "I wondered if men would get it or if it would just hit with women."

"Oh, yeah, he died over it."

"Pardon me." With what he considered admirable restraint, Preston held up a hand. "I'd like to know if the two of you sit around here discussing your various sexual encounters and then rating them on a scale of one to ten before you then give the American public a good chuckle over it with their corn flakes."

"Discussing them?" Eyes wide and innocent, Cybil stared up at Preston. "Honestly, McQuinn, this is a comic strip. You're taking it too seriously."

"So all this about the no scale is just a bit?"

"What else?"

He studied her face. "I wouldn't like to think that when I finally get you into bed, I'm going to read about my performance in five sections in the morning paper."

"Oh, my. Oh, well." Jody patted a hand on her heart. "I think I'll just take Charlie and go put him down for his nap." She eased him out of Preston's arms and hurried out.

"McQuinn." Cybil smiled, tapped her pencil. "I have a feeling that event would be worth the full Sunday spread."

"Is that a threat or a joke?"

When she only laughed, he spun her stool around, then knocked the air out of her lungs with a fierce and demanding kiss. "Tell your friend to go away, and we'll find out."

"No, I'm keeping her. She's all that stopped me from biting your throat when you came in."

"Are you trying to drive me crazy?"

"Not really. It's kind of a side effect." Her pulse had gone from slow shuffle to manic tap dance. "You've got to go. I've finally found a distraction I can't work through. And you're it."

Seeing no reason he should go crazy alone, he leaned down one last time and took her mouth. "When you speak of this—" he caught her bottom lip between his teeth, drawing it erotically through them "—and I expect you will, be accurate."

He walked to the doorway, turning back in time to see her shudder. "No scale?" he said, realizing he suddenly found it not just amusing but gratifying.

When she managed to do nothing more than make one helpless gesture with her hands, he laughed. And was still grinning when he jogged down her steps and out the door.

"Safe?" Jody whispered, poking her head into the doorway.

"Oh, God, God, Jody, what am I going to do here?" Shaken, Cybil stabbed the second pencil behind her ear, knocked the first out of place, and didn't even bother to curse. "I thought I had it all figured out. I mean what's wrong with easing yourself into what promises to be a blistering, roof-raising affair with an incredibly intense, gorgeous, interesting man?"

"Let me think." Holding up a finger, Jody strolled in and picked up the coffee Preston had never touched. "Okay, I've got it. Nothing. The answer to that question is nothing."

"And if you're a little bit in love with him, that only sweetens the deal, right?"

"Absolutely. Otherwise it's fun but sort of like eating too much chocolate at one sitting. You enjoy it when it's going on, then you feel a little queasy and ashamed."

"But what if you went all the way in. What do you do when you've gone over the brink?"

Jody set down the coffee. "You went over the brink?"

"Just now."

"Oh, honey." All sympathy, Jody wrapped her arms around Cybil and rocked. "It's all right. It had to happen sooner or later."

"I know, but I always thought it would be later."

"We all do."

"He won't want me to be in love with him. It'll just annoy him." Turning her face to Jody's shoulder, she let out a shaky breath. "I'm not too happy about it myself, but I'll get used to it."

"Sure you will. Poor Frank." With a sigh, Jody patted Cybil's shoulder, then stepped back. "He never really had a shot, did he?"

"Sorry."

"Oh, well." Jody dismissed her favorite cousin with an absent flick of the wrist. "What are you going to do?"

"I don't know. I guess running and hiding's out."

"That's for wimps."

"Yeah. Wimps. How about pretending it'll go away?"

"That's for morons."

Cybil drew a bracing breath. "How about shopping?"

"Now you're talking." On a quick salute, Jody headed for the door. "I'll see if Mrs. Wolinsky will watch Charlie, then we'll handle this problem like real women."

She bought a new dress. A slinky length of black sin that made Jody roll her eyes and declare, "The man's a goner," when Cybil tried it on.

She bought new shoes. Mile-high heels as thin as honed scalpels.

She bought new lingerie. The kind women wear when they expect it to be seen by a man who'll then be compelled to rip it off.

And she imagined Preston's wide hands and long fingers peeling the silky-as-cobwebs hose down her legs.

Then there were flowers to choose, candles, wine.

Marketing for a meal she would design to tease the senses and whet the palate for a more primitive kind of appetite.

By the time she got home she was loaded down, and she was calm.

There was a scene to be set, and doing so gave her focus. Because she wanted to take the rest of the day to prepare, because she needed it to be perfect, she wrote a note to Preston and stuck it to her door.

Then she locked herself in, drew a deep breath and took everything up to the bedroom.

She arranged tender lilies and fragrant rosebuds in vases, in bowls, and set them on tables, the dresser, the windowsills. Then she grouped candles, all white, a trio here, a single there, a half-dozen scented tealights on a circle of mirrored glass.

Some she lit so the room would fill with soft light and gentle fragrance while she worked.

She unwrapped two slender-stemmed wineglasses, placed them just so on the low table in front of the curved wicker chaise. Reminded herself to chill the wine.

Facing the bed, she stopped, considered. Would turning down the duvet and sheets be too obvious? Then she laughed at herself. Why stop now?

When it was done, when she could look around the room and see there was nothing that wasn't as she needed it to be, she went down to make the early preparations for the meal she intended to cook.

She listened, hoping he'd begin to play so that some of him would come inside her rooms with her. But his apartment remained silent.

With careful deliberation she chose music for mood, arranging CDs in her changer.

Satisfied, she went back up, laid her new dress on the bed, shivered in anticipation as she set the black lace bra and the blatantly provocative matching garter belt beside it and imagined what it would feel like to wear them.

Powerful, she decided. Secretive and certain.

She shivered again, thrilling to the clutch of lust deep in her center, then went to draw a hot, frothy bath.

She poured wine, lit more candles to promote the mood, before she slipped into the tub. And closing her eyes, she imagined Preston's hands, rather than the frothy water, on her.

Nearly an hour later, she was slathering every inch of her body with cream, sliding her fingers along to make certain her skin was silky and scented, when Preston tugged her note off the front door:

McQuinn, I've got plans. I'll see you later. Cybil

Plans? Plans? She had plans when he'd worked himself into a turmoil over her all day? He read the note again, furious with both of them, as he hadn't been able to get the image of spending yet another foolish evening with her out of his head.

For God's sake, he'd gone out and bought her flowers. He hadn't bought flowers for a woman since…

He crumpled the note in his hand. What else could he expect? Women were, first and foremost, tuned to their own agenda. He'd known it, accepted it, and if he'd let himself forget that single relevant detail with Cybil, he had no one to blame but himself.

She'd see him later?

It appeared she was a game player after all. But he didn't have to step up to bat.

He turned, marched back into his apartment, where he tossed the lilacs that had inexplicably reminded him of her on the kitchen counter. He flipped her balled note across the room, picked up his sax and stalked out to work off his temper at Delta's.

At exactly seven-thirty, Cybil took the stuffed mushrooms she'd slaved over out of the oven. The table was set for two, with more candles, more flowers precisely arranged. There was a wonderfully colorful avocado-and-tomato salad chilling along with the wine.

Once they'd enjoyed their appetizers and first course, she intended to destroy him with her seafood crepes.

If all went according the plan, they'd polish off the meal with icy champagne and fresh raspberries and cream. In bed.

"Okay, Cybil."

She took off her apron, marched to the mirror to check the fit and line of the dress. She slipped on her heels, added another dash of perfume, then gave her reflection a bracing smile.

"Let's go get him."

She sauntered across the hall, pressed his buzzer, then waited with her heart hammering. Shifting from foot to foot, she buzzed again.

"How could you not be home? How *could* you? Didn't you get the note? You must have. It's not on the door, is it? Didn't I specifically say I'd see you later?"

Groaning, she thumped her fist against the door. Then she jerked upright and blinked.

"I said I had plans. Oh, my God, you didn't get it, did you, you thick-headed jerk? *You're* the plans. Oh, hell." She made a dash back through her open door for her key, realized she didn't have anywhere to put it. With a shrug, she stuck it into her bra rather than waste time running upstairs for a bag.

In thirty seconds flat, she was risking a broken neck by running down the stairs.

"Woman trouble, sugar lips?"

Preston looked over at Delta as he took a break to wet his throat. "No woman. No trouble."

"This is Delta." She tapped a finger to his cheek. "Every night this week you come in here late and you play like a man who's got a woman on his mind. And this man doesn't much mind having her there. Now tonight, you come in early and you're playing like a man who's got trouble with the woman. Did you have a fight with that pretty little girl?"

"No. We've both got other things to do."

"Still holding you off, is she?" She laughed, but not without sympathy. "Some woman take more romance than others."

"It has nothing to do with romance."

"Maybe that's your problem." Delta wrapped an arm around his shoulders and squeezed. "Do you ever buy her flowers? Tell her she has beautiful eyes."

"No." Damn it, he had brought her flowers. She hadn't bothered to stick around to take them. "It's sex, not a courtship."

"Oh, sweetheart. You want one, you better do the other with a woman like that."

"That's why I'm better off without a woman like that. I want it simple." He picked up the sax, lifted a brow. "Now, are you going to let me play, or do you want to give me more advice on my love life?"

With a shake of her head, she stepped back. "When you have a love life, *cher,* I'll have advice."

He blew off a riff, listening to the music inside his head. Inside his blood. He let the notes come, but the music didn't take his mind off her. He could use that, as well, he told himself. Here, where sharing was a pleasure. Not with words, where it was often pain.

The notes slipped out, throbbed in the air, sobbed into a wail.

And she walked in the door.

Her eyes, full of secrets, met his through the haze of smoke, held. And the smile she sent him as she slid into a chair made his palms go damp. She moistened her lips, trailed a finger up from the center of the low bodice of the slinky black dress to the base of her throat. And back again.

He watched, his blood swimming, as she crossed long, long legs with a movement so slow, so studied, it had to be deliberate. Surely the way she ran her hand from calf to knee to thigh was designed to make a man's gaze follow the movement.

His did, and his pulse leaped like a wolf on the hunt.

She sat through the song, leaning back in the chair, hooking one arm provocatively over the back. When the notes faded, she traced the tip of her tongue lazily over those hot red lips.

Nora Roberts

Then she rose, her gaze still locked with his as the music pumped. She ran a hand down her hip, turned on those man-killer heels and started back out. She glanced over her shoulder, sent him a sultry invitation with no more than a lift of eyebrow and left the door swinging behind her.

The oath that came out of his mouth when he lowered the sax was absolutely reverent.

"You going after that, brother?"

Preston crouched to push his sax into its case. "Do I look stupid, André?"

"No." André chuckled and kept on playing. "No, you don't."

Chapter 7

She was waiting on the sidewalk when he came out, standing in the white wash of a streetlight with one hand resting on a cocked hip, her head angled, her lips curved in the barest hint of a smile. It made him think of a photograph, some arty shot perfectly framed and cropped for a classy magazine.

Sex in black and white.

He started toward her, taking more in the closer he came. The short, whiskey-colored hair sleeked to frame her face. The short black dress sleeked to frame her body.

No jewelry to distract the eye.

Mile-high heels designed to showcase mile-long legs.

The only color was on those huge green eyes under sooty lashes and the siren red of her mouth. A mouth, he noted, that was curved in smug, female satisfaction.

He was three steps away when her scent reached out like a crooked finger and beckoned him the rest of the way.

"Hello, neighbor." She purred it—one more hot bullet to his loins.

He tilted his head, lifted a brow. "Change of plans... neighbor?"

"I hope not." She took the last step, moving into him, deliberately sliding her hands up his sides, over his shoulders, around his neck. Her body fit suggestively to his as she purred again.

Then she laughed, shook her head. "You were the plans, you knothead."

She wondered if it was the announcement or the mild insult that had his eyes narrowing in speculation.

"Is that so?"

"McQuinn." She tilted her head, brought her mouth a whisper from his. Then, with her eyes on his, slowly licked. "Didn't I tell you you'd be the first to know?"

"Yeah." With his free hand he cupped her neck, keeping that wet red mouth tantalizingly close to his. "How fast can you walk in those heels?"

She laughed again, just a little breathlessly now. "Not very. But we've got all night, don't we?"

"It might just take longer than that." He stepped back, and after a moment, held out a hand for hers. "Where did you get the lethal weapon? The dress," he added when she gave him a blank look.

"Oh, this old thing." This time her laugh was warm and rich. "I bought it today, thinking of you. And when I put it on tonight, I was thinking of what it was going to be like when you took it off me."

"You must have been practicing," he said when he could manage to form words again. "Because you're damn good at this."

"Actually, I'm making it up as I go along."

"Don't stop on my account."

It was amazing, she thought, that a balmy spring evening

could suddenly seem as sultry as summer in the Tropics. "Sorry I wasn't more specific in my note. I had a lot on my mind." She turned, delighted that the heels brought her eye level with his mouth. "A lot of you on my mind."

"It pissed me off." It didn't seem so hard to admit it.

"Pardon me if I find that very flattering. When I knocked on your door and you didn't answer, I had essentially the same reaction. I spent a lot of time getting ready for you. You can be flattered."

"It must have taken a while to paint on what there is of that dress."

"Not just that." She'd managed to keep her heartbeat fairly steady, but as she paused at the entrance to their building, it began to plunge and kick. "I made dinner."

"You did?" He wasn't just flattered, he realized. He wasn't just aroused. He was touched.

"A fairly fabulous one, if I do say so myself," she added, backing into the building. "With a sassy little white wine to set it off—and an elegant and icy champagne to go with dessert."

She led the way into the elevator, pushed the button for three, then leaned back against the wall. "Which I thought we could enjoy in bed."

He kept a step away, knowing if he touched her they wouldn't be leaving the elevator for a very long time. "Anything else I should know about these plans of yours?"

"Oh, I don't think you're going to need me to write anything down." She stepped off the elevator, tossed one of those slow smiles over her shoulder and strolled to her door.

He thought if he managed to get inside without exploding, he'd show her he could make plans of his own. "Key?"

"Hmm." Keeping her eyes on his, she slid a finger under the deep scoop of her bodice, touched metal and watched his gaze drop, heat, linger. "Gee." She slid her finger up again, circled it lazily at the base of her throat. "I can't seem to find it. Maybe you can get it for me."

He decided he had news for medical science. It was possible to remain conscious and upright after all the blood had drained out of your head.

He trailed his finger along the inviting swell above the black silk—felt her shiver, heard the catchy intake of her breath. Then dipped down, taking his time, gliding his finger lazily over heated flesh, gently abrading her nipple until her eyes clouded and closed.

"I'd say you're the one who's been practicing," she managed, and made him smile.

"I'm just making it up as I go along."

"Mmm-hmm. Don't stop on my account."

He didn't intend to. Not for hours. "Looks like I found it," he murmured, hooking the key.

"Yeah." She let out a long, long breath. "I just knew you would."

He slid the key home, released locks. "Ask me in, Cybil."

"Come in."

He pushed open the door, backed her inside. Reaching behind, he locked the door. Clamping his hands on her hips, he kept walking.

"Dinner?"

"Can wait." He lifted the phone off the hook as they passed it.

"The wine?"

"Later. Much later." Her heels bumped into the bottom step. This time he smiled. "Keep going."

On legs that had gone weak, she moved up the stairs with her hands braced on his shoulders.

"Ask me to touch you."

"Touch me." She sighed as his hands traveled up.

"Ask me to taste you."

"Taste me." And moaned as his mouth brushed over the rise of her breasts.

When they reached the bedroom door, his teeth scraped along her throat, her jaw, and left her mouth aching for attention.

"Kiss me."

"I will." But he only teased the corners of her lips with the tip of his tongue. "I want the light."

"No, I have candles. They're everywhere." She broke free to grab a matchbook, then fumbled. "I can't. I'm shaking. Isn't that ridiculous?"

He took the matches from her and danced his fingertips along her thigh. "I want you to. Don't move," he ordered, then worked his way around the room setting the candles alight.

The glow shimmered. The scent whispered.

Tossing the matches aside, he moved back to where she stood, her eyes huge and full of nerves, needs and candlelight.

"Now." His hands slid around her waist, down. "Ask me to take you."

She kept her eyes on his. "Take me."

His mouth captured hers, plundered, rocking her with the first punch of the power they'd built between them. She grabbed on, as much to add to the storm as ride it. This was what she wanted, this bold, blistering, battering heat. The crash of senses, the war of needs.

"I want you." She raced wild kisses over his face. "I want you in bed."

Then she gasped as he whirled her around, dragged her back against him. It stunned her to see them reflected in the mirror, to see the gleam of desire in his gaze as it traveled down her body.

"We have all night," he reminded her. "Watch."

He dipped his head to the curve of her neck and shoulder, sharp little bites that had the first helpless sounds catching in her throat.

She watched his hands travel up, saw them, felt them cup her breasts, squeeze, release, slide over silk, his fingers sliding under it, tugging the material. She braced for him to rip.

Then shuddered as he simply let his hands glide over her again, then down. She cried out in aroused shock as he pressed against her center.

His head lifted, his teeth catching the lobe of her ear as their gazes met in the mirror. She'd driven him crazy when she'd walked into the club. He intended to return the favor.

"Tell me you want more."

Her muscles had gone lax, her bones to jelly. "Preston."

He traced his fingers up and down her thighs, felt the muscles quiver and the flesh heat. "Tell me you want more."

"God." Her head fell back on his shoulder as she fought for air. "I want more."

"So do I."

He moved from silky hose to silky flesh, torturing himself. Her scent was destroying him, the feel of her urging him to take all of her. But he drew it out, even as his own breath became labored; he held back the animal pacing inside him.

Because when he let it go, he knew it would devour them both.

He nipped his way around the back of her neck, her shoulders, while he tugged down the zipper of her dress. He peeled it off her, then bit back a groan.

Sex in black and white, he thought again.

Even through the haze of desire she saw his eyes change. Saw something dangerous flash into them. It shocked her to realize that was what she wanted. The danger, the risk, the glory of breaking whatever choke chain he had on his control.

Power swirled into her as she covered his hands with hers and guided them over her. "I bought this today," she whispered, holding his hands to her breasts. "So you could rip it off me tonight."

She curled her fingers with his, nudged them over the thin silk connecting the lace. And let out one sharp gasp when he yanked the dress apart.

And with that single movement, he broke.

He spun her around, his mouth ravishing hers now, his hands close to brutal as he dragged her to the bed.

He was going to eat her alive, and couldn't stop it. He felt her arch and buck when his hand covered her. Heard her choked scream as he drove her over the first ragged edge. Then he was tearing at silk and lace, desperate for more.

He feasted on her breasts, the firm fragrant swell of them, while her heart hammered against his mouth. Her hands drove him wild as they pulled at his shirt, as her nails scraped down his back.

Her mouth was as greedy as his, her hands as rough and impatient as they tugged and dragged at his jeans. And when they closed around him, fire burst in his blood.

She rolled with him, tangling in the sheets she'd so carefully smoothed. Panting, shuddering, she wrapped herself around him, bowed up in urgent demand.

When he drove into her, heat into heat, the explosion of pleasure was huge, a fast, hard, turbulent wave that drenched the skin and swamped the soul. With one throaty moan, she matched him for speed and fury.

More was all he could think. He had to have more of her. Clamping her hands on the slim iron poles of the headboard, he plunged deeper. She arched, accepted. Mad on the pleasure of her, he watched her face, absorbing every flicker of shock and delight as he took her higher, and faster, then over so that she sobbed out his name, so that her eyes went dark and blind.

As her body melted under his, he let himself pour into her. Surrendered himself.

His hands continued to hold hers on the rungs, though her fingers had gone limp. His body continued to cover hers while she quaked. He stayed inside her. Mated.

"Are we still breathing?"

He turned his head, felt the pulse in her throat scrambling. "Your heart's still beating."

"Good, that's good. Is yours?"

"Seems to be."

"Okay, then it's probably safe for us to stay here like this for the next five or ten years. I'm pretty sure I'll be able to move by then."

He lifted his head. Though she kept her eyes closed, Cybil was aware she was being studied, imagined that clear blue and focused gaze. And smiled. "I seduced the hell out of you, McQuinn. It was awfully nice of you to return the favor."

"No problem. It was the least I could do."

"Nobody ever made me feel like this before." She opened her eyes. "No one ever touched me this way."

She saw her mistake immediately. The way his eyes shuttered, the way he retreated from the intimacy. If it was light, if it was sexy, if it was dangerous, he was with her. But there was to be no tenderness, no heart, no slippery sentiment, to change the balance.

It made her ache for both of them.

"You've got great hands." She made her smile sassy as she wiggled her fingers under his. "Definitely major-league hands."

"You've got some real contenders yourself." He rolled onto his back, relieved and annoyed with himself for feeling that deep inner jolt when she'd looked at him with so much dazzled emotion in her eyes.

He wasn't going to let things shift into that area between them. Because once it did, it was over. That part of him that was hope and heart had long ago been calcified.

She wanted to curl into him, to curve her body into the warmth of his, but imagined that was another taboo. Keep it simple, she warned herself, or he'll walk right out the door.

So she sat up, instead, flicked her fingers through her disordered hair. "I think that wine would go down well right now, don't you?"

"Oh, yeah." He skimmed his fingers along her calf, because he had to touch, had to keep that connection. "You mentioned something about dinner."

"McQuinn, I have an amazing meal in store for you." She leaned down to give him a careless kiss. "Everything's done but the crepes—seafood crepes, which I will whip up in front of your astonished eyes."

"You're going to cook?"

"Mmm-hmm."

He watched her slide out of bed, walk to the closet on legs that had his blood stirring again. "What's that for?"

"This? It's called a robe," she said with a laugh as she slipped into it. "It's often used to cover nakedness."

He got up, crossed to her and tugged the belt loose again. "Take it off."

A quick thrill shimmied down her spine. "I thought you wanted dinner."

"I do. And I want to watch you cook it."

"Then—oh." She laughed again and pulled the robe together. "I am not cooking crepes naked. That little fantasy of yours is doomed."

He didn't think so. "Actually, I was wondering if you had any more of…" He turned to the bed, found what was left of the lacy black garter belt. "This sort of thing."

Surprised, then intrigued, she lifted her eyebrows. "No intelligent shopper buys only one. I have another little ensemble in red. Break-your-heart, tart red."

His smile spread slowly as he tossed the black lace aside. "Why don't you put it on? I'm really hungry."

Preparing crepes in sexy underwear was not without its risks. Cybil discovered just what it was like to be ravished against the pantry door.

Amazing.

And plundered on the living-room rug.

Incredible.

And being savaged under the hot, beating spray of the shower was an experience she would be more than willing to repeat.

Through the hours of the night he'd reached for her, thrilled her, had never seemed quite able to get enough of her. Or she of him. They'd been so completely in tune, so utterly together, that at times it had seemed his heart had beat inside hers.

The candles had gutted out in their own fragrant pools, and light had been seeping softly through the windows when she'd fallen into an exhausted sleep.

Only to wake alone.

She knew it shouldn't hurt her that he hadn't slept with her, hadn't woken with her. It wasn't to be like that between them. She knew that, accepted that. There would be no soft and foolish words between them, no baring of souls.

The border of intimacy stopped at the physical, with his side of it walled thick. Her heart was her own problem, not his.

How could he know she'd never given herself so absolutely to any other man? Why should he be expected to know that the primitive power of their desire for each other was driven by love on her side?

She rubbed her tired eyes and ordered herself up and out of bed.

She'd walked into the relationship with her eyes open, she thought as she tidied up the bedroom. She'd known its limitations. His limitations. They could be together, enjoy each other, as long as certain lines weren't crossed.

Well, that was fine. She wasn't going to pine and sigh over it. She was in charge of her own emotions; she was responsible for her own actions; and she was hardly going to mope around because she was involved with an exciting, fascinating, interesting man.

"Damn it!" She hurled her shoes into the closet. "Damn it, damn it, damn it!"

Cybil leaped on the bed, grabbed the phone. She had to tell someone, talk to someone. And when it was this vital, there was really only one someone.

"Mama? Mama, I'm in love," she said, then burst into wild tears.

Preston's fingers flew over the keyboard. He'd had less than three hours' sleep, but his system was revved, his mind clear as crystal. His first major play had been wrenched out of him, every word a wound. But this was pouring out, streaming like wine out of a magic bottle that had only been waiting to be decanted.

It was so fully alive. And for the first time in longer than he could remember, so was he.

He could see it all perfectly, the sets, the staging, the characters and everything inside them. The doomed, the damned, the triumphant.

A world in three acts.

There was an energy here, inside these people who formed on the page and lived on the stage already set inside his head. He knew them, knew how their hearts would leap and how they would break.

The thread of hope that ran through their lives hadn't been planned, but it was there, woven through and tangled so that he found himself riding on it with them.

He wrote until he ran dry; then, disoriented, glanced around the room. It was dark but for the lamp he'd switched on and the steady glow from his computer screen. He hadn't a clue what time it was—what day, for that matter. But his neck and shoulders were stiff, his stomach empty, and the coffee in the cup on his desk looked faintly revolting.

Standing, he worked out the worst of the kinks, then walked to the window, pushed open the curtains. There was a hell of a spring storm going on. He hadn't noticed. Now he watched the flashing of lightning, the scurry of desperate pedestrians rushing to appointments or shelter.

The entrepreneur on the corner was doing a brisk business in the umbrellas, which no one in New York seemed to own for longer than it took the pavement to dry.

He wondered if Cybil was looking out her window, watching the same scene. What she would think of it, how she would turn something so simple and ordinary as a thunderstorm in the city into the bright and ridiculous.

She'd use the Umbrella Man, he decided, work up an entire biography for him, give the figure in black slicker and hood a name, a background, a personality full of quirks. And the anonymous street vendor would become part of her world.

She had such a gift for drawing people into her world.

He was in it now, Preston mused. He hadn't been able to stop himself from opening that colorful door and stepping inside the confusion, the delights, the energy.

She didn't seem to understand he didn't belong there.

When he was inside, when he was surrounded by her, it seemed as though he could stay. That if he let it, life could be just that simple and extraordinary.

Like a storm in the city, he thought. But storms pass.

He'd nearly let himself sink into it that morning. Nearly let himself sink in and stay in that warm bed, with that warm body that had turned to curl around him in sleep.

She'd looked so…soft, he thought now. So welcoming. What had moved through him as he'd watched her in that fragile light had been a different kind of hunger. One that yearned to hold, to sigh out all the troubles and doubts and hold on to dreams.

It had been safer for both of them to leave her sleeping.

He flicked the curtains closed and walked downstairs.

He started fresh coffee, foraged for food, toyed with the idea of a nap.

But he thought of her, and of the night, and knew the restlessness inside him wouldn't allow him to rest.

What was she doing over there?

He had no business knocking on her door, interrupting her work just because his was finished for now. Just because the drum of rain made him feel edgy and alone. Just because he wanted her.

He liked being alone, he reminded himself as he prowled the living area. He needed the edge for his work.

He wanted to sit with her and watch the rain. To make slow, lazy love with her while it pounded the streets and sidewalks and cocooned them from everything but each other.

Wanted her, he admitted, just a little too much for comfort.

He told himself it was safe enough to want. It was crossing the line from want to need that was dangerous. Just how close, he wondered, was he already skirting that very thin, very shaky line?

When a woman got inside a man this way, it changed him, left him wide-open so that he made mistakes and exposed pieces of himself better left alone.

She wasn't Pamela. He wasn't so blind he believed every woman was a liar and a cheat and cold as stone. If he'd ever known anyone with less potential for cruelty and deceit, it was Cybil Campbell.

But that didn't change the bottom line.

From want to need to love were short, skidding steps. Once a man had taken the fall and ended up broken, he learned to keep his balance at all costs. He didn't want the desperation, the vulnerability, the loss of self that went hand in hand with genuine intimacy. And he'd stopped believing himself capable of those things.

Which meant there was nothing to worry about, he told himself, sipping his coffee and staring at his door as if he could see through it and through the one across the hall. She wasn't asking for anything more than passion, companionship, enjoyment.

Exactly as he was.

She was perfectly aware the arrangement was temporary.

He'd be gone in a few weeks, and their lives would go comfortably in other directions. She with her crowds of friends, he with his contented solitude.

He'd set his cup down with a violent snap before he realized the idea annoyed him.

They could still see each other from time to time, he told

himself as he began to pace again. His house in Connecticut was a reasonable commute from the city. Isn't that why he'd chosen it in the first place?

He came into the city often enough. There was no reason he couldn't make it more often.

Until she got involved with someone else, he thought, jamming his hands in his pockets. Why should a woman like that wait around for him to breeze in and out of her life?

And that was fine, too, he decided as his temper began to rumble like the thunder outside. Who was asking her to wait around? She could damn well hook herself up with any idiot her interfering friends tossed at her.

But not, by God, while he was still across the hall.

He strode to her door, intending to make a few things clear. And opened it just in time to watch Cybil launch herself joyfully into the arms of a tall man with sun-streaked brown hair.

"Still the prettiest girl in New York," he said in a voice that hinted of beignets and chicory. "Give me a kiss."

And as she did, lavishly, Preston wondered which method of murder would be most satisfying.

Chapter 8

"Matthew! Why didn't you tell me you were coming? When did you get in? How long are you staying? Oh, I'm so happy to see you! You're all wet. Come inside, take off your jacket—when are you going to buy a new one? This one looks like it's been through a war."

He only laughed, hefted her off her feet and kissed her again. "You still never shut up."

"I babble when I'm happy. When are you—oh, Preston." She beamed at him out of eyes shining with joy. "I didn't see you there."

"Obviously." Bare hands, he thought, would be the most satisfying. He would simply take the guy with the smug brown eyes and the scarred leather jacket apart piece by piece. And feed each one to Cybil. "Don't let me interrupt the reunion."

"It's great, isn't it? Matthew, this is Preston McQuinn."

"McQuinn?" Matthew ran his tongue around his teeth. He was fairly sure the man braced in the hallway wanted to break them. "The playwright. I caught your work the last time I was in the city. Cyb cried buckets. I practically had to carry her out of the theater."

"I wasn't that bad."

"Yes, you were. Of course, you used to tear up during greeting-card commercials, so you're an easy mark."

"That's ridiculous, and—oh, my phone. Hang on a minute." She darted inside, leaving the men eyeing each other narrowly.

"I'm a sculptor," Matthew said in the same lazy drawl. "And since I really need my hands to work, I'll tell you I'm Cybil's brother before I offer to shake."

"Brother?" The murderous gleam shifted but didn't quite fade. "Not much family resemblance."

"Not especially. Want to see my ID, McQuinn?"

"That was Mrs. Wolinsky," Cybil announced as she dashed back. "She saw you come in but couldn't get to her door in time to waylay you. I'm supposed to tell you she thinks you're more handsome than ever." Chuckling, Cybil grabbed both his cheeks. "Isn't he pretty?"

"Don't start."

"Oh, but you are. Such a pretty face. All the female hearts flutter." She laughed again, then snagged Preston's hand. "Come on, let's have a drink to celebrate."

He started to refuse, then shrugged. It wouldn't do any harm to take a few minutes to size up Cybil's brother.

"What kind of sculptor?"

"I work in metal primarily." Matthew peeled off his jacket, tossed it carelessly over the arm of a chair. It barely had time to land before Cybil snatched it off.

"I'll just hang this in the bathroom to dry. Preston pour us some wine, will you?"

"Sure."

"She have any beer?" Matthew wanted to know and sauntered over to lean on the counter while Preston moved through the kitchen with a familiarity that had the big brother arching a brow.

"Yeah." He plucked out two, popped the tops, then took out the wine for Cybil. "You work in the South?"

"That's right. New Orleans suits me better than New England. Weather-wise, it gives me more room to work outside if I want. Cyb hasn't mentioned you. When did you move in?"

Preston lifted his beer, noted Matthew's eyes were nearly the exact color of Cybil's hair. Like good aged whiskey. "Not long ago."

"Work fast, do you?"

"Depends."

"Preston." Cybil heaved a sigh as she came back. "Couldn't you have used glasses?"

"We don't need glasses." Matthew grinned, keeping a challenging eye on Preston. "We'll just drink our beer like real men, then chew up the bottle."

"Then you probably don't want any dainty cheese and crackers, or girlie pâté to go with it."

"Says who?" Matthew demanded, and slid onto a stool. "You used to have four of these, didn't you?"

"Oh, Preston borrowed one. What are you doing in New York, Matthew?" She stuck her head in the fridge.

"Just some quick preliminary business for my show this fall. I'm only here for a couple days."

"And you checked into a hotel, didn't you?"

"Your revolving-door policy drives me crazy." Matthew gestured toward Preston with his beer. "You've lived across the hall for a bit, right? So you know what goes on in here. It's terrifying. She lets…" He shuddered dramatically. "People in here."

"Matthew is a professional recluse," Cybil said dryly as she began preparing a small feast. "You two should get along famously. Preston doesn't like people, either."

"Ah, finally. A man of sense." Matthew aimed one of his quick, crooked smiles at Preston and decided he might like him after all. "I let her talk me into staying here once," Matthew continued, stealing a cracker. "Oh, the horror. Three days, people dropping in, talking, eating, drinking, standing around, bringing their relatives and pets."

"It was only one little dog."

"Who insisted on sitting in my lap, without invitation, then ate my socks."

"If you hadn't left them lying on the floor, he wouldn't have eaten them. Besides, he only chewed them a bit."

"It's all a matter of perspective," Matthew concluded. "And you see, in a civilized hotel, the only people who drop in are housekeeping and room service—and they knock first and very rarely bring along small, toothy dogs." He reached over, pinched her chin. "But I'll let you cook me dinner, darling."

"You're so good to me."

"You ever had Cyb's homemade chicken potpie, McQuinn?"

"Can't say I have."

"Well, watch me sweet-talk us into some."

It was an interesting way to spend the evening, Preston thought later, watching Cybil relate to her brother. The ease of affection, humor, occasional exasperation. He remembered it had been like that between him and his sister. Before Pamela.

After that, there had still been affection, but the ease of it had vanished. All too often he had felt an awkwardness that had never been there before.

But awkwardness wasn't a problem with the Campbells. They cheerfully told embarrassing stories about each other, and when that paled ganged up to tell him about their absent and therefore defenseless sister and any number of cousins.

By the time he left, he was wondering if he could work bits of them into act 2, for a little comic relief.

Work, Preston decided, since Cybil was likely to be occupied with family for quite some time yet, was his best hope for the rest of the night.

"I like your friend." Matthew stretched out his legs and swirled the brandy Cybil had opened in his honor.

"That's handy—so do I."

"A little on the sober side for you."

"Ah, well." She settled in beside him on the sofa. "A little change of pace now and again can't hurt."

"Is that what he is?" Matthew gave her earlobe a tug. "I noticed you two didn't waste any time getting locked together when I so accommodatingly strolled upstairs to make a phone call."

"If you were making a phone call, how do you know what we were doing down here? Unless you were spying." She smiled sweetly, fluttered her lashes and got another jerk on the ear.

"I wasn't spying. I just happened to glance down the stairs at one very strategic moment. And since he looked at you any number of times during the evening like he knew you'd be a lot more tasty than your chicken potpie—which was great, by the way—I cleverly put two and two together."

"You were always bright, Matthew. I suppose it's reasonable to say, since you're being nosy, that Preston and I are together."

"You're sleeping with him."

Deliberately, Cybil widened her eyes. "Why, no—we've decided to be canasta partners. We realize it's a big commitment, but we think we can handle it."

"You always were a smart-ass," he muttered.

"That's how I make my fame and fortune."

"Now you're making it turning McQuinn across the hall into Emily's elusive and irritable Quinn."

"How could I resist?"

Matthew drummed his fingers, shifted. "Emily thinks she's in love with him."

Cybil said nothing for a moment, then shook her head. "Emily is a cartoon character who pretty much does what I tell her to do. She's not me."

"She has pieces of you—some of your most endearing and annoying pieces."

"True. That's why I like her."

Matthew blew out a breath, frowned into his brandy. "Look, Cyb, I don't want to horn into your personal life, but I'm still your big brother."

"And you're so good at it, Matthew." She leaned over to kiss his cheek. "You don't have to worry about this. Preston didn't and isn't taking advantage of your baby sister." She took Matthew's brandy, sipped, handed it back. "I took advantage of him. I baked him cookies, and ever since he's been my love slave."

"There's that mouth again." Uncomfortable, he pushed off the sofa, paced a bit. "Okay, I don't want the details, but—"

"Oh, and I was so looking forward to sharing all of them with you, especially the home videos."

"Shut up, Cybil." Working his way from uncomfortable to embarrassed, Matthew dragged a hand through his hair. "I know you're grown-up, and you're seriously cute in spite of that nose."

"My nose is very attractive." She sniffed with it.

"We all worked hard to make you believe that, and you've overcome that little deformity so well."

She had to laugh. "Shut up, Matthew."

"All I want to say is...be careful. You know? Careful."

Her eyes went soft as she rose. "I love you, Matthew. In spite of that annoying facial tic."

"I don't have a facial tic."

"We worked hard to make you believe that." Laughing again, she slipped her arms around him for a fierce hug. "It's so nice to have you here. Can't you stay longer?"

"Can't." He rested his cheek on the top of her head. "I'm going up to Hyannis for a couple days. I'll hang out, do some sketching. Grandpa wheedled."

"He's the champ. Is Grandma pining for you?" Cybil asked, leaning back to grin.

"Fretting herself down to skin and bones. Why don't you come up? Give him a bonus. And that way we can spot each other when he starts on why we're not settled down and raising a pack of little people."

"Hmm. Well, he has called here a couple times in the last few weeks—hasn't given me a chance to call first." She considered, juggling time and duties in her head. "I'm enough strips ahead to take a couple of days. I do have a meeting day after tomorrow, though, that I shouldn't break."

"Come up afterward." He angled his head when he saw her mull it over, hesitate. "You can ask your canasta partner to drive up with you. We'll have a tournament."

"He might enjoy that," she murmured. "I'll check with him. Either way, I'll come."

"Good." And, Matthew thought, he hoped Preston accepted the invitation. He would love to see Daniel Mac-Gregor work him over.

* * *

Since it was after midnight when Matthew went off to his hotel, Cybil told herself to go upstairs to bed. She hadn't gotten much sleep the night before—and neither had Preston. The reasonable, the practical, thing to do was climb into bed, shut off the light and get some much-needed rest.

So she walked across the hall and pushed his buzzer.

She was beginning to think he'd gone to bed, or down to the club, when she heard the rattle of locks.

"Hi. I never offered you a nightcap."

He glanced over her shoulder, back at her face. "Where's your brother?"

"On his way to his hotel. I opened some brandy, and—"

She didn't manage the rest, or even much of a squeak of surprise as he yanked her inside, kicked the door closed and shoved her against it. Her mouth was much too busy being assaulted by his.

When he switched to her neck, she managed to suck in a breath. "I guess you don't want any brandy." Since he was already dragging off her shirt, she returned the favor. "Or after-dinner mints."

The force of need that had slammed into him the moment he'd seen her was outrageous. He couldn't stem it, even with his hands rushing over her to take. Greedy, his mouth crushed back on hers while he pulled her head back to dive yet deeper.

And she strained against him, just as urgently, just as desperately, groaning in pleasure as he tugged her trousers down her hips.

Whatever she had was his.

He filled his hands with her breasts, then his mouth descended, sucking, nipping while her nails bit, arousing points of pain, into his back. Her skin, like warmed silk, drove him to possess. Desire, a freshly whetted blade, twisted as he moved down her until her hands vised on his shoulder and her breath was only gasping sobs.

Not possible, not possible to feel so much and survive, was her last coherent thought. Then he used his mouth on her, his fingernails raking lightly down her body as with lips and teeth and tongue he drove her beyond reason.

She heard her own cry of shocked release dimly, struggling for air as her system rocked from the hot explosion of pleasure. Destroyed, she sagged against the door, utterly open to him.

Surrender only fanned the flames.

His hands slipped, slid, over her damp skin. His mouth continued its relentless assault, demanding more, still more, until her body began to quiver again. Until he felt her begin to heat and move and stretch toward the next peak.

He left her groaning, traveling back up her body, slicking his tongue over flesh that tasted erotically of salt and woman. His hands were rougher than he intended as he dragged her to the chair, pulled her down on him, lifted her hips.

His eyes met hers, watching, watching as that soft, clouded green darkened and blurred, watching as those long lids flickered, watching still as he lowered her.

Now, as she closed around him, surrounded him in hot, slippery heat, their groans mixed. Her head fell back, exposing that lovely white arch of throat where a pulse beat in wild hammer blows.

And she began to ride.

The pace was hers now, and it was fast and fierce. Each thrust of hips slapped them both toward the dark swirl of delirium. He craved it, that moment when sanity ripped away.

Bright arrows of sensation, each separate and sharp, stabbed through him. The sumptuous taste of her flesh in his mouth, the wet silk texture of it as his hands sought more of her, those low, animal sounds in her throat and the sheer wonder of her face flushed with pleasure and purpose.

He teetered on the edge, struggling to hold on another instant, just one more instant where he could no longer tell where she began and he left off. But she closed around him, a glorious fist of triumph, and, breathing his name, dragged him over with her.

Then, as she had before, she melted onto him. The sensation of having her head lie on his shoulder, her lips against his throat, spread a hazy glow through him. Closing his eyes, he held on to it, and to her.

He remembered what she had said to him before. No one had ever touched her as he had.

No one, he thought, had ever reached him as she had. But, however clever he was with words on paper, he didn't know how to begin to tell her.

"I wanted to get my hands on you all evening." That, at least, he could say without risking either of them.

"Mmm. And to think I nearly went up to bed." With a long, contented sigh, she nuzzled his hair. "I knew this chair was perfect for you."

A chuckle rumbled in his chest. "I was thinking of having it recovered. But now I'm having it bronzed."

She leaned back, cupping her hands on his face. "I love those little unexpected pockets of humor in you."

"It's not funny," he said in serious tones. "It's going to cost me a fortune."

He expected her to laugh, a sound he'd grown to depend on. But her smile was wistful, her eyes soft. "Preston." She murmured it, then lowered her mouth to his.

The slow, deep, gentle kiss stirred the soul rather than the blood. It reached into him, brushed hesitant fingers over his heart and made him yearn for something he refused to believe in.

Something struggled to shift inside him, made his hands tremble with the effort to hold it still and steady. But the sweetness of it seeped in, left him reeling.

He crossed over that thin line between want and need, and felt himself stumble terrifyingly close to the edge of love.

She sighed, pressed her cheek to his. And wished.

"You're cold," he murmured, feeling her skin chill.

"A little." She kept her eyes squeezed tight another moment, reminding herself you couldn't always have everything you wished for. "Thirsty. Want some water?"

"Yeah, I'll get it."

"No, that's all right." She slid off him, leaving him slightly baffled by the sense of loss. "Do you have a robe?"

He worked up a smile again. "What is this obsession you have with robes?"

"Never mind." She snatched up his shirt and pulled it on. "Matthew likes you," she commented as she walked into the kitchen.

"I like him." He could take a deep breath now. Could, he told himself, regain his balance now. "The piece up in your studio. That's his work?"

"Yeah. Terrific, isn't it? He's got such a unique vision of things. And watching him work—if he doesn't murder you—is an amazing experience."

She opened a bottle of water, poured a tall glass to the rim, then drank down nearly a third before moving back to Preston. She didn't notice his blink of surprise when she settled, cozy as a cat, into his lap.

"So anyway," she began, offering him the glass, "how do you feel about taking a little trip?"

"A trip?"

"A couple of days in Hyannis Port. Matthew's going up to see our grandparents—the MacGregors—and I thought I might do the same. Grandpa loves to complain that we don't visit enough. It's a great place. The house is…well, I can't describe it. But you'd like it. You'd like them. Want to get out of Dodge for a bit, McQuinn?"

"It sounds like a family thing." It struck him as odd, and totally out of character, that he should feel so unhappy with the idea of her being away for a couple of days.

"With The MacGregor, everything is a family thing. Grandpa loves people. He's over ninety, and has the most amazing energy."

"I know. He's fascinating. They both are." He glanced back as she frowned at him. "I know them. Slightly. They're acquaintances of my parents."

"Oh? I didn't realize. I told you the rather convoluted family connection, didn't I? MacGregor to Blade. Blade to Grandeau. Grandeau to Campbell. Campbell to MacGregor, not necessarily in that order."

"Don't start. It makes my ears ring."

She laughed, dutifully kissed them. "Well, since you know them and you've met Matthew, it wouldn't be like dropping yourself in on a group of strangers. Come with me." She ran her lips from his ear to his neck. "It'll be fun."

"We could stay right here in this chair and have even more fun."

She chuckled warmly. "There are dozens and dozens of rooms in Castle MacGregor," she murmured. "And in many of them, there are big…soft…beds."

"When do we leave?"

"Really?" Thrilled at the idea, she leaned back. "Day after tomorrow? I have a meeting midmorning. We can leave right after. I can rent a car."

"I have a car."

"Oh." She cocked her head. "Hmm. Is it a sexy car?"

"How do you feel about four-door sedans?"

"It's probably very sturdy, very reliable. I appreciate a sensible car."

"Then you're not going to like my Porsche."

"A Porsche?" She giggled in delight. "Oh, tell me it's a convertible."

"What else?"

"Oh, yeah. Tell me it's a five-speed."

"Sorry. it's a six-speed."

Her eyes widened. "Really? *Really?* Can I drive?"

"Of course. If by the day after tomorrow the icicles have finished forming in Hell, you're at the wheel."

Pouting only a little, she began to play with his hair. "I'm an excellent driver."

"I'm sure you are." He decided it would be much more productive to distract her than to listen to her try to change his mind. He rolled the cold glass over her naked back, making her gasp and arch so that her breasts flattened delightfully against his chest.

"Now…what do you think we could accomplish if we laid this recliner back?"

"All manner of amazing things," she murmured, turning her neck to give his teeth better access. "Did you know my grandfather owns this building?"

"Sure. He told me about the apartment when I was looking for a place. Turn like…yeah, that's the way."

"He told you about the apartment?" Somehow he'd managed to shift so that his body covered hers, distracting her from a niggling thought just beginning to form in her mind. "When did he… Oh God, you're so awfully good at that."

"Thank you. But I'm about to get much better."

Chapter 9

The house The MacGregor built stood arrogantly on the cliffs above a surging sea. Nothing about the old gray stone was sober. Everything about it, from its spearing towers and jutting turrets, to the snapping flag that carried the crest of the clan, shouted pride.

He had built as he'd intended to, on a sturdy foundation, with grandiose vision. And he had built to last.

The wild and rambling roses that would bloom brilliantly come summer did nothing to soften the effect but only added to that sense of magic.

"Stop," Preston murmured, and laid a hand on Cybil's arm. "Stop the car."

Because she understood, and was pleased to see the sight of that fanciful structure affect him as it always did her, she braked gently.

"It's like a fairy tale, isn't it?" She leaned on the steering wheel to study the house through a driving curtain of rain. "Not one of the wimpy G-rated versions, but one with blood and guts."

"I've seen photographs. They don't come close."

"It's not just a house. It's the most generous of homes. Whenever we visited we'd always find something new. Something marvelous."

As she would this time, she thought. With Preston. "It shows well in the rain, doesn't it?" she commented.

"I imagine it always shows well."

"You're right. You should see it in the winter. We always come up during Christmas. The snow and the wind turn it into something frozen out of time. And last year, just at the end of summer when the roses were tumbling and the sky was so hard and blue you waited for it to crack like an egg, my cousin Duncan got married here. But in the rain..." She smiled dreamily, leaning on the wheel. "It feels like Scotland."

"Have you ever been?"

"Mmm. Twice. Have you?"

"No."

"You should. It's your roots. You'll be surprised how much they tug at you when you breathe the air in the highlands or look out at a lowland loch."

"Maybe I will. I might want a couple of weeks to decompress when the play's finished." He turned his head, lifted his eyebrows. "How's the car handling for you?"

"Since you've only let me drive it for approximately forty-five seconds, it's difficult to be sure. Now, if you let me take it out for a spin tomorrow..."

"Even your powers of persuasion aren't going to get you behind the wheel longer than it takes to go up the drive."

Cybil shrugged carelessly, thought, *We'll see about that,* and drove decorously up the hill, parked. "Thank you very much." She gave him a light kiss, and the keys.

"You're welcome."

"Let's not worry about the bags now. We'll make a dash

for it and see how long it takes to have whiskey and scones by the fire."

She pushed open the car door, ran like a bullet through the rain, then stopped on the covered porch to shake her head like a wet dog and laugh.

For ten full seconds, he couldn't move. He could only stare at her, through the shimmering curtain of rain, her cap of hair sleek and soaked, her face alive with the delight of it. He wanted to think it was desire, straight and uncomplicated. But desire rarely struck so deeply or had fingers of fear clawing at the gut.

If he couldn't ignore it, he'd deny it. He stepped into the rain, let the wind slap at his cheeks like a teasing woman as he walked to her. And while she laughed, he yanked her hard against him and took her mouth with a kind of violent possession.

For once her hands only fluttered helplessly as the sudden, almost brutal, kiss staggered her. But she tasted the desperation on his mouth, felt the barely restrained fury in the body that pressed to hers. And her hands reached for him, stroked once, then held.

"Preston."

He heard her murmur through the roaring in his brain that was like the rain and the sea battering against him. The soft sound of her voice had him gentling his hold, then the kiss, before he forced himself to draw back.

"With all your family around," he managed, and skimmed her dripping hair behind her ear in an absent gesture that made her heart flutter foolishly, "I might not be able to do that for a while."

"Well." She breathed deep, hoping to settle herself. "That ought to hold me." And smiling, she took his hand and pulled him inside.

There was warmth, immediate and welcoming.

Bright swords and shields glowed on the walls. It was, after all, the home of a warrior and one who had never forgotten it. There was the scent of flowers and wood, and of age that speaks of dignity rather than dust.

"Cybil!" Anna MacGregor came down the wide stairs, her soft face aglow with pleasure. Her sable hair was swept back, her deep-brown eyes clear and smiling as she held out her arms to take Cybil into them.

"Grandma." She breathed deep, exhaled lavishly. "How can you always be so beautiful?"

With a laugh, Anna squeezed tighter. "At my age the best you can hope for is presentable."

"Not you. You're always beautiful. Isn't she, Preston?"

"Very."

"You're never too old to appreciate a considerate lie from a handsome young man." Anna shifted, keeping one arm around Cybil's waist as she held out a hand. "Hello, Preston. I doubt you'll remember me. You couldn't have been more than sixteen the last I saw you."

"About," he agreed, taking her hand. "But I remember you very well, Mrs. MacGregor. It was at the Spring Ball in Newport, and you were very kind to a young boy who wanted to be anywhere else."

"You remember. Now I am flattered. Come, let's get you warmed up. Rain's cold this time of year."

"Where are Grandpa and Matthew?"

"Oh." Anna laughed lightly as she led them down the hall into what the family called the Throne Room. "Daniel's got poor Matthew hammering on the pump for the pool. He says it's acting up, and you know how your grandfather is about his daily swim. Claims it keeps him young."

"Everything keeps him young."

The term for the room was apt, with Daniel's regal high-back chair dominating a great space carpeted in scarlet. The furnishings were old and massive, the carvings deep. Lamps were already lit against the gloom, and a fire blazed boldly in the big hearth.

"We'll have tea. I imagine Daniel will insist we add whiskey to that and use company as an excuse for it. Sit, be comfortable," she invited. "If I don't let him know you're here, I'll never hear the end of it."

"You sit," Cybil insisted. "I'll go. I'll have the tea sent along on the way."

"You're a good girl." Anna patted Cybil's hand as she sat by the fire. "You always were." Anna gestured to the chair beside hers. "Preston, Daniel and I saw your play in Boston some months ago. It was powerful, and wrenching. Your family must be so proud of what you've accomplished."

"Actually, I think they were more surprised."

"Sometimes that amounts to the same thing. We never really expect our children or our siblings, no matter how we admire them, to exhibit real genius. It brings us a jolt, and we think—how could I have missed that all those years?"

"You know my family," he said quietly. "So you'd know the play cut very close to home."

"Yes, I know. Sometimes a wound needs to be lanced or it festers. Is your sister well?"

"Yes, she has the children. They center her."

"And you, Preston? Is it your work that centers you?"

"Apparently."

"I'm sorry." Annoyed with herself, Anna lifted her hands. "I'm prying—and I usually leave that to my husband. I'm interested because I remember that young boy at the Spring Ball and the way he looked after his sister. It reminded me of the way Alan and Caine always looked after Serena—and how it irritated her as it appeared to irritate…it's Jenna, isn't it?"

"Yes." He smiled now. "It used to drive her crazy." But the smile soon faded. "If I'd done a better job of it years later, she'd never have been hurt."

"Preston, you didn't hurt her," Anna reminded him. "And, truly, I didn't mean to take you back there. Will you tell me about what you're working on now, or do you keep such matters secret?"

"It's a love story, set in New York. At least, that's the way it's turning out."

His gaze flicked past her shoulder when he heard laughter rolling down the hall. Yes, Anna thought, that seemed to be the way it was turning out.

"Haven't you given the man a whiskey yet, Anna?"

Daniel stepped into the room and simply dominated it. Size, presence and that great booming voice that refused to thin with age. His eyes glittered blue as the lochs of his homeland; his hair and rich full beard were stunningly white.

"Is that any way to welcome a man after he's come in out of the rain and brought up my favorite grandchild from the city?"

"Oh, fine," Matthew muttered, trailing in behind him. "When you wanted your pool fixed *I* was your favorite grandchild."

"Well, it's fixed now, isn't it?" Daniel said, and with a bark of laughter slapped Matthew on the back with the affection a father grizzly might show to his cub.

"It's good to see you, Mr. MacGregor." Preston crossed the room, hand extended to shake. But for Daniel this was rarely sufficient when he'd taken an interest in a man. He clapped Preston into a hug with the force of a steel trap biting closed.

"You're looking fit, McQuinn, and a good drink of whiskey always makes a Scotsman fitter."

"You'll have a drop in your tea, Daniel," Anna warned him as she rose to fetch the decanter.

"A drop." For a big man, he could still manage to sulk like a child. "Anna."

"Two drops," she conceded with a smile tugging at her mouth. "Tell me, Preston, do you smoke cigars?"

"Not as a rule, no."

Anna turned, angled her head in warning at Daniel. "Then if I come across you with one in your hand, I'll know who stuck it there before he dashed out of the room."

"The woman'll nag you to death," Daniel muttered. "Well, sit down, boy, and tell me how you and Cybil are getting on."

Little alarm bells sounded in Preston's head. "Getting on?"

"Neighbors, aren't you?"

"Yeah." Relieved, Preston sat. "Across-the-hall neighbors."

"Pretty as a primrose, isn't she?"

"Grandpa." Cybil sighed as she wheeled in a loaded tea tray. "Don't start on McQuinn. He hasn't even been here ten minutes."

"Start what?" Daniel narrowed his eyes at her. "Are you pretty or not?"

"I'm adorable." She laughed and kissed his nose. While she was close, she whispered in his ear. "Behave and I might tip a bit of my whiskey into your tea while she's not looking."

Daniel's teeth flashed in a grin; his eyebrows wiggled. "There's a lass."

"You won't believe these scones, McQuinn." Satisfied she'd bribed The MacGregor, Cybil loaded a small plate.

"I can't quite pull them off. Mine are close, but not quite there."

"Cybil's a fine cook," Daniel agreed, scowling when he watched his wife measure a measly two drops of whiskey into a cup for him. "You've been feeding the man a bit from time to time, haven't you, lass? Like a proper neighbor."

"She made us all a potpie last night." Matthew loaded a scone with strawberry jam. He'd promised to be a buffer, he remembered. "Preston, you want whiskey or are you making do with tea?"

"I'll take the whiskey, thanks. Neat."

"And how else would a man drink it?" Daniel muttered, pouting into his teacup. "So you've had a taste of our Cybil," he added, and watched with a barely suppressed grin as Preston nearly bobbled a scone.

"Excuse me?"

"Her cooking." Daniel's eyes radiated innocence. Oh, aye, he thought, I've got you on the reel, laddie. "Woman who can cook like my darling here ought to have a family to feed."

"Grandpa." Cybil tapped her finger on her whiskey glass.

When a man was torn between his drink of choice and his granddaughter's future, what choice did he have? Sacrifices, Daniel mused, had to be made. "What man doesn't appreciate a hot meal well made, I'd like to know? You can't disagree with that, can you, lad?"

Somehow, somewhere, there was dangerous ground, was all Preston could think. "No."

"There!" Daniel pounded a fist, made plates rattle. "Hah! McQuinn's a good and honorable name. You've done proud by it."

"Thanks," Preston said cautiously.

"But a man your age should be thinking of what comes after him. You must be thirty by now."

"That's right." And how the hell do you know that? Preston wondered.

"A man gets to be thirty, it's time to take stock, to consider his duties to name and family."

"I've got a few years left," Matthew whispered to Cybil. She merely elbowed him. "Do something," she hissed.

"If he turns it on me, it's gonna cost you."

"Name your price."

"Oh, I will." And cheerfully throwing himself on the sword, Matthew dropped into a chair. "Grandpa, I haven't told you about this woman I've been seeing lately."

"Woman?" Distracted, Daniel blinked, then zeroed in on his grandson. "What woman would that be? I thought you were too busy building your big metal toys to pay any mind to women."

"I pay them plenty of mind." Matthew grinned, lifted his whiskey in salute. "This one's something special."

"Is she, now?" Shifting gears, Daniel settled back. "Well, it would take a special lass to catch your eye for more than a blink."

"Oh, I've been looking at this one for a while. Name's Lulu," Matthew decided on the spot. "Lulu LaRue, though I think that's her stage name. She's a table dancer."

"Dances on tables!" Daniel roared as his wife choked back a laugh, then continued to drink her tea. "Naked on tables?"

"Of course naked. What's the point otherwise? She's got the most amazing tattoo on her—"

"Naked, tattooed dancing girls! I'll be damned, Matthew Campbell. You want to break your dear mother's heart? Anna, are you listening to this?"

"Yes, of course I am, Daniel. Matthew, stop teasing your grandfather."

"Yes, ma'am." Matthew shrugged, grinned and watched

Daniel's eyes narrow into blue slits. "But I don't see why I can't have a naked, tattooed dancing girl if I want."

Much later, after the rain had passed and night had fallen and Preston had slipped into her room to take advantage of her and the big four-poster bed, Cybil hummed in contentment.

It had been a near perfect day.

Perfect enough that she let herself curl up against the man she loved and pretend, in this fairy tale world, that he had scaled the walls of the castle to find her. And love her. And stay with her for always.

"Tell me something," he murmured, too relaxed to worry about how soothing it was to lie there with her arm draped over him, her head in the curve of his shoulder and their bodies sharing a lazy, intimate warmth.

"Okay. Despite exhaustive research, the exact number of angels who can dance on the head of a pin has never been fully documented."

"I thought it was 634."

"That's mere speculation. Nor in related studies has it ever been fully discovered precisely how many frogs one must kiss before finding the prince."

"That goes without saying. But..." He loved the way she chuckled as she shifted closer. "What I really wanted to know—and you would be the handiest authority on the subject—is what the hell was all that with your grandfather at tea?"

"Which all?" She lifted her head, skimmed her hair back from her brow, then rolled her eyes. "Oh, that all. I didn't warn you because I had the pathetic hope that it wouldn't be necessary. The fault is entirely mine."

She shifted, rolling over so that her body lounged cozily

over his. "Do you know you have wonderful eyes, McQuinn? They're almost translucent, like I could dive right into that moonlight blue and just disappear."

"Is that a genuine comment or an evasion of the subject at hand?"

"Both." But since it had to be dealt with, she sat up, kissed him, then reached for the robe she'd tossed at the foot of the bed earlier.

"Why do you have to cover up whenever you talk to me?"

She glanced over, and to his surprise, flushed a little. "A latent puritanical streak?"

"Incredibly latent," he noted, but only smiled as she belted the robe. "Now, about your grandfather and his sudden interest in my family name—or as he put it during dinner—the good blood, strong stock in my ancestry."

"Well, McQuinn, you're a Scotsman."

"Third-generation Rhode Islander."

"Hardly matters in the vast and historic scheme of things." She rose and poured them a glass to share from the pitcher of ice water that had been placed on the bedside table. "I'll apologize first," she said, without looking at him. "But hope you'll understand Grandpa means well. It's all out of love, and he wouldn't have done it if he didn't like you."

Something much too akin to nerves moved into Preston's stomach. "Done what, exactly?"

"I didn't realize it—or it didn't sink in fully until we got here. It should have," she murmured, sitting on the bed and handing him the glass before she'd sipped herself. "The other night when you mentioned how you knew each other and he'd put you onto the apartment across from mine, I should have latched on to it. Well." She jerked her shoulders. "It wouldn't have mattered anyway."

"What, Cybil?"

She blew out a breath, lifted her lashes and looked directly into his eyes. "He's picked you out for me. It's just that he loves me," she said quickly. "And he wants what he thinks is best for me—that's marriage, a family, a home. And that appears to be you."

It wasn't nerves, Preston discovered. It was outright terror. "How the hell did he come to that conclusion?" he demanded, and set his water back on the table with a hard click of glass on wood.

"It's not an insult, McQuinn." Her voice chilled several frigid degrees. "It's a compliment. As I said, he loves me very much, so he obviously thinks a great deal of you if he believes you'd make me a proper husband and be a good father for the many great-grandchildren he hopes I'll give him."

"I thought you didn't want marriage."

"I didn't say I did. I said he wanted it for me." Her chin jerked up before she got out of bed again, stalking to the bureau to snatch up her brush and drag it over her hair. "And the fact that you're so obviously appalled is incredibly insulting."

"I suppose you think it's amusing."

"I think it's sweet."

"You think it's sweet for your ninety-something grandfather to pick out men for you?"

"He isn't grabbing them off the street corner for me to audition." Ridiculously hurt, she slammed down the brush. "You needn't panic, McQuinn. I'm not buying my trousseau or booking chapels. I'm perfectly capable of finding my own husband when and if I want one. Which I've already said I don't."

She tossed her head and, for lack of something better to do with her hand, wrenched open a jar of cream and began to slather it on her hands.

"Now, I'm tired, and I'd like to go to bed. And since you don't care to sleep with me after sex, you should go."

Was it just temper, he wondered, or was there something more in the reflection of her eyes in the mirror? "Why are you angry?"

"Why am I angry?" she said quietly, unsure if she wanted to weep or scream. "How can someone who writes about what's inside people with such insight, such sensitivity, ask a question like that? Why am I angry, Preston?"

She turned then because it was best to face the issue head-on. "Because you're sitting there in the bed we just shared, still warm from me and utterly baffled, completely shocked that someone who loves me thinks there could or should be something more between us than sex."

"Of course there's more between us than sex." His own temper started to twitch as he grabbed his jeans and tugged them on.

"Is there? Is there really?"

The cool, flat tone had him looking over, had the sneaky worm of guilt sliding into him. "I care about you, Cybil. You know I do."

"You find me amusing. That's not the same thing."

Yes, there was more than temper, he realized before she turned away. There was hurt. Somehow he'd hurt her again without plan or purpose. He took her arm, firmly turned her back. "I care about you."

Her heart, already too much his, softened. "All right." She touched a hand to his, squeezed, released. "Let's forget about it."

He wanted to agree, to keep it simple. But the smile she'd tossed him before she'd walked to the window hadn't reached her eyes. And those eyes had been wounded. "Cybil, I don't have more than that."

"I didn't ask for more than that. The moon's come out. All the clouds have been blown away. We can walk the cliffs tomorrow. It's a little chilly, though." Absently, her heart weeping in her breast, she rubbed her arms. "I think we need another log on the fire."

"I'll do it."

The fire in the fieldstone hearth still burned bright and cheerful. But he took a log from the carved box, sat it on the flames, then watched them rise up, lick, curve greedily around it.

For a time the only sound in the room was the crack and the hiss of wood being consumed.

Maybe it was because she didn't ask, so deliberately didn't ask, that he was compelled to tell her. "Would you sit down?"

"I like standing here looking at the stars. You can't see the stars in New York. It's all the lights. You forget to look up, much less wonder where the stars are. In Maine, where I grew up, they filled the sky. I never realize I miss them until I see them again. You can get along, very well, for long periods, without a lot of things. Hardly even noticing you're missing them."

When his hands came to her shoulders, she tensed, an instinctive movement it took concentrated effort to undo. But she smiled when she turned. "Why don't we go out and get a better look at them while they're there."

"I want you to sit down and listen to me."

"All right." Struggling to be casual, she walked to one of the deep chairs in front of the fire. "I'm listening."

He sat beside her, leaned forward in his chair and kept his eyes on her face. "I always wanted to write. I can't remember otherwise. Not the novels my father had hoped for. It was always plays. Everything was very clear in my head. The stage, each set, the movement of the actors, the precise angle and quality of the lights. Often, maybe too often, that was the world I lived in. You come from a prominent family, one with a lot of social obligations and demands."

"I suppose that's true."

"So do I. I tolerated that end of it, enjoyed it occasionally, but for the most part just tolerated or eluded it."

"You value your privacy," she said. "I understand that. My father's the same, and Matthew."

"I valued it. I needed it." Too restless to sit, he rose to wander the room. "I love my parents, my sister, no matter how little we sometimes understand one another. I'm sure I hurt them countless times with small acts of carelessness, but I do love them, Cybil."

"Of course you do," she began, but said nothing more when he shook his head.

"My sister, Jenna, she was always so outgoing, so easy with people. She's a lovely woman. She wasn't quite twenty-one when she married. Married my best friend from college. I introduced them."

It still scraped him raw to think of that. The first step in the whole miserable journey had been his. Glancing at the water, he wished it were whiskey.

"They were great together," he murmured. "Shining with love, full to bursting with hope and plans. Jacob came along just over a year later. And less than a year after that she was pregnant again and glowing with it."

He stuck his hands in his pockets, moved to the window. But he didn't see the stars. "About that time, my first play was being produced. Locally, just a small theater group, but a place with cachet. My father's an important writer, so that made his son's work of some interest."

"It's of interest on its own," Cybil declared, and he

glanced back, grateful to her for understanding his need for that separate legitimacy. But she would, he thought, because of who she was and from what she'd come.

"Now I certainly hope so. But not then, not right at the start. And it was vital to me that my work stand on its own and not lean on his. Part of that was pride," he continued thoughtfully. "But part of it was respect. Whatever the reason, this play, this first of mine to be produced, was incredibly important to me."

Because he turned away, seemed to need a moment to gather himself, she spoke again. "I didn't sleep at all the night before my first strip came out. However much I loved the work, I couldn't have stood it if people thought I was using my father's accomplishments as a stepping stone."

"Some always will," Preston murmured. "You can't let it matter. The work has to matter most, and this play did to me. There wasn't any aspect of it I wasn't involved in—the set designs, the staging, the casting, the rehearsals, lighting cues. All of it."

She smiled a little. "I imagine you drove everyone, including yourself, insane."

"I'm sure I did. The company had a lot of talent. The actress who played the lead was stunning, certainly the most beautiful woman I'd ever seen. She dazzled me."

He faced her. "I'd just turned twenty-five, and I was hopelessly in love with her. Every minute I spent with her was a gift. Just to watch her onstage, saying lines I'd written, that had come from me. Having her look at me and smile and ask me if that was how I meant it to be. The more I became involved with her, the less the play meant to me."

Even now it burned inside him, what he'd tossed aside. And what he'd had stolen. "She was gentle. Oh, and sweet. Even a little shy when she wasn't onstage. I made excuses to be with her, then began to realize she was making them to be with me. We became lovers on a Sunday afternoon, in her bed, and afterward, she cried on my shoulder and told me she loved me. I think I would have cut off my arm for her at that moment."

Cybil folded her hands in her lap and wondered what it would be like to be loved like that by a man like him. She didn't speak because she could see there was more. And what was left still caused him pain.

"For weeks," he continued, "my world revolved around her. The play opened, garnered very decent reviews. All I could think was that the play had been the vehicle that had given her to me. That was all that mattered."

"Love should matter most."

"Should it?" He laughed shortly and the cynical light was back in his eyes. "But words last, Cybil. That's why a writer should take care with them."

Love lasts. She wanted to say it, nearly did, but she could already see his hadn't.

"I bought her gifts," he continued, "because they made her happy, took her dancing or to the club because she loved to be with people. She was so beautiful I thought she deserved to be showcased. She needed the right clothes, the right jewelry, to be showcased in, didn't she? So why not buy them for her? And if she needed a little to tide her over, why not write her a check? It was only money, and I had more than enough."

Cybil could see where it was going, or thought she could. She wanted, so badly, to go to him, to slip her arms around him in comfort. But it wasn't unhappiness in his voice, in his eyes; it was bitterness.

"She had talent, and I wanted to help her become an important actress. Why not use my influence—or my father's, my family's—to boost her career?"

"You loved her," Cybil said quietly, already hurting for him. "What you wouldn't have used for yourself, you would use for someone you loved."

"And that makes it right?" He shook his head. "No, it's never right to use someone else. But I did. She talked about marriage, shyly again, almost wistfully. I hesitated there. Her career needed her attention. We could wait to settle down. After the play, I told her, after she began to move up, we'd go to New York and we'd both *own* theater. We'd own it together."

Together, he thought, was all too often a word that didn't hold true. "Then one day she came to me, weeping, shaking, so pale you could almost see through that beautiful skin. She told me she was pregnant, and lovely, terrified tears slipped out of her eyes and down her cheeks. She blamed herself, begged me not to abandon her. Where would she go, what would she do? She had little money. She was afraid. She thought I would hate her."

"No," Cybil whispered. "You wouldn't hate her."

"Of course I didn't. I didn't hate her, I didn't blame her. I was afraid, I was shaken, but part of me was thrilled. The decision had been taken out of my hands. I didn't need to be practical now but could marry her, start a life with her."

He prowled now, restless in the cage of his own past. "Money was no problem. I'd come into a large part of my inheritance at twenty-five, would come into more at thirty. Money wasn't a problem," he said again, then lifted the poker and jabbed viciously at the logs blazing.

"I dried her tears, and I held her, told her everything would be fine. It would be wonderful. We'd be married right away. We'd stay in Newport until the baby was born, then we'd go to New York just as we'd planned. It would be three of us instead of two, but we'd be happy. We had a touching parting scene as she left to go back to her little apartment—to rest and call her family and tell them the wonderful news. We agreed to go to my parents after the show that evening and tell them.

"I started making plans almost immediately. Imagined myself as her husband, as the father of the child we'd made together."

"You wanted the baby," Cybil said, remembering the ease with which he'd held little Charlie.

"Yes, I did."

He turned to her then, his back to the fire. But the heat that pumped from the flames couldn't reach the cold memories left inside him. "I wanted her, and the child, and the life I imagined we could make together. And while I was floating on that particular cloud my sister came to my door."

He could still see it, still bring it back. Every movement, every gesture. Another play on another stage. "Like Pamela, she was weeping, she was trembling, she was pale. And like Pamela, she was pregnant. Further along, just showing, so I was worried at the state she was in. She clung to me, sobbing and sobbing, and finally managed to tell me her husband was having an affair."

His voice changed now, darkened, flattened, as did his eyes. "She told me that she'd dashed back home, leaving Jacob with my mother, because she'd forgotten something. They were to be out all day, so she wasn't expected back only an hour after she'd left. Wasn't expected to walk in and find her husband scrambling back into his trousers and a woman in her bed. Her own bed."

"Oh, Preston, how horrible for her." She rose then, wanting to comfort. "How awful for your family. She must have…" She trailed off as it clicked. The scenes he'd been painting for her, the scenes he'd painted in his play. "Oh, no. Oh, God."

He stepped back from the sympathy she offered. "Her name was Leanna in *Tangle of Souls,* but she was pure Pamela. Beautiful and clever and cold. A woman who could act without rehearsing the lines. Who could play a man brilliantly, all for money, for power, for the possibilities. She would have married me for those things, and to give a socially prominent name to the baby my closest friend, my sister's husband, had planted in her. But I was no longer in the mood."

"You loved her, and she hurt you. Hurt all of you. I'm so sorry."

"Yes, I loved her, but she taught me. You can't trust the heart. My sister trusted hers, and it almost destroyed her. If she hadn't had Jacob and the baby on the way, I think it would have. They needed her, and that's what got her through."

"But you didn't have that."

"I had my work, and the satisfaction of facing the woman who'd cut through our lives. She wept and she swore it was all a lie. Some terrible mistake. She begged me to believe her, and I very nearly did. She was that good."

"No," Cybil murmured. "You were in love. You'd have wanted to believe her."

"Either way. We argued, and some of the layers on that perfectly presented mask of hers fell away. I saw her for what she was. A schemer, a liar, a cheat. A woman who thought nothing of seducing and sleeping with another's husband for pleasure and going from him to another man for gain. But she finished the run of the play." He smiled thinly. "The show must go on."

"How did you stand it?"

"She was good, and it was only a matter of reminding

myself the work was more important than she was, more important than anything else." He arched a brow. "You think that was a cold decision on my part?"

"No." She laid her hands on his shoulders, then on his cheeks, wondering that he couldn't see the hurt was still there. "No, I think it was brave." Then she leaned into him, held him, sighing when his arms finally came around her. "She didn't deserve even the smallest piece of your heart, Preston. Then or now."

"Now she's only an interesting character in a play. I won't give anyone that much ever again. I don't have it to give."

"If you believe that, you've let her take more." She lifted her head, and her eyes were drenched. "You've let her win."

"Nobody won, my sister, my friend, me. Three lives damaged, and all she got from it was a few auditions. Nobody won," he murmured, and brushed a tear from her cheek with his thumb. "Don't cry. I didn't tell you to make you cry, just to help you understand who I am."

"I know who you are, and I can't help hurting for you."

"Cybil." He brought her close again. "If you keep wearing your heart that close to the surface, someone's going to come along and break it."

She closed her eyes but didn't tell him someone already had.

Chapter 10

It was time, Daniel decided, to have a private little chat with young Preston McQuinn. It was simple enough to lure the man up into his tower office while Cybil was busy with Anna in another part of the house. And Matthew—well, the boy was likely off somewhere or other looking for inspiration for one of his metal toys.

Matthew's sculptures invariably brought Daniel both puzzlement and pride.

"Have a seat, lad. Stretch out your legs." Daniel walked to the bookshelf, took out a copy of *War and Peace* and chose a cigar out of the hollow. "Will you have one?"

Preston only lifted a brow. "No, thanks. Interesting literature, Mr. MacGregor."

"Well, a man does what he can to keep his woman off his back." Daniel ran the length of the cigar under his nose, sniffing in appreciation, sighed in anticipation as he sat, then took his time lighting it. Part of the pleasure was in the small and delightful steps.

He unlocked the bottom drawer in his huge oak desk, took out a large carved shell and set it in the center of his blotter as an ashtray. Following that came a tiny battery-operated fan. It was the newest of Daniel's attempts to keep Anna from sniffing him out.

"Wife doesn't want me smoking." The pity of it had Daniel shaking his head. "And the older she gets, the sharper her nose. Got one like a bloodhound," he muttered, then settled back, sighed. "Now, then."

"What if she comes up?" Preston wanted to know.

"We worry about that if and when, boy, if and when." But his healthy fear of his wife's wrath had him nudging the little fan closer. "So tell me, your play's going well for you?"

"Yes, it is."

"I'm not only asking as an investor, I want you to know. I'm interested in you."

"Mmm-hmm."

"Admire your father's work. Got some of his books around here." Daniel leaned back in the enormous leather chair, puffed out smoke. "A bird tells me that Hollywood's taken quite an interest in your work, McQuinn."

"You've got a good ear for birds."

"I do indeed. How does it sit with you, this movie business?"

"Well enough."

"You play poker, don't you, McQuinn?"

"I've been known to ante up occasionally."

"I'll wager you play a fine game of it. You're not one to give your hand away. I like that." Contemplatively, Daniel tapped his cigar on the shell. "You'll be in New York a few more weeks?"

"Another month, anyway. Most of the work on the house should be done by then."

"A fine big house, too, by the sea." Daniel smiled as Preston narrowed his eyes. "The birds tell me all manner of things. It's good for a man to have a house of his own. Some of us aren't meant to live in a hive, with people buzzing through the next wall. We need our own space, for ourselves, for our family. Room to spread out," he continued, gesturing. "A place where a man can go to have a damn cigar in his own house without being nagged half to death."

As Daniel scowled, took another puff, Preston's lips twitched.

"True enough," Preston agreed. "Though I wouldn't say my house is anywhere near the scale of yours."

"Young yet, aren't you? You build as you go. And you'd need the sea, as I did, having grown up with it outside your door."

"I prefer it to the city." Since he wasn't quite sure where the conversation was headed, Preston didn't relax quite yet. "And if I had to live in a suburban development I'd likely slit my throat in a week."

Daniel laughed, puffed and eyed Preston through the cloud of smoke. "You're a man who needs his privacy, and that's a reasonable thing. But when solitude and privacy become isolation, it's not always healthy, is it?"

Preston angled his head. "I don't see any neighbors mowing their yards and trimming their hedges when I look out the windows of Castle MacGregor."

Daniel's grin flashed in his beard. "That you don't, McQuinn. But while private we are, isolated we aren't. You know Cybil grew up by the sea, as well." He clamped the cigar between his teeth. "Along the coast of Maine, where her father guarded his privacy like a pit bull."

"So I've heard," Preston said mildly.

"Her father's a good man for all he's a Campbell." Idly,

Daniel drummed his fingers on the edge of his desk. "Time was a highlander'd sooner bed down with rats and weasels than let a Campbell through the front door. You don't hold the '45 against him and his, do you, McQuinn?"

It took him a minute, possibly longer, to realize Daniel referred to the Jacobite Rebellion over two hundred years before. Thinking a laugh would be out of place, he disguised it with a cough. "No," he said, very seriously. "Times change. We have to move on."

"Right enough." Pleased, Daniel thumped a fist on the desk. "And as I said, he's a good man, and his wife's a fine woman. Comes from good stock herself. Their children do them proud."

At sea, Preston merely nodded. "I'm sure you're right."

"Of course I'm right. You've seen for yourself, haven't you? She's a bright and lovely woman, my Cybil. A heart big as the moon, warm as the sun. She draws people to her just by being. There's a light about her, don't you think?"

"I think she's unique."

"That she is. There's no deceit in her, or guile," Daniel continued, his blue eyes sharp and focused. "Too often she puts her own feelings aside to spare another's. Not that she's a doormat, not with that good Scots' blood in her. She'll spit when she's cornered, but she's more likely to hurt herself before she'd hurt another. Causes me some worry."

Though he was hearing no more than he'd seen for himself, Daniel's words had Preston shifting uncomfortably in the chair. "I don't think you have to worry about Cybil."

"It's a grandparent's right, duty, and pleasure if it comes down to it, to worry about his chicks. She wants a place to put all the love she holds inside her. The man who engages that heart of hers will live his life lucky."

"Yes, he will."

"You've had your eye on her, McQuinn." Daniel leaned forward now. "I don't need birds to tell me that."

More than my eye, Preston thought with an inward wince. "As you said, she's a lovely woman."

"And you're a single man of thirty. What are your intentions?"

Well, Preston thought, that was cutting straight to the core. "I don't have any."

"Then it's time you got some." To punctuate, Daniel banged his fist on the desk. "You're not blind or stupid, are you?"

"No."

"Well then, what's stopping you? The girl's exactly what you need to lighten up that serious nature of yours, to keep you from burrowing into a cave like a bear with indigestion." Eyes narrowed, he jabbed out with the cigar. "And if I didn't know you were just what's best for her, you wouldn't be within arm's reach, I can tell you that."

"You put me in arm's reach, Mr. MacGregor." Feeling trapped, and furious because of it, Preston pushed out of his chair. "You dumped me on her doorstep, under the guise of doing me a favor."

"I did you the finest favor of your life, lad, and you should be thanking me for it, instead of looking murderous."

"I don't know how the rest of the family and acquaintances handle your button pushing, but I can tell you I don't appreciate or need it."

"If you didn't need it," Daniel disagreed in a roar, "why are you still moping about something that's gone—and never really was—instead of taking hold of what is?"

The temper that had been heating Preston's eyes turned to ice. "That's my business."

"It's your flaw," Daniel disagreed, more pleased than not

to watch the anger, and the control. "And a man's entitled to one or two. I've had over ninety years in this world to watch people, to measure them, to see them as they are. I'll tell you something, McQuinn, that you're either too young or too stubborn to see for yourself—you match, the pair of you. One balancing the other."

"You're wrong."

"Hah! Damned if I am. The lass wouldn't have asked you to this house if she wasn't already in love with you. And you'd not have come unless you were already in love with her."

So he goes pale at that, Daniel thought, sitting back again with satisfaction. Love, for some, was a scary business.

"You've miscalculated." Preston spoke softly as his stomach clenched into a dozen tight fists. "Love has nothing to do with what's between Cybil and me. And if I hurt her. When I hurt her," Preston corrected, "you'll own part of the blame for it."

He stalked out, leaving Daniel puffing on his cigar. Hurt was part of love, he acknowledged. Though he'd suffer for knowing his precious girl would ache a bit along the way. And yes, he'd own part of the blame for it. But when the man stopped wriggling like a stubborn trout on the line and made her happy… Well then, who would own the credit, he'd like to know, if it wasn't Daniel MacGregor?

And laughing, he finished his cigar in secret delight.

Cybil was sorry the trip to Hyannis had put Preston in a prickly mood. One, she thought, that hadn't completely reversed itself after a week back in New York.

He was a difficult man. She accepted that. Now that she knew the full story of what he'd been through, what had been done to him, she didn't see how he could be otherwise.

It would take him, a man with that much sensitivity, that much heart, a long time to trust again. A long time to allow himself to feel again.

She could wait.

But it hurt. She couldn't stop it from hurting when he turned away from her just a little too quickly, or barricaded himself against her with his work, his music or the long, solitary walks he'd begun to take at odd hours.

Walks where he made it clear he wanted to be alone, that he didn't want to share with her.

She told herself his work was giving him trouble—though he never talked about his play with her any longer. She imagined he didn't think she could understand the pain, the joy, the frustration of his work or what parts of himself it could swallow. That stung, but she told herself she accepted it.

She'd always been able to lie to herself more easily than she had to others.

Her own work had taken a new turn and was involving more of her time and energy. The meeting she'd had just before leaving for Hyannis had been a vital one. But she'd told no one. Not family, not friends, not her lover.

Superstitious, she supposed, as she climbed out of a cab in front of her building. She'd been afraid to say it out loud and jinx it before it was real.

Now it was.

She pressed a hand to her heart, felt it thud in hard, excited beats. Heard herself giggle. Now it was very real, and she couldn't wait to tell everyone.

Maybe she'd have a party to celebrate. A loud, silly, joyful bash of a party.

Champagne and balloons. Pizza and caviar.

As if preparing for it, she danced up the steps. She had to

call her parents, her family, to grab Jody so they could squeal at each other.

But first, she had to tell Preston.

She used the knuckles of both fists, rapping a cheerful tattoo on his door. He'd be working, she thought, but this couldn't wait. He'd understand.

They had to celebrate. Glug champagne in the middle of the afternoon, get a little drunk and stupid and make crazy love.

When he opened the door she was shining like a sunbeam.

"Hi! I just got back. You won't believe it."

He was rumpled, unshaven, and resented the fact that one look at her could yank his mind right out of his play. Just one look. "I'm working, Cybil."

"I know. I'm sorry. But I'm going to burst if I don't tell somebody." She lifted her hands to his face, rubbed them over the stubble. "You look like you could use a quick break anyway."

"I'm in the middle of things," he began, but she was already breezing in.

"I bet you haven't eaten lunch. I just had the most incredible lunch at this new hot spot uptown. Why don't I fix you a sandwich and we'll—"

"I don't want a sandwich." He heard the edgy snap to his voice, didn't bother to soften it as he stalked to the stove to pour coffee that had been ripening for hours. "And I don't have time for one. I want to work."

"You have to eat." She had her head inside his fridge, then brought it out again when she heard him go upstairs. "Oh, for heaven's sake." She blew out a breath, rolled her eyes and started up after him.

"Okay, forget the sandwich. I just have to tell you how I spent my day. God, McQuinn, it's dark as a tomb in here."

Instinctively, she marched to the window, started to throw open the drapes.

"Leave them alone. Damn it, Cybil."

Her hand froze, then dropped away, as slowly, as completely, as her mood. He was already at the keyboard, she noted, already closed off from her, just as he closed himself off from the life that surged and pulsed outside his curtained window.

He worked with lamplight and stale coffee. And with his back to her.

Nothing that was inside her, that had been bubbling like a geyser, mattered to him.

"It's so easy for you to ignore me," she murmured. "To dismiss me."

There was no mistaking the hurt in her voice. He braced himself against it, refused to feel guilty. "It's not easy, but right now it's necessary."

"Yes, you're working, and I've got some nerve, don't I, interrupting genius, interfering with such a grand enterprise. One I couldn't possibly understand."

Irritated, he flicked a glance at her. "You can work with people hovering. I can't."

"Then again," she continued, "it's easy for you to ignore and dismiss me at other times, too, when work has nothing to do with it."

He pushed away from the keyboard, shifted toward her. "I'm not in the mood to argue with you."

"And, of course, it always comes down to your moods. If you're in the mood to be with me or be alone. To talk to me or be quiet. To touch me or turn away."

There was a hint of finality in her tone that had panic skating up his spine. "If that didn't suit you, you should have said so."

"You're right. Absolutely. Exactly right. And just now it doesn't suit me, Preston, to be treated like a mild annoyance easily swatted aside, then picked up again when you have a moment. It doesn't suit me to have what matters to me shrugged off as unimportant."

"You want me to stop work and listen to how you spent the day shopping and having lunch?"

She opened her mouth, closed it again, but not before one small sound of hurt had escaped.

"I'm sorry." Furious with himself, he got to his feet. She looked as if he'd slapped her. "I'm streaming toward the end of this, and I'm distracted, nasty." He dragged his hands through his hair because she hadn't moved, hadn't stopped staring at him with those wide, wounded eyes. "Let's go downstairs."

"No, I have to go." Because she could feel ridiculous tears stirring in her throat, burning there. "I have some calls to make, and I have a headache," she said, lifting a hand to rub at her throbbing temple. "It makes me irritable. I think I need some aspirin and a nap."

She started out, stopping when he laid a hand on her arm. He felt her tremble and absorbed a hard wash of shame. "Cybil—"

"I don't feel well, Preston. I'm going home to lie down."

She broke free, rushed out. He winced as he heard the slam of the door. "You stupid son of a bitch," he muttered, rubbing his fingers against his eyes. "Why didn't you just kick her a couple of times while you were at it?"

Disgusted with himself, he paced the room, shoving his hands in his pocket, then pulling them out again to yank at the drapes.

The sun was brilliant, streaming through the glass, making him narrow his eyes in defense. Maybe he did close himself off from what was on the other side, he thought. He worked better that way. And he didn't have to justify or explain his work habits to anyone.

He didn't have to hurt her that way.

But damn it, she'd burst in on him at the worst possible time. He was entitled to his privacy, to his space when the work and the words were racing through him.

He didn't dismiss her. He didn't ignore her. How the hell did you ignore someone who wouldn't get out of your mind no matter what else was sharing the space with her?

But he'd been trying to, hadn't he? Very deliberately trying to do both, ever since the little session with Daniel MacGregor in his tower office in Hyannis Port.

Because the clever, canny, meddling old man was right.

He was already in love with her.

If he ignored it, dismissed it, kept pushing it just a little further out of reach, it might go away before it got a good, firm grip on him.

He wasn't risking love again, not when he knew exactly what it could do to twist heart and soul, to wring every drop of blood out of them. He wasn't going to allow himself to become that vulnerable to her.

He'd get over it, he told himself, and pulled the curtains shut again. He'd put things back on balance and they'd both be happier.

And as far as his insufferable behavior of the last few days, he'd make it up to her. She hadn't done anything to deserve it, except exist. She'd done nothing but give, he thought. He'd done nothing but take.

Knowing work was out of the question, he went downstairs. He considered going across the hall, knocking, leading in with the apology he owed her. But she was entitled to her privacy, as well, he decided. He'd give it to her and take a walk.

He didn't think about buying her flowers until he saw them, bright and sunny in an outdoor cart. Not roses, he mused. Too formal. Not the daisies—they were cheerful but ordinary. He settled on tulips in butter yellow and creamy white.

The minute they were in his hand, he felt lighter.

He kept walking, realizing he'd gone on too long without taking the time to really let his mind clear. As it did, he thought more about what she'd said in that brief, dark scene in his room.

Just how often had she nudged aside her own moods, her own needs, to accommodate his? The MacGregor had hit that one, as well. It was her nature to think about the needs of those she cared about before her own.

He'd never known anyone as selfless, generous or unfailingly happy in her own skin. He'd stopped being all those things, except when he was with her. When he let himself really *be* with her.

She'd been so excited when she'd burst into his apartment. He'd become so used to seeing her that way he hadn't considered it might have been something special that had put that shine in her eyes.

He'd taken care of that quickly enough, he thought viciously.

And he'd taken her for granted, he realized, almost from the first moment.

He could change that. And would. He'd give her back as much as he took, put them on equal ground. So when the time came to step back from each other—and it would—they might have a chance to do so as friends.

He simply couldn't imagine his life without her as part of it any longer.

He stayed out the rest of the afternoon, into early evening. When he went to her door with flowers he didn't feel foolish. He felt settled. And when she opened it, he felt right.

"Did you get some rest?"

"Yes." She'd dived into sleep the way a rabbit dives into a thicket. To hide. "Thanks."

"Feel like company?" He brought the tulips up into her line of sight. And when she stared at them, he recognized simple shock. "And tulips?"

"Ah…sure. They're wonderful. I'll get a vase."

Just how much had he left out, he wondered, if his bringing her a handful of flowers stunned her? "I'm sorry about this afternoon."

"Oh." So the flowers were an apology, she thought, as she took a blue glass vase from a cupboard. She shook off the vague disappointment that they hadn't been for no reason at all and turned to smile. "It doesn't matter. It's what you get when you disturb a bear in his den."

"It matters." He laid a hand on hers over the tulips. "And I'm sorry."

"All right."

"That's it? A lot of women would make a man grovel a little."

"I don't care for groveling much. Aren't you lucky?"

He lifted her hand, turning it over to press his lips to the palm. "Yes. I am." And for the second time he saw blank shock on her face.

He'd never given her tenderness, he realized, amazed at his own stupidity. Never given her the simple glow of romance. "I thought, if you're feeling better, you might like to go out to dinner."

She blinked. "Out?"

"If you like. Or if you're not feeling up to it," he continued, coming around the counter, "we can have a quiet dinner in. Whatever you want," he murmured, cupping her face to brush his lips over her forehead.

"Who are you? And what are you doing in Preston's body?"

He chuckled, then kissed her cheeks, one, the other. "Tell me what you want, Cybil."

To be touched like this. Looked at like this. "I...I can just fix something here."

"If you want to stay in, I'll take care of dinner."

"You? *You?* All right, that's it. I'm calling the cops."

He drew her into his arms, held her. "I'm not threatening to cook. We'd never survive the night that way." He nuzzled her hair, stroked it. "I'll order in."

"Oh, well, all right." He was holding her, she thought dizzily. Just holding her, as if that was enough, as if that was everything.

"You're tight." He murmured it, sliding his hands up to rub at the tension in her shoulders. "I don't think I've ever known you to be knotted up. The headache still bothering you?"

"No, not much."

"Why don't you go up. Soak in the tub until you're relaxed. Then you can put on one of those robes you're so fond of and we'll have a quiet dinner."

"I'm fine. I can..." She trailed off as his mouth skimmed hers, retreated, then returned, softly, gently, sweetly enough to dissolve her knees.

"Go on up." He drew her away, smiling as she stared up at him with slumberous, confused eyes. "I'll take care of everything."

"All right. I guess I'm a little unsteady yet." Which might explain why she wasn't entirely sure how to get upstairs in her own apartment. "The, ah, number for the pizza place is on the phone."

"I'll take care of it." He gave her a nudge toward the steps. "Go relax."

"Okay." She started to the steps, up, then stopped and turned back to study him. "Preston?"

"Yeah?"

"Are you..." With a half laugh she shook her head. "Nothing. Never mind. I won't be long."

"Take your time," he told her. It was going to require a bit of his to make certain everything was ready for her when she came back down.

If the hint of romance nearly shocked her speechless, he thought she'd have a hard time forming a single word by the time the evening he was planning was over.

He picked up the phone, punched the button on memory next to Jody's name. "Jody? Preston McQuinn. Yeah. Listen, does Cybil have a favorite restaurant around here? No, not the diner," he said with a laugh. "We're moving upscale. Let's try French and fancy."

He had to grin at Jody's long, three-toned "Oh," then scribbled down the name she gave him. "I don't suppose you'd have the number handy. You do, huh? You're a genius. Now, let's see if you can hit three for three. Which dessert on their menu sends her into a coma? Got it, thanks. Special?" He glanced upstairs, grinned. "No, nothing special. Just a quiet dinner in. Thanks for the tip."

He laughed again as Jody continued to shoot out questions. "Hey, we both know she'll tell you all about it tomorrow."

He hung up, dialed the restaurant and outlined his needs. Then, metaphorically pushing up his sleeves, got down to work.

Chapter 11

She did as he'd suggested and took her time. She needed it to adjust to this strange new mood of his. Or was it a side of him, she wondered, he just hadn't shown her before?

How could she have known he had such sweetness in him? And how could she have predicted that his showing her, giving her that sweetness, would make it so much more difficult for her to stay in control of her own feelings?

She loved him when he was careless and cross, when he was amused and amusing, when he was hot and hungry. How much more could she love him when he was kind and caring?

He was making an effort, she thought, to apologize to her for hurting her. And he didn't even know, not really, just what he'd done. But it mattered enough—she mattered enough—for him to want to make it right again.

How could she say no?

A quiet, casual evening at home would be good for both of them. He didn't like crowds, and at the moment, she didn't have the energy for them herself. So they'd eat pizza in front of the TV, be easy with each other again. They'd laugh, talk about something unimportant and make love on the sofa while an old movie flickered on the screen.

They'd make things simple again. Because simple was really what was best for both of them.

Steadier, she belted a long, silky blue robe, flicked her fingers through her nearly dry hair, and started downstairs.

She heard the music first. Low, dreamy. The kind that set the pulse for seduction. It didn't puzzle her for long. After all, the man liked his music. But when she was halfway down the steps, she saw the candles burning. Dozens of them, with pinpoint flames that flickered and swayed.

He was standing in that shimmering light, waiting for her.

He'd changed into trousers and a black shirt and had shaved off the two days' growth of beard. His hand was already held out for hers, and she stepped down to take it, more than a little dazzled at the way the light glinted on his hair and deepened the blue of his eyes.

"Feeling better?"

"I'm fine. What's going on here?"

"We're having dinner."

"The set's a little elaborate for..." He raised her hand to his lips, nibbled lightly at her knuckles, and had the breath strangling in her throat. "Pizza," she managed, and he only smiled.

"I like looking at you in candlelight. Seeing what it does to your eyes. Those exotic, enormous eyes," he murmured, and drew her close to kiss them gently closed. "And your skin." He trailed his lips over her cheek. "That impossibly soft skin. I'm afraid I've put bruises on it forgetting just how soft it is."

"What?" Her head seemed to be circling slowly.

"I've been careless with you, Cybil. I won't be tonight." He lifted her hands again, kissed them again, and had her heart stumbling.

"I have something for you," he told her, and picked up a small square box with an elaborate pink bow from the counter.

Instantly, she whipped her hands behind her back. "I don't need gifts. I don't want them."

He frowned, puzzled at the shaky edge in her voice. Then realized she was thinking of Pamela. "It's not because you need them, or ask for them, or anything else for that matter. It's because they made me think of you." He held the box out. "Open it before you decide. Please."

Feeling foolish, she took the box, gently removed the bow. "Well, who doesn't like presents?" she said lightly. "And you missed my birthday."

"I did?"

He said it with such guilty surprise she laughed. "Yes, it was in January, and just because you didn't know me is really no excuse for not giving me a present. So this will…" She stopped, stared into the box at the earrings, two long dangles of hematite in the shape of a dozen tiny, foolish fish. Like minnows on the line.

She laughed, rolled with it as she took them out, held them up and shook so they would clack together. "They're ridiculous."

"I know."

"I love them."

"I figured you would."

Eyes sparkling, she slipped the thin wire backs through her ears. "Well, what do you think?"

"They're you. Definitely."

"It's such a sweet thing to do."

She tossed her arms around him, kissed him lavishly enough to have his blood heating. Then he heard the sniffle.

"Oh, God, don't. Don't do that."

"Sorry." She pressed her face to his throat. "It's just— flowers and candles and silly fish all in one night. It's so thoughtful." But she drew a long breath, blew it out, stepped back. "There, all clear."

"Thank God." He brushed his thumb over her lashes where a tiny tear clung. "Ready for champagne?"

"Champagne?" Baffled, she lifted her hands. "Well, it's tough not to be ready for champagne."

She watched as he stepped into the kitchen, took a bottle from her own crystal ice bucket and began to open it. What in the world had gotten into him? she wondered. Suddenly, he was relaxed, happy, romantic...

"You finished your play! Oh, Preston, you finished it."

"No, I didn't. Not quite." He popped the cork, poured the wine.

"Oh." Trying to puzzle it out, she angled her head as he turned, handed her a glass full of straw-colored, bubbling wine. "Then what are we celebrating?"

"You." He touched his glass to hers. "Just you." He laid a hand on her cheek, then lifted his own glass to her lips.

She tasted the wine, a froth on the tongue, silk in the throat. But it was the way he looked at her that made her head spin. "I don't know what to say to you."

"Well, there's an unprecedented event." Smiling, he brought the wine to his own lips, tasted it. Tasted her.

"Ah, so this is all a ploy to shut me up." Chuckling, relaxed again, she enjoyed the champagne. "Very clever, aren't you?"

"I haven't even started." He took the glass from her, set it aside, then drew her into his arms. Even as she lifted her mouth, expecting the kiss—expecting, he was sure, demand and heat—he skimmed his cheek over hers and began to move to the rhythm of the music. "I've never asked you to dance."

"No." Her eyes drifted closed. "You haven't."

"Dance with me, Cybil."

She ran her hands up his back, laid her head on his shoulder and fell into the music and him. They danced, swaying together in the kitchen washed with candle glow.

When his lips grazed her jaw, she turned her head so that his mouth cruised over hers. Her pulse was slow, slow and thick, her limbs weak as water.

"Preston." She murmured it, rising on her toes to give him more.

"That must be dinner," he said against her lips.

"What?"

"Dinner. The buzzer."

"Oh." She'd thought the buzzing was in her head, and had to brace a hand on the counter for balance when he left her to release the outer door.

"I hope you're not disappointed," he commented, unlocking her door. "It isn't pizza."

"Oh, that's all right. Anything's fine." How was a woman supposed to eat when her stomach was full of tiny, energetic butterflies?

But her eyes widened when, rather than a delivery boy, two tuxedoed waiters appeared at the door.

She watched, astonished, as with discretion and efficiency they arranged food on the table Preston had already set with her best dishes. In less than ten minutes, they were gone, and she'd yet to find her voice.

"Hungry?"

"I... It looks wonderful."

"Come, sit down." He took her hand again, led her to the table in front of the window, then bent to brush a kiss at her nape.

She must have eaten. She would never be able to remember what, or how it had tasted. Her innate powers of observation had deserted her. All she could see was Preston. All she would remember was the way his fingers had brushed hers, how his mouth had skimmed over her knuckles. How he had smiled and poured more wine, until her head was swimming with it.

How he had looked at her when he'd risen and held out a hand for hers to bring her to her feet. The way her heart had tripped when he'd lifted her right off them and into his arms.

She suddenly seemed so delicate. So vulnerable when she trembled. Even if he'd wished it otherwise, he couldn't have been anything but gentle.

He carried her up the steps, into the bedroom, and laid her on the pillows. He lit the candles as he had once before, but this time when he turned to her, when he came to her, his touch was feather soft.

And he took her, dreaming, into the kiss.

He gave more than he'd thought he had left in him. Found more in her open response than he'd believed possible. If she trembled, it wasn't triumph he felt but tenderness.

And he gave it back to her.

Slow, silky, sumptuous kisses. Long, liquid, lingering caresses. He had her floating on some high, lace-edged cloud where the air was full of perfume and the world beyond it insignificant.

Gently, he slipped the robe from her, the glide of his hands sending silvery shivers along her skin and shimmering warmth beneath it. Through dazed eyes she watched as he drew back, as his gaze followed the lazy trail of a single fingertip over her body.

"You're so lovely, Cybil." Those suddenly intense blue eyes met hers. "How many times have I forgotten to tell you? To show you?"

"Preston—"

"No. Let me do both. Let me watch you enjoy being touched as I should have touched you before. Like this," he murmured, skimming his fingertips over her.

Her breath caught, and the cloud beneath her began to rock. Then he lowered his head and let his mouth follow the path his fingertips had blazed.

Now she was drowning, slowly floating beneath the surface of a warm dark sea. Helpless there, drifting with only his hands and lips to anchor her. And that first wave came in a long, liquid crest that washed through her system to leave it weak and heavy with pleasure.

He wanted to have her steep in it, sate her with it. No sharp flash this time but a slow burn. He explored and exploited every inch of her, lingering when her breath quickened, savoring when her body arched on each steadily building delight.

And his blood swam with it; his heart jolted until he was as lost and open as she.

He murmured her name as he slipped into her, moaned it as she wrapped around him in welcome.

With long, deep thrusts, he moved in her while their mouths met in a soft and stirring kiss. In a slow, sleek rhythm, she moved under him while their hands met to complete yet another link.

They swallowed each other's sighs, gripped each other's hands as they let themselves shatter.

And he was there when she awoke, holding her, as he'd held her while they slept.

"It's definitely number one of the modern-day Top Ten Most Romantic Evenings." Jody expertly changed Charlie's diaper, cooing at him between commentary. "It knocks that Valentine's Day carriage ride around the park and dozen white roses with diamond-chip earrings attached that my cousin Sharon experienced down to a poor second place. She's going to be peeved."

"No one's ever paid that much attention," Cybil murmured, hugging one of the teddy bears in Charlie's vast collection. "Not just the you-know."

"But the you-know." Jody cocked her eyebrows as she fastened Charlie's fresh diaper. "That was excellent, right?"

"It was spectacular. You know that scene in *Through the Mist,* where Dorian and Alessa find each other after being cruelly separated by her evil, ambitious uncle?"

"Oh." Jody rolled her eyes, lifting Charlie up to bounce him. "Do I ever. I was up till two reading that book, then I woke up Chuck." She smiled reminiscently. "We were both a little tired the next day but very, very loose. Anyway—" she shook herself, before carrying Charlie into the living room so he could practice his crawling "—it was that good?"

"It was better."

"No way."

"It was like having him take my heart out and hold it, then give it back to me."

"Oh, man." Weak-kneed, Jody slipped into a chair. "That's beautiful, Cyb. Just beautiful. You ought to write a romance novel yourself."

"But it wasn't just that. It was all of it. Everything." Still giddy, she threw her arms out and twirled in a circle, making Charlie rock back on his butt and clap in delight.

"I'm so in love with him, Jody. I didn't think you could be this much in love and not have it all just come steaming out of you. There shouldn't be room inside for it all."

"Oh." Jody's sigh was long and loud. "When are you going to tell him?"

"I can't." With a sigh of her own, Cybil picked up Charlie's red plastic hammer and tapped the oversize head on her palm. "I'm not brave enough to tell him something he doesn't want to hear."

"Cyb, the guy's crazy about you."

"He's got feelings for me, and maybe, maybe if I can wait, if he realizes I'm not going to let him down, he'll let himself feel more."

"Let him down?" The very idea ruffled Jody's feathers. "You never let anyone down. But maybe this time you're letting Cybil down."

"He's got reasons to be careful," she said, then shook her head before Jody could speak. "I can't tell you about it. They're his own."

"Okay."

"Thanks. I've got to go. I have a million errands to run. Need anything?"

"Actually, I do. If you're going out anyway."

"I'll just add it to the list. I've got a few things to pick up for Mrs. Wolinsky, and I told Mr. Peebles I'd see if the green grapes looked good at the market. Just let me find my shopping list."

"I'm only asking because you're going out anyway and because it's you." Jody bit her lip, then grinned. "Don't tell anybody what you're getting for me, okay?"

"I won't." Absently, Cybil dug through her purse. "I know that list is in here somewhere."

* * *

It took longer than she'd expected—but Cybil found shopping usually did. Then, by the time she'd delivered the goods to Mrs. Wolinsky, the grapes—which had looked appetizing enough for her to buy a pound of her own—to Mr. Peebles and knocked on Jody's door, it was after five o'clock.

She hissed in frustration when Jody didn't answer. It appeared her friend could stand the suspense, though Cybil herself wanted instant gratification. But either Jody had taken Charlie out for a little walk or she was visiting one of the other neighbors and they'd both just have to wait.

Arms loaded, Cybil took the elevator up.

And grinned like a fool when she saw Preston waiting for her in the hall. "Hi."

"Hi, neighbor." He scooped the bags out of her arms, then bent down and kissed her. "Hold it," he said when she dropped back from her toes to the balls of her feet. "Let's do that again."

"Okay." Laughing, she wound her arms around his neck, shifted back to her toes and put a great deal more energy into the greeting. "How's that?"

"That was fine. What have you got in here? Bricks?"

Searching for her ever-elusive key, she laughed again. "Food mostly, and some cleaning supplies. Some this and some that. I picked up a few things for you. The apples looked very good, and they're better for you to snack on while you're working than candy bars or stale bagels."

She found her key with a little *aha!* and unlocked the door. "Oh, and I got you some ammonia—it'll take care of that grime you're letting build up on your windows."

"Apples and ammonia." He set the bags on the counter. "What else could a man ask for?"

"Cheesecake, straight from the deli. It was irresistible."

"It'll have to wait." He spun her around, off her feet, and began to twirl with her.

"Well, you're in a mood, aren't you?" Grinning, she bent down to kiss him. "If your smile got any bigger, I might fall in."

"You'd be better than cheesecake. I finished the play."

"You did?" The hands that were braced on his shoulders slid around to hug his neck. "That's wonderful. That's great."

"I've never had anything move so fast. It still needs work, but it's there. All there. You had a lot to do with it."

"Me?"

"So much of you kept jumping into it. Once I stopped trying to push you back out, it just raced."

"I'm speechless. What did you write about me? What was I like? What did I do in it? Can I read it?"

"So much for speechless," he noted, and set her back on her feet. "After I fiddle with it a bit more you can read it. Let's go to the diner and celebrate."

"The diner? You want to go celebrate something like this with spaghetti and meatballs?"

"Exactly." And he didn't give a damn if it was sentimental. "With you, where you once took a struggling musician out for a hot meal."

"Did you put that in there? About me paying you? God."

"You'll like it, don't worry."

"What's my name—in the play, what's my name?"

"Zoe."

"Zoe." She pursed her lips, considered, then the dimple fluttered at the corner of her mouth. "I like it."

"Nothing ordinary quite fit. She kept tossing them back at me." He laughed a little, shook it off.

"You look so happy." She reached up, brushing at his hair. "It's nice to see you look so happy."

"I've been doing a lot of that lately. Come on. Let's go."

"I have to put the groceries away, fix my face. Then we'll go."

"Go fix whatever you think's wrong with your face. I'll put them away."

"All right. They actually have places," she called out as she ran up the stairs. "They don't just get tossed into cupboards."

"Just make it fast," he told her, and started pulling things out of the first bag.

He'd been going crazy for the past hour, just waiting for her to get back so he could tell her. Tell her first. And to tell her, to find a way to tell her, that somehow, somewhere, over the last few weeks, everything had changed for him.

And though he'd fought it, ignored it, denied it, it had changed nonetheless. He realized that for the first time in much, much too long, the sensation he continued to feel was simple happiness.

She was right. He looked happy. He was happy. But it wasn't just the play. It was Cybil, and it had been all along.

She made him happy.

It had come out in his work. There was an underlying glow of hope in this play he hadn't intended to put there when he'd begun. But it was just there—shimmering and impossible to resist. The way she was.

It had come out in his life when she had come into his life. With cookies and chatter and compassion. With generosity and laughter and verve.

What he felt for her—what she, being who she was, had given him no choice but to feel—filled him, completed him and, he thought, in a very real sense saved him.

The last line of his play said it, he mused.

Love heals.

With a little time, a little effort, he thought, he had a chance of making the kind of life with her he'd stopped believing really existed.

He reached in the second bag, pulled out a box. And felt the world that had so recently gone rock steady, waver, shake and fall away under his feet.

"I was going to change, but I decided not to waste the time when we could be celebrating." She clattered down the steps at a dead run, the foolish earrings he'd given her swinging. "I just have to call Jody, see if she's back yet. Then we're out of here."

"What the hell is this, Cybil?" Pale, coldly furious, he tossed the home pregnancy test kit on the counter. "Are you pregnant?"

"I—"

"You think you're pregnant, but you don't tell me. What? Were you going to pick your time, your place, your *mood,* then let me in on it?"

The color excitement and pleasure that had been glowing in her cheeks drained so that she was as pale as he now. "Is that what you think, Preston?"

"What the hell am I supposed to think? You waltz in, all smiles, not a care in the world, and there's this." He rapped a finger on the box. "And you're the one who claims she doesn't play games, doesn't tell lies. What else is keeping this from me but both of those?"

"And that makes me like Pamela, doesn't it?" All the joy that had shimmered in her heart throughout the day turned to ashes, cold and gray. "Calculating, deceitful. Just one more user."

He had to steady himself, to calm, but the slash of betrayal where he had finally, finally, decided to trust was ripping through him. "This is you and me, no one else. I want an explanation."

"I wonder if there's ever really been a you and me and no one else," she murmured. "I'll give you an explanation, Preston. I picked up apples for you, grapes for 1B and several small items for Mrs. Wolinsky. And I picked up that handy little will-it-be-pink-or-blue kit for Jody. She and Chuck are hoping they're expecting a baby brother or sister for Charlie."

"Jody?"

"That's right." Every word she spoke hurt her throat. "I'm not pregnant, so you can relax on that score."

"I'm sorry."

"Oh, so am I. I'm terribly sorry." Her eyes ached as she picked up the box, examined it. "Jody was so excited when she asked me to buy this. So hopeful. For some people the idea of making a child is a joyful one. But for you," she went on, putting the box down, making herself look at him, "it's a threat, just a bad memory of a bad time."

"It was a poor reaction, Cybil. Knee-jerk."

"You could say instinctive, I suppose. What would you have done, Preston, if it had been mine? If I'd been pregnant? Would you have thought I'd tricked you, trapped you, done it on purpose to ruin your life? Or maybe you'd have wondered if I'd been with another man and was laughing at you behind your back."

"No, I wouldn't have thought that." The very idea shocked him. "Don't be ridiculous. Of course I wouldn't have thought that."

"What's ridiculous about it? She did it—why not me? Why the hell not me? You let her jump right back in here. You're the one who left the door open for her."

"You're right. Cybil—"

She stepped back sharply when he reached for her. "Oh, don't. I can't quite figure out if you think I'm just another calculating bitch or pathetically malleable. But I'm neither. I'm just me, and I've been nothing but honest with you. You had no right to hurt me like this, and I had no right to let you. But that stops now. I want you to go."

"I'm not going until we settle this."

"It's settled. I don't blame you for it. I'm just as much at fault. I gave too much and expected too little. You were honest with me. 'This is all I have. Don't ask for more,' you said. 'This is what I am. Take it or leave it.' It's my own fault that's what I did. But I won't be doing it anymore. I need someone in my life who respects me, who trusts me. I'm not settling for less. So I want you out."

She strode to the door, flung it open. "Get the hell out."

Because in spite of the fire in her eyes, they were swimming with tears; despite the fists her hands were clenched in, they were shaking. He went to the door, but he stopped, looked at her.

"I was wrong. Completely wrong. Cybil, I'm sorry."

"So am I." She started to slam the door, then drew a deep breath. "I lied. I haven't always been honest with you, but now I will be. I'm in love with you, Preston. And that's the pity of it."

He said her name, started toward her, but she shut the door. He heard the locks snap into place.

He pounded on the door, cursed through it. He paced the hallway, then stalked into his own apartment to call her. But she wouldn't answer.

He tried pounding again, and finally feeling that everything he'd begun to treasure in his life was slipping away, he tried begging. But she was upstairs, with that door closed, as well, and couldn't hear him as she wept in the dark.

Chapter 12

"I ought to go find the son of a bitch and break his legs, his arms. Then his neck." Grant Campbell paced the kitchen of the home he'd built with his wife, his mood as dark and rough as the sea that thrashed outside.

"That wouldn't stop her from hurting." Gennie turned from the window where she'd been watching for her daughter and studied her husband.

Long and lean, she mused, and still just a bit dangerous. So much the man she'd fallen in love with all those years ago. And so much more.

"It'd make me feel a hell of a lot better," Grant muttered. "I'm going out to get her."

"No, don't." Gennie laid a hand on his arm before he could storm out the door. "Let her be awhile."

"It's dark," he said, and felt helpless.

"She'll come in when she's ready."

"I can't stand it. I can't stand the look he put in her eyes."

"She has to hurt before she can heal. We both know that."

Because they both needed it, Gennie slipped into his arms, rested her head on his shoulder. "She knows we're here."

"It was easier when one of them would fall down. Scrape or break something."

"You didn't think so then." Her laugh was as warm as it had been when he'd first met her; her voice was rich and recalled the scent of magnolias in full bloom. She tipped back her head, cupped his face. "You always hurt more than they did."

"I just want to put her on my lap, make it go away." He lowered his brow to Gennie's. "Then I want to rip the bastard's lungs out."

"Me, too," she said, pleased when he chuckled.

That was how Cybil saw them when she came in the room. The two of them standing in the kitchen, standing close, their eyes on each other's.

And that, she decided, that bond, that intimacy, was what she wanted. What she'd been willing to give.

She walked to them, slipped an arm around each to make a circle. "Do you know how many times in my life I've come in here and seen the two of you just like this? And how lovely it is?"

"Your hair's wet." Grant rubbed his cheek over it.

"I was watching the waves crash." She tilted her head to kiss him. "Stop worrying so, Daddy."

"I will. When you're fifty. Maybe." He patted her cheek. "Want some coffee?"

"Mmm, no. Nothing really. I think I'll take a hot bath, then snuggle into bed with a book. It always worked for me when I was a teenager working off a crush."

"During those crises, I ran your bath," her mother reminded her. "Why break tradition?"

"You don't have to do that, Mama."

"Let me fuss." Gennie slipped an arm around her shoulders.

With a sigh, Cybil let herself be guided out. "I was sort of hoping you would."

"Your father needs to be alone to pace and curse your young man."

"He's not my 'young man,'" Cybil muttered as they started up the wide, circular stairs Grant had designed to echo the narrow, metal ones in the lighthouse just beyond the house. "He never was."

"But you're not a teenager now." Gently, Gennie turned Cybil as they moved into the bedroom where Cybil had dreamed her young-girl dreams. "And this isn't a crush."

The tears came again, spurting out of her center, flooding her heart, throat, eyes, as she shook her head. "Oh, Mama."

"There, baby." She led Cybil to the bed, still covered with its colorful quilt, and, sitting beside her, opened her arms.

"I want to hate him." Burrowing into the comfort, Cybil wept and clung. "I want to hate him. If I could, for just a little while, I'd stop loving him."

"I wish I could tell you that you would. I wish I knew. Some men are so hard, so baffling." Gennie rocked her daughter as she spoke. "I know you, sweet baby. I know if you love him there's something in him that makes him worthy of it."

"He's wonderful. He's horrible. Oh, Mama." Cybil leaned back, weeping still. "He's just like Daddy."

"Oh, God help you." With a half laugh, Gennie gathered her close again.

"I always loved the story." Her breath hitched, and she gratefully took the tissue Gennie snagged from the box near the bed. "The story about how you met—when your car broke down in the storm and you were lost, and you stumbled on the lighthouse where he was living like a hermit. And he was so cranky and rude."

She paused to blow her nose, while Gennie stroked her hair and added, "He couldn't wait to get rid of me."

"The way he tells it, you burst in on him. And he was annoyed because you were wet and beautiful." Cybil sighed and studied her mother's face with its honey-toned skin, its strong bones, the lovely fall of dark hair that framed it. "You're so beautiful, Mama."

"You have my eyes," Gennie said softly. "That makes me feel beautiful."

Tired after the storm of tears, Cybil wiped them dry. "We're just wrong for each other," she said at length. "Preston and I. He's so fiercely private, so absorbed in his work. But it's not that he doesn't have humor."

She sighed, rose, walked to the window so that she could see the moon on the water. "Sometimes it can be incredibly charming, unexpected, delightful. He's so moody you never know what's going to pop up. And there's this amazing sensitivity, and you realize he's almost afraid to trust, to feel. Then he touches you, and you're lost. All the things that he is, all of those complicated things he is, are there when he touches you. But he still doesn't quite let you in."

"Good Lord. He *is* like your father. Cybil, you have to do what's right for you. But if you love him this much, you may never be happy unless you at least try to work things out with him."

"He thinks I'm frivolous." The fighting edge came back in her voice, pleasing Gennie enormously. "And that my work is less important than his just because it's different. He doesn't trust me. He thinks he can flick me off like a gnat one minute, and he can't keep his hands off me the next."

She whirled around, ready to spew out more complaints, and saw her mother smiling. "What?"

"How did you find another? I thought I had the only one."

"Grandpa found him."

Gennie's smile sharpened, her aristocratic eyebrows arched. "Oh," she said in the regal tone Cybil recognized as dangerous. "Oh, really."

For the first time in more than twenty-four hours, Cybil smiled.

Preston scowled and shoved his sax back in his case. Damn the woman. He couldn't even play out his frustration. He certainly couldn't work, which he'd proven after spending most of a miserable day between staring at his screen and going across the hall to bang on Cybil's door.

That was before he'd finally realized she wasn't inside anymore.

She'd left him. Which he decided was the smartest thing she'd done since she'd met him. And after brooding over it, he'd figured out the best thing he could do for both of them was to be gone when she got back. From wherever the hell she'd gone.

He was going back to Connecticut in the morning. He could tolerate construction workers, plumbers, electricians and whoever else would descend on him on a daily basis for the next few weeks. But he couldn't tolerate living across the hall from a woman he loved and couldn't have due to his own stupidity.

Everything she'd said to him had been completely true. He had no defense.

"I won't be around for a while, André."

The piano player looked up through the haze of smoke from the cigarette between his lips. "That so?"

"I'm heading back to Connecticut tomorrow."

"Uh-huh. Woman chase you away?" Brow cocked, André stretched back. "That your tail I see between your legs, brother?"

With a short, humorless laugh, Preston picked up his case. "See you around."

"I'll be right here." When Preston's back was turned, André jerked up his chin, signaling his wife, then stabbed a thumb in Preston's direction.

With a nod, she glided over to block Preston's exit. "Leaving early tonight, sugar lips."

"I haven't got anything in me. And I want an early start in the morning. I'm going back to Connecticut."

"Back to the boonies?" She smiled, hooked her arm around his shoulders. "Well, let's have us a goodbye drink, 'cause I'm gonna miss your pretty face."

"I'll miss yours, too."

"Not just mine," she said, then held up two fingers to the bartender. "That little girl put the blues into you, and you can't put them all in your sax. Not this time. Not with her."

"No, not with her." He lifted his glass. "That's over."

"Why's that?"

"Because she said it is." He drank, let the fire course through him, but found it didn't quite warm his insides.

Delta let out a short laugh. "When did a man take that for an answer?"

"When the woman means it, this man takes it."

"McQuinn." Delta patted his cheek. "You sure are a fool."

"No argument. That's why it's over. I ruined it—I have to live with it."

"You ruin it—you have to fix it."

"When you hurt someone that much, they've got the right to lock you out."

"Honey, when you love someone that much, you've got the right to pick that lock, then do a lot of crawling on your hands and knees." She turned, studied him eye to eye. "You love her that much?"

He turned his glass, watched the whiskey through the smoke. "I didn't know there was this much. That there could be."

"Sugar lips." She kissed him. "Go pick yourself a lock."

He shook his head, tossed back the rest of his drink, then started the walk home.

Delta was wrong, he told himself. Sometimes you couldn't fix it. You couldn't pick the lock, and you were better off not trying. Why should she let him back in? He carried the image of how her face had paled, how her eyes had gone huge and hollow—and how the tears had swirled in them over the heat of anger.

He didn't have any right to ask her to listen. To let him crawl or beg or play on her sympathies.

And he didn't realize he'd started to run until he'd reached Jody's door, out of breath, and was pounding on it.

"For God's sake." After checking the peep, Jody wrenched open the door and hitched her robe closed. If Chuck didn't sleep like a rock, she wouldn't have had to race out of bed before the noise woke the baby. "It's after midnight. Are you crazy?"

"Where is she, Jody? Where did she go?"

She wrinkled her nose, lifting her chin with a dignity that was difficult to maintain in a robe covered with pink kittens. "Are you drunk?"

"I had one drink. No, I'm not drunk." He'd never felt more sober, or more desperate. "Where's Cybil?"

"Like I'd tell you after you broke her heart. Go back up to your hole," she ordered, pointing dramatically. "Before I wake up Chuck and some of the other people around here.

They might just lynch you on the spot." Her bottom lip trembled. "Everyone loves Cybil."

"So do I."

"Right. That's why you made her cry her eyes out." As her own threatened to fill, Jody dug a ratty tissue out of the pocket of her robe.

All Preston could do was close his eyes against the vicious guilt. "Please tell me where she is."

"Why should I?"

"So I can crawl, and give her a chance to kick me while I'm down. So I can beg. For God's sake, Jody, tell me where she is. I have to see her."

Jody sniffled into the tissue, but the eyes over it had cleared. And now they narrowed as they studied Preston's face and saw pale desperation. "You really love her?"

"Enough to let her send me away if that's what she wants. But I have to see her first."

What could a romantic heart do but sigh? "She's at her parents in Maine. I'll write it down for you."

Rocked with relief, stunned with gratitude, he had to close his eyes again. "Thanks."

"If you hurt her again," she muttered as she scribbled on the back of an envelope, "I'll hunt you down and kill you with my bare hands."

"I won't even put up a fight." He blew out a breath. "Are you, ah…"

She glanced over, then smiled and laid a hand on her belly. "Yeah, I'm 'ah.' I'm due on Valentine's Day. Isn't that perfect?"

"It's great. Congratulations." He took the envelope she handed him. Then stuffed it into his pocket, framed her face in his hands and kissed her. "Thank you."

She waited until he'd dashed out, then exhaled, long and

sharp. "Oh, yeah," she murmured as she closed and locked the door. "I can see how that could work into a no scale. Definitely no-scale potential." Then she closed her eyes, crossed the fingers of both hands. "Good luck, Cybil."

"The MacGregor." Grant said the words through clenched teeth, his dark-brown eyes snapping as visions of murder and mayhem danced through his mind. "Interfering old goat."

Because it was a sentiment Grant had expressed in various terms any number of times since she'd told him the night before of Daniel's matchmaking plot, Gennie didn't bother to suppress the grin. Her husband adored Daniel MacGregor.

"I thought it was 'meddling old blockhead.'"

"That, too. If he wasn't six hundred years old, I'd kick his butt."

"Grant." Gennie set down her sketch pad, deciding the lovely old maple she'd been sketching would be in full leaf rather than tender bud before her husband stopped pacing. "You know he did it out of love."

"Didn't work, did it?"

Gennie started to speak; then, hearing the sound of a car, turned, shielding her eyes against the slant of the midmorning sun. She felt a little ripple go through her heart. "I'm not so sure of that," she murmured.

"Who the hell is that?" It was Grant's usual sentiment when someone dared to trespass on his staunchly guarded privacy. "If that's another tourist, I'm getting the gun."

"You don't have a gun."

"I'm buying one."

She couldn't help it. Gennie sprang to her feet, tossed the sketchbook down on the glider and threw her arms around him. "Oh, Grant, I love you."

The feel of her broke through his darkening mood like sun through storm clouds. "Genviève." He lowered his head, took her mouth. His blood stirred and his heart warmed. "Tell whoever that is to go away and never come back."

Gennie kept her arms around him, laid her head on his shoulder and watched the gorgeous little car fight its way down the narrow, rutted road Grant refused to have repaired. "I think that's going to be up to Cybil."

"What?" Grant's eyes narrowed as he shifted his gaze to watch the car's progress. "You figure that's him? Well, well," he said, and would have pushed his way clear if his wife's arms hadn't tightened around him. "I'm going to be able to kick some butt after all."

"Behave."

"The hell I will."

Preston spotted them as a particularly nasty bump snapped his teeth together. He'd been too busy cursing whoever considered this ditch in the middle of nowhere a road to notice much more than the next rut, but as his gaze was drawn up, he saw the couple standing in the yard of a rambling white farmhouse.

Not really standing, he thought. Embracing. There on the grass just greening with spring, beside an old-fashioned glider positioned to nestle between graceful shrubs, were the parents of the woman he loved.

He wondered which one of them would kill him first.

Resigned, he muscled the car down the lane and scanned the place where he would likely be buried in a shallow grave.

He'd seen it before, he realized, in the work of Genviève Campbell. She'd painted here, he thought, with love and with brilliance. The romantic old whitewashed lighthouse that loomed over the cliff, the tumbling rocks that showed color and age in the morning light, the bent and twisted trees—all had been pulled together to form a place and a painting of wild beauty.

The house, with its gleaming white paint, its many windows and cozily covered porch, the tidy flower beds waiting for the spring that would come late to this part of the world, offered simple comfort.

Cybil had grown up here, he thought, in this wild and wonderful place.

He stopped the car, but the sense of relief that his bones could now stop rattling couldn't compete against nerves. The couple on the lawn had turned to watch him. Even at a distance, Preston could see the sentiment on the rugged face of Cybil's father.

And the sentiment wasn't *welcome.*

He stepped out of the car, determined to live long enough to see Cybil and say his piece. After that, he supposed, all bets were off.

No wonder, Gennie thought, as she watched Preston cross the yard. No wonder she'd fallen so hard. Feeling Grant tense, she dug her fingers into his waist in warning. He vibrated like a pit bull on a choke chain.

"Mrs. Campbell. Mr. Campbell." Preston nodded but knew better than to offer his hand. It would be very hard to type with a stub. "I'm Preston McQuinn. I need Cybil—need to see Cybil," he corrected, flustered.

"How old are you, McQuinn?"

Preston's brows knit at the unexpected question delivered in slow, measured tones that didn't dilute the threat. "Thirty."

Grant inclined his head. "You want to live to see thirty-one you get back in that car, put it in reverse and just keep going."

Preston kept his eyes level, unconsciously rolling his shoulders like a boxer preparing for a bout. "Not until I've seen Cybil. After that, you can take me apart. Or try to."

"You're not getting within ten feet of her." Grant set Gennie aside as if she weighed little more than a child's doll.

As he took a menacing step forward, Preston kept his hands at his sides. Cybil's father could have first blood, he decided. He'd earned it.

"Stop it!" Gennie dashed between them, slapped a hand on each of their chests. She sent her husband one withering look, then offered Preston the same.

He had a moment to think he'd just been chastised by a queen, then his heart stumbled. "She has your eyes." He had to swallow. "Cybil. She has your eyes."

And the soft green of them warmed. "Yes, she does. She's on the cliff, behind the lighthouse."

"Damn it, Gennie."

Before he could stop himself, Preston lifted a hand to the one she pressed to his heart. He could feel his own thundering beat. "Thank you."

He lifted his gaze to Grant's, held it. "I won't hurt her. Not ever again."

"Damn it," Grant muttered again when Preston started for the cliffs in long, determined strides. "Why did you do that?"

With a sigh, Gennie turned back, took her husband's face in her hands. "Because he reminded me of someone."

"Like hell."

She laughed. "And I think our daughter's going to be a very happy woman very shortly."

He let out one exasperated sigh. "I should've gotten just one punch in, on principle. Damn, if he wasn't going to let me."

Then Grant glanced over, watched Preston disappear behind the wide white base of the tower. "I might've been able to do it if one look at your eyes hadn't cut him off at the knees. He's stupid in love with her."

"I know. Remember how scary that is?"

"It's still scary." With a laugh, he pulled her against him again. "The boy's got guts," Grant mused. "And being your daughter, Cybil will twist them into knots for a while before she forgives him."

"Of course she will. He deserves it. Daniel was right about them," she added.

"I know." Grant grinned down at his wife. "But let's not tell him for a while and make him suffer."

She was sketching, sitting on a rock with the wind ruffling through her dark hair, her head bent over the pad, her pencil flying.

The sight of her stole his breath. He'd driven through the night, through the morning, all the while trying to image how he would feel when he saw her again. For once his imagination had fallen far short.

He said her name, then realized his shaky whisper wouldn't carry over the sounds of wind and water. He started down the narrow beaten path toward the sea.

Maybe she heard him, or perhaps his shadow changed her light. Or maybe she simply sensed him. But her head came up, and her eyes whipped to him. Emotions stormed through them before they turned the chilly green of a winter sea.

Then, as if his presence didn't matter in the least, she began to sketch again. "You're a long way from home, McQuinn."

"Cybil." His throat felt rusty.

"We're not much on visitors around here. My father often talks about mining the road. Too bad he hasn't gotten around to it."

"Cybil," he said again, while his fingers itched to touch her.

"If I'd had any more to say to you, I'd have said it in New York." Go away! her mind screamed. Go away before the tears come back.

"I have something to say to you."

She flicked him a disinterested glance. "If I'd wanted to hear it…same goes." She closed her sketchbook, rose. "Now—"

"Please." He lifted a hand, but when her eyes flared in warning dropped it again. "Hear me out. Then if you want me to go, I'll go. You're too…fair," he said for a lack of a better word, "not to listen."

"All right." She sat back on the rock, opened her sketchbook again. "I'll just keep working, if you don't mind."

"I—" He didn't know where to begin. All the speeches he'd rehearsed, all the pleas and promises, deserted him. "My agent ran into yours yesterday."

"Really? What a small, insular world we live in."

He might have winced at that biting tone, but he was too busy looking at her. "He told her about the series—the television series they're going to do based on your strip. She said it was a major deal."

"For some."

"You didn't tell me."

She spared him another glance. "You're not interested in my work."

"That's not true, but I can't blame you for thinking it. I worked it out, time-wise. The day you came to see me, almost bursting with excitement. You'd come to tell me, and I ruined it for you. I—" He broke off, had to turn away and stare out over the green and restless sea. "I was distracted by the play, and more, what I was feeling for you. What I didn't want to feel for you."

Her fingers tightened and she broke the tip of her pencil.

Furious with herself, she stuck it behind her ear and dug in her small tool bag for another. "If that's what you came to say, you've said it. Now you can go."

"No, that's not what I came to say, but I'll apologize for it, and tell you I'm happy for you."

"Whoopee."

He shut his eyes, fisted his hands. So, she could be cruel, he thought, when it was deserved. "Everything you said to me the night you threw me out of your life was right. I let something that had happened a long time ago stand in front of now. I used it to cut myself off from the best thing that's ever happened to me. I watched my sister's world shatter, saw her struggle to function over the betrayal and the pain, to raise her son alone and give birth to another before the ink was dry on her divorce papers."

How could she hold herself aloof from that, Cybil thought, as she closed her book again? How could she be unmoved? "I know it was hell for her, for both of you. No one should have gone through what your sister did, Preston."

"No, they shouldn't. But people do."

He turned back, met her eyes. Already, he thought in wonder, already there was sympathy in them. "It would work, wouldn't it, if I used my sister to play on your compassion? That's not what I want to do. Not what I'm going to do."

He walked to where the land fell off, where it seemed to have been hacked by an ax to form a wall that faced the churning sea. Gulls screamed overhead, swooping down with flashes of white wings, then rising up again to soar.

She came here, he thought, here to this place whenever she visited her childhood home. Came here on those rare times when she needed to be alone with her thoughts.

It was only right, he supposed, that he finally gave her his thoughts, and the feelings behind them, in a place that was hers.

"I loved Pamela. What happened between us changed me."

"I know." She would have to forgive him, Cybil realized as she could feel her heart softening. Before she let him go.

"I loved her," he repeated, turning toward her again, stepping forward. "But what I felt for her isn't a shadow, isn't even a pale substitute, for what I feel for you. What I feel when I think of you, when I look at you. It overwhelms me, Cybil. It makes me ache. It makes me hope."

Her lips trembled open. Her heart began to beat in a quick, almost painful rhythm she recognized as joy. She saw on his face what she'd never really believed she would see. Struggling to absorb it, she looked away, down the long, rocky coast that seemed to stretch into forever.

"For what?" she managed. "What does it make you hope for?"

"Miracles. I hurt you. I've no excuse for it." He spoke quickly, terrified she would tell him it no longer mattered, that it was too late. "I attacked when I thought you might be pregnant because I was angry at myself. Angry that part of me was thinking that having a baby with you would be a way I could keep you."

When her head whipped around, her eyes wide with shock, he dragged his hands through his hair. "I knew you didn't want marriage, but if you'd been…I could have pushed you into it. And my only defense against that kind of thinking, against using something like that, was to turn on you."

"Pushed me into marriage?" was all she could say. Staggered, she rose, walked a few feet away to stare blindly down into the thrashing waves. How was she supposed to keep up with this? she wondered. How had it all changed so fast?

"It's no excuse, but you have a right to know I never thought you'd planned it or tricked me. I've never known anyone less calculating than you. Cybil, you're a warm, generous woman, with a capacity for joy unlike anyone else I've ever known. Having you in my life…you made me happy, and I think I'd forgotten how to be."

"Preston." She turned back, her vision blurry with tears.

"Please, let me finish. Just hear me out." He grabbed her hands now, gripping hard. "I love you. Everything about you staggers me. You said you loved me. You don't lie."

"No." She saw him clearly now. The exhaustion in his eyes, the tension in his face. If he hadn't been holding her hands so tightly she would have tried to smooth it all away. "I don't lie."

"I need you, so much more than you need me. I know you can get over me and move on. You're too resilient, too open to life, not to. Nothing would stop you from being what you are. You can tell me to go. You'll forget me. Whatever part I played in your life won't keep you from being happy."

He kept his eyes on her face, surrendering everything to the desperate whirl of emotion inside him. "And I'll never in my life get over you. I'll never stop loving you or stop regretting everything I did to push you away from me. You can tell me to go," he said in a voice strained taut with emotion. "And I will. Please God." Helpless, he lowered his brow to hers. "Please don't tell me to go."

"Do you believe that?" she said quietly. "Do you really believe I could forget you?" Amazed at how steady her voice, and her heart was, she waited until he lifted his head and looked down at her. "Maybe I could get over you and be happy. But why should I risk it? Why should I tell you to go when I want you to stay?"

He let out the air clogging his lungs. Even as her lips began to curve, he pulled her against him, kept her there, swaying with relief. She felt him shudder once as he pressed his face to her shoulder.

"You didn't let me ruin it." His voice was raw, and his heart seemed to batter against hers until it moved inside her.

"No, I didn't." She held on, rocked with the knowledge that he had so much feeling for her in him. This strong, stubborn, serious man was weak for love of her. "I couldn't. I need you, too."

He held her away from him, his heart in his eyes as he skimmed his thumbs over her cheeks. "I love this face. I thought I lost it." He brushed his lips over her brow, her eyelids. "I thought I lost you. Cybil. I can't…"

His mouth covered hers. He meant to be gentle, to show her she would be cherished, but emotion raged through him, wild and strong as the sea below them. All of it poured into the kiss.

When he drew back, her eyes were wet. "Don't cry."

"You're going to have to get used to it. We Campbells are an emotional lot."

"I figured that out. Your father wants to break me into very small pieces."

"When he sees you make me happy, he'll let you live." She grinned, and laughter bubbled out. "He'll love you, Preston, and so will my mother. First because I do, then because of who you are."

"Moody, rude, short-tempered?"

"Yes." She laughed again when he winced. "I could deny it, but I'm such a lousy liar. She took his hand in hers and began to walk. "I love it here. This is where my parents met and fell in love. He lived in the lighthouse then, like a hermit, guarding his work, irritated that a woman had come along to distract him."

She shot him a sidelong look. "He's moody, rude, short-tempered."

The similarity had him grinning. "Sounds like a very sensible man." He brought their joined hands to his lips. "Cybil, will you go to Newport with me and meet my family?"

"I'd like that." She glanced up, her head angling when she saw that familiar intense expression in his eyes. "What?"

He stopped, turned to her in the shadow of the great light with the water warring against the rocks below. "I know you don't want marriage or a house in the country. You like living in New York in the center of things, and I don't expect—you'd like the house," he said, interrupting his own thoughts. "It's a great old place, near the coast like this. Anyway," he continued, shaking his head as she remained silent, just looking at him, "I don't expect you to change your lifestyle. But if you decide, later on, that you want to marry me, make a home and a family with me, will you tell me?"

Her heart did three wonderful and stylish handsprings, but she only nodded. "You'll be the first to know."

Telling himself to be content with that, he gave her hand a quick squeeze. "Okay."

He started to walk again, surprised when she stopped, pulling back so that both their arms were extended, linked only by warm fingers. "Preston?"

"Yeah?"

"I want to marry you, make a home and a family with you." The smile lit up her face as he gaped at her. "See, you're the first to know."

Hope spun cheerfully into bliss. "Sure." He brought her

stumbling into him with one quick jerk. "But did you have to keep me dangling for so long?"

Then she was laughing as he swung her off her feet, spinning her in dizzy circles.

* * * * *

Untamed

For my sons.
Life's a circus.
Go for it!

Chapter 1

At the crack of the whip, twelve lions stood on their haunches and pawed the air. On command, they began to leap from pedestal to pedestal in a quick, close-formation, figure-eight pattern. This required split-second timing. With voice and hand commands the trainer kept the tawny, springing bodies moving.

"Well done, Pandora."

At her name and the signal, the muscular lioness leaped to the ground and lay down on her side. One by one the others followed suit, until, snarling and baring their teeth, they stretched across the tanbark. A male was positioned beside each female; at a sharp reproof from the trainer, Merlin ceased nibbling on Ophelia's ear.

"Heads up!" They obeyed as the trainer walked briskly in front of them. The whip was tossed aside with a flourish, then, with apparent nonchalance, the trainer reclined length-wise across the warm bodies. The center cat, a full-maned African, let out a great, echoing bellow. As a reward for his response to the cue, his ear was given a good scratching. The trainer rose from the feline couch, clapped hands and brought the lions to their feet. Then, with a hand signal, each was called by name and sent through the chute and into their cages. One stayed behind, a huge, black-maned cat who, like an ordinary tabby, circled and rubbed up against his trainer's legs.

Deftly, a rope was attached to a chain that was hidden under his mane. Then, with swift agility, the trainer mounted the lion's back. As the door of the big cage opened, lion and rider passed through for a tour of the practice ring. When they reached the back door of the ring barn, Merlin, the obliging lion, was transferred to a wheel cage.

"Well, Duffy." Jo turned after the cage was secured. "Are we ready for the road?"

Duffy was a small, round man with a monk's fringe of chestnut hair and a face that exploded with ginger freckles. His open smile and Irish blue eyes gave him the look of an aging choirboy. His mind was sharp, shrewd and scrappy. He was the best manager Prescott's Circus Colossus could have had.

"Since we open in Ocala tomorrow," he replied in a raspy voice, "you'd better be ready." He shifted his fat cigar stump from the right side of his mouth to the left.

Jo merely smiled, then stretched to loosen muscles grown taut during the thirty minutes in the cage. "My cats are ready, Duffy. It's been a long winter. They need to get back on the road as much as the rest of us."

Duffy frowned. As circumstances had it, he stood only inches higher than his animal trainer. Widely spaced, almond-shaped eyes stared back at him. They were as sharp and green as emeralds, surrounded by thick, inky lashes. At the moment they were fearless and amused, but Duffy had seen them frightened, vulnerable and lost. He shifted his cigar again and took two quick puffs as Jo gave a cage hand instructions.

He remembered Steve Wilder, Jo's father. He had been one of the best cat men in the business. Jo was as good with the cats as Wilder had been. In some ways, Duffy acknowledged, even better. But she had the traits of her mother: delicate build; dark, passionate looks. Jolivette Wilder was as slender as her aerialist mother had been, with bold green eyes and straight, raven black hair that fell to just below her waist. Her brows were delicately arched, her nose small and straight, her cheekbones high and elegant, while her mouth was full and soft. Her skin was tawny from the Florida sun; it added to her gypsy-like appearance. Confidence added spark to the beauty.

Finishing her instructions, Jo tucked her arm through Duffy's. She had seen that frown before. "Somebody quit?" she asked as they began to walk toward Duffy's office.

"Nope."

His monosyllabic reply caused Jo to lift a brow. It was not often Duffy answered any question briefly. Years of experience told her to hold her tongue as they moved across the compound.

Rehearsals were going on everywhere. Vito the wire walker informally sharpened his act on a cable stretched between two trees. The Mendalsons called out to each other as they tossed their juggling pins high in the air, while the equestrian act led their horses into the ring barn. She saw one of the Stevenson girls walking on stilts. She'd be six now, Jo mused, tossing the hair from her eyes as she watched the young girl's wavering progress. Jo remembered the year she had been born. It had been that same year that she had been allowed to work the big cage alone. She had been sixteen, and it had been another full year before she had been permitted to work an audience.

For Jo, there had never been any home but the circus. She had been born during the winter break, had been tucked into her parents' trailer the following spring to spend her first year and each subsequent one of her life thereafter on the road. She had inherited both her fascination and her flair with animals from her father, her style and grace of movement from her mother. Though she had lost both parents fifteen years before, they continued to influence her. Their legacy to her had been a world of restlessness, a world of fantasies. She had grown up playing with lion cubs, riding elephants, wearing spangles and traveling like a gypsy.

Jo glanced down at a cluster of daffodils growing by the side of Prescott's winter office and smiled. She remembered planting them when she had been thirteen and in love with a tumbler. She remembered, too, the man who had stooped beside her, offering advice on bulb planting and broken hearts. As Jo thought of Frank Prescott, her smile grew sad.

"I still can't believe he's gone," she murmured as she and Duffy moved inside.

Duffy's office was sparsely furnished with a wooden desk, metal filing cabinets and two spindly chairs. A collage of posters adorned the walls. They promised the amazing, the astounding, the incredible:
elephants that danced, men who flew through the air, beautiful girls who spun by their teeth, raging tigers that rode horseback. Tumblers, clowns, lions, strong men, fat ladies, boys who could balance on their forefingers; they brought the magic of the circus into the drab little room.

As Jo glanced over at a narrow pine door, Duffy followed her gaze. "I keep expecting him to come busting through there with some crazy new idea," he mumbled as he began to fiddle with his prize possession, an automatic coffee maker.

"Do you?" With a sigh Jo straddled a chair, then rested her chin on its back. "We all miss him. It's not going to seem the same without him this year." She looked up suddenly, and her eyes were angry. "He wasn't an old man, Duffy. Heart attacks should be for old men." She brooded into space, touched again with the injustice of Frank Prescott's death.

He had been barely into his fifties and full of laughter and simple kindness. Jo had loved him and trusted him without reservation. At his death she had grieved for him more acutely than she had for her own parents. In her longest memory he had been the core of her life.

"It's been nearly six months," Duffy said gruffly as he studied her face. When Jo glanced up, he stuck out a mug of coffee.

"I know." She took the mug, letting it warm her hands in the chilly March morning. Resolutely, she shook off the mood. Frank would not have wanted to leave sadness behind. Jo studied the coffee, then sipped. It was predictably dreadful. "Rumor has it we're following last year's route to the letter. Thirteen states." Jo smiled, watching Duffy wince over his coffee before he downed it. "Not superstitious, are you?" She grinned, knowing he kept a four-leaf clover in his billfold.

"*Pah!*" he said indignantly, coloring under his freckles. He set down his empty cup, then moved around his desk and sat behind it. When he folded his hands on the yellow blotter, Jo knew he was getting down to business. Through the open window she could hear the band rehearsing. "We should be in Ocala by six tomorrow," he began. Dutifully, Jo nodded. "Should have the tents up before nine."

"The parade should be over by ten, and the matinee will start at two," Jo finished with a smile. "Duffy, you're not going to ask me to work the menagerie in the side show again, are you?"

"Should be a good crowd," he replied, adroitly skirting her question. "Bonzo predicts clear skies."

"Bonzo should stick with pratfalls and unicycles." She watched as Duffy chewed on the stub of a now dead cigar. "Okay," she said firmly, "let's have it."

"Someone's going to be joining us in Ocala, at least temporarily." He pursed his lips as his eyes met Jo's. His were blue, faded with age. "I don't know if he'll finish out the season with us."

"Oh, Duffy, not some first of mayer we have to break in this late?" Jo demanded, using the circus term for novice. "What is he, some energetic writer who wants an epic on the vanishing tent circus? He'll spend a few weeks as a roustabout and swear he knows all there is to know about it."

"I don't think he'll be working as a roustabout," Duffy muttered. Striking a match, he coaxed the cigar back to life. Jo frowned, watching the smoke struggle toward the ceiling.

"It's a bit late to work in a new act now, isn't it?"

"He's not a performer." Duffy swore lightly under his breath, then met Jo's eyes again. "He owns us."

For a moment Jo said nothing. She sat unmoving, as Duffy had seen her from time to time when she trained a young cat. "No!" She rose suddenly, shaking her head. "Not him. Not now. Why does he have to come? What does he want here?"

"It's his circus," Duffy reminded her. His voice was both rough and sympathetic.

"It'll never be his circus," Jo retorted passionately. Her eyes lit and glowed with a temper she rarely let have sway. "It's Frank's circus."

"Frank's dead," Duffy stated in a quiet, final tone. "Now the circus belongs to his son."

"Son?" Jo countered. She lifted her fingers to press them against her temple. Slowly, she moved to the window. Outside, the sun was pouring over the heads of troupers. She watched the members of the trapeze act, in thick robes worn over their tights, head toward the ring barn. The chatter of mixed languages was so familiar she failed to notice it. She placed her palms on the window sill and with a little sigh, steadied her temper. "What sort of son is it who never bothers to visit his father? In thirty years he never came to see Frank. He never wrote. He didn't even come to the funeral." Jo swallowed the tears of anger that rose to her throat and thickened her voice. "Why should he come now?"

"You've got to learn that life's a two-sided coin, kiddo," Duffy said briskly. "You weren't even alive thirty years ago. You don't know why Frank's wife up and left him or why the boy never visited."

"He's not a boy, Duffy, he's a man." Jo turned back, and he saw that she again had herself under control. "He's thirty-one, thirty-two years old now, a very successful attorney with a fancy Chicago office. He's very wealthy, did you know?" A small smile played on her lips but failed to reach her eyes. "And not just from court cases and legal fees; there's quite a lot of money on his mother's side. Nice, quiet, old money. I can't understand what a rich city lawyer would want with a tent circus."

Duffy shrugged his broad, round shoulders. "Could be he wants a tax shelter. Could be he wants to ride an elephant. Could be anything. He might want to take inventory and sell us off, piece by piece."

"Oh, Duffy, no!" Emotion flew back into Jo's face. "He couldn't do that."

"The heck he couldn't," Duffy muttered as he stubbed out his cigar. "He can do as he pleases. If he wants to liquidate, he liquidates."

"But we have contracts through October…."

"You're too smart for that, Jo." Duffy frowned, scratching his rim of hair. "He can buy them off or let them play through. He's a lawyer. He can figure the way out of a contract if he wants to. He can wait till August when we start to negotiate again and let them all lapse." Seeing Jo's distress, he backpedaled. "Listen, kiddo, I didn't say he was going to sell, I said he *could*."

Jo ran a hand through her hair. "There must be something we can do."

"We can show a profit by the end of the season," Duffy said wryly. "We can show the new owner what we have to offer. I think it's important that he sees we're not just a mud show but a profitable three-ring circus with class acts. He should see what Frank built, how he lived, what he wanted to do. I think," Duffy added, watching Jo's face, "that you should be in charge of his education."

"Me?" Jo was too incredulous to be angry. "Why? You're better qualified in the public relations department than I am. I train lions, not lawyers." She could not keep the hint of scorn from her voice.

"You were closer to Frank than anyone. And there isn't anyone here who knows this circus better than you." Again he frowned. "And you've got brains. Never thought much use would come of all those fancy books you read, but maybe I was wrong."

"Duffy." Her lips curved into a smile. "Just because I like to read Shakespeare doesn't mean I can deal with Keane Prescott. Even thinking about him makes me furious. How will I act when I meet him face to face?"

"Well." Duffy shrugged before he pursed his lips. "If you don't think you can handle it…"

"I didn't say I *couldn't* handle it," Jo muttered.

"Of course, if you're afraid…"

"I'm not afraid of anything, and I'm certainly not afraid of some Chicago lawyer who doesn't know sawdust from tanbark." Sticking her hands in her pockets, she paced the length of the small room. "If Keane Prescott, attorney-at-law, wants to spend his summer with the circus, I'll do my best to make it a memorable one."

"Nicely," Duffy cautioned as Jo moved to the door.

"Duffy," she paused and gave him an innocent smile. "You know what a gentle touch I have." To prove it, Jo slammed the door behind her.

Dawn was hovering over the horizon as the circus caravan drew up in a large, grassy field. Colors were just a promise in a pale gray sky. In the distance was grove upon grove of orange trees. As Jo stepped from the cab of her truck, the fragrance met her. It's a perfect day, she decided, then took a long, greedy breath. To her, there was no more beautiful sight than dawn struggling to life.

The air was vaguely chilly. She zipped up her gray sweat jacket as she watched the rest of the circus troupe pouring out of their trucks and cars and trailers. The morning quiet was soon shattered by voices. Work began immediately. As the Big Top canvas was being unrolled out of the spool truck, Jo went to see how her lions had fared the fifty-mile journey.

Three handlers unloaded the traveling cages. Buck had been with Jo the longest. He had worked for her father, and during the interim between his death and Jo's professional debut, he had worked up a small act with four male lions.

His shyness had made his retirement from performing a relief. To Buck, two people were a crowd. He stood six-feet-four, and his build was powerful enough for him to pad the sideshow from time to time as Hercules the Strong Man. He had an impressive head of wild blond hair and a full, curling beard. His hands were wide, with thick, strong fingers, but Jo remembered their gentleness when the two of them had delivered a lioness of a pair of cubs.

Pete's small frame seemed puny beside Buck's. He was of indeterminable age. Jo guessed between forty and fifty, but she was never certain. He was a quiet man with skin like polished mahogany and a rich, low-pitched voice. He had come to Jo five years before, asking for a job. She had never asked where he had come from, and he had never told her. He wore a fielder's cap and was never seen without a wad of gum moving gently in his teeth. He read Jo's books and was the undisputed king of the poker table.

Gerry was nineteen and eager. He was nearly six feet and still carried the lankiness of his youth. His mother sewed, and his father was a souvenir salesman, or a candy butcher, as circus jargon had it. Working the big cage was Gerry's dream, and because it had been hers, Jo had finally agreed to tutor him.

"How are my babies?" she demanded as she approached. At each cage she paused and soothed a nervous cat, calling each by name until they had settled. "They've traveled well. Hamlet's still edgy, but it's his first year on the road."

"He's a mean one," Buck muttered, watching Jo move from cage to cage.

"Yes, I know," she replied absently. "He's smart, too." She had twisted her hair into one thick braid and now tossed it to her back. "Look, here come some towners." A few cars and a smattering of bikes drew into the field.

These were the people from the outlying towns who

wanted to see a Big Top raised, who wanted to see the circus, if only for a moment, from the other side. Some would watch while others would lend a hand with tent poles, stretching canvas and rigging. They would earn a show pass and an unforgettable experience.

"Keep them clear of the cages," Jo ordered, nodding to Pete before she moved toward the still flaccid canvas. Buck lumbered beside her.

The field was alive with ropes and wire and people. Six elephants were harnessed but idle, with their handlers standing by the stake line. As workers pulled on guy ropes, the dusky brown canvas billowed up like a giant mushroom.

The poles were positioned—side, quarter, center—while the canvas muffled the sounds of scrambling workers. In the east the sun was rising fast, streaking the sky with pink. There were shouted instructions from the head canvas man, laughter from adventuresome boys and an occasional oath. As the quarter poles were driven into the sag of canvas, Jo signaled Maggie, the large African elephant. Obligingly, Maggie lowered her trunk. Jo stepped nimbly into the *u,* then scrambled onto the wide, gray back.

The sun grew higher by the second, shooting the first streams of light onto the field. The scent of orange blossoms mingled with the odor of leather harnesses. Jo had watched the canvas rise under a lightening sky countless times. Each time it was special, and the first raising each season was the most special of all. Maggie lifted her head and trumpeted as if pleased to be around for another season. With a laugh Jo reached back and swatted her rough, wrinkled rump. She felt free and fresh and incredibly alive. If there were a moment, she thought suddenly, that I could capture and bottle, it would be this one. Then, when I'm very old, I could take it out and feel young again. Smiling, she glanced down at the people swarming below her.

Her attention was caught by a man who stood by a coil of cable. Typically, she noted his build first. A well-proportioned body was essential to a performer. He was lean and stood straight. She noted he had good shoulders but doubted if there was much muscle in his arms. Though he was dressed casually in jeans, *city* stood out all over him. His hair was a dark, rich blond, and the early breeze had disturbed it so that it teased his forehead. He was clean-shaven, with a narrow, firm-jawed face. It was an attractive face. It was not, Jo mused, smoothly handsome like Vito the wire walker's but more aware, more demanding. Jo liked the face, liked the shape of the long, unsmiling mouth, liked the hint of bone beneath his tawny skin. Most of all she liked the directness of the amber eyes that stared back at her. They're like Ari's, she observed, thinking of her favorite lion. She was certain that he had been watching her long before she had looked down. Knowing this, Jo was impressed with his unselfconsciousness. He continued to stare, making no effort to camouflage his interest. She laughed, unperturbed, and tossed her braid from her shoulder.

"Want a ride?" she called out. Too many strangers had walked in and out of her world for her to be aloof. She watched his brow lift in acknowledgment of her offer. She would see if it was only his eyes that were like Ari's. "Maggie won't hurt you. She's gentle as a lamb, just bigger." Instantly, she saw he had understood the challenge. He walked across the grass until he stood beside her. He moved well, she noted. Jo tapped Maggie's side with the bull hook she carried. Wearily, the elephant knelt down on her trunk-like front legs. Jo held out her hand. With an agility that surprised her, the man mounted the elephant and slid into place behind her.

For a moment she said nothing, a bit stunned by the trem-

bling that had coursed up her arm as her palm had met his.
The contact had been brief. Jo decided she had imagined it.
"Up, Maggie," she said, giving her mount another tap. With
an elephantine sigh, Maggie obeyed, rocking her passengers
gently from side to side.

"Do you always pick up strange men?" the voice behind
her inquired. It was a smooth, well-keyed voice, a good
pitchman's voice.

Jo grinned over her shoulder. "Maggie's doing the
picking up."

"So she is. Are you aware that she's remarkably uncomfortable?"

Jo laughed with genuine enjoyment. "You should try
riding her a few miles in a street parade while keeping a
smile on your face."

"I'll pass. Are you in charge of her?"

"Maggie? No, but I know how to handle her. You have eyes
like one of my cats," she told him. "I like them. And since you
seemed to be interested in Maggie and me, I asked you up."

This time it was he who laughed. Jo twisted her head,
wanting to see his face. There was humor in his eyes now,
and his teeth were white and straight. Liking his smile, she
answered with one of her own. "Fascinating. You asked me
to take a ride on an elephant because I have eyes like your
cat's. And no offense to the lady beneath me, but I was
looking at you."

"Oh?" Jo pursed her lips in thought. "Why?"

For several seconds he studied her in silence. "Strange, I
believe you really don't know."

"I wouldn't ask if I did," she returned, shifting her weight
slightly. "It would be a waste of time to ask a question if I
knew the answer." She shifted again and turned away from
him. "Hold on now. Maggie's got to earn her bale of hay."

The poles hung between the canvas and the ground at forty-five degree angles. Quickly the elephant's chains were hooked to the metal rings at the base of the quarter poles. Jo urged Maggie forward in unison with her coworkers. Poles skidded along the ground, then up into place, pushing the canvas with it. The Big Top billowed to life under the early morning sky.

Her job done, Maggie moved through the flaps and into the light. "Beautiful, isn't it?" Jo murmured. "It's born fresh every day."

Vito walked by, calling out to Jo in Italian. Sending him a wave, she called back in his own language, then signaled to Maggie to kneel again. Jo waited until her passenger had dismounted before she slid off. It surprised her, when they stood face to face, that he was so tall. Tilting back her head, she judged him to be only two inches shy of Buck.

"You looked shorter when I was up on Maggie," she told him with her usual candor.

"You looked taller."

Jo chuckled, patting Maggie behind the ear. "Will you see the show?" She knew that she wanted him to, knew as well that she wanted to see him again. She found this both strange and intriguing. Men had always taken a second place to her cats, and towners had never interested her.

"Yes, I'm going to see the show." There was a slight smile on his face, but he was studying her thoughtfully. "Do you perform?"

"I have an act with my cats."

"I see. Somehow I pictured you in an aerial act, flying from the trapeze."

She sent him an easy smile. "My mother was an aerialist." Someone called her name, and looking, Jo saw Maggie was needed for raising the sideshow tent. "I have to go. I hope you like the show."

He took her hand before she could lead Maggie away. Jo stood still, again surprised by a trembling up her arm. "I'd like to see you tonight."

Glancing up, she met his eyes. They were direct and unselfconscious. "Why?" The question was sincere. Jo knew she wanted to see him as well but was unsure why.

This time he did not laugh. Gently, he ran a finger down the length of her braid. "Because you're beautiful, and you intrigue me."

"Oh." Jo considered. She had never thought of herself as beautiful. Striking, perhaps, in her costume, surrounded by her cats, but in jeans, without makeup, she doubted it. Still, it was an interesting thought. "All right, if there's no trouble with the cats. Ari hasn't been well."

A smile played at the corners of his mouth. "I'm sorry to hear that."

There was another loud summons for Jo, and both looked toward it. "I see you're needed," he said with a nod. "Perhaps you could point out Bill Duffy for me before you go."

"Duffy?" Jo repeated, surprised. "You can't be looking for a job?" There was incredulity in her voice, and he grinned.

"Why can't I?"

"Because you don't fit any of the types."

"Are there types?" he asked, both interested and amused. Jo shook her head in annoyance.

"Yes, of course, and you don't fit into any of them."

"Actually, I'm not looking for a job, so to speak," he told her, still smiling. "But I am looking for Bill Duffy."

It was against Jo's nature to probe. Privacy was both guarded and respected in the circus. Shielding her eyes with her hand, Jo looked around until she spotted Duffy supervising the raising of the cookhouse tent. "There," she said, pointing. "Duffy's the one with the red checked jacket. He still dresses like an outside talker."

"A what?"

"You'd call it a barker, I imagine." With easy grace she mounted the patient Maggie. "That's a towner's term, not a circus one." She smiled at him, then urged Maggie into a walk. "Tell Duffy Jo said to give you a pass," she called over her shoulder, then waved and turned away.

Dawn was over, and it was morning.

Chapter 2

Jo stood at the back door of the Big Top waiting for her cue. Beside her was Jamie Carter, alias Topo. He was a third generation clown and wore his bright face and orange wig naturally. He was young and limber and used these traits as well as his makeup to bring enthusiasm to his craft. To Jo, Jamie was more brother than friend. He was tall and thin, and under his greasepaint his face was mobile and pleasant. He and Jo had grown up together.

"Did she say anything?" Jamie demanded for the third time. With a sigh, Jo tossed closed the flap of the tent. Inside, clowns were performing around the hippodrome track while hands set up the big cage.

"Carmen said nothing. I don't know why you waste your time." Her voice was sharp, and Jamie bristled.

"I don't expect you to understand," he said with great dignity. His thin shoulders drew straight under his red polka dot shirt. "After all, Ari's the closest you've come to being involved with the opposite sex."

"That's very cute," Jo replied, unoffended by the jibe. Her annoyance stemmed from seeing Jamie make a fool of himself over Carmen Gribalti, the middle sister of the flying Gribaltis. She was darkly beautiful, graceful, talented, selfish and sublimely indifferent to Jamie. Looking into his happy, painted face and moody eyes, Jo's irritation dissipated. "She probably hasn't had a chance to answer the note you sent her," she soothed. "The first day of a new season's always wild."

"I suppose," Jamie muttered with a grudging shrug. "I don't know what she sees in Vito."

Jo thought of the wire walker's dark, cocky looks and rippling muscles. Wisely, she refrained from mentioning them. "Who can account for taste?" She gave him a smacking kiss on his round, red nose. "Personally, I get all wobbly when I see a man with thick, orange hair."

Jamie grinned. "Proves you know what to look for in a man."

Turning, Jo lifted the flap again, noting Jamie's cue was nearly upon them. "Did you happen to notice a towner hanging around today?"

"Only a couple dozen of them," Jamie answered dryly as he lifted the pail of confetti he used to finish the gag now being performed inside.

Jo shot him a half-hearted glare. "Not the usual type. About thirty, I think," she continued. "Wearing jeans and a T-shirt. He was tall, six-one, six-two," she went on as laughter poured out of the open flap to drown out her words. "He had dark blond straight hair."

"Yeah, I saw him." Jamie nudged her out of his way and prepared to make his entrance. "He was going into the red wagon with Duffy." With a wild, high-pitched scream, Topo the clown bounded into the Big Top in size fifteen tennis shoes, brandishing his bucket of confetti.

Thoughtfully, Jo watched Jamie chase three other clowns around the track. It was odd, she thought, for Duffy to take a towner into the administration trailer. He had said he wasn't looking for a job. He wasn't a drifter; there was an unmistakable air of stability about him. He wasn't a circus hand from another show, either. His palm had been too smooth. And, her mind added as she vaulted onto Babette, a pure white mare, there had been an undeniable aura of urbanity about him. Success, as well, she thought. And authority. No, he had not been looking for a job.

Jo shrugged, annoyed that a stranger was crowding into her thoughts. It irritated her further that she had scanned the crowds for him during the parade and that even now she wondered if he sat somewhere in the circular arena. He hadn't been at the matinee. Jo patted the mare's neck absently, then straightened as she heard the ringmaster's whistle.

"Ladies and gentlemen," he called in deep, musical tones. "Presenting the most spectacular exhibition of animal subjugation under the Big Top. Jovilette, Queen of the Jungle Cats!"

Jo nudged Babette with her heels and raced into the arena. The applause rose to meet her as the audience appreciated the dashing figure she cut. Swathed in a black cape, raven hair flying free under a glittering tiara, she galloped bareback on the snow white mare. In each hand she held a long, thin whip, which she cracked alternately overhead. At the entrance to the big cage she leaped from the still racing horse. While Babette galloped out of the back door and into the care of a handler, Jo shifted both whips into one hand, then removed the cape with a flourish. Her costume was a close-fitting, one-piece jumpsuit, dazzling in white and spangled with gold sequins. In dramatic contrast, her hair hung straight and severe down her back.

Make an entrance, Frank had always said. And Jovilette made an entrance.

The twelve cats were already in the cage, banding its inside edge as they perched on blue and white pedestals. Entering the main cage appeared routine to the audience, but Jo knew it was one of the most dangerous moments of the act. To enter, she had to pass directly between two cats as she moved from the safety cage to the main arena. She always stationed her best behaved cats there, but if one was irritated, or even playful, he could easily strike out with a powerful paw. Even with sharp claws retracted, the damage could be deadly.

She entered swiftly and was surrounded by cats on all sides. Her spangles and tiara caught the lights and played with them as she began to move around the cage, cracking the whip for showmanship while using her voice to command the cats to rise on their haunches. She moved them through their routine, adjusting the timing to compensate for any feline reluctance, letting one trick begin where the last ended.

Jo disliked overdone propping, preferring action and movement. The contrast of the big, tawny cats and the small white and gold woman were the best props available to her. She used them well. Hers was a *picture act,* relying on style and flash, rather than a *fighting act,* which emphasized the ferocity of the big cats by employing blank-bulleted guns and rehearsed charges, or *bounces.* Her confidence transmitted itself to the audience, making her handling of the cats appear effortless. In truth, her body was coiled for any danger, and her mind was focused so intently on her cats, there might have been no audience at all.

She stood between two high pedestals as the cats leaped over her head from both directions. They set up a light breeze, which stirred her hair. They roared when she cued them, setting up an echoing din. Now and then one reached out to paw at the stock of her whip, and she stopped him with a quick command. She sent her best leaper through a hoop of flame and coaxed her best balancer to walk on a glistening silver ball. She ended to waves of applause by trotting Merlin around the hippodrome track.

At the back door Merlin jumped into a wheel cage and was turned over to Pete. "Nice show," he said as he handed her a long chenille robe. "Smooth as silk."

"Thanks." Cold, she bundled into the robe. The spring night was frigid in contrast to the hot lights and heat in the big cage. "Listen, Pete, tell Gerry he can feed the cats tonight. They're behaving themselves."

Pete snapped his gum and chuckled. "Won't he be riding high tonight." As he moved to the truck that would pull the cage to the cat area, Jo called after him.

"Pete." She bit her lip, then shrugged when he twisted his head. "You'll keep an eye on him, won't you?"

Pete grinned and climbed into the cab of the truck. "Who you worried about, Jo? Those big cats or that skinny boy?"

"Both," she answered. The rhinestones in her tiara sparkled as she tossed her head and laughed. Knowing she had nearly an hour before the finale parade, Jo walked away from the Big Top. She thought of wandering to the cook-house for some coffee. Mentally, she began replaying every segment of her act. It had gone well, she thought, pleased with the timing and the flow. If Pete had said it had been smooth, Jo knew it had. She had heard his criticisms more than once over the past five years. True, Hamlet had tested her once or twice, but no one knew that but Jo and the cat. She doubted if anyone but Buck would have seen that he had given her trouble. Closing her eyes a moment, Jo rolled her shoulders, loosening tight, tensed muscles.

"That's quite an act you have."

Jo whirled around at the sound of the voice. She could feel her heart rate accelerate. Though she wondered at her interest in a man she barely knew, Jo was aware that she had been waiting for him. There was a quick surge of pleasure as she watched him approach, and she allowed it to show on her face.

"Hello." She saw that he smoked a cigar, but unlike Duffy's, his was long and slim. Again she admired the elegance of his hands. "Did you like the show?"

He stopped in front of her, then studied her face with a thoroughness that made her wonder if her makeup had smeared. Then he gave a small, surprised laugh and shook his head. "Do you know," he began, "when you told me this morning that you did an act with cats, I had Siamese in mind rather than African."

"Siamese?" Jo repeated blankly, then laughed. "House cats?" He brushed her hair behind her back while Jo giggled at the thought of coaxing a Siamese to jump through a flaming hoop.

"From my point of view," he told her as he let a strand of her hair linger between his fingers, "it made more sense than a little thing like you walking into a cage with a dozen lions."

"I'm not little," Jo corrected good-naturedly. "Besides, size hardly matters to twelve lions."

"No, I suppose it doesn't." He lifted his eyes from her hair and met hers. Jo continued to smile, enjoying looking at him. "Why do you do it?" he asked suddenly.

Jo gave him a curious look. "Why? Because it's my job." By the way he studied her, Jo could see that he was not satisfied with the simplicity of her answer. "Perhaps I should ask *how* you became a lion tamer."

"Trainer," Jo corrected automatically. To her left, she could hear the audience's muffled applause. "The Beirots are starting," she said with a glance toward the sound. "You shouldn't miss their act. They're first-rate acrobats."

"Don't you want to tell me?" His voice was soft.

She lifted a brow, seeing that he truly wanted to know. "Why, it's not a secret. My father was a trainer, and I have a knack for working with cats. It just followed." Jo had never thought about her career past this point, and she shrugged it aside. "You shouldn't waste your ticket standing out here. You can stand by the back door and watch the rest of the act." Jo turned to lead the way to the performer's entrance but stopped when his hand took hers.

He stepped forward until their bodies were nearly touching. Jo could feel the heat from his as she watched his face. Her heart was thudding in a quick, steady rhythm. She could hear it vibrate through her the same way it did when she approached a new cat for the first time. Here was something new, something untested. She tingled with the excitement of the unknown when he lifted his hand to touch her cheek. She did not move but let the warmth spread while she watched him carefully, gauging him. Her eyes were wide, curious and unafraid.

"Are you going to kiss me?" she asked in a tone that expressed more interest than desire.

His eyes lit with humor and glittered in the dim light. "I had given it some thought," he answered. "Do you have any objections?"

Jo considered a moment, dropping her eyes to his mouth. She liked its shape and wondered how it would feel against hers. He brought her no closer. One hand still held hers while the other slid around to cradle her neck. Jo shifted her gaze until their eyes met again. "No," she decided. "I haven't any objections."

The corners of his mouth twitched as he tightened his hold slightly on the base of her neck. Slowly, he lowered his head toward hers. Curious and a bit wary, Jo kept her eyes open, watching his. She knew from experience that you could tell more about people and about cats from the eyes. To her surprise, his remained open as well, even as their lips met.

It was a gentle kiss, without pressure, only a whisper of a touch. Amazed, Jo thought she felt the ground tremble under her feet. Dimly, she wondered if the elephants were being led by. But it can't be time, she thought in confusion. His lips moved lightly over hers, and his eyes remained steady. Jo's pulse drummed under her skin. They stood, barely touching, as the Big Top throbbed with noise behind them. Lazily, he traced her lips with the tip of his tongue, teasing them open. Still there was no demand in the kiss, only testing. Unhurried, confident, he explored her mouth while Jo felt her breath accelerating. A soft moan escaped her as her lids fluttered down.

For an instant she surrendered utterly to him, to the new sensations swimming through her. She leaned against him, straining toward pleasure, sighing with it as the kiss lingered.

He drew her away, but their faces remained close. Dizzily, Jo realized that she had risen to her toes to compensate for their difference in height. His hand was still light on the back of her neck. His eyes were gold in the darkening night.

"What an incredible female you are, Jovilette," he murmured. "One surprise after another."

Jo felt stunningly alive. Her skin seemed to tingle with new feelings. She smiled. "I don't know your name."

He laughed, releasing her neck to take her other hand in his. Before he could speak, Duffy called out from the direction of the Big Top. Jo turned to watch as he moved toward them in his quick, rolling walk.

"Well, well, well," he said in his jolly, rough voice. "I didn't know you two had met. Has Jo been showing you around already?" Reaching them, he squeezed Jo's shoulder. "Knew I could count on you, kiddo." Jo glanced at him in puzzlement, but he continued before she could form a question. "Yes, sir, this little girl puts on quite a show, doesn't she? Always a grabber. And she knows this circus like the back of her hand. Born and raised to it," he continued. Jo relaxed. She recognized that Duffy was into one of his spiels, and there was no stopping him. "Yessiree, any questions you got, you just ask our Jo, and she'll tell you. 'Course, I'm always at your disposal, too. Anything I can tell you about the books or accounts or contracts and the like, you just let me know." Duffy puffed twice on his cigar as Jo felt her first hint of unease.

Why was Duffy rambling about books and contracts? Jo glanced at the man who still held her hands in his. He was watching Duffy with an easy, amused smile.

"Are you a bookkeeper?" Jo asked, perplexed. Duffy laughed and patted her head.

"You know Mr. Prescott's a lawyer, Jo. Don't miss your cue." He gave them both a friendly nod and toddled off.

Jo had stiffened almost imperceptibly at Duffy's offhand information, but Keane had felt it. His brows lowered as he studied her. "Now you know my name."

"Yes." All warmth fled from Jo. Her voice was as cool as her blood. "Would you let go of my hands, Mr. Prescott?"

After a brief hesitation Keane inclined his head and obliged. Jo stuffed her hands quickly into the pockets of her robe. "Don't you think we've progressed to the first name stage of our relationship, Jo?"

"I assure you, Mr. Prescott, if I had known who you were, we wouldn't have progressed at all." Jo's words were stiff with dignity. Inside, though she tried to ignore it, she felt betrayal, anger, humiliation. All pleasure had died from the evening. Now the kiss that had left her feeling clean and alive seemed cheap and shabby. No, she would not use his first name, she vowed. She would never use it. "If you'll excuse me, I have some things to do before my cue."

"Why the turnaround?" he asked, halting her with a hand on her arm. "Don't you like lawyers?"

Coldly, Jo studied him. She wondered how it was possible that she had completely misjudged the man she had met that morning. "I don't categorize people, Mr. Prescott."

"I see." Keane's tone became detached, his eyes assessing. "Then it would appear that you have an aversion to my name. Should I assume you hold a grudge against my father?"

Jo's eyes glittered with quick fury. She jerked her arm from his hold. "Frank Prescott was the most generous, the kindest, most unselfish man I've ever known. I don't even associate you with Frank, Mr. Prescott. You have no right to him." Though it was nearly impossible, Jo forced herself to speak in a normal tone of voice. She would not shout and draw anyone's attention. This would be kept strictly between Keane Prescott and herself. "It would have been much better if you had told me who you were right away, then there would have been no mix-up."

"Is that what we've had?" he countered mildly. "A mix-up?"

His cool tone was nearly Jo's undoing. He watched her with a dispassionate curiosity that tempted her to slap him. She fought to keep her fury from spilling over into her voice. "You have no right to Frank's circus, Mr. Prescott," she managed quietly. "Leaving it to you is the only thing I've ever faulted him for." Knowing her control was slipping, Jo whirled, running across the grass until she merged with the darkness.

Chapter 3

The morning was surprisingly warm. There were no trees to block the sun, and the smell of the earth was strong. The circus had moved north in the early hours. All the usual scents merged into the aroma of circus: canvas, leather, sweating horses, greasepaint and powder, coffee and oilcloth. The trailers and trucks sat in the accustomed spots, forming the "back yard" that would always take the same formation each time the circus made a stop along the thousands of miles it traveled. The flag over the cookhouse tent signaled that lunch was being served. The Big Top stood waiting for the matinee.

Rose hurried along the midway toward the animal cages. Her dark hair was pinned neatly in a bun at the back of her neck. Her big brown eyes darted about searchingly, while her mouth sat softly in a pout. She was wrapped in a terry cloth robe and wore tennis shoes over her tights. When she saw Jo standing in front of Ari's cage, she waved and broke into a half-run. Watching her, Jo shifted her attention from Ari. Rose was always a diversion, and Jo felt in need of one.

"Jo!" She waved again as if Jo had not seen her the first time, then came to a breathless halt. "Jo, I only have a few minutes. Hello, Ari," she added out of politeness. "I was looking for Jamie."

"Yes, I gathered." Jo smiled, knowing Rose had set her heart on capturing Topo's alter ego. And if he had any sense, she thought, he'd let himself be caught instead of pining over Carmen. Silly, she decided, dismissing all affairs of the heart. Lions were easier to understand. "I haven't seen him all morning, Rose. Maybe he's rehearsing."

"Drooling over Carmen, more likely," Rose muttered, sending a sulky glare in the direction of the Gribalti trailer. "He makes a fool of himself."

"That's what he's paid for," Jo reminded her, but Rose did not respond to the humor. Jo sighed. She had a true affection for Rose. She was bright and fun and without pretentions. "Rose," she said, keeping her voice both light and kind. "Don't give up on him. He's a little slow, you know," she explained. "He's just a bit dazzled by Carmen right now. It'll pass."

"I don't know why I bother," she grumbled, but Jo saw the dark mood was already passing. Rose was a creature of quick passions that flared and soon died. "He's not so very handsome, you know."

"No," Jo agreed. "But he has a cute nose."

"Lucky for him I like red," Rose returned and grinned. "Ah, now we're speaking of handsome," she murmured as her eyes drifted from Jo. "Who is this?"

At the question, Jo glanced over her shoulder. The humor fled from her eyes. "That's the owner," she said colorlessly.

"Keane Prescott? No one told me he was so handsome. Or so tall," she added, admiring him openly as he crossed the back yard. Jo noted that Rose always became more

Mexican around men. "Such shoulders. Lucky for Jamie I'm a one-man woman."

"Lucky for you your mama can't hear you," Jo muttered, earning an elbow in the ribs.

"But he comes here, *amiga,* and he looks at you. La, la, my papa would have Jamie to the altar *pronto* if he looked at me that way."

"You're an idiot," Jo snapped, annoyed.

"Ah, Jo," Rose said with mock despair. "I am a romantic."

Jo was helpless against the smile that tugged at her lips. Her eyes were laughing when she glanced up and met Keane's. Hastily, she struggled to dampen their brilliance, turning her mouth into a sober line.

"Good morning, Jovilette." He spoke her name too easily, she thought, as if he had been saying it for years.

"Good morning, Mr. Prescott," she returned. Rose gave a loud, none-too-subtle cough. "This is Rose Sanches."

"It's a pleasure, Mr. Prescott." Rose extended a hand, trying out a smile she had been saving for Jamie. "I heard you were traveling with us."

Keane accepted the hand and smiled in return. Jo noticed with annoyance that it was the same easy, disarming smile of the stranger she had met the morning before. "Hello, Rose, it's nice to meet you."

Seeing her friend's Mexican blood heat her cheeks, Jo intervened. She would not permit Keane Prescott to make a conquest here. "Rose, you only have ten minutes to get back and into makeup."

"Holy cow!" she said, forgetting her attempt at sophistication. "I've got to run." She began to do so, then called over her shoulder, "Don't tell Jamie I was looking for him, the pig!" She ran a little further, then turned and ran backwards.

"I'll look for him later," she said with a laugh, then turned back and streaked toward the midway.

Keane watched her dart across the compound while holding up the long skirts of her robe in one hand. "Charming."

"She's only eighteen," Jo offered before she could stop herself.

When Keane turned to her, his look was one of amusement. "I see," he said. "I'll take that information under advisement. And what does the eighteen-year-old Rose do?" he asked, slipping his thumbs into the front pockets of his jeans. "Wrestle alligators?"

"No." Jo returned without batting an eye. "Rose is Serpentina, your premier sideshow attraction. The snake charmer." She was pleased with the incredulous look that passed over his face. It was replaced quickly, however, with one of genuine humor.

"Perfect." He brushed Jo's hair from her cheek before she could protest by word or action. "Cobras?" he asked, ignoring the flash in her eyes.

"And boa constrictors," she returned sweetly. Jo brushed the dust from the knees of her faded jeans. "Now, if you'll excuse me…"

"No, I don't think so." Keane's voice was cool, but she recognized the underlying authority. She did her best not to struggle against it. He *was* the owner, she reminded herself.

"Mr. Prescott," she began, banking down hard on the urge to mutiny. "I'm very busy. I have to get ready for the afternoon show."

"You've got an hour and a half until you're on," he countered smoothly. "I think you might spare me a portion of that time. You've been assigned to show me around. Why don't we start now?" The tone of the question left room for only one answer. Jo's mind fidgeted in search of a way out.

Tilting her head back, she met his eyes. He won't be easy
to beat, she concluded, studying his steady, measuring gaze.
I'd better study his moves more carefully before I start a
battle. "Where would you like to begin?" she asked aloud.

"With you."

Keane's easy answer brought a deep frown to Jo's brows.
"I don't understand what you mean."

For a moment Keane watched her. There was no coyness
or guile in her eyes as they looked into his. "No, I can see
you don't," he agreed with a nod. "Let's start with your
cats."

"Oh." Jo's frown cleared instantly. "All right." She
watched as he pulled out a thin cigar, waiting until the flame
of his lighter licked the tip before speaking. "I have
thirteen—seven males, six females. They're all African lions
between four-and-a-half and twenty-two years."

"I thought you worked with twelve," Keane commented
as he dropped his lighter into his pocket.

"That's right, but Ari's retired." Turning, Jo indicated the
large male lion dozing in a cage. "He travels with me because
he always has, but I don't work him anymore. He's twenty-
two, the oldest. My father kept him, even though he was born
in captivity, because he was born the same day I was." Jo
sighed, and her voice became softer. "He's the last of my
father's stock. I couldn't sell him to a zoo. It seemed like
shoving an old relative into a home and abandoning him.
He's been with this circus every day of his life, just as I have.
His name is Hebrew for *lion*." Jo laughed, forgetting the
man beside her as she sifted through memories. "My father
always gave his cats names that meant lion somehow or
other. Leo, Leonard, Leonara. Ari was a first-class leaper in
his prime. He could climb, too; some cats won't. I could teach
Ari anything. Smart cat, aren't you, Ari?" The altered tone

of her voice caused the big cat to stir. Opening his eyes, he stared back at Jo. The sound he made was more grumble than roar before he dozed again. "He's tired," Jo murmured, fighting a shaft of gloom. "Twenty-two's old for a lion."

"What is it?" Keane demanded, touching her shoulder before she could turn away. Her eyes were drenched with sadness.

"He's dying," she said unsteadily. "And I can't stop it." Stuffing her hands in her pockets, Jo moved away to the main group of cages. To steady herself, she took two deep breaths while waiting for Keane to join her. Regaining her composure, she began again. "I work with these twelve," she told him, making a sweeping gesture. "They're fed once a day, raw meat six days a week and eggs and milk on the seventh. They were all imported directly from Africa and were cage broken when I got them."

The faint sound of a calliope reached them, signaling the opening of the midway. "This is Merlin, the one I ride out on at the finish. He's ten, and the most even-tempered cat I've ever worked with. Heathcliff," she continued as she moved down the line of cages, "he's six, my best leaper. And this is Faust, the baby at four and a half." The lions paced their cages as Jo walked Keane down the line. Unable to prevent herself, Jo gave Faust a signal by raising her hand. Obediently, he sent out a huge, deafening roar. To Jo's disappointment, Keane did not scramble for cover.

"Very impressive," he said mildly. "You put him in the center when you lie down on them, don't you?"

"Yes." She frowned, then spoke her thoughts candidly. "You're very observant—and you've got steady nerves."

"My profession requires them, too, to an extent," he returned.

Jo considered this a moment, then turned back to the lions.

"Lazareth, he's twelve and a natural ham. Bolingbroke, he's ten, from the same lioness as Merlin. Hamlet," she said stopping again, "he's five. I bought him to replace Ari in the act." Jo stared into the tawny eyes. "He has potential, but he's arrogant. Patient, too. He's just waiting for me to make a mistake."

"Why?" Keane glanced over at Jo. Her eyes were cool and steady on Hamlet's.

"So he can get a good clean swipe at me," she told him without altering her expression. "It's his first season in the big cage. Pandora," Jo continued, pointing out the females. "A very classy lady. She's six. Hester, at seven, my best all-around. And Portia; it's her first year, too. She's mostly a seat-warmer."

"Seat-warmer?"

"Just what it sounds like," Jo explained. "She hasn't mastered any complicated tricks yet. She evens out the act, does a few basics and warms the seat." Jo moved on. "Dulcinea, the prettiest of the ladies. Ophelia, who had a litter last year; and Abra, eight, a bit bad-tempered but a good balancer."

Hearing her name, the cat rose, stretched her long, golden body, then began to rub it against the bars of the cage. A deep sound rumbled in her throat. Jo scowled and jammed her hands into her pockets. "She likes you," she muttered.

"Oh?" Lifting a brow, Keane studied the three-hundred-pound Abra more carefully. "How do you know?"

"When a lion likes you, it does exactly what a house cat does. It rubs against you. Abra's rubbing against the bars because she can't get any closer."

"I see." Humor touched his mouth. "I must admit, I'm at a loss on how to return the compliment." He drew on his cigar, then regarded Jo through a haze of smoke. "Your choice of names is fascinating."

"I like to read," she stated, leaving it at that. "Is there anything else you'd like to know about the cats?" Jo was determined to keep their conversation on a professional level. His smile had reminded her all too clearly of their encounter the night before.

"Do you drug them before a performance?"

Fury sparked Jo's eyes. "Certainly not."

"Was that an unreasonable question?" Keane countered. He dropped his cigar to the ground, then crushed it out with his heel.

"Not for a first of mayer," Jo decided with a sigh. She tossed her hair carelessly behind her back. "Drugging is not only cruel, it's stupid. A drugged animal won't perform."

"You don't touch the lions with that whip," Keane commented. He watched the light breeze tease a few strands of her hair. "Why do you use it?"

"To get their attention and to keep the audience awake." She smiled reluctantly.

Keane took her arm. Instantly, Jo stiffened. "Let's walk," he suggested. He began to lead her away from the cages. Spotting several people roaming the back yard, Jo refrained from pulling away. The last thing she wanted was the story spreading that she was having a tiff with the owner. "How do you tame them?" he asked her.

"I don't. They're not tame, they're trained." A tall blond woman walked by carrying a tiny white poodle. "Merlin's hungry today," Jo called out with a grin.

The woman bundled the dog closer to her breast in mock alarm and began a rapid scolding in French. Jo laughed, telling her in the same language that Fifi was too tough a mouthful for Merlin.

"Fifi can do a double somersault on the back of a moving horse," Jo explained as they began to walk again. "She's trained just as my cats are trained, but she's also domesticated. The cats are wild." Jo turned her face up to Keane's. The sun cast a sheen over her hair and threw gold flecks into her eyes. "A wild thing can never be tamed, and anyone who tries is foolish. If you take something wild and turn it into a pet, you've stolen its character, blanked out its spark. And still, there's always an essence of the wild that can come back to life. When a dog turns on his master, it's ugly. When a lion turns, it's lethal." She was beginning to become accustomed to his hand on her arm, finding it easy to talk to him because he listened. "A full-grown male stands three feet at the shoulder and weighs over five hundred pounds. One well-directed swipe can break a man's neck, not to mention what teeth and claws can do." Jo gave a smile and a shrug. "Those aren't the virtues of a pet."

"Yet you go into a cage with twelve of them, armed with a whip?"

"The whip's window dressing." Jo discounted it with a gesture of her hand. "It would hardly be a defense against even one cat at full charge. A lion is a very tenacious enemy. A tiger is more bloodthirsty, but it normally strikes only once. If it misses, it takes it philosophically. A lion charges again and again. Do you know the line Byron wrote about a tiger's spring? 'Deadly, quick and crushing.'" Jo had completely forgotten her animosity and began to enjoy her walk and conversation with this handsome stranger. "It's a true description, but a lion is totally fearless when he charges, and stubborn. He's not the razzle-dazzle fighter the tiger is, just accurate. I'd bet on a lion against a tiger any day. And a man simply hasn't a prayer against one."

"Then how do you manage to stay in one piece?"

The calliope music was just a hint in the air now. Jo turned, noting with surprise that they had walked a good distance from camp. She could see the trailers and tents, hear occasional shouts and laughter, but she felt oddly separated from it all. She sat down cross-legged on the grass and plucked a blade. "I'm smarter than they are. At least I make them think so. And I dominate them, partly by a force of will. In training, you have to develop a rapport, a mutual respect, and if you're lucky, a certain affection. But you can't trust them to the point where you grow careless. And above all," she added, glancing over as he sat down beside her, "you have to remember the basic rule of poker. Bluff." Jo grinned, leaning back on her elbows. "Do you play poker?"

"I've been known to." Her hair trailed out along the grass, and he lifted a strand. "Do you?"

"Sometimes. My assistant handler, Pete…" Jo scanned the back yard, then smiled and pointed. "There he is, by the second trailer, sitting with Mac Stevenson, the one with the fielder's cap. Pete organizes a game now and then."

"Who's the little girl on stilts?"

"That's Mac's youngest, Katie. She wants to walk on them in the street parade. She's getting pretty good. There's Jamie," she said, then laughed as he did a pratfall and landed at Katie's wooden stilts.

"Rose's Jamie?" Keane asked, watching the impromptu show in the back yard.

"If she has her way. He's currently dazzled by Carmen Gribalti. Carmen won't give Jamie the time of day. She bats her lashes at Vito, the wire walker. He bats his at everyone."

"A complicated state of affairs," Keane commented. He twisted Jo's hair around his fingers. "Romance seems to be very popular in circus life."

"From what I read," she countered, "it's popular everywhere."

"Who dazzles you, Jovilette?" He gave her hair a tug to bring her face around to his.

Jo hadn't realized he was so close. She need do no more than sway for her mouth to touch his. Her eyes measured his while she waited for her pulse to calm. It was odd, she thought, that he had such an effect on her. With sudden clarity, she could smell the grass, a clean, sweet scent, and feel the sun. The sounds of the circus were muted in the background. She could hear birds call out with an occasional high-pitched trill. She remembered the taste of his mouth and wondered if it would be the same.

"I've been too busy to be dazzled," she replied. Her voice was steady, but her eyes were curious.

For the first time, Jo truly *wanted* to be kissed by a man. She wanted to feel again what she had felt the night before. She wanted to be held, not lightly as he had held her before, but close, with his arms tight around her. She wanted to renew the feeling of weightlessness. She had never experienced a strong physical desire, and for a moment she explored the sensation. There was a quiver in her stomach which was both pleasant and disturbing. Throughout her silent contemplations Keane watched her, intrigued by the intensity of her eyes.

"What are you thinking of?"

"I'm wondering why you make me feel so odd," she told him with simple frankness. He smiled, and she noticed that it grew in his eyes seconds before it grew on his mouth.

"Do I?" He appeared to enjoy the information. "Did you know your hair catches the sunlight?" Keane took a handful, letting it spill from between his fingers. "I've never seen another woman with hair like this. It's a temptation all in itself. In what way do I make you feel odd, Jovilette?" he asked as his eyes trailed back up to hers.

"I'm not sure yet." Jo found her voice husky. Abruptly, she decided it would not do to go on feeling odd or to go on wanting to be kissed by Keane Prescott. She scrambled up and brushed off the seat of her pants.

"Running away?" As Keane rose, Jo's head snapped up.

"I never run away from anything, Mr. Prescott." Ice sharpened her voice. She was annoyed that she had allowed herself to fall under his charm again. "I certainly won't run from a city-bred lawyer." Her words were laced with scorn. "Why don't you go back to Chicago and get someone thrown in jail?"

"I'm a defense attorney," Keane countered easily. "I get people out of jail."

"Fine. Go put a criminal back on the streets, then."

Keane laughed, bringing Jo's temper even closer to the surface. "That covers both sides of the issue, doesn't it? You dazzle me, Jovilette."

"Well, it's strictly unintentional." She took a step back from the amusement in his eyes. She would not tolerate him making fun of her. "You don't belong here," she blurted out. "You have no business here."

"On the contrary," he disagreed in a cool, untroubled voice. "I have every business here. I own this circus."

"Why?" she demanded, throwing out her hands as if to push his words aside. "Because it says so on a piece of paper? That's all lawyers understand, I imagine—pieces of paper with strange little words. Why did you come? To look us over and calculate the profit and loss? What's the liquidation value of a dream, Mr. Prescott? What price do you put on the human spirit? Look at it!" she demanded, swinging her arm to encompass the lot behind them. "You only see tents and a huddle of trailers. You can't possibly understand what it all means. But Frank understood. He loved it."

"I'm aware of that." Keane's voice was still calm but had taken on a thin edge of steel. Jo saw that his eyes had grown dark and guarded. "He also left it to me."

"I don't understand why." In frustration, Jo stuffed her hands in her pockets and turned away.

"Neither do I, I assure you, but the fact remains that he did."

"Not once in thirty years did you visit him." Jo whirled back around. Her hair followed in a passionate arch. "Not once."

"Quite true," Keane agreed. He stood with his weight even on both legs and watched her. "Of course, some might look at it differently. Not once in thirty years did he visit me."

"Your mother left him and took you to Chicago—"

"I won't discuss my mother," Keane interrupted in a tone of clipped finality.

Jo bit off a retort, spinning away from him again. Still she could not find the reins to her control. "What are you going to do with it?" she demanded.

"That's my business."

"Oh!" Jo spun back, then shut her eyes and muttered in a language he failed to understand. "Can you be so arrogant? Can you be so dispassionate?" Her lashes fluttered up, revealing eyes dark with anger. "Do the lives of all those people mean nothing to you? Does Frank's dream mean nothing? Haven't you enough money already without hurting people to get more? Greed isn't something you inherited from Frank."

"I'll only be pushed so far," Keane warned.

"I'd push you all the way back to Chicago if I could manage it," she snapped.

"I wondered how much of a temper there was behind

those sharp green eyes," Keane commented, watching her passion pour color into her cheeks. "It appears it's a full-grown one." Jo started to retort, but Keane cut her off. "Just hold on a minute," he ordered. "With or without your approval, I own this circus. It might be easier for you if you adjusted to that. Be quiet," he added when her mouth opened again. "Legally, I can do with my—" He hesitated a moment, then continued in a mordant tone. "—inheritance as I choose. I have no obligation or intention of justifying my decision to you."

Jo dug her nails into her palms to help keep her voice from shaking. "I never knew I could grow to dislike someone so quickly."

"Jovilette." Keane dipped his hands into his pockets, then rocked back on his heels. "You disliked me before you ever saw me."

"That's true," she replied evenly. "But I've learned to dislike you in person in less than twenty-four hours. I have a show to do," she said, turning back toward the lot. Though he did not follow, she felt his eyes on her until she reached her trailer and closed the door behind her.

Thirty minutes later Jamie sprang through the back door of the Big Top. He was breathless after a lengthy routine and hooked one hand through his purple suspenders as he took in gulps of air. He spotted Jo standing beside the white mare. Her eyes were dark and stormy, her shoulders set and rigid. Jamie recognized the signs. Something or someone had put Jo in a temper, and she had barely ten minutes to work her way out of it before her cue.

He crossed to her and gave a tug on her hair. "Hey."

"Hello, Jamie." Jo struggled to keep her voice pleasant, but he heard the traces of emotion.

"Hello, Jo," he replied in precisely the same tone.

"Cut it out," she ordered before taking a few steps away. The mare followed docilely. Jo had been trying for some time to put her emotions back into some semblance of order. She was not succeeding.

"What happened?" Jamie asked from directly behind her.

"Nothing," Jo snapped, then hated herself for the short nastiness of the word.

Jamie persisted, knowing her too well to be offended. "Nothing is one of my favorite topics of conversation." He put his hands on her shoulders, ignoring her quick, bad-tempered jerk. "Let's talk about it."

"There's nothing to talk about."

"Exactly." He began massaging the tension in her shoulders with his white gloved hands.

"Oh, Jamie." His good-heartedness was irresistible. Sighing, she allowed herself to be soothed. "You're an idiot."

"I'm not here to be flattered."

"I had an argument with the owner." Jo let out a long breath and shut her eyes.

"What're you doing having arguments with the owner?"

"He infuriates me." Jo whirled around. Her cape whipped and snapped with the movement. "He shouldn't be here. If he were back in Chicago..."

"Hold it." With a slight shake of her shoulders, Jamie halted Jo's outburst. "You know better than to get yourself worked up like this right before a show. You can't afford to have your mind on anything but what you're doing when you're in that cage."

"I'll be all right," she mumbled.

"Jo." There was censure in his voice mixed with affection and exasperation.

Reluctantly, Jo brought her gaze up to his. It was impossible to resist the grave eyes in the brightly painted face. With something between a sigh and a moan, she dropped her forehead to his chest. "Jamie, he makes me so mad! He could ruin everything."

"Let's worry about it when the time comes," Jamie suggested, patting her hair.

"But he doesn't understand us. He doesn't understand anything."

"Well, then it's up to us to make him understand, isn't it?"

Jo looked up and wrinkled her nose. "You're so logical."

"Of course I am," he agreed and struck a pose. As he wiggled his orange eyebrows, Jo laughed. "Okay?" he asked, then picked up his prop bucket.

"Okay," she agreed and smiled.

"Good, 'cause there's my cue."

When he disappeared behind the flap, Jo leaned her cheek against the mare and nuzzled a moment. "I don't think I'm the one to make him understand, though."

I wish he'd never come, she added silently as she vaulted onto the mare's back. I wish I'd never noticed how his eyes are like Ari's and how nice his mouth is when he smiles, she thought. Jo ran the tip of her tongue gingerly over her lips. I wish he'd never kissed me. *Liar.* Her conscience spoke softly in her ear: *Admit it, you're glad he kissed you. You've never felt anything like that before, and no matter what, you're glad he kissed you last night. You even wanted him to kiss you again today.*

She forced her mind clear, taking deep, even breaths until she heard the ringmaster announce her. With a flick of her heels, she sent the mare sprinting into the tent.

It did not go well. The audience cheered her, oblivious to any problem, but Jo was aware that the routine was far from smooth. And the cats sensed her preoccupation. Again and again they tested her, and again and again Jo was forced to alter her timing to compensate. When the act was over, her head throbbed from the strain of concentration. Her hands were clammy as she turned Merlin over to Buck.

The big man came back to her after securing the cage. "What's the matter with you?" he demanded without preamble. By the underlying and very rare anger in his voice, Jo knew he had observed at least a portion of her act. Unlike the audience, Buck would note any deviation. "You go in the cage like that again, one of those cats is going to find out what you taste like."

"My timing was a little off, that's all." Jo fought against the trembling in her stomach and tried to sound casual.

"A little?" Buck glowered, looking formidable behind the mass of blond beard. "Who do you think you're fooling? I've been around these ugly cats since before you were born. When you go in the cage, you've got to take your brain in with you."

Only too aware that he was right, Jo conceded. "I know, Buck. You're right." With a weary hand she pushed back her hair. "It won't happen again. I guess I was tired and a little off-balance." She sent him an apologetic smile.

Buck frowned and shuffled. Never in his forty-five years had he managed to resist feminine smiles. "All right," he muttered, then sniffed and made his voice firm. "But you go take a nap right after the finale. No coffee. I don't want to see you around again until dinner time."

"Okay, Buck." Jo kept her voice humble, though she was tempted to grin. The weakness was going out of her legs, and the dull buzz of fear was fading from between her temples. Still she felt exhausted and agreeable to Buck's un-characteristic tone of command. A nap, she decided as Buck drove Merlin away, was just what she needed, not to mention that it was as good a way as any to avoid Keane Prescott for the rest of the day. Shooing this thought aside, Jo decided to while away the time until the finale in casual conversation with Vito the wire walker.

Chapter 4

It rained for three days. It was a solid downpour, not heavy but insistent. As the circus wound its way north, the rain followed. Nevertheless, canvas men pitched the tents in soggy fields and muddy lots while straw was laid on the hippodrome track and performers scurried from trailers to tents under dripping umbrellas.

The lot near Waycross, Georgia, was scattered with puddles under a thick, gray sky. Jo could only be grateful that no evening show had been scheduled. By six, it was nearly dark, with a chill teasing the damp air. She hustled from the cookhouse after an early supper. She would check on the cats, she decided, then closet herself in her trailer, draw the curtains against the rain and curl up with a book. Shivering, she concluded that the idea was inspired.

She carried no umbrella but sought questionable shelter under a gray rolled-brimmed hat and thin windbreaker. Keeping her head lowered, she jogged across the mud, skimming around or hopping over puddles. She hummed lightly, anticipating the simple pleasures of an idle evening. Her humming ended in a muffled gasp as she ran into a solid object. Fingers wrapped around her upper arms. Even before she lifted her head, Jo knew it was Keane who held her. She recognized his touch. Through some clever maneuvering, she had managed to avoid being alone with him since they had walked together and looked back on the circus.

"Excuse me, Mr. Prescott. I'm afraid I wasn't looking where I was going."

"Perhaps the weather's dampened your radar, Jovilette." He made no move to release her. Annoyed, Jo was forced to hold her hat steady with one hand as she tilted her head to meet his eyes. Rain fell cool on her face.

"I don't know what you mean."

"Oh, I think you do," Keane countered. "There's not another soul around. You've been careful to keep yourself in a crowd for days."

Jo blinked rain from her lashes. She admitted ruefully that it had been foolish to suppose he wouldn't notice her ploy. She saw he carried no umbrella either, nor did he bother with a hat. His hair was darkened with rain, much the same color that one of her cats would be if caught in an unexpected shower. It was difficult, in the murky light, to clearly make out his features, but the rain could not disguise his mockery.

"That's an interesting observation, Mr. Prescott," Jo said coolly. "Now, if you don't mind, I'm getting wet." She was surprised when she remained in his hold after a strong attempt on her part to pull away. Frowning, she put both hands against his chest and pushed. She discovered that she had been wrong; under the lean frame was an amazing amount of strength. Infuriated that she had misjudged him and that she was outmatched, Jo raised her eyes again. "Let me go," she demanded between clenched teeth.

"No," Keane returned mildly. "I don't believe I will."

Jo glared at him. "Mr. Prescott, I'm cold and wet and I'd like to go to my trailer. Now, what do you want?"

"First, I want you to stop calling me Mr. Prescott." Jo pouted but she kept silent. "Second, I'd like an hour of your time for going over a list of personnel." He paused. Through her windbreaker Jo could feel his fingers unyielding on her arms.

"Is there anything else?" she demanded, trying to sound bored.

For a moment there was only the sound of rain drumming on the ground and splashing into puddles. "Yes," Keane said quietly. "I think I'll just get this out of my system."

Jo's instincts were swift but they were standing too close for her to evade him. And he was quick. Her protest was muffled against his mouth. Her arms were pinioned to her sides as his locked around her. Jo had felt a man's body against her own before—working out with the tumblers, practicing with the equestrians—but never with such clarity as this. She was aware of Keane in every fiber of her being. His body was whipcord lean and hard, his arms holding the strength she had discounted the first time she had seen him. But more, it was his mouth that mystified her. Now it was not gentle or testing; it took and plundered and demanded more before she could withhold a response.

Jo forgot the rain, though it continued to fall against her face. She forgot the cold. The warmth spread from inside, where her blood flowed fast, as her body was molded to Keane's. She forgot herself, or the woman she had thought herself to be, and discovered another. When he lifted his mouth, Jo kept her eyes closed, savoring the lingering pleasures, inviting fresh ones.

"More?" he murmured as his hand trailed up, then down her spine. Heat raced after it. "Kissing can be a dangerous pastime, Jo." He lowered his mouth again, then nipped at her soft bottom lip. "But you know all about danger, don't you?" He kissed her hard, leaving her breathless. "How courageous are you without your cats?"

Suddenly her heart raced to her throat. Her legs became rubbery, and a tingle sprinted up her spine. Jo recognized the feeling. It was the way she felt when she experienced a close call with the cats. Reaction would set in after the door of the safety cage locked behind her and the crisis had passed. It was then that fear found her. She studied Keane's bold, amber eyes, and her mouth went dry. She shuddered.

"You're cold." His voice was abruptly brisk. "Small wonder. We'll go to my trailer and get you some coffee."

"No!" Jo's protest was sharp and instantaneous. She knew she was vulnerable and she knew as well that she did not yet possess the experience to fight him. To be alone with him now was too great a risk.

Keane drew her away, but his grip remained firm. She could not read his expression as he searched her face. "What happened just now was personal," he told her. "Strictly man to woman. I'm of the opinion that love making should be personal. You're an appealing armful, Jovilette, and I'm accustomed to taking what I want, one way or another."

His words were like a shot of adrenaline. Jo's chin thrust forward, and her eyes flamed. "No one *takes* me, one way or another." She spoke with the deadly calm of fury. "If I make love with anyone, it's only because I want to."

"Of course," Keane agreed with an easy nod. "We're both aware you'll be willing when the time comes. We could make love quite successfully tonight, but I think it best if we know each other better first."

Jo's mouth trembled open and closed twice before she could speak. "Of all the arrogant, outrageous…"

"Truthful," Keane supplied, tossing her into incoherency again. "But for now, we have business, and while I don't mind kissing in the rain, I prefer to conduct business in a drier climate." He held up a hand as Jo started to protest. "I told you, the kiss was between a man and a woman. The business we have now is between the owner of this circus and a performer under contract. Understood?"

Jo took a long, deep breath to bring her voice to a normal level. "Understood," she agreed. Without another word she let him lead her across the slippery lot.

When they reached Keane's trailer, he hustled Jo inside without preliminaries. She blinked against the change in light when he hit the wall switch. "Take off your coat," he said briskly, pulling down her zipper before she could perform the task for herself. Instinctively, her hand reached for it as she took a step backward. Keane merely lifted a brow, then stripped off his own jacket. "I'll get the coffee." He moved down the length of the narrow trailer and disappeared around the corner where the tiny kitchen was set.

Slowly, Jo pulled off her dripping hat, letting her hair tumble free from where it had been piled under its confinement. With automatic movements she hung both her hat and coat on the hooks by the trailer door. It had been almost six months since she had stood in Frank's trailer, and like a woman visiting an old friend, she searched for changes.

The same faded lampshade adorned the maple table lamp that Frank had used for reading. The shade sat straight now, however, not at its usual slightly askew angle. The pillow that Lillie from wardrobe had sewn for him on some long-ago Christmas still sat over the small burn hole in the seat cushion of the couch. Jo doubted that Keane knew of the hole's existence. Frank's pipe stand sat, as always, on the counter by the side window. Unable to resist, Jo crossed over to run her finger over the worn bowl of his favorite pipe.

"Never could pack it right," she murmured to his well-loved ghost. Abruptly, her senses quivered. She twisted her head to see Keane watching her. Jo dropped her hand. A rare blush mantled her cheeks as she found herself caught unguarded.

"How do you take your coffee, Jo?"

She swallowed. "Black," she told him, aware that he was granting her the privacy of her thoughts. "Just black. Thank you."

Keane nodded, then turned to pick up two steaming mugs. "Come, sit down." He moved toward the Formica table that sat directly across from the kitchen. "You'd better take off your shoes. They're wet."

After squeaking her way down the length of the trailer, Jo sat down and pulled at the damp laces. Keane set both mugs on the table before disappearing into the back of the trailer. When he returned, Jo was already sipping at the coffee.

"Here." He offered her a pair of socks.

Surprised, Jo shook her head. "No, that's all right. I don't need..."

Her polite refusal trailed off as he knelt at her feet. "Your feet are like ice," he commented after cupping them in his palms. Briskly, he rubbed them while Jo sat mute, oddly disarmed by the gesture. The warmth was spreading dangerously past her ankles. "Since I'm responsible for keeping you out in the rain," he went on as he slipped a sock over her foot, "I'd best see to it you don't cough and sneeze your way through tomorrow's show. Such small feet," he murmured, running his thumb over the curve of her ankle as she stared wordlessly at the top of his head.

Raindrops still clung to and glistened in his hair. Jo found herself longing to brush them away and feel the texture of his hair beneath her fingers. She was sharply aware of him and wondered if it would always be this way when she was near him. Keane pulled on the second sock. His fingers lingered on her calf as he lifted his eyes. Hers were darkened with confusion as they met his. The body over which she had always held supreme control was journeying into frontiers her mind had not yet explored.

"Still cold?" Keane asked softly.

Jo moistened her lips and shook her head. "No. No, I'm fine."

He smiled a lazy, masculine smile that said as clearly as words that he was aware of his effect on her. His eyes told her he enjoyed it. Unsmiling, Jo watched him rise to his feet.

"It doesn't mean you'll win," she said aloud in response to their silent communication.

"No, it doesn't." Keane's smile remained as his gaze roamed possessively over her face. "That only makes it more interesting. Open and shut cases are invariably boring, hardly worth the trouble of going on if you've won before you've finished your opening statement."

Jo lifted her coffee and sipped, taking a moment to settle her nerves. "Are we here to discuss the law or circus business, counselor?" she asked, letting her eyes drift to his again as she set the mug back on the table. "If it's law, I'm afraid I'm going to disappoint you. I don't know much about it."

"What do you know about, Jovilette?" Keane slid into the chair beside hers.

"Cats," she said. "And Prescott's Circus Colossus. I'll be glad to let you know whatever I can about either."

"Tell me about you," he countered, and leaning back, pulled a cigar from his pocket.

"Mr. Prescott—" Jo began.

"Keane," he interrupted, flicking on his lighter. He glanced at the tip of his cigar, then back up at her through the thin haze of smoke.

"I was under the impression you wanted to be briefed on the personnel."

"You are a member of this circus, are you not?" Casually, Keane blew smoke at the ceiling. "I have every intention of being briefed on the entire troupe and see no reason why you shouldn't start with yourself." His eyes traveled back to hers. "Humor me."

Jo decided to take the line of least resistance. "It's a short enough story," she said with a shrug. "I've been with the circus all my life. When I was old enough, I started work as a generally useful."

"A what?" Keane paused in the action of reaching for the coffeepot.

"Generally useful," Jo repeated, letting him freshen her cup. "It's a circus term that means exactly what it says. Rose's parents, for instance, are generally usefuls. We get a lot of drifters who work that way, too. It's also written into every performer's contract, after the specific terms, that they make themselves generally useful. There isn't room in most circuses, and certainly not in a tent circus, for performers with star complexes. You do what's necessary, what's needed. Buck, my handler, fills in during a slump at the sideshow, and he's one of the best canvas men around. Pete is the best mechanic in the troupe. Jamie knows as much about lighting as most shandies—electricians," she supplied as Keane lifted a brow. "He's also a better-than-average tumbler."

"What about you?" Keane interrupted the flow of Jo's words. For a moment she faltered, and the hands that had been gesturing became still. "Besides riding a galloping horse without reins or saddle, giving orders to elephants and facing lions?" He lifted his cup, watching her as he sipped. A smile lurked in his eyes. Jo frowned, studying him.

"Are you making fun of me?"

His smile sobered instantly. "No, Jo, I'm not making fun of you."

She continued. "In a pinch, I run the menagerie in the sideshow or I fill in the aerial act. Not the trap," she explained, relaxing again. "They have to practice together constantly to keep the timing. But sometimes I fill in on the Spanish Web, the big costume number where the girls hang from ropes and do identical moves. They're using butterfly costumes this year."

"Yes, I know the one." Keane continued to watch her as he drew on his cigar.

"But mostly Duffy likes to use girls who are more curvy. They double as showgirls in the finale."

"I see." A smile tugged at the corners of Keane's mouth. "Tell me, were your parents European?"

"No." Diverted, Jo shook her head. "Why do you ask?"

"Your name. And the ease with which I've heard you speak both French and Italian."

"It's easy to pick up languages in the circus," Jo said.

"Your accent was perfect in both cases."

"What? Oh." She shrugged and absently shifted in her chair, bringing her feet up to sit cross-legged. "We have a wide variety of nationalities here. Frank used to say that the world could take a lesson from the circus. We have French, Italian, Spanish, German, Russian, Mexican, Americans from all parts of the country and more."

"I know. It's like a traveling United Nations." He tipped his cigar ash in a glass tray. "So you picked up some French and Italian along the way. But if you've traveled with the circus all your life, what about the rest of your schooling?"

The hint of censure in his voice brought up her chin. "I went to school during the winter break and had a tutor on the road. I learned my ABC's, counselor, and a bit more, besides. I probably know more about geography and world history than you, and from more interesting sources than textbooks. I imagine I know more about animals than a third-year veterinary student and have more practical experience healing them. I can speak seven languages and—"

"Seven?" Keane interrupted. "Seven languages?"

"Well, five fluently," she corrected grudgingly. "I still have a bit of trouble with Greek and German, unless I can really take my time, and I can't read Greek yet at all."

"What else besides French, Italian and English?"

"Spanish and Russian." Jo scowled into her coffee. "The Russian's handy. I use it for swearing at the cats during the act. Not too many people understand Russian cursing, so it's safe."

Keane's laughter brought Jo's attention from her coffee. He was leaning back in his chair, his eyes gold with their mirth. Jo's scowl deepened. "What's so funny?"

"You are, Jovilette." Stung, she started to scramble up, but his hands on her shoulders stopped her. "No, don't be offended. I can't help but find it amusing that you toss out so offhandedly an accomplishment that any language major would brag about." Carelessly, he ran a finger over her sulky mouth. "You continually amaze me." He brushed a hand through her hair. "You mumbled something at me the other day. Were you swearing at me in Russian?"

"Probably."

Grinning, Keane dropped his hand and settled into his chair again. "When did you start working with the cats?"

"In front of an audience? When I was seventeen. Frank wouldn't let me start any earlier. He was my legal guardian as well as the owner, so he had me both ways. I was ready when I was fifteen."

"How did you lose your parents?"

The question caught her off guard. "In a fire," she said levelly. "When I was seven."

"Here?"

She knew Keane was not referring to their locale but to the circus. Jo sipped her cooling coffee. "Yes."

"Didn't you have any other family?"

"The circus is a family," she countered. "I was never given the chance to be an orphan. And I always had Frank."

"Did you?" Keane's smile was faintly sarcastic. "How was he as a father figure?"

Jo studied him for a moment. Was he bitter? she wondered. Or amused? Or simply curious? "He never took my father's place," she replied quietly. "He never tried to, because neither of us wanted it. We were friends, as close as I think it's possible for friends to be, but I'd already had a father, and he'd already had a child. We weren't looking for substitutes. You look nothing like him, you know."

"No," Keane replied with a shrug. "I know."

"He had a comfortable face, all creases and folds." Jo smiled, thinking of it while she ran a finger absently around the rim of her mug. "He was dark, too, just beginning to gray when..." She trailed off, then brought herself back with a quick shake of her head. "Your voice is rather like his, though; he had a truly beautiful voice. I'll ask you a question now."

Keane's expression became attentive, then he gestured with the back of his hand. "Go ahead."

"Why are you here? I lost my temper when I asked you before, but I do want to know." It was against her nature to probe, and some of her discomfort found its way into her voice. "It must have caused you some difficulty to leave your practice, even for a few weeks."

Keane frowned at the end of his cigar before he slowly crushed it out. "Let's say I wanted to see firsthand what had fascinated my father all these years."

"You never came when he was alive." Jo gripped her hands together under the table. "You didn't even bother to come to his funeral."

"I would've been the worst kind of hypocrite to attend his funeral, don't you think?"

"He was your father." Jo's eyes grew dark and her tone sharp in reproof.

"You're smarter than that, Jo," Keane countered calmly. "It takes more than an accident of birth to make a father. Frank Prescott was a complete stranger to me."

"You resent him." Jo felt suddenly torn between loyalty for Frank and understanding for the man who sat beside her.

"No." Keane shook his head thoughtfully. "No, I believe I actively resented him when I was growing up, but..." He shrugged the thought aside. "I grew rather ambivalent over the years."

"He was a good man," Jo stated, leaning forward as she willed him to understand. "He only wanted to give people pleasure, to show them a little magic. Maybe he wasn't made to be a father—some men aren't—but he was kind and gentle. And he was proud of you."

"Of me?" Keane seemed amused. "How?"

"Oh, you're hateful," Jo whispered, hurt by his careless attitude. She slipped from her chair, but before she could step away, Keane took her arm.

"No, tell me. I'm interested." His hold on her arm was light, but she knew it would tighten if she resisted.

"All right." Jo tossed her head to send her hair behind her back. "He had the Chicago paper delivered to his Florida office. He always looked for any mention of you, any article on a court case you were involved in or a dinner party you attended. Anything. You have to understand that to us a write-up is very important. Frank wasn't a performer, but he was one of us. Sometimes he'd read me an article before he put it away. He kept a scrapbook."

Jo pulled her arm away and strode past Keane into the bedroom. The oversize wooden chest was where it had always been, at the foot of Frank's bed. Kneeling down, Jo tossed up the lid. "This is where he kept all the things that mattered to him." Jo began to shift through papers and mementos quickly; she had not been able to bring herself to sort through the chest before. Keane stood in the doorway and watched her. "He called it his memory box." She pushed at her hair with an annoyed hand, then continued to search. "He said memories were the rewards for growing old. Here it is." Jo pulled out a dark green scrapbook, then sat back on her heels. Silently, she held it out to Keane. After a moment he crossed the room and took it from her. Jo could hear the rain hissing on the ground outside as their eyes held. His expression was unfathomable as he opened the book. The pages rustled to join the quiet sound of the rain.

"What an odd man he must have been," Keane murmured, "to keep a scrapbook on a son he never knew." There was no rancor in his voice. "What was he?" he asked suddenly, shifting his eyes back to Jo.

"A dreamer," she answered. "His watch was always five minutes slow. If he hung a picture on the wall, it was always crooked. He'd never straighten it because he'd never notice. He was always thinking about tomorrow. I guess that's why he kept yesterday in this box." Glancing down, she began to straighten the chaos she had caused while looking for the book. A snatch of red caught her eye. Reaching for it, her fingers found a familiar shape. Jo hesitated, then drew the old doll out of the chest.

It was a sad piece of plastic and faded silk with its face nearly washed away. One arm was broken off, leaving an empty sleeve. The golden hair was straggled but brave under its red cap. Ballet shoes were painted on the dainty feet. Tears backed up behind Jo's eyes as she made a soft sound of joy and despair.

"What is it?" Keane demanded, glancing down to see her clutching the battered ballerina.

"Nothing." Her voice was unsteady as she scrambled quickly to her feet. "I have to go." Though she tried, Jo could not bring herself to drop the doll back into the box. She swallowed. She did not wish to reveal her emotions before his intelligent, gold eyes. Perhaps he would be cynical, or worse, amused. "May I have this, please?" She was careful with the tone of the request.

Slowly, Keane crossed the distance between them, then cradled her chin in his hand. "It appears to be yours already."

"It was." Her fingers tightened on the doll's waist. "I didn't know Frank had kept it. Please," she whispered. Her emotions were already dangerously heightened. She could feel a need to rest her head against his shoulder. The evening had been a roller coaster for her feelings, climaxing now with the discovery of her most prized childhood possession. She knew that if she did not escape, she would seek comfort in his arms. Her own weakness frightened her. "Let me by."

For a moment, Jo read refusal in his eyes. Then he stepped aside. Jo let out a quiet, shaky breath. "I'll walk you back to your trailer."

"No," she said quickly, too quickly. "It isn't necessary," she amended, moving by him and into the kitchen. Sitting down, she pulled on her shoes, too distraught to remember she still wore his socks. "There's no reason for us both to get wet again." She rambled on, knowing he was watching her hurried movement, but unable to stop. "And I'm going to check on my cats before I go in, and…"

She stopped short when he took her shoulders and pulled her to her feet. "And you don't want to take the chance of being alone in your trailer with me in case I change my mind."

A sharp denial trembled on her lips, but the knowledge in his eyes crushed it. "All right," she admitted. "That, too."

Keane brushed her hair from her neck and shook his head. He kissed her nose and moved down to pluck her hat and coat from their hooks. Cautiously, Jo followed him. When he held out her coat, she turned and slipped her arms into the sleeves. Before she could murmur her thanks, he turned her back and pulled up the zipper. For a moment his fingers lingered at her neck, his eyes on hers. Taking her hair into his hand, he piled it atop her head, then dropped on her hat. The gestures were innocent, but Jo was rocked by a feeling of intimacy she had never experienced.

"I'll see you tomorrow," he said, pulling the brim of her hat down further over her eyes.

Jo nodded. Holding the doll against her side, she pushed open the door. The sound of rain was amplified through the trailer. "Good night," she murmured, then moved quickly into the night.

Chapter 5

The morning scent was clean. In the new lot rainbows glistened in puddles. At last the sky was blue with only harmless white puffs of clouds floating over its surface. In the cookhouse a loud, crowded breakfast was being served. Finding herself without appetite, Jo skipped going to the cookhouse altogether. She was restless and tense. No matter how she disciplined her mind, her thoughts wandered back to Keane Prescott and to the evening they had spent together. Jo remembered it all, from the quick passion of the kiss in the rain to the calmness of his voice when he had said good-night. It was odd, she mused, that whenever she began to talk to him, she forgot he was the owner, forgot he was Frank's son. Always she was forced to remind herself of their positions.

Deep in thought, Jo slipped into tights and a leotard. It was true, she admitted, that she had failed to keep their relationship from becoming personal. She found it difficult to corral her urge to laugh with him, to share a joke, to open for him the doorway to the magic of the circus. If he could feel it, she thought, he would understand. Though she could admit her interest in him privately, she could not find a clear reason for his apparent interest in her.

Why me? she wondered with a shake of her head. Turning, she opened her wardrobe closet and studied herself in the full-length glass on the back of the door. There she saw a woman of slightly less-than-average height with a body lacking the generous curves of Duffy's showgirls. The legs, she decided, were not bad. They were long and well-shaped with slim thighs. The hips were narrow, more, she thought with a pout, like a boy's than a woman's; and the bustline was sadly inadequate. She knew many women in the troupe with more appeal and a dozen with more experience.

Jo could see nothing in the mirror that would attract a sophisticated Chicago attorney. She did not note the honesty that shone from the exotically shaped green eyes or the strength in her chin or the full promise of her mouth. She saw the touch of gypsy in the tawny complexion and raven hair but remained unaware of the appeal that came from the hint of something wild and untamed just under the surface. The plain black leotard showed her firm, lithe body to perfection, but Jo thought nothing of the smooth satiny sheen of her skin. She was frowning as she pulled her hair back and began to braid it.

He must know dozens of women, she thought as her hands worked to confine her thick mane of hair. He probably takes a different one to dinner every night. They wear beautiful clothes and expensive perfume, she mused, torturing herself with the thought. They have names like Laura and Patricia, and they have low, sophisticated laughs. Jo lifted a brow at the reflection in the mirror and gave a light, low laugh. She wrinkled her brow at the hollowness of the sound. They discuss mutual friends, the Wallaces or the Jamesons, over candlelight and Beaujolais. And when he takes the most beautiful one home, they listen to Chopin and drink brandy in front of the fire. Then they make love. Jo felt an odd tightening in her stomach but pursued the fantasy to the finish. The lovely lady is experienced, passionate and worldly. Her skin is soft and white. When he leaves, she is not devastated but mature. She doesn't even care if he loves her or not.

Jo stared at the woman in the glass and saw her cheeks were wet. On a cry of frustration, she slammed the door shut. *What's wrong with me?* she demanded, brushing all traces of tears from her face. I haven't been myself for days! I need to shake myself out of this—this…whatever it is that I'm in. Slipping on gymnastic shoes and tossing a robe over her arm, Jo hustled from the trailer.

She moved carefully, avoiding puddles and any further speculation on Keane Prescott's romantic life. Before she was halfway across the lot, she saw Rose. From the expression on her face, Jo could see she was in a temper.

"Hello, Rose," she said, strategically stepping aside as the snake charmer splashed through a puddle.

"He's hopeless," Rose tossed back. "I tell you," she continued, stopping and wagging a finger at Jo, "I'm through this time. Why should I waste my time?"

"You've certainly been patient," Jo agreed, deciding that sympathy was the wisest course. "It's more than he deserves."

"Patient?" Rose raised a dramatic hand to her breast. "I have the patience of a saint. Yet even a saint has her limits!" Rose tossed her hair behind her shoulders. She sighed heavily. "*Adios.* I think I hear Mama calling me."

Jo continued her walk toward the Big Top. Jamie walked by, his hands in his pockets. "She's crazy," he muttered. He stopped and spread his arms wide. His look was that of a man ill-used and innocent. Jo shrugged. Shaking his head, Jamie moved away. "She's crazy," he said again.

Jo watched him until he was out of sight, then darted to the Big Top.

Inside, Carmen watched adoringly while Vito practiced a new routine on the incline wire. The tent echoed with the sounds of rehearsals: voices and thumps, the rattle of rigging, the yapping of clown dogs. In the first ring Jo spotted the Six Beirots, an acrobatic act that was just beginning its warm-ups. Pleased with her timing, Jo walked the length of the arena. A raucous whistle sounded over her head, and she glanced up to shake a friendly fist at Vito. He called from fifteen feet above her as he balanced on a slender wire set at a forty-five-degree angle.

"Hey, chickie, you have a nice rear view. You're almost as cute as me."

"No one's as cute as you, Vito," she called back.

"Ah, I know." With a weighty sigh, he executed a neat pivot. "But I have learned to live with it." He sent down a lewd wink. "When you going into town with me, chickie?" he asked as he always did.

"When you teach my cats to walk the wire," Jo answered as she always did. Vito laughed and began a light-footed cha-cha. Carmen fired Jo a glare. She must have it bad, Jo decided, if she takes Vito's harmless flirting seriously. Stopping beside her, Jo leaned close and spoke in a conspirator's whisper. "He'd fall off his wire if I said I'd go."

"I'd go," Carmen said with a lovely pout, "if he'd just ask me."

Jo shook her head, wondering why romances were invariably complicated. She was lucky not to have the problem. Giving Carmen an encouraging pat on the shoulder, Jo set off toward the first ring.

The Six Beirots were brothers. They were all small-statured, dark men who had immigrated from Belgium. Jo worked out with them often to keep herself limber and to keep her reflexes sharp. She liked them all, knew their wives and children, and understood their unique blending of French and English. Raoul was the oldest, and the stockiest of the six brothers. Because of his build and strength, he was the under-stander in their human pyramid. It was he who spotted Jo and first lifted a hand in greeting.

"Halo." He grinned and ran his palm over his receding hairline. "You gonna tumble?"

Jo laughed and did a quick handspring into the ring. She stuck out her tongue when the unanimous critique was "sloppy." "I just need to warm up," she said, assuming an air of injured dignity. "My muscles need tuning."

For the next thirty minutes Jo worked with them, doing muscle stretches and limbering exercises, rib stretches and lung expanders. Her muscles warmed and loosened, her heart pumped steadily. She was filled with energy. Her mind was clear. Because of her lightened mood, Jo was easily cajoled into a few impromptu acrobatics. Leaving the more complicated feats to the experts, she did simple back flips, handsprings or twists at Raoul's command. She did a brief, semi-successful thirty seconds atop the rolling globe and earned catcalls from her comrades at her dismount.

She stood back as they began the leaps. One after another they lined up to take turns running along a ramp, bounding upon a springboard and flying up to do flips or twists before landing on the mat. There was a constant stream of French as they called out to each other.

"Hokay, Jo." Raoul gestured with his hand. "Your turn."

"Oh, no." She shook her head and reached for her robe. "Uh-uh." There was a chorus of coaxing, teasing French. "I've got to give my cats their vitamins," she told them, still shaking her head.

"Come on, Jo. It's fun." Raoul grinned and wiggled his eyebrows. "Don't you like to fly?" As she glanced at the ramp, Raoul knew she was tempted. "You take a good spring," he told her."Do one forward somersault, then land on my shoulders." He patted them to show their ability to handle the job.

Jo smiled and nibbled pensively on her lower lip. It had been a long while since she had taken the time to go up on the trapeze and really fly. It did look like fun. She gave Raoul a stern look. "You'll catch me?"

"Raoul never misses," he said proudly, then turned to his brothers. *"Ne c'est pas?"* His brothers shrugged and rolled their eyes to the ceiling with indistinguishable mutters. "Ah." He waved them away with the back of his hand.

Knowing Raoul was indeed a top flight under-stander, Jo approached the ramp. Still she gave him one last narrow-eyed look. "You catch me," she ordered, shaking her finger at him.

"Cherie." He took his position with a stylish movement of his hand. "It's a piece of pie."

"Cake," Jo corrected, took a deep breath, held it and ran. When she came off the springboard, she tucked into the so-mersault and watched the Big Top turn upside down. She felt good. As the tent began to right itself, she straightened for her landing, keeping herself loose. Her feet connected with Raoul's powerful shoulders, and she tilted only briefly before he took her ankles in a firm grip. Straightening her poor posture, Jo styled elaborately with both arms while she received exaggerated applause and whistles. She leaped down nimbly as Raoul took her waist to give her landing bounce.

"When do you want to join the act?" he asked her, giving her a friendly pat on the bottom. "We'll put you up on the sway pole."

"That's okay." Grinning, Jo again reached for her robe. "I'll stick with the cats." After a cheerful wave, she slipped one arm into a sleeve and started back down the hippodrome track. She pulled up short when she spotted Keane leaning up against the front seat rail.

"Amazing," he said, then straightened to move to her. "But then, the circus is supposed to be amazing, isn't it?" He lifted the forgotten sleeve to her robe, then slipped her other arm into it. "Is there anything here you can't do?"

"Hundreds of things," Jo answered, taking him seriously. "I'm only really proficient with animals. The rest is just show and play."

"You looked amazingly proficient to me for the last half hour or so," he countered as he pulled out her braid from where it was trapped by her robe.

"Have you been here that long?"

"I walked in as Vito was commenting on your rear view."

"Oh." Jo laughed, glancing back to where Vito now stood flirting with Carmen. "He's crazy."

"Perhaps," Keane agreed, taking her arm. "But his eyesight's good enough. Would you like some coffee?"

Jo was reminded instantly of the evening before. Leery of being drawn to his charms again, she shook her head. "I've got to change," she told him, belting her robe. "We've got a show at two. I want to rehearse the cats."

"It's incredible how much time you people devote to your art. Rehearsals seem to run into the beginning of a show, and a show seems to run into more rehearsals."

Jo softened when he referred to circus skills as art. "Performers always look for just a bit more in themselves. It's a constant struggle for perfection. Even when a performance goes beautifully and you know it, you start thinking about the next time. How can I do it better or bigger or higher or faster?"

"Never satisfied?" Keane asked as they stepped out into the sunlight.

"If we were, we wouldn't have much of a reason to come back and do it all over again."

He nodded, but there was something absent in the gesture, as if his mind was elsewhere. "I have to leave this afternoon," he said almost to himself.

"Leave?" Jo's heart skidded to a stop. Her distress was overwhelming and so unexpected that she was forced to take an extra moment to steady herself. "Back to Chicago?"

"Hmm?" Keane stopped, turning to face her. "Oh, yes."

"And the circus?" Jo asked, thoroughly ashamed that it had not been her first concern. She didn't want him to leave, she suddenly realized.

Keane frowned a moment, then continued to walk. "I see no purpose in disrupting this year's schedule." His voice was brisk now and businesslike.

"This year's?" Jo repeated cautiously.

Keane turned and looked at her. "I haven't decided its ultimate fate, but I won't do anything until the end of the summer."

"I see." She let out a long breath. "So we have a reprieve."

"In a manner of speaking," Keane agreed.

Jo was silent for a moment but could not prevent herself from asking, "Then you won't—I mean, you'll be staying in Chicago now; you won't be traveling with us?"

They negotiated their way around a puddle before Keane

answered. "I don't feel I can make a judicious decision about the circus after so brief an exposure. There's a complication in one of my cases that needs my personal attention, but I should be back in a week or two."

Relief flooded through her. He would be back, a voice shouted in her ear. It shouldn't matter to you, another whispered. "We'll be in South Carolina in a couple of weeks," Jo said casually. They had reached her trailer, and she took the handle of her door before she turned to face him. *It's just that I want him to understand what this circus means,* she told herself as she looked up into his eyes. *That's the only reason I want him to come back.* Knowing she was lying to herself made it difficult to keep her gaze steady.

Keane smiled, letting his eyes travel over her face. "Yes, Duffy's given me a route list. I'll find you. Aren't you going to ask me in?"

"In?" Jo repeated. "Oh, no, I told you, I have to change, and…" He stepped forward as she talked. Something in his eyes told her a firm stand was necessary. She had seen a similar look in a lion's eyes while he contemplated taking a dangerous liberty. "I simply don't have time right now. If I don't see you before you go, have a good trip." She turned and opened the door. Aware of a movement, she turned back, but not before he had nudged her through the door and followed. As it closed at his back, Jo bristled with fury. She did not enjoy being outmaneuvered. "Tell me, counselor, do you know anything about a law concerning breaking and entering?"

"Doesn't apply," he returned smoothly. "There was no lock involved." He glanced around at the attractive simplicity of Jo's trailer. The colors were restful earth tones without frills. The beige- and brown-flecked linoleum floor was spotlessly clean. It was the same basic floorplan as

Frank's trailer, but here there were softer touches. There were curtains rather than shades at the windows; large, comfortable pillows tossed onto a forest green sofa; a spray of fresh wildflowers tucked into a thin, glass vase. Without comment Keane wandered to a black lacquer trunk that sat directly opposite the door. On it was a book that he picked up while Jo fumed. *"The Count of Monte Cristo,"* he read aloud and flipped it open. "In French," he stated, lifting a brow.

"It was written in French," Jo muttered, pulling it from his hand. "So I read it in French." Annoyed, she lifted the lid on the trunk, preparing to drop the book inside and out of his reach.

"Good heavens, are those all yours?" Keane stopped the lid on its downswing, then pushed books around with his other hand. "Tolstoy, Cervantes, Voltaire, Steinbeck. When do you have time in this crazy, twenty-four-hour world you live in to read this stuff?"

"I make time," Jo snapped as her eyes sparked. "My *own* time. Just because you're the owner doesn't mean you can barge in here and poke through my things and demand an account of my time. This is my trailer. I own everything in it."

"Hold on." Keane halted her rushing stream of words. "I wasn't demanding an account of your time, I was simply astonished that you could find enough of it to do this type of reading. Since I can't claim to be an expert on your work, it would be remarkably foolish of me to criticize the amount of time you spend on it. Secondly," he said, taking a step toward her—and though Jo stiffened in anticipation, he did not touch her—"I apologize for 'poking through your things,' as you put it. I was interested for several reasons. One being I have quite an extensive library myself. It seems we have a common interest, whether we like it or not. As for barging into your trailer, I can only plead guilty. If you choose to prosecute, I can recommend a couple of lousy attorneys who overcharge."

His last comment forced a smile onto Jo's reluctant lips. "I'll give it some thought." With more care than she had originally intended, Jo lowered the lid of the trunk. She was reminded that she had not been gracious. "I'm sorry," she said as she turned back to him.

His eyes reflected curiosity. "What for?"

"For snapping at you." She lifted her shoulders, then let them fall. "I thought you were criticizing me. I suppose I'm too sensitive."

Several seconds passed before he spoke. "Unnecessary apology accepted if you answer one question."

Mystified, Jo frowned at him. "What question?"

"Is the Tolstoy in Russian?"

Jo laughed, pushing loose strands of hair from her face. "Yes, it is."

Keane smiled, enjoying the two tiny dimples that flickered in her cheeks when she laughed. "Did you know that though you're lovely in any case, you grow even more so when you smile?"

Jo's laughter stilled. She was unaccustomed to this sort of compliment and studied him without any idea of how to respond. It occurred to her that any of the sophisticated women she had imagined that morning would have known precisely what to say. She would have been able to smile or laugh as she tossed back the appropriate comment. That woman, Jo admitted, was not Jovilette Wilder. Gravely, she kept her eyes on his. "I don't know how to flirt," she said simply.

Keane tilted his head, and an expression came and went in his eyes before she could analyze it. He stepped toward her. "I wasn't flirting with you, Jo, I was making an observation. Hasn't anyone ever told you that you're beautiful?"

He was much too close now, but in the narrow confines of the trailer, Jo had little room to maneuver. She was forced to tilt back her head to keep her eyes level with his. "Not precisely the way you did." Quickly, she put her hand to his chest to keep the slight but important distance between them. She knew she was trapped, but that did not mean she was defeated.

Gently, Keane lifted her protesting hand, turning it palm up as he brought it to his lips. An involuntary breath rushed in and out of Jo's lungs. "Your hands are exquisite," he murmured, tracing the fine line of blue up the back. "Narrow-boned, long-fingered. And the palms show hard work. That makes them more interesting." He lifted his eyes from her hand to her face. "Like you."

Jo's voice had grown husky, but she could do nothing to alter it. "I don't know what I'm supposed to say when you tell me things like that." Beneath her robe her breasts rose and fell with her quickening heart. "I'd rather you didn't."

"Do you really?" Keane ran the back of his hand along her jaw line. "That's a pity, because the more I look at you, the more I find to say. You're a bewitching creature, Jovilette."

"I have to change," she said in the firmest voice she could muster. "You'll have to go."

"That's unfortunately true," he murmured, then cupped her chin. "Come, then, kiss me goodbye."

Jo stiffened. "I hardly think that's necessary…."

"You couldn't be more wrong," he told her as he lowered his mouth. "It's extremely necessary." In a light, teasing whisper, his lips met hers. His arms encircled her, bringing her closer with only the slightest pressure. "Kiss me back, Jo," he ordered softly. "Put your arms around me and kiss me back."

For a moment longer she resisted, but the lure of his mouth nibbling at hers was too strong. Letting instinct rule her will, Jo lifted her arms and circled his neck. Her mouth grew mobile under his, parting and offering. Her surrender seemed to lick the flames of his passion. The kiss grew urgent. His arms locked, crushing her against him. Her quiet moan was not of protest but of wonder. Her fingers found their way into his hair, tangling in its thickness as they urged him closer. She felt her robe loosen, then his hands trail up her rib cage. At his touch, she shivered, feeling her skin grow hot, then cold, then hot again in rapid succession.

When his hand took her breast, she shied, drawing in her breath quickly. "Steady," he murmured against her mouth. His hands stroked gently, coaxing her to relax again. He kissed the corners of her mouth, waiting until she quieted before he took her deep again. The thin leotard molded her body. It created no barrier against the warmth of his searching fingers. They moved slowly, lingering over the peak of her breast, exploring its softness, wandering to her waist, then tracing her hip and thigh.

No man had ever touched her so freely. Jo was helpless to stop him, helpless against her own growing need for him to touch her again. Was this the passion she had read of so often? The passion that drove men to war, to struggle against all reason, to risk everything? She felt she could understand it now. She clung to him as he taught her—as she learned— the demands of her own body. Her mouth grew hungrier for the taste of him. She was certain she remained in his arms while seasons flew by, while decades passed, while worlds were destroyed and built again.

But when he drew away, Jo saw the same sun spilling through her windows. Eternity had only been moments.

Unable to speak, she merely stared up at him. Her eyes

were dark and aware, her cheeks flushed with desire. But somehow, though it still tingled from his, her mouth maintained a youthful innocence. Keane's eyes dropped to it as his hands loitered at the small of her back.

"It's difficult to believe I'm the first man to touch you," he murmured. His eyes roamed to hers. "And quite desperately arousing. Particularly when I find you've passion to match your looks. I think I'd like to make love with you in the daylight first so that I can watch that marvelous control of yours slip away layer by layer. We'll have to discuss it when I get back."

Jo forced strength back into her limbs, knowing she was on the brink of losing her will to him. "Just because I let you kiss me and touch me doesn't mean I'll let you make love to me." She lifted her chin, feeling her confidence surging back. "If I do, it'll be because it's what I want, not because you tell me to."

The expression in Keane's eyes altered. "Fair enough," he agreed and nodded. "It'll simply be my job to make it what you want." He took her chin in his hand and lowered his mouth to hers for a brief kiss. As she had the first time, Jo kept her eyes open and watched him. She felt him grin against her mouth before he raised his head. "You are the most fascinating woman I've ever met." Turning, he crossed to the door. "I'll be back," he said with a careless wave before it closed behind him. Dumbly, Jo stared into empty space.

Fascinating? she repeated, tracing her still warm lips with her fingertips. Quickly, she ran to the window, and kneeling on the sofa below it, watched Keane stride away.

She realized with a sudden jolt that she missed him already.

Chapter 6

Jo learned that weeks could drag like years. During the second week of Keane's absence she had searched each new lot for a sign of him. She had scanned the crowds of towners who came to watch the raising of the Big Top, and as the days stretched on and on, she balanced between anger and despair at his continued absence. Only in the cage did she manage to isolate her concentration, knowing she could not afford to do otherwise. But after each performance Jo found it more and more difficult to relax. Each morning she felt certain he would be back. Each night she lay restless, waiting for the sun to rise.

Spring was in full bloom. The high grass lots smelled of it. Often there were wildflowers crushed underfoot, leaving their heavy fragrances in the air. Even as the circus caravan traveled north, the days grew warm, sunlight lingering further into evening. While other troupers enjoyed the balmy air and providentially sunny skies, Jo lived on nerves.

It occurred to her that after returning to his life in Chicago, Keane had decided against coming back. In Chicago he had comfort and wealth and elegant women. Why should he come back? Jo closed her mind against the ultimate fate of the circus, unwilling to face the possibility that Keane might close the show at the end of the season. She told herself the only reason she wanted him to come back was to convince him to keep the circus open. But the memory of being in his arms intruded too often into her thoughts. Gradually, she grew resigned, filling the strange void she felt with her work.

Several times each week she found time to give the eager Gerry more training. At first she had only permitted him to work with the two menagerie cubs, allowing him, with the protection of leather gloves, to play with them and to feed them. She encouraged him to teach them simple tricks with the aid of small pieces of raw meat. Jo was as pleased as he when the cats responded to his patience and obeyed.

Jo saw potential in Gerry, in his genuine affection for animals and in his determination. Her primary concern was that he had not yet developed a healthy fear. He was still too casual, and with casualness, Jo knew, came carelessness. When she thought he had progressed far enough, Jo decided to take him to the next step of his training.

There was no matinee that day, and the Big Top was scattered with rehearsing troupers. Jo was dressed in boots and khakis with a long-sleeved blouse tucked into the waist. She studied Gerry as she ran the stock of her whip through her hand. They stood together in the safety cage while she issued instructions.

"All right, Buck's going to let Merlin through the chute. He's the most tractable of the cats, except for Ari." She paused a moment while her eyes grew sad. "Ari isn't up to even a short practice session." She pushed away the depression that threatened and continued. "Merlin knows you, he's familiar with your voice and your scent." Gerry nodded and swallowed. "When we go in, you're to be my shadow. You move when I move, and don't speak until I tell you. If you get frightened, don't run." Jo took his arm for emphasis. "That's *important,* understand? Don't run. Tell me if you want out, and I'll get you to the safety cage."

"I won't run, Jo," he promised and wiped hands, damp with excitement, on his jeans.

"Are you ready?"

Gerry grinned and nodded. "Yeah."

Jo opened the door leading to the big cage and let Gerry through behind her before securing it. She walked to the center of the arena in easy, confident strides. "Let him in, Buck," she called and heard the immediate rattle of bars. Merlin entered without hurry, then leaped onto his pedestal. He yawned hugely before looking at Jo. "A solo today, Merlin," she said as she advanced toward him. "And you're the star. Stay with me," she ordered as Gerry merely stood still and stared at the big cat. Merlin gave Gerry a disinterested glance and waited.

With an upward move of her arm, she sent Merlin into a sit-up. "You know," she told the boy behind her, "that teaching a cat to take his seat is the first trick. The audience won't even consider it one. The sit-up," she continued while signaling Merlin to bring his front paws back down, "is usually next and takes quite a bit of time. It's necessary to strengthen the cat's back muscles first." Again she signaled Merlin to sit up, then, with a quick command, she had him pawing the air and roaring. "Marvelous old ham," she said with a grin and brought him back down. "The primary move of each cue is always given from the same position with the same tone of voice. It takes patience and repetition. I'm going to bring him down off the pedestal now."

Jo flicked the whip against the tanbark, and Merlin leaped down. "Now I maneuver him to the spot in the arena where I want him to lie down." As she moved, Jo made certain her student moved with her. "The cage is a circle, forty feet in diameter. You have to know every inch of it inside your head. You have to know precisely how far you are from the bars at all times. If you back up into the bars, you've got no room to maneuver if there's trouble. It's one of the biggest mistakes a trainer can make." At her signal Merlin laid down, then shifted to his side. "Over, Merlin," she said briskly, sending him into a series of rolls. "Use their names often; it keeps them in tune with you. You have to know each cat and their individual tendencies."

Jo moved with Merlin, then signaled him to stop. When he roared, she rubbed the top of his head with the stock of her whip. "They like to be petted just like house cats, but they are not tabbies. It's essential that you never give them your complete trust and that you remember always to maintain your dominance. You subjugate not by poking them or beating or shouting, which is not only cruel but makes for a mean, undependable cat, but with patience, respect and will. Never humiliate them; they have a right to their pride. You bluff them, Gerry," she said as she raised both arms and brought Merlin up on his hind legs. "Man is the unknown factor. That's why we use jungle-bred rather than captivity-bred cats. Ari is the exception. A cat born and raised in captivity is too familiar with man, so you lose your edge." She moved forward, keeping her arms raised. Merlin followed, walking on his hind legs. He spread seven feet into the air and towered over his trainer. "They might have a sense of affection for you, but there's no fear and little respect. Unfortunately, this often happens if a cat's been with a trainer a long time. They don't become more docile the longer they're in an act, but they become more dangerous. They test you constantly. The trick is to make them believe you're indestructible."

She brought Merlin down, and he gave another yawn before she sent him back to his seat. "If one swipes at you, you have to stop it then and there, because they try again and again, getting closer each time. Usually, if a trainer's hurt in the cage, it's because he's made a mistake. The cats are quick to spot them; sometimes they let them pass, sometimes they don't. This one's given me a good smack on the shoulder now and again. He's kept his claws retracted, but there's always the possibility that one time he'll forget he's just playing. Any questions?"

"Hundreds," Gerry answered, wiping his mouth with the back of his hand. "I just can't focus on one right now."

Jo chuckled and again scratched Merlin's head when he roared. "They'll come to you later. It's hard to absorb anything the first time, but it'll come back to you when you're relaxed again. All right, you know the cue. Make him sit up."

"Me?"

Jo stepped to the side, giving Merlin a clear view of her student. "You can be as scared as you like," she said easily. "Just don't let it show in your voice. Watch his eyes."

Gerry rubbed his palm on the thighs of his jeans, then lifted it as he had seen Jo do hundreds of times. "Up," he told the cat in a passably firm voice.

Merlin studied him a moment, then looked at Jo. This, his eyes told her clearly, was an amateur and beneath his notice. Carefully, Jo kept her face expressionless. "He's testing you," she told Gerry. "He's an old hand and a bit harder to bluff. Be firm and use his name this time."

Gerry took a deep breath and repeated the hand signal. "Up, Merlin."

Merlin glanced back at him, then stared with measuring, amber eyes. "Again," Jo instructed and heard Gerry swallow audibly. "Put some authority into your voice. He thinks you're a pushover."

"Up, Merlin!" Gerry repeated, annoyed enough by Jo's description to put some dominance into his voice. Though his reluctance was obvious, Merlin obeyed. "He did it," Gerry whispered on a long, shaky breath. "He really did it."

"Very good," Jo said, pleased with both the lion and her student. "Now bring him down." When this was accomplished, Jo had him bring Merlin from the seat. "Here." She handed Gerry the whip. "Use the stock to scratch his head. He likes it best just behind the ear." She felt the faint tremble in his hand as he took the whip, but he held it steady, even as Merlin closed his eyes and roared.

Because he had performed well, Jo afforded Merlin the liberty of rubbing against her legs before she called for Buck to let him out. The rattle of the bars was the cat's cue to exit, and like a trouper, he took it with his head held high. "You did very well," she told Gerry when they were alone in the cage.

"It was great." He handed her back the whip, the stock damp from his sweaty palms. "It was just great. When can I do it again?"

Jo smiled and patted his shoulder. "Soon," she promised. "Just remember the things I've told you and come to me when you remember all those questions."

"Okay, thanks, Jo." He stepped through the safety cage. "Thanks a lot. I want to go tell the guys."

"Go ahead." Jo watched him scramble away, leaping over the ring and darting through the back door. With a grin, she leaned against the bars. "Was I like that?" she asked Buck, who stood at the opposite end of the cage.

"The first time you got a cat to sit up on your own, we heard about it for a week. Twelve years old and you thought you were ready for the big show."

Jo laughed, and wiping the damp stock of her whip against her pants, turned. It was then she saw him standing behind her. "Keane!" she used the name she had sworn not to use as pleasure flooded through her. It shone on her face. Just as she had given up hope of seeing him again, he was there. She took two steps toward him before she could check herself. "I didn't know you were back." Jo gripped the stock of the whip with both hands to prevent herself from reaching out to touch him.

"I believe you missed me." His voice was as she remembered, low and smooth.

Jo cursed herself for being so naïve and transparent. "Perhaps I did, a little," she admitted cautiously. "I suppose I'd gotten used to you, and you were gone longer than you said you'd be." He looks the same, she thought rapidly, exactly the same. She reminded herself that it had only been a month. It had seemed like years.

"*Mmm,* yes. I had more to see to than I had expected. You look a bit pale," he observed and touched her cheek with his fingertip.

"I suppose I haven't been getting much sun," she said with quick prevarication. "How was Chicago?" Jo needed to turn the conversation away from personal lines until she had an opportunity to gauge her emotions; seeing him suddenly had tossed them into confusion.

"Cool," he told her, making a long, thorough survey of her face. "Have you ever been there?"

"No. We play near there toward the end of the season, but I've never had time to go all the way into the city."

Nodding absently, Keane glanced into the empty cage behind her. "I see you're training Gerry."

"Yes." Relieved that they had lapsed into a professional discussion, Jo let the muscles of her shoulders ease. "This was the first time with an adult cat and no bars between. He did very well."

Keane looked back at her. His eyes were serious and probing. "He was trembling. I could see it from where I stood watching you."

"It was his first time—" she began in Gerry's defense.

"I wasn't criticizing him," Keane interrupted with a tinge of impatience. "It's just that he stood beside you, shaking from head to foot, and you were totally cool and in complete control."

"It's my job to be in control," Jo reminded him.

"That lion must have stood seven feet tall when he went up on his hind legs, and you walked under him without any protection, not even the traditional chair."

"I do a picture act," she explained, "not a fighting act."

"Jo," he said so sharply she blinked. "Aren't you ever frightened in there?"

"Frightened?" she repeated, lifting a brow. "Of course I'm frightened. More frightened than Gerry was—or than you would be."

"What are you talking about?" Keane demanded. Jo noted with some curiosity that he was angry. "I could see that boy sweat in there."

"That was mostly excitement," Jo told him patiently. "He hasn't the experience to be truly frightened yet." She tossed back her hair and let out a long breath. Jo did not like to talk of her fears with anyone and found it especially difficult with Keane. Only because she felt it necessary that he understand this to understand the circus did she continue. "Real fear comes from knowing them, working with them, understanding them. You can only speculate on what they can do to a man. I *know.* I know exactly what they're capable of. They have an incredible courage, but more, they have an incredible guile. I've seen what they can do." Her eyes were calm and clear as they looked into his. "My father almost lost a leg once. I was about five, but I remember it perfectly. He made a mistake, and a five-hundred-pound Nubian sunk into his thigh and dragged him around the arena. Luckily, the cat was diverted by a female in season. Cats are unpredictable when they have sex on their minds, which is probably one of the reasons he attacked my father in the first place. They're fiercely jealous once they've set their minds on a mate. My father was able to get into the safety cage before any of the other cats took an interest in him. I can't remember how many stitches he had or how long it was before he could walk properly again, but I do remember the look in that cat's eyes. You learn quickly about fear when you're in the cage, but you control it, you channel it or you find another line of work."

"Then why?" Keane demanded. He took her shoulders before she could turn away. "Why do you do it? And don't tell me because it's your job. That's not good enough."

It puzzled Jo why he seemed angry. His eyes were darkened with temper, and his fingers dug into her shoulders. As if wanting to draw out her answer, he gave her one quick shake. "All right," Jo said slowly, ignoring the ache in her flesh. "That is part of it, but not all. It's all I've ever known, that's part of it, too. It's what I'm good at." While she spoke, she searched his face for a clue to his mood. She wondered if perhaps he had felt it wrong of her to take Gerry into the cage. "Gerry's going to be good at it, too," she told him. "I imagine everyone needs to be good—really good— at something. And I enjoy giving the people who come to see me the best show I can. But over all, I suppose it's because I love them. It's difficult for a layman to understand a trainer's feeling for his animals. I love their intelligence, their really awesome beauty, their strength, the un-quenchable streak of wildness that separates them from well-trained horses. They're exciting, challenging and ter-rifying."

Keane was silent for a moment. She saw that his eyes were still angry, but his fingers relaxed on her shoulders. Jo felt a light throbbing where bruises would certainly show in the morning. "I suppose excitement becomes addicting— difficult to live without once it's become a habit."

"I don't know," Jo replied, grateful that his temper was apparently cooling. "I've never thought about it."

"No, I suppose you'd have little reason to." With a nod, he turned to walk away.

Jo took a step after him. "Keane." His name raced through her lips before she could prevent it. When he turned back to her, she realized she could not ask any of the dozens of questions that flew through her mind. There was only one she felt she had any right to ask. "Have you thought any more about what you're going to do with us…with the circus?"

For an instant she saw temper flare again into his eyes. "No." The word was curt and final. As he turned his back on her again, she felt a spurt of anger and reached for his arm.

"How can you be so callous, so unfeeling?" she demanded. "How is it possible to be so casual when you hold the lives of over a hundred people in your hands?"

Carefully, he removed her hand from his arm. "Don't push me, Jo." There was warning in his eyes and in his voice.

"I'm not trying to," she returned, then ran a frustrated

hand through her hair. "I'm only asking you to be fair, to be…kind," she finished lamely.

"Don't ask me anything," he ordered in a brisk, authoritative tone. Jo's chin rose in response. "I'm here," he reminded her. "You'll have to be satisfied with that for now."

Jo battled with her temper. She could not deny that in coming back he had proved himself true to his word. She had the rest of the season if nothing else. "I don't suppose I have any choice," she said quietly.

"No," he agreed with a faint nod. "You don't."

Frowning, Jo watched him stride away in a smooth, fluid gait she was forced to admire. She noticed for the first time that her palms were as damp as Gerry's had been. Annoyed, she rubbed them over her hips.

"Want to talk about it?"

Jo turned quickly to find Jamie behind her in full clown gear. She knew her preoccupation had been deep for her to be caught so completely unaware. "Oh, Jamie, I didn't see you."

"You haven't seen anything but Prescott since you stepped out of the cage," Jamie pointed out.

"What are you doing in makeup?" she asked, skirting his comment.

He gestured toward the dog at her feet. "This mutt won't respond to me unless I'm in my face. Do you want to talk about it?"

"Talk about what?"

"About Prescott, about the way you feel about him."

The dog sat patiently at Jamie's heels and thumped his tail. Casually, Jo stopped and ruffled his gray fur.

"I don't know what you're talking about."

"Look, I'm not saying it can't work out, but I don't want to see you get hurt. I know how it is to be nuts about somebody."

"What in the world makes you think I'm nuts about Keane Prescott?" Jo gave the dog her full attention.

"Hey, it's me, remember?" Jamie took her arm and pulled her to her feet. "Not everybody would've noticed, maybe, but not everybody knows you the way I do. You've been miserable since he went back to Chicago, looking for him in every car that drove on the lot. And just now, when you saw him, you lit up like the midway on Saturday night. I'm not saying there's anything wrong with you being in love with him, but—"

"In love with him?" Jo repeated, incredulous.

"Yeah." Jamie spoke patiently. "In love with him."

Jo stared at Jamie as the realization slid over her. "In love with him," she murmured, trying out the words. "Oh, no." She sighed, closing her eyes. "Oh, no."

"Didn't you have enough sense to figure it out for yourself?" Jamie said gently. Seeing Jo's distress, he ran a hand gently up her arm.

"No, I guess I'm pretty stupid about this sort of thing." Jo opened her eyes and looked around, wondering if the world should look any different. "What am I going to do?"

"Heck, I don't know." Jamie kicked sawdust with an oversized shoe. "I'm not exactly getting rave notices myself in that department." He gave Jo a reassuring pat. "I just wanted you to know that you always have a sympathetic ear here." He grinned engagingly before he turned to walk away, leaving Jo distracted and confused.

Jo spent the rest of the afternoon absorbed with the idea of being in love with Keane Prescott. For a short time she allowed herself to enjoy the sensation, the novel experience of loving someone not as a friend but as a lover. She could feel the light and the power spread through her, as if she had caught the sun in her hand. She daydreamed.

Keane was in love with her. He'd told her hundreds of times as he'd held her under a moonlit sky. He wanted to marry her, he couldn't bear to live without her. She was suddenly sophisticated and worldly enough to deal with the country club set on their own ground. She could exchange droll stories with the wives of other attorneys. There would be children and a house in the country. How would it feel to wake up in the same town every morning? She would learn to cook and give dinner parties. There would be long, quiet evenings when they would be alone together. There would be candlelight and music. When they slept together, his arms would stay around her until morning.

Idiot. Jo dragged herself back sternly. As she and Pete fed the cats, she tried to remember that fairy tales were for children. None of those things are ever going to happen, she reminded herself. I have to figure out how to handle this before I get in any deeper.

"Pete," she began, keeping her voice conversational as she put Abra's quota of raw meat on a long stick. "Have you ever been in love?"

Pete chewed his gum gently, watching Jo hoist the meat through the bars. "Well, now, let's see." Thrusting out his lower lip, he considered. "Only 'bout eight or ten times, I guess. Maybe twelve."

Jo laughed, moving down to the next cage. "I'm serious," she told him. "I mean *really* in love."

"I fall in love easy," Pete confessed gravely. "I'm a pushover for a pretty face. Matter of fact, I'm a pushover for an ugly face." He grinned. "Yes sir, the only thing like being in love is drawing an ace-high flush when the pot's ripe."

Jo shook her head and continued down the line. "Okay, since you're such an expert, tell me what you do when you're in love with a person and the person doesn't love you back and you don't want that person to know that you're in love because you don't want to make a fool of yourself."

"Just a minute." Pete squeezed his eyes tight. "I got to think this one through first." For a moment he was silent as his lips moved with his thoughts. "Okay, let's see if I've got this straight." Opening his eyes, he frowned in concentration. "You're in love—"

"I didn't say *I* was in love," Jo interrupted hastily.

Pete lifted his brows and pursed his lips. "Let's just use *you* in the general sense to avoid confusion," he suggested. Jo nodded, pretending to absorb herself with the feeding of the cats. "So, you're in love, but the guy doesn't love you. First off, you've got to be sure he doesn't."

"He doesn't," Jo murmured, then added quickly, "let's say he doesn't."

Pete shot her a look out of the corner of his eye, then shifted his gum to the other side of his mouth. "Okay, then the first thing you should do is change his mind."

"Change his mind?" Jo repeated, frowning at him.

"Sure." Pete gestured with his hand to show the simplicity of the procedure. "You fall in love with him, then he falls in love with you. You play hard to get, or you play easy to get. Or you play flutter and smile." He demonstrated by coyly batting his lashes and giving a winsome smile. Jo giggled and leaned on the feeding pole. Pete in fielder's cap, white T-shirt and faded jeans was the best show she'd seen all day. "You make him jealous," he continued. "Or you flatter his ego. Girl, there're so many ways to get a man, I can't count them, and I've been gotten by them all. Yes, sir, I'm a real pushover." He looked so pleased with his weakness, Jo smiled. How easy it would be, she thought, if I could take love so lightly.

"Suppose I don't want to do any of those things. Suppose I

don't really know how and I don't want to humiliate myself by making a mess of it. Suppose the person isn't—well, suppose nothing could ever work between us, anyway. What then?"

"You got too many supposes," Pete concluded, then shook his finger at her. "And I got one for you. Suppose you ain't too smart because you figure you can't win even before you play."

"Sometimes people get hurt when they play," Jo countered quietly. "Especially if they aren't familiar with the game."

"Hurting's nothing," Pete stated with a sweep of his hand. "Winning's the best, but playing's just fine. This whole big life, it's a game, Jo. You know that. And the rules keep changing all the time. You've got nerve," he continued, then laid his rough, brown hand on her shoulder. "More raw nerve than most anybody I've ever known. You've got brains, too, hungry brains. You going to tell me that with all that, you're afraid to take a chance?"

Meeting his eyes, Jo knew hypothetical evasions would not do. "I suppose I only take calculated risks, Pete. I know my turf; I know my moves. And I know exactly what'll happen if I make a mistake. I take a chance that my body might be clawed, not my emotions. I've never rehearsed for anything like this, and I think playing it cold would be suicide."

"I think you've got to believe in Jo Wilder a little more," Pete countered, then gave her cheek a quick pat.

"Hey, Jo." Looking over, Jo saw Rose approaching. She wore straight-leg jeans, a white peasant blouse and a six-foot boa constrictor over her shoulders.

"Hello, Rose." Jo handed Pete the feeding pole. "Taking Baby out for a walk?"

"He needed some air." Rose gave her charge a pat. "I

think he got a little carsick this morning. Does he look peaked to you?"

Jo looked down at the shiny, multicolored skin, then studied the tiny black eyes as Rose held Baby's head up for inspection. "I don't think so," she decided.

"Well, it's a warm day," Rose observed, releasing Baby's head. "I'll give him a bath. That might perk him up."

Jo noticed Rose's eyes darting around the compound. "Looking for Jamie?"

"*Hmph.*" Rose tossed her black curls. "I'm not wasting my time on that one." She stroked the latter half of Baby's anatomy. "I'm indifferent."

"That's another way to do it," Pete put in, giving Jo a nudge. "I forgot about that one. It's a zinger."

Rose frowned at Pete, then at Jo. "What's he talking about?"

With a laugh, Jo sat down on a water barrel. "Catching a man," she told her, letting the warm sun play on her face. "Pete's done a study on it from the male point of view."

"Oh." Rose threw Pete her most disdainful look. "You think I'm indifferent so he'll get interested?"

"It's a zinger," Pete repeated, adjusting his cap. "You get him confused so he starts thinking about you. You make him crazy wondering why you don't notice him."

Rose considered the idea. "Does it usually work?"

"It's got an eighty-seven percent success average," Pete assured her, then gave Baby a friendly pat. "It even works with cats." He jerked his thumb behind him and winked at Jo. "The pretty lady cat, she sits there and stares off into space like she's got important things occupying her mind. The boy in the next cage is doing everything but standing on his head to get her attention. She just gives herself a wash, pretending she doesn't even know he's there. Then, maybe after she's got him banging his head against the bars, she looks over, blinks her big yellow eyes and says, 'Oh, were you talking to me?'" Pete laughed and stretched his back muscles. "He's hooked then, brother, just like a fish on a line."

Rose smiled at the image of Jamie dangling from her own personal line. "Maybe I won't put Baby in Carmen's trailer after all," she murmured. "Oh, look, here comes Duffy and the owner." An inherent flirt, Rose instinctively fluffed her hair. "Really, he is the most handsome man. Don't you think so, Jo?"

Jo's eyes had already locked on Keane's. She seemed helpless to release herself from the gaze. Gripping the edge of the water barrel tightly, she reminded herself not to be a fool. "Yes," she agreed with studied casualness. "He's very attractive."

"Your knuckles are turning white, Jo," Pete muttered next to her ear.

Letting out a frustrated breath, Jo relaxed her hands. Straightening her spine, she determined to show more restraint. Control, she reminded herself, was the basic tool of her trade. If she could train her emotions and outbluff a dozen lions, she could certainly outbluff one man.

"Hello, Duffy." Rose gave the portly man a quick smile, then turned her attention to Keane. "Hello, Mr. Prescott. It's nice to have you back."

"Hello, Rose." He smiled into her upturned face, then lifted a brow as his eyes slid over the reptile around her neck and shoulders. "Who's your friend?"

"Oh, this is Baby." She patted one of the tan-colored saddle marks on Baby's back.

"Of course." Jo noticed how humor enhanced the gold of his eyes. "Hello, Pete." He gave the handler an easy nod before his gaze shifted and then lingered on Jo.

As on the first day they had met, Keane did not bother to camouflage his stare. His look was cool and assessing. He was reaffirming ownership. It shot through Jo that yes, she was in love with him, but she was also afraid of him. She feared his power over her, feared his capacity to hurt her. Still, her face registered none of her thoughts. Fear, she reminded herself as her eyes remained equally cool on his, was something she understood. Love might cause impossible problems, but fear could be dealt with. She would not cower from him, and she would honor the foremost rule of the arena. She would not turn and run.

Silently, they watched each other while the others looked on with varying degrees of curiosity. There was the barest touch of a smile on Keane's lips. The battle of wills continued until Duffy cleared his throat.

"Ah, Jo."

Calmly, without hurry, she shifted her attention. "Yes, Duffy?"

"I just sent one of the web girls into town to see the local dentist. Seems she's got an abscess. I need you to fill in tonight."

"Sure."

"Just for the web and the opening spectacular," he continued. Unable to prevent himself, he cast a quick look at Keane to see if he was still staring at her. He was. Duffy shifted uncomfortably and wondered what the devil was going on. "Take your usual place in the finale. We'll just be one girl shy in the chorus. Wardrobe'll fix you up."

"Okay." Jo smiled at him, though she was very much aware of Keane's eyes on her. "I guess I'd better go practice walking in those three-inch heels. What position do I take?"

"Number four rope."

"Duffy," Rose chimed in and tugged on his sleeve. "When are you going to let me do the web?"

"Rose, how's a pint-sizer like you going to stand up with that heavy costume on?" Duffy shook his head at her, keeping a respectable distance from Baby. After thirty-five years of working carnies, sideshows and circuses, he still was uneasy around snakes.

"I'm pretty strong," Rose claimed, stretching her spine in the hope of looking taller. "And I've been practicing." Anxious to demonstrate her accomplishments, Rose deftly unwound Baby. "Hold him a minute," she requested and dumped several feet of snake into Keane's arms.

"Ah…" Keane shifted the weight in his arms and looked dubiously into Baby's bored eyes. "I hope he's eaten recently."

"He had a nice breakfast," Rose assured him, going into a fluid backbend to show Duffy her flexibility.

"Baby won't eat owners," Jo told Keane. She did not bother to suppress her grin. It was the first time she had seen him disconcerted. "Just a stray towner, occasionally. Rose keeps him on a strict diet."

"I assume," Keane began as Baby slithered into a more comfortable position, "that he's aware I'm the owner."

Grinning at Keane's uncomfortable expression, Jo turned to Pete. "Gee, I don't know. Did anybody tell Baby about the new owner?"

"Haven't had a chance, myself," Pete drawled, taking out a fresh stick of gum. "Looks a lot like a towner, too. Baby might get confused."

"They're just teasing you, Mr. Prescott," Rose told him as she finished her impromptu audition with a full split. "Baby doesn't eat people at all. He's docile as a lamb. Little kids come up and pet him during a demonstration." She rose and brushed off her jeans. "Now, you take a cobra…"

"No, thank you," Keane declined, unloading the six-foot Baby back into Rose's arms.

Rose slipped the boa back around her neck. "Well, Duffy, I'm off. What do you say?"

"Get one of the girls to teach you the routine," he said with a nod. "Then we'll see." Smiling, he watched Rose saunter away.

"Hey, Duffy!" It was Jamie. "There's a couple of towners looking for you. I sent them over to the red wagon."

"Fine. I'll just go right on along with you." Duffy winked at Jo before turning to catch up with Jamie's long stride.

Keane was standing very close to the barrels. Jo knew getting down from her perch was risky. She knew, too, however, that her pulse was beginning to behave erratically despite her efforts to control it. "I've got to see about my costume." Nimbly, she came down, intending to skirt around him. Even as her boots touched the ground, his hands took her waist. Exercising every atom of willpower, she neither jerked nor struggled but lifted her eyes calmly to his.

His thumbs moved in a lazy arch. She could feel the warmth through the fabric of her blouse. With her entire being she wished he would not hold her. Then, perversely, she wished he would hold her closer. She struggled not to weaken as her lips grew warm under the kiss of his eyes. Her heart began to hammer in her ears.

Keane ran a hand down the length of her long, thick braid. Slowly, his eyes drifted back to hers. Abruptly, he released her and backed up to let her pass. "You'd best go have wardrobe take a few tucks in that costume."

Deciding she was not meant to decipher his changing moods, Jo stepped by him and crossed the compound. If she spent enough time working, she could keep her thoughts from dwelling on Keane Prescott. Maybe.

Chapter 7

The Big Top was packed for the evening show. Jo watched the anticipation in the range of faces as she took her temporary position in the opening spectacular. The band played jumpy, upbeat music, leaning heavily on brass as the theme parade marched around the hippodrome track. As the substitute Bo Peep, Jo wore a demure mopcap and a wide crinoline skirt and led a baby lamb on a leash. Because her act came so swiftly on the tail of the opening, she rarely participated in the spectacular. Now she enjoyed a close-up look at the audience. In the cage, she blocked them out almost completely.

They were, she decided, a well-mixed group: young babies, older children, parents, grandparents, teenagers. They gave the pageant enthusiastic applause. Jo smiled and waved as she performed the basic choreography with hardly a thought.

After a quick costume change, she took her cue as Queen of the Jungle Cats. After that followed another costume change that transformed her into one of the Twelve Spinning Butterflies.

"Just heard," Jamie whispered in her ear as she took the customary pose by the rope. "You got the job for the next week. Barbara won't be able to handle the teeth grip."

Jo shifted her shoulders to compensate for the weight of her enormous blue wings. "Rose is going to learn the routine," she mumbled back, smiling in the flood of the sunlight. "Duffy's giving her the job if she can stand up under this blasted costume." She made a quick, annoyed sound and smiled brightly. "It weighs a ton."

Slowly, to the beat of the waltz the band played, Jo climbed hand over hand up the rope. "Ah, show biz," she heard Jamie sigh. She vowed to poke him in the ribs when she took her bow. Then, hooking her foot in the hoop, she began the routine, imitating the other eleven Spinning Butterflies.

She was able to share a cup of coffee with Rose's mother when she returned the butterfly costume to wardrobe and changed into her own white and gold jumpsuit. Her muscles complained a bit due to the unfamiliar weight of the wings, and she gave a passing thought to a long, luxurious bath. That was a dream for September, she reminded herself. Showers were the order of the day on the road.

Jo's last duty in the show was to stand on the head of Maggie, the key elephant in the finale's long mount. Sturdy and dependable, Maggie stood firm while four elephants on each side of her rose on their hind legs, resting their front legs on the back of the one in front. Atop Maggie's broad head, Jo stood glittering under the lights with both arms lifted in the air. It was here, more than any other part of the show, that the applause washed over her. It merged with the music, the ringmaster's whistle, the laughter of children. Where she had been weary, she was now filled with energy. She knew the fatigue would return, so she relished the power of the moment all the more. For those few seconds there was no work, no long hours, no predawn drives. There was only magic. Even when it was over and she slid from Maggie's back, she could still feel it.

Outside the tent, troupers and roustabouts and shandies mingled. There were anecdotes to exchange, performances to dissect, observations to be made. Gradually, they drifted away alone, in pairs or in groups. Some would change and help strike the tents, some would sleep, some would worry over their performances. Too energized to sleep, Jo planned to assist in the striking of the Big Top.

She switched on a low light as she entered her trailer, then absently braided her hair as she moved to the tiny bath. With quick moves she creamed off her stage makeup. The exotic exaggeration of her eyes was whisked away, leaving the thick fringe of her lashes and the dark green of her irises unenhanced. The soft bloom of natural rose tinted her cheeks again, and her mouth, unpainted, appeared oddly vulnerable. Accustomed to the change, Jo did not see the sharp contrast between Jovilette the performer and the small, somewhat fragile woman in the glittering jumpsuit. With her face naked and the simple braid hanging down her back, the look of the wild, of the gypsy, was less apparent. It remained in her movements, but her face rinsed of all artifice and unframed, was both delicate and young, part ingenue, part flare. But Jo saw none of this as she reached for her front zipper. Before she could pull it down, a knock sounded on her door.

"Come in," she called out and flicked her braid behind her back as she started down the aisle. She stopped in her tracks as Keane stepped through the door.

"Didn't anyone ever tell you to ask who it is first?" He shut the door behind him and locked it with a careless flick of his wrist. "You might not have to lock your door against the circus people," he continued blandly as she remained still, "but there are several dozen curious towners still hanging around."

"I can handle a curious towner," Jo replied. The offhand quality of his dominance was infuriating. "I never lock my door."

There was stiffness and annoyance in her voice. Keane ignored them both. "I brought you something from Chicago."

The casual statement succeeded in throwing Jo's temper off the mark. For the first time, she noticed the small package he carried. "What is it?" she asked.

Keane smiled and crossed to her. "It's nothing that bites," he assured her, then held it out.

Still cautious, Jo lifted her eyes to his, then dropped her gaze back to the package. "It's not my birthday," she murmured.

"It's not Christmas, either," Keane pointed out.

The easy patience in the tone caused Jo to lift her eyes again. She wondered how it was he understood her hesitation to accept presents. She kept her gazed locked on his. "Thank you," she said solemnly as she took the gift.

"You're welcome," Keane returned in the same tone.

The amenities done, Jo recklessly ripped the paper. "Oh! It's Dante," she exclaimed, tearing off the remaining paper and tossing it on the table. With reverence she ran her palm over the dark leather binding. The rich scent drifted to her. She knew her quota of books would have been limited to one a year had she bought a volume so handsomely bound. She opened it slowly, as if to prolong the pleasure. The pages were heavy and rich cream in color. The text was Italian, and even as she glanced over the first page, the words ran fluidly through her mind.

"It's beautiful," she murmured, overcome. Lifting her

eyes to thank him again, Jo found Keane smiling down at her. Shyness enveloped her suddenly, all the more intense because she had so rarely experienced it. A lifetime in front of crowds had given her a natural confidence in almost any situation. Now color began to surge into her cheeks, and her mind was a jumble of words that would not come to order.

"I'm glad you like it." He ran a finger down her cheek. "Do you always blush when someone gives you a present?"

Because she was at a loss as to how to answer his question, Jo maneuvered around it. "It was nice of you to think of me."

"It seems to come naturally," Keane replied, then watched Jo's lashes flutter down.

"I don't know what to say." She was able to meet his eyes again with her usual directness, but he had again touched her emotions. She felt inadequate to deal with her feelings or with his effect on her.

"You've already said it." He took the book from Jo's hand and paged through it. "Of course, I can't read a word of it. I envy you that." Before Jo could ponder the idea of a man like Keane Prescott envying her anything, he looked back up and smiled. Her thoughts scattered like nervous ants. "Got any coffee?" he asked and set the book back down on the table.

"Coffee?"

"Yes, you know, coffee. They grow it in quantity in Brazil." Jo gave him a despairing look. "I don't have any made. I'd fix you a cup, but I've got to change before I help strike the tents. The cookhouse will still be serving."

Keane lifted a brow as he let his eyes wander over her face. "Don't you think that between Bo Peep, lions and butterflies, you've done enough work tonight? By the way, you make a very appealing butterfly."

"Thank you, but—"

"Let's put it this way," Keane countered smoothly. He took the tip of her braid in his fingers. "You've got the night off. I'll make the coffee myself if you show me where you keep it."

Though she let out a windy sigh, Jo was more amused than annoyed. Coffee, she decided, was the least she could do after he had brought her such a lovely present. "I'll make it," she told him, "but you'll probably wish you'd gone to the cookhouse." With this dubious invitation, Jo turned and headed toward the kitchen. He made no sound, but she knew he followed her. For the first time, she felt the smallness of her kitchen.

Setting an undersized copper kettle on one of the two burners, Jo flicked on the power. It was a simple matter to keep her back to him while she plucked cups from the cupboard. She was well aware that if she turned around in the compact kitchen, she would all but be in his arms.

"Did you watch the whole show?" she asked conversationally as she pulled out a jar of instant coffee.

"Duffy had me working props," Keane answered. "He seems to be making me generally useful."

Amused, Jo twisted her head to grin at him. Instantly, she discovered her misstep in strategy. Keane's face was only inches from hers, and in his eyes she read his thoughts. He wanted her, and he intended to have her. Before she could shift her position, Keane took her shoulders and turned her completely around. Jo knew she had backed up against the bars.

Leisurely, he began to loosen her hair, working his fingers through it until it pooled over her shoulders. "I've wanted to do that since the first time I saw you. It's hair to get lost in." His voice was soft as he took a generous handful. The gesture itself seemed to stake his claim. "In the sun it shimmers with red lights, but in the dark it's like night itself." It came to her that each time she was close to him, she was less able to resist him. She became more lost in his eyes, more beguiled by his power. Already her mouth tingled with the memory of his kiss, with the longing for a new one. Behind them the kettle began a feverish whistle.

"The water," she managed and tried to move around him. With one hand in her hair, Keane kept her still as he turned off the burner. The whistle sputtered peevishly, then died. The sound echoed in Jo's head.

"Do you want coffee?" he murmured as his fingers trailed to her throat.

Jo's eyes clung to his. Hers were enormous and direct, his quiet and searching. "No," she whispered, knowing she wanted nothing more at that moment than to belong to him. He circled her throat with his hand and pressed his fingers against her pulse. It fluttered wildly.

"You're trembling." He could feel the light tremor of her body as he brought her closer. "Is it fear?" he demanded as his thumbs brushed over her lips. "Or excitement?"

"Both," she answered in a voice thickened with emotion. She made a tiny, confused sound as his palm covered her heart. Its desperate thudding increased. "Are you…" She stopped a moment because her voice was breathless and unsteady. "Are you going to make love to me?" Did his eyes really darken? she wondered dizzily. Or is it my imagination?

"Beautiful Jovilette," he murmured as his mouth lowered to hers. "No pretentions, no evasions…irresistible." The quality of the kiss altered swiftly. His mouth was hungry on hers, and her response leaped past all caution. If loving him was madness, her heart reasoned, could making love take her further beyond sanity? Past wisdom and steeped in sensation, she let her heart rule her will. When her lips parted under his, it was not in surrender but in equal demand.

Keane gentled the kiss. He kept her shimmering on the razor's edge of passion. His mouth teased, promised, then fed her growing need. He found the zipper at the base of her throat and pulled it downward slowly. Her skin was warm, and he sought it, giving a low sound of pleasure as her breast swelled under his hand. He explored without hurry, as if memorizing each curve and plane. Jo no longer trembled but became pliant as her body moved to the rhythm he set. Her sigh was spontaneous, filled with wonder and delight.

With a suddenness that took her breath away, Keane crushed her mouth beneath his in fiery urgency. Jo's instincts responded, thrusting her into a world she had only imagined. His hands grew rougher, more insistent. Jo realized he had relinquished control. They were both riding on the tossing waves of passion. This sea had no horizon and no depth. It was a drowning sea that pulled the unsuspecting under while promising limitless pleasure. Jo did not resist but dove deeper.

At first she thought the knocking was only the sound of her heart against her ribs. When Keane drew away, she murmured in protest and pulled him back. Instantly, his mouth was avid, but as the knocking continued, he swore and pulled back again.

"Someone's persistent," he muttered. Bewildered, Jo stared up at him. "The door," he explained on a long breath.

"Oh." Flustered, Jo ran a hand through her hair and tried to collect her wits.

"You'd better answer it," Keane suggested as he pulled the zipper to her throat in one quick move. Jo broke the surface into reality abruptly. For a moment Keane watched her, taking in her flushed cheeks and tousled hair before he moved aside. Willing her legs to carry her, Jo walked to the front of the trailer. The door handle resisted, then she remembered that Keane had locked it, and she turned the latch.

"Yes, Buck?" she said calmly enough when she opened the door to her handler.

"Jo." His face was in shadows, but she heard the distress in the single syllable. Her chest tightened. "It's Ari."

He had barely finished the name before Jo was out of the trailer and running across the compound. She found both Pete and Gerry standing near Ari's cage.

"How bad?" she demanded as Pete came to meet her.

He took her shoulders. "Really bad this time, Jo."

For a moment she wanted to shake her head, to deny what she read in Pete's eyes. Instead, she nudged him aside and walked to Ari's cage. The old cat lay on his side as his chest lifted and fell with the effort of breathing. "Open it," she ordered Pete in a voice that revealed nothing. There was the jingle of keys, but she did not turn.

"You're not going in there." Jo heard Keane's voice and felt a restraining grip on her shoulders. Her eyes were opaque as she looked up at him.

"Yes, I am. Ari isn't going to hurt me or anyone else. He's just going to die. Now leave me alone." Her voice was low and toneless. "Open it," she ordered again, then pulled out of Keane's loosened hold. The bars rattled as he slid the door open. Hearing it, Jo turned, then hoisted herself into the cage.

Ari barely stirred. Jo saw, as she knelt beside him, that his eyes were open. They were glazed with weariness and pain. "Ari," she sighed, seeing there would be no tomorrow for him. His only answer was a hollow wheezing. Putting a hand to his side, she felt the ragged pace of his breathing.

He made an effort to respond to her touch, to his name, but managed only to shift his great head on the floor. The gesture tore at Jo's heart. She lowered her face to his mane, remembering him as he had once been: full of strength and a terrifying beauty. She lifted her face again and took one long, steadying breath. "Buck." She heard him approach but kept her eyes on Ari. "Get the medical kit. I want a hypo of pentobarbital." She could feel Buck's brief hesitation before he spoke.

"Okay, Jo."

She sat quietly, stroking Ari's head. In the distance were the sounds of the Big Top going down, the call of men, the rattle of rigging, the clang of wood against metal. An elephant trumpeted, and three cages down, Faust roared half-heartedly in response.

"Jo." She turned her head as Buck called her and pushed her hair from her eyes. "Let me do it."

Jo merely shook her head and held out her hand.

"Jo." Keane stepped up to the bars. His voice was gentle, but his eyes were so like the cat's at her knees, Jo nearly sobbed aloud. "You don't have to do this yourself."

"He's my cat," she responded dully. "I said I'd do it when it was time. It's time." Her eyes shifted to Buck. "Give me the hypo, Buck. Let's get it done." When the syringe was in her hand, Jo stared at it, then closed her fingers around it. Swallowing hard, she turned back to Ari. His eyes were on her face. After more than twenty years in captivity there was still something not quite tamed in the dying cat. But she saw trust in his eyes and wanted to weep. "You were the best," she told him as she passed a hand through his mane. "You were always the best." Jo felt a numbing cold settling over her and prayed it would last until she had finished. "You're tired now. I'm going to help you sleep." She pulled the safety from the point of the hypodermic and waited until she was certain her hands were steady. "This won't hurt, nothing is going to hurt you anymore."

Involuntarily, Jo rubbed the back of her hand over her mouth, then, moving quickly, she plunged the needle into Ari's shoulder. A quiet whimper escaped her as she emptied the syringe. Ari made no sound but continued to watch her face. Jo offered no words of comfort but sat with him, methodically stroking his fur as his eyes grew cloudy. Gradually, the effort of his breathing lessened, becoming quieter and quieter until it wasn't there at all. Jo felt him grow still, and her hand balled into a fist inside the mass of his mane. One quick, convulsive shudder escaped her. Steeling herself, she moved from the cage, closing the door behind her. Because her bones felt fragile, she kept them stiff, as though they might shatter. Even as she stepped back to the ground, Keane took her arm and began to lead her away.

"Take care of things," he said to Buck as they moved past.

"No." Jo protested, trying and failing to free her arm. "I'll do it."

"No, you won't." Keane's tone held a quiet finality. "Enough's enough."

"Don't tell me what to do," she said sharply, letting her grief take refuge in anger.

"I *am* telling you," he pointed out. His hand was firm on her arm.

"You *can't* tell me what to do," she insisted as tears rose treacherously in her throat. "I want you to leave me alone."

Keane stopped, then took her by the shoulders. His eyes caught the light of a waning moon. "There's no way I'm going to leave you alone when you're so upset."

"My emotions have nothing to do with you." Even as she spoke, he took her arm again and pulled her toward her trailer. Jo wanted desperately to be alone to weep out her grief in private. The mourning belonged to her, and the tears were personal. As if her protests were nonexistent, he pulled her into the trailer and closed the door behind them. "Will you get out of here?" she demanded, frantically swallowing tears.

"Not until I know you're all right." Keane's answer was calm as he walked back to the kitchen.

"I'm perfectly all right." Her breath shuddered in and out quickly. "Or I will be when you leave me alone. You have no right to poke your nose in my business."

"So you've told me before," Keane answered mildly from the back of the trailer.

"I just did what had to be done." She held her body rigid and fought against her own quick, uneven breathing. "I put a sick animal out of his misery; it's as simple as that." Her voice broke, and she turned away, hugging her arms. "For heaven's sake, Keane, go away!"

Quietly, he walked back to her carrying a glass of water. "Drink this."

"No." She whirled back to him. Tears spilled out of her eyes and trickled down her cheeks despite her efforts to banish them. Hating herself, she pressed the heel of her hand between her brows and closed her eyes. "I don't want you here." Keane set down the glass, then gathered her into his arms. "No, don't. I don't want you to hold me."

"Too bad." He ran a hand gently up and down her back. "You did a very brave thing, Jo. I know you loved Ari. I know how hard it was to let him go. You're hurting, and I'm not leaving you."

"I don't want to cry in front of you." Her fists were tight balls at his shoulders.

"Why not?" The stroking continued up and down her back as he cradled her head in the curve of his shoulder.

"Why won't you let me be?" she sobbed as her control slipped. Her fingers gripped his shirt convulsively. "Why am I always losing what I love?" She let the grief come. She let his arms soothe her. As desperately as she had protested against it, she clung to his offer of comfort.

She made no objection as he carried her to the couch and cradled her in his arms. He stroked her hair, as she had stroked Ari, to ease the pain of what couldn't be changed. Slowly, her sobbing quieted. Still she lay with her cheek against his chest, with her hair curtaining her face.

"Better?" he asked as the silence grew calmer. Jo nodded, not yet trusting her voice. Keane shifted her as he reached for the glass of water. "Drink this now."

Gratefully, Jo relieved her dry throat, then went without resistance back against his chest. She closed her eyes, thinking it had been a very long time since she had been held in anyone's lap and soothed. "Keane," she murmured. She felt his lips brush over the top of her head.

"Hmm?"

"Nothing." Her voice thickened as she drifted toward sleep. "Just Keane."

Chapter 8

Jo felt the sun on her closed lids. There was the summer morning sound of excited birds. Her mind, levitating slowly toward the surface, told her it must be Monday. Only on Monday would she sleep past sunrise. That was the enroute day, the only day in seven the circus held no show. She thought lazily of getting up. She would set aside two hours for reading. Maybe I'll drive into town and see a movie. What town are we in? With a sleepy sigh she rolled onto her stomach.

I'll give the cats a good going over, maybe hose them down if it gets hot enough. Memory flooded back and snapped her awake. *Ari.* Opening her eyes, Jo rolled onto her back and stared at the ceiling. Now she recalled vividly how the old cat had died with his eyes trusting on her face. She sighed again. The sadness was still there, but not the sharp, desperate grief of the night before. Acceptance was settling in. She realized that Keane's insistence on staying with her during the peak of her mourning had helped her. He had given her someone to rail at, then someone to hold on to. She remembered the incredible comfort of being cradled in his lap, the solid dependability of his chest against her cheek. She had fallen asleep with the sound of his heart in her ear.

Turning her head, Jo looked out the window, then at the patch of white light the sun tossed on the floor. But it isn't Monday, she remembered suddenly. It's Thursday. Jo sat up, pushing at her hair, which seemed to tumble everywhere at once. What was she doing in bed on a Thursday when the sun was up? Without giving herself time to work out the answer, she scrambled out of bed and hurried from the room. She gave a soft gasp as she ran headlong into Keane.

His hand ran down the length of her hair before he took her shoulder. "I heard you stirring," he said easily, looking down into her stunned face.

"What are you doing here?"

"Making coffee," he answered as he gave her a critical study. "Or I was a moment ago. How are you?"

"I'm all right." Jo lifted her hand to her temple as if to gain her bearings. "I'm a bit disoriented, I suppose. I overslept. It's never happened before."

"I gave you a sleeping pill," Keane told her matter-of-factly. He slipped an arm around her shoulder as he turned back to the kitchen.

"A pill?" Jo's eyes flew to his. "I don't remember taking a pill."

"It was in the water you drank." On the stove the kettle began its piercing whistle. Moving to it, Keane finished making the coffee. "I had my doubts as to whether you'd take it voluntarily."

"No, I wouldn't have," Jo agreed with some annoyance. "I've never taken a sleeping pill in my life."

"Well, you did last night." He held out a mug of coffee.

"I sent Gerry for it while you were in the cage with Ari."
Again he gave her a quick, intense study. "It didn't seem to
do you any harm. You went out like a light. I carried you to
bed, changed your clothes—"

"Changed my…" All at once Jo became aware that she
wore only a thin white nightshirt. Her hand reached instinctively for the top button that nestled just above her bosom.
Thinking hard, she found she could recall nothing beyond
falling asleep in his arms.

"I don't think you'd have spent a very comfortable night
in your costume," Keane pointed out. Enjoying his coffee,
he smiled at the nervous hand she held between her breasts.
"I've had a certain amount of experience undressing women
in the dark." Jo dropped her hand. It was an unmistakable
movement of pride. Keane's eyes softened. "You needed a
good night's sleep, Jo. You were worn out."

Without speaking, Jo lifted her coffee to her lips and
turned away. Walking to the window, she could see that the
back yard was deserted. Her sleep must indeed have been
deep to have kept her unaware of camp breaking.

"Everyone's gone but a couple of roustabouts and a genera-
tor truck. They'll take off when you don't need power
anymore."

The vulnerability Jo felt was overwhelming. Several times
in the course of the evening before, she had lost control,
which had always been an essential part of her. Each time,
it had been Keane who had been there. She wanted to be
angry with him for intruding on her privacy but found it impossible. She had needed him, and he had known it.

"You didn't have to stay behind," she said, watching a
crow swoop low over the ground outside.

"I wasn't certain you'd be in any shape to drive fifty miles
this morning. Pete's driving my trailer."

Her shoulders lifted and fell before she turned around. Sunlight streamed through the window at her back and poured through the thin folds of her nightshirt. Her body was a slender shadow. When she spoke, her voice was low with regret. "I was horribly rude to you last night."

Keane shrugged and lifted his coffee. "You were upset."

"Yes." Her eyes were an open reflection of her sorrow. "Ari was very important to me. I suppose he was an ongoing link with my father, with my childhood. I'd known for some time he wouldn't make it through the season, but I didn't want to face it." She looked down at the mug she held gripped in both hands. A faint wisp of steam rose from it and vanished. "Last night was a relief for him. It was selfish of me to wish it otherwise. And I was wrong to strike out at you the way I did. I'm sorry."

"I don't want your apology, Jo." Because he sounded annoyed, she looked up quickly.

"I'd feel better if you'd take it, Keane. You've been very kind."

To her astonishment, he swore under his breath and turned back to the stove. "I don't care for your gratitude any more than your apology." He set down his mug and poured in more coffee. "Neither of them is necessary."

"They are to me," Jo replied, then took a step toward him. "Keane…" She set down her coffee and touched his arm. When he turned, she let impulse guide her. She rested her head on his shoulder and slipped her arms around his waist. He stiffened, putting his hands to her shoulders as if to draw her away. Then she heard his breath come out in a long sigh as he relaxed. For an instant he brought her closer.

"I never know precisely what to expect from you," he murmured. He lifted her chin with his finger. In automatic response, Jo closed her eyes and offered her mouth. She felt his fingers tighten on her skin before his lips brushed hers lightly. "You'd better go change." His manner was friendly but cool as he stepped away. "We'll stop off in town, and I'll buy you some breakfast."

Puzzled by his attitude but satisfied he was no longer annoyed, Jo nodded. "All right."

Spring became summer as the circus wound its way north. The sun stayed longer, peeking into the Big Top until well after the evening show began. Heavy rain came infrequently, but there were quick summer storms with thunder and lightning. Through June, Prescott's Circus Colossus snaked through North Carolina and into western Tennessee.

During the long weeks while spring tripped over into summer, Jo found Keane's attitude a paradox. His friendliness toward her was offhand. He laughed if she said something amusing, listened if she had a complaint and to her confusion, slipped a thin barrier between them. At times she wondered if the passion that had flared between them the night he had returned from Chicago had truly existed. Had the desire she had tasted on his lips been a fantasy? The closeness she had felt blooming between them had withered and blown away. They were only owner and trouper now.

Keane flew back to Chicago twice more during this period, but he brought no surprise presents back with him. Not once during those long weeks did he come by her trailer. Initially, his altered manner confused her. He was not angry. His mood was neither heated nor icy with temper but fell into an odd middle ground she could not understand. Jo ached with love. As days passed into weeks, she was forced to admit that Keane did not seem to be interested in a close relationship.

* * *

On the eve of the July Fourth show, Jo sat sleepless in her bed. In her hand she held the volume of Dante, but the book was only a reminder of the emptiness she felt. She closed it, then stared at the ceiling. It's time to snap out of it, she lectured herself. It's time to stop pretending he was ever really part of my life. Loving someone only makes him a part of your wishes. He never talked about love, he never promised anything, never offered anything but what he gave to me. He's done nothing to hurt me. Jo squeezed her eyes shut and pressed the book between her fingers. How I wish I could hate him for showing me what life could be like and then turning away, she thought.

But I can't. Jo let out a shaky breath and relaxed her grip on the book. Gently, she ran a finger down its smooth, leather binding. I can't hate him, but I can't love him openly, either. How do I stop? I should be grateful he stopped wanting me. I would have made love with him. Then I'd hurt a hundred times more. Could I hurt a hundred times more? For several moments she lay still, trying to quiet her thoughts.

It's best not to know, she told herself sternly. It's best to remember he was kind to me when I needed him and that I haven't a right to make demands. Summer doesn't last forever. I may never see him again when it's over. At least I can keep the time we have pleasant.

The words sounded hollow in her heart.

Chapter 9

The Fourth of July was a full day with a run to a new lot, the tent raising, a street parade and two shows. But it was a holiday. Elephants wore red, white and blue plumes atop their massive heads. The evening performance would be held an hour earlier to allow for the addition of a fireworks display. Traditionally, Prescott's circus arranged to spend the holiday in the same small town in Tennessee. The license and paperwork for the display were seen to in advance, and the fireworks were shipped ahead to be stored in a warehouse. The procedure had been precisely the same for years. It was one of the circus's most profitable nights. Concessions thrived.

Jo moved through the day with determined cheerfulness. She refused to permit the distance between her and Keane to spoil one of the highlights of the summer. Brooding, she decided, would not change things. The mood of the crowd helped to keep her spirits light.

Between shows came the inevitable lull. Some troupers sat outside their trailers exchanging small talk and enjoying the sun. Others got in a bit more practice or worked out a few kinks. Bull hands washed down the elephants, causing a minor flood in the pen area.

Jo watched the bathing process with amusement. She never ceased to enjoy this particular aspect of circus life, especially if there were one or two inexperienced bull hands involved. Invariably, Maggie or one of the other veteran bulls would spray a trunkful of water over the new hands to initiate them. Though Jo knew the other hands encouraged it, they always displayed remarkable innocence.

Spotting Duffy, Jo moved away from the elephant area and wandered toward him. She could see he was deep in discussion with a towner. He was as short as Duffy but wider, with what she had once heard Frank call a successful frame. His stomach started high and barreled out to below his waist. He had a ruddy complexion and pale eyes that squinted hard against the sun. Jo had seen his type before. She wondered what he was selling and how much he wanted for it. Since Duffy was puffing with annoyance, Jo assumed it was quite a lot.

"I'm telling you, Carlson, we've already paid for storage. I've got a signed receipt. And we pay fifteen bucks delivery, not twenty."

Carlson was smoking a small, unfiltered cigarette and dropped it to the ground. "You paid Myers for storage, not me. I bought the place six weeks ago." He shrugged his wide shoulders. "Not my problem you paid in advance."

Looking over, Jo saw Keane approaching with Pete. Pete was talking rapidly, Keane nodding. As Jo watched, Keane glanced up and gave Carlson a quick study. She had seen that look before and knew the older man had been assessed. Keane caught her eye, smiled and began to move past her. "Hello, Jo."

Unashamedly curious, Jo fell into step beside him. "What's going on?"

"Why don't we find out?" he suggested as they stopped in front of Duffy and Carlson. "Gentlemen," Keane said in an easy tone. "Is there a problem?"

"This character," Duffy spouted, jerking a scornful thumb at Carlson's face, "wants us to pay twice for storage on the fireworks. Then he wants twenty for delivery when we agreed on fifteen."

"Myers agreed on fifteen," Carlson pointed out. He smiled without humor. "I didn't agree on anything. You want your fireworks, you gotta pay for them first—cash," he added, then spared Keane a glance. "Who's this guy?"

Duffy began to wheeze with indignation, but Keane laid a restraining hand on his shoulder. "I'm Prescott," he told him in untroubled tones. "Perhaps you'd like to fill me in."

"Prescott, huh?" Carlson stroked both his chins as he studied Keane. Seeing youth and amiable eyes, he felt closer to success. "Well, now we're getting somewhere," he said jovially and stuck out his hand. Keane accepted it without hesitation. "Jim Carlson," he continued as he gave Keane's hand a brisk pump. "Nice circus you got here, Prescott. Me and the missus see it every year. Well, now," he said again and hitched up his belt. "Seeing as you're a businessman, too, I'm sure we can straighten all this out. Problem is, your fire-works've been stored in my warehouse. Now, I gotta make a living, they can't just sit there for free. I bought the place off Myers six weeks ago. I can't be held responsible for a deal you made with him, can I?" Carlson gave a stretched-lip smile, pleased that Keane listened so politely. "And as for delivery, well…" He made a helpless gesture and patted Keane's shoulder. "You know about gas prices these days, son. But we can work that out after we settle this other little problem."

Keane nodded agreeably. "That sounds reasonable." He ignored Duffy's huffing and puffing. "You do seem to have a problem, Mr. Carlson."

"I don't have a problem," Carlson countered. His smile suffered a fractional slip. "You've got the problem, unless you don't want the fireworks."

"Oh, we'll have the fireworks, Mr. Carlson," Keane corrected with a smile Jo thought more wolfish than friendly. "According to paragraph three, section five, of the small business code, the lessor is legally bound by all contracts, agreements, liens and mortgages of the previous lessor until such time as all aforesaid contracts, agreements, liens and mortgages are expired or transferred."

"What the..." Carlson began with no smile at all, but Keane continued blandly.

"Of course, we won't pursue the matter in court as long as we get our merchandise. But that doesn't solve your problem."

"My problem?" Carlson sputtered while Jo looked on in frank admiration. "I haven't got a problem. If you think..."

"Oh, but you do, Mr. Carlson, though I'm sure there was no intent to break the law on your part."

"Break the law?" Carlson wiped damp hands on his slacks.

"Storing explosives without a license," Keane pointed out. "Unless, of course, you obtained one after your purchase of the warehouse."

"Well, no, I..."

"I was afraid of that." Keane lifted his brow in pity. "You see, in paragraph six of section five of the small business code it states that all licenses, permits and warrants shall be nontransferable. Authorization for new licenses, permits or warrants must be requested in writing by the current owner.

Notarized, naturally." Keane waited a bit to allow Carlson to wrestle with the idea. "If I'm not mistaken," he continued conversationally, "the fine's pretty hefty in this state. Of course, sentencing depends on—"

"Sentencing?" Carlson paled and mopped the back of his neck with a handkerchief.

"Look, tell you what." Keane gave Carlson a sympathetic smile. "You get the fireworks over here and off your property. We don't have to bring the law in on something like this. Just an oversight, after all. We're both businessmen, aren't we?"

Too overwrought to detect sarcasm, Carlson nodded.

"That was fifteen on delivery, right?"

Carlson didn't hesitate but stuck the damp handkerchief back in his pocket and nodded again.

"Good enough. I'll have the cash for you on delivery. Glad to help you out."

Relieved, Carlson turned and headed for his pickup. Jo managed to keep her features grave until he pulled off the lot. Simultaneously, Pete and Duffy began to hoot with laughter.

"Was it true?" Jo demanded and took Keane's arm.

"Was what true?" Keane countered, merely lifting a brow over the hysterics that surrounded him.

"'Paragraph three, section five, of the small business code,'" Jo quoted.

"Never heard of it," Keane answered mildly, nearly sending Pete into orbit.

"You made it up," Jo said in wonder. "You made it all up!"

"Probably," Keane agreed.

"Smoothest con job I've seen in years," Duffy stated and gave Keane a parental slap on the back. "Son, you could go into business."

"I did," Keane told him and grinned.

"I ever need a lawyer," Pete put in, pushing his cap further back on his head, "I know where to go. You come on by the cookhouse tonight, Captain. We're having ourselves a poker game. Come on, Duffy, Buck's gotta hear about this."

As they moved off, Jo realized that Keane had been officially accepted. Before, he had been the legal owner but an outsider, a towner. Now he was one of them. Turning, she lifted her face to his. "Welcome aboard."

"Thank you." She saw he understood precisely what had been left unsaid.

"I'll see you at the game," she said before her smile became a grin. "Don't forget your money."

She turned away, but Keane touched her arm, bringing her back to him. "Jo," he began, puzzling her by the sudden seriousness of his eyes.

"Yes?"

There was a brief hesitation, then he shook his head. "Nothing, never mind. I'll see you later." He rubbed his knuckles over her cheek, then walked away.

Jo studied her hand impassively. On the deal, she had missed a heart flush by one card and now waited for someone to open. Casually, she moved her glance around the table. Duffy was puffing on a cigar, apparently unconcerned with the dwindling chips in front of him. Pete chewed his gum with equal nonchalance. Amy, the wife of the sword swallower, sat beside him, then Jamie, then Raoul. Directly beside Jo was Keane, who, like Pete, was winning consistently.

The pot grew. Chips clinked on the table. Jo discarded and was pleased to exchange a club for the fifth heart. She slipped it into her hand without blinking. Frank had taught her the game. Before the second round of betting, Jamie folded in disgust. "Should never have taken Buck's seat," he muttered and frowned when Pete raised the bet.

"You got out cheap, kiddo," Duffy told him dolefully as he tossed in chips. "I'm only staying in so I don't change my standard of living. Money'll do that to you," he mumbled obscurely.

"Three kings," Pete announced when called, then spread his cards. Amid a flutter of complaints cards were tossed down.

"Heart flush," Jo said mildly before Pete could rake in the pot. Duffy leaned back and gave a hoot of laughter.

"Atta, girl, Jo. I hate to see him win all my money."

During the next two hours the cookhouse tent grew hot and ripe with the scents of coffee and tobacco and beer. Jamie's luck proved so consistently poor that he called for Buck to relieve him.

Jo found herself with an indifferent pair of fives. Almost immediately the betting grew heavy as Keane raised Raoul's opening. Curiosity kept Jo in one round, but practicality had her folding after the draw. Divorced from the game, she watched it with interest. Leaning on her elbows, she studied each participant. Keane played a good game, she mused. His eyes gave nothing away. They never did. Casually, he nursed the beer beside him while Duffy, Buck and Amy folded. Studying him closely, Pete chewed his gum. Keane returned the look, keeping the stub of his cigar clamped between his teeth. Raoul muttered in French and scowled at his cards.

"Could be bluffing," Pete considered, seeing Keane's raise. "Let's raise it five more and see what's cooking." Raoul swore in French, then again in English, before he tossed in his hand. Taking his time, Keane counted out the necessary chips and tossed them into the pot. It was a plastic mountain of red, white and blue. Then, he counted out more.

"I'll see your five," he said evenly, "and raise it ten."

There was mumbling around the table. Pete looked into his hand and considered. Shifting his eyes, he took in the generous pile of chips in front of him. He could afford to risk another ten. Glancing up, he studied Keane's face while he fondled his chips. Abruptly, he broke into a grin.

"Nope," he said simply, turning his cards face down. "This one's all yours."

Setting down his cards, Keane raked in a very sweet pot. "Gonna show 'em?" Pete asked. His grin was affable.

Keane pushed a stray chip into the pile and shrugged. With his free hand he turned over the cards. The reaction ranged from oaths to laughter.

"Trash," Pete mumbled with a shake of his head. "Nothing but trash. You've got nerve, Captain." His grin grew wide as he turned over his own cards. "Even I had a pair of sevens."

Raoul gnashed his teeth and swore elegantly in two languages. Jo grinned at his imaginative choice of words. She rose on a laugh and snatched off the soft felt hat Jamie wore. Deftly, she scooped her chips into it. "Cash me in later," she requested, then gave him a smacking kiss on the mouth. "But don't play with them."

Duffy scowled over at her. "Aren't you cashing in early?"

"You've always told me to leave 'em wanting more," she reminded him. With a grin and a wave, she swung through the door.

"That Jo," said Raoul, chuckling as he shuffled the cards. "She's one smart cracker."

"Cookie," Pete corrected, opening a fresh stick of gum. He noticed that Keane's gaze had drifted to the door she had closed behind her. "Some looker, too," he commented and watched Keane's eyes wander back to his. "Don't you think, Captain?"

Keane slipped his cards into a pile as they were dealt to him. "Jo's lovely."

"Like her mother," Buck put in, frowning at his cards. "She was a beaut, huh, Duffy?" Duffy grunted in agreement and wondered why Lady Luck refused to smile on him. "Always thought it was a crime for her to die that way. Wilder, too," he added with a shake of his head.

"A fire, wasn't it?" Keane asked as he picked up his cards and spread them.

"Electrical fire." Buck nodded and lifted his beer. "A short in their trailer's wiring. What a waste. If they hadn't been in bed asleep, they'd probably still be alive. The trailer was halfway gone before anybody set up an alarm. Just plain couldn't get to the Wilders. Their side of the trailer was like a furnace. Jo's bedroom was on the other side, and we nearly lost her. Frank busted in the window and pulled her out. Poor little tyke. She was holding onto this old doll like it was the last thing she had left. Kept it with her for I don't know how long. Remember, Duffy?" He glanced into his hand and opened for two. "It only had one arm." Duffy grunted again and folded. "Frank sure knew how to handle that little girl."

"She knew how to handle him, more likely," Duffy mumbled. Raoul bumped the pot five, and Keane folded.

"Deal me out the next hand," he said as he rose and moved to the door. One of the Gribalti brothers took the chair Jo had vacated, and Jamie slipped into Keane's. Curious, he lifted the tip of the cards. He saw a jack-high straight. With a thoughtful frown, he watched the door swing shut.

Outside, Jo moved through the warm night. With a glance at the sky, she thought of the fireworks. They had been wonderful, she mused, stirring up the stars with exploding color. Though it was over and a new day hovered, she felt some magic remained in the night. Far from sleepy, she wandered toward the Big Top.

"Hello, pretty lady."

Jo looked into the shadows and narrowed her eyes. She could just barely make out a form. "Oh, you're Bob, aren't you?" She stopped and gave him a friendly smile. "You're new."

He stepped toward her. "I've been on for nearly three weeks." He was young, Jo guessed about her own age, with a solid build and sharp-featured face. Just that afternoon she had watched Maggie give him a shower.

Jo pushed her hands into the pockets of her cut-offs and continued to smile. It appeared he thought his tenure made him a veteran. "How do you like working with the elephants?"

"It's okay. I like putting up the tent."

Jo understood his feeling. "So do I. There's a game in the cookhouse," she told him with a gesture of her arm. "You might like to sit in."

"I'd rather be with you." As he moved closer, Jo caught the faint whiff of beer. He's been celebrating, she thought and shook her head.

"It's a good thing tomorrow's Monday," she commented. "No one's going to be in any shape to pitch a tent. You should go to bed," she suggested. "Or get some coffee."

"Let's go to your trailer." Bob weaved a little, then took her arm.

"No." Firmly, Jo turned in the opposite direction. "Let's go to the cookhouse." His advances did not trouble her. She was close enough to the cookhouse tent that if she called out, a dozen able-bodied men would come charging. But that was precisely what Jo wanted to avoid.

"I want to go with you," he said, stumbling over the words

as he veered away from the cookhouse again. "You look so pretty in that cage with those lions." He put both arms around her, but Jo felt it was as much for balance as romance. "A fella needs a pretty lady once in a while."

"I'm going to feed you to my lions if you don't let me go," Jo warned.

"Bet you can be a real wildcat," he mumbled and made a fumbling dive for her mouth.

Though her patience was wearing thin, Jo endured the kiss that landed slightly to the left of bull's-eye. His hands, however, had better aim and grabbed the firm roundness of her bottom. Losing her temper, Jo pushed away but found his hold had taken root. In a quick move, she brought up her fist and caught him square on the jaw. With only a faint sound of surprise, Bob sat down hard on the ground.

"Well, so much for rescuing you," Keane commented from behind her.

Turning quickly, Jo pushed at her hair and gave an annoyed sigh. She would have preferred no witnesses. Even in the dim light, she could see he was furious. Instinctively, she stepped between him and the man who sat on the ground fingering his jaw and shaking the buzzing from his ears.

"He—Bob just got a bit overenthusiastic," she said hastily and put a restraining hand on Keane's arm. "He's been celebrating."

"I'm feeling a bit enthusiastic myself," Keane stated. As he made to brush her aside, Jo clung with more fervor.

"No, Keane, please."

Looking down, he fired a glare. "Jo, would you let go so that I can deal with this?"

"Not until you listen." The faint hint of laughter in her eyes only enraged him further, and Jo fought to suppress it. "Keane, please, don't be hard on him. He didn't hurt me."

"He was attacking you," Keane interrupted. He barely resisted the urge to shake her off and drag the still seated Bob by the scruff of the neck.

"No, he was really more just leaning on me. His balance is a trifle impaired. He only tried to kiss me," she pointed out, wisely deleting the wandering hands. "And I hit him much harder than I should have. He's new, Keane, don't fire him."

Exasperated, he stared at her. "Firing was the least of what I had in mind for him."

Jo smiled, unable to keep the gleam from her eyes. "If you were going to avenge my honor, he really didn't do much more than breathe on it. I don't think you should run him through for that. Maybe you could just put him in the stocks for a couple of days."

Keane swore under his breath, but a reluctant smile tugged at his mouth. Seeing it, Jo loosened her hold. "Miss Wilder wants to give you a break," he told the dazed Bob in a tough, no-nonsense voice that Jo decided he used for intimidating witnesses. "She has a softer heart than I do. Therefore, I won't knock you down several more times or kick you off the lot, as I had entertained doing." He paused, allowing Bob time to consider this possibility. "Instead, I'll let you sleep off your—enthusiasm." In one quick jerk, he pulled Bob to his feet. "But if I ever hear of you breathing uninvited on Miss Wilder or any other of my female employees, we'll go back to the first choice. And before I kick you out," he added with low menace, "I'll let it be known that you were decked by one punch from a hundred-pound woman."

"Yes, sir, Mr. Prescott," said Bob as clearly as possible.

"Go to bed," Jo said kindly, seeing him pale. "You'll feel better in the morning."

"Obviously," Keane commented as Bob lurched away, "you haven't done much drinking." He turned to Jo and grinned. "The one thing he's not going to feel in the morning is better." Jo smiled, pleased to have Keane talk to her without the thin shield of politeness. "And where," he asked and took her hand for examination, "did you learn that right jab?"

Jo laughed, allowing Keane's fingers to interlock with hers. "It would hardly have knocked him down if he hadn't already been tilting in that direction." Her face turned up to his and sparkled with starlight. In his eyes an expression she couldn't comprehend came and went. "Is something wrong?"

For a moment he said nothing. In her breast her heart began to hammer as she waited to be kissed. "No, nothing," he said. The moment was shattered. "Come on, I'll walk you back to your trailer."

"I wasn't going there." Wanting to put him back into an easy mood, she linked her arm with his. "If you come with me, I'll show you some magic." Her smile slanted invitingly. "You like magic, don't you, Keane? Even a sober, dedicated lawyer must like magic."

"Is that how I strike you?" Jo almost laughed at the trace of annoyance in his voice. "As a sober, dedicated lawyer?"

"Oh, not entirely, though that's part of you." She enjoyed feeling that for the moment she had him to herself. "You've also got a streak of adventure and a rather nice sense of humor. And," she added with generous emphasis, "there's your temper."

"You seem to have me all figured out."

"Oh, no." Jo stopped and turned to him. "Not at all. I only know how you are here. I can only speculate on how you are in Chicago."

His brow lifted as she caught his attention. "Would I be different there?"

"I don't know." Jo's forehead wrinkled in thought. "Wouldn't you be? Circumstances would. You probably have a house or a big apartment, and there's a housekeeper who comes in once—no, twice—a week." Caught up in the picture, she gazed off into the distance and built it further. "You have an office with a view of the city, a very efficient secretary and a brilliant law clerk. You go to business lunches at the club. In court you're deadly and very successful. You have your own tailor and work out at the gym three times a week. There's the theater on the weekends, along with something physical. Tennis maybe, not golf. No, handball."

Keane shook his head. "Is this the magic?"

"No." Jo shrugged and began to walk again. "Just guesswork. You don't have to have a great deal of money to know how people who do behave. And I know you take the law seriously. You wouldn't choose a career that wasn't very important to you."

Keane walked in silence. When he spoke, his voice was quiet. "I'm not certain I'm comfortable with your little outline of my life."

"It's very sketchy," Jo told him. "I'd have to understand you better to fill in the gaps."

"Don't you?"

"What?" Jo asked, pausing. "Understand you?" She laughed, tickled at the absurdity of his question. "No, I don't understand you. How could I? You live in a different world." With this, she tossed aside the flap of the Big Top and stepped into its darkness. When she hit the switch, two rows of overhead lights flashed on. Shadows haunted the corners and fell over the arena seats.

"It's wonderful, isn't it?" Her clear voice ran the length of the tent and echoed back. "It's not empty, you know. They're always here—the troupers, the audience, the animals." She walked forward until she stood beside the third ring. "Do you know what this is?" she asked Keane, tossing out her arms and turning a full circle. "It's an ageless wonder in a changing world. No matter what happens on the outside, this is here. We're the most fragile of circuses, at the mercy of the elephants, of emotions, of mechanics, of public whims. But six days a week for twenty-nine weeks we perform miracles. We build a world at dawn, then disappear into the dark. That's part of it—the mystery." She waited until Keane moved forward to join her.

"Tents pop up on an empty lot, elephants and lions walk down Main Street. And we never grow old, because each new generation discovers us all over again." She stood slender and exquisite in a circle of light. "Life here's crazy. And it's hard. Muddy lots, insane hours, sore muscles, but when you've finished your act and you get that feeling that tells you it was special, there's nothing else like it in the world."

"Is that why you do it?" Keane asked.

Jo shook her head and moved out of the circle of light into the dark and into another ring. "It's all part of the same thing. We all have our own reasons, I suppose. You've asked me that before; I'm not certain I can explain. Maybe it's that we all believe in miracles." She turned under the light, and it shimmered around her. "I've been here all my life. I know every trick, every illusion. I know how Jamie's dad gets twenty clowns into a two-seater car. But each time I see it, I laugh and I believe it. It's not just the excitement, Keane, it's the anticipation of the excitement. It's knowing you're going to see the biggest or the smallest or the fastest or the highest." Jo ran to the center ring and threw up her arms.

"Ladies and gentlemen," she announced with a toss of her head. "For your amazement and astonishment, for the first time in America, a superabundance of mountainous, mighty pachyderms led in a stupendous exhibition of choreography by the Great Serena." Jo laughed and shifted her hair to her back with a quick movement of her hand. "Dancing elephants!" she said to Keane, pleased that he was smiling. "Or you listen to the talker in the sideshow when he starts his spiel. Step right up. Come a little closer." She curled her fingers in invitation. "See the Amazing Serpentina and her monstrous, slithering vipers. Watch the beautiful young girl charm a deadly cobra. Watch her accept the reptilian embrace of the gargantuan boa. Don't miss the chance to see the enchantress of the evil serpent!"

"I suppose Baby might sue for slander."

Jo laughed and stepped up on the ring. "But when the crowds see little Rose with a boa constrictor wrapped around her shoulders, they've gotten their money's worth. We give them what they come for: color, fantasy, the unique. Thrills. You've seen the audience when Vito does his high wire act without a net."

"A net seems little enough protection when he's balancing on a wire at two hundred feet." Keane stuck his hands in his pockets and frowned. "He risks his life every day."

"So does a police officer or a fire fighter." Jo spoke quietly and rested her hands on his shoulders. It seemed more necessary than ever that she make him understand his father's dream. "I know what you're saying, Keane, but you have to understand us. The element of danger is essential to many of the acts. You can hear the whole audience suck in their breath when Vito does his back somersault on the wire. They'd be impressed if he used a net, but they wouldn't be terrified."

"Do they need to be?"

Jo's sober expression lightened. "Oh, yes! They need to be terrified and fascinated and mesmerized. It's all included in the price of a ticket. This is a world of superlatives. We test the limit of human daring, and every day it changes. Do you know how long it took before the first man accomplished the triple on the trapeze? Now it's nearly a standard." A light of anticipation flared in her eyes. "One day someone will do a quadruple. If a man stands in this ring and juggles three torches today, tomorrow someone will juggle them on horseback and after that there'll be a team tossing them back and forth while swinging on a trap. It's our job to do the incredible, then, when it's done, to do the impossible. It's that simple."

"Simple," Keane murmured, then lifted a hand to caress her hair. "I wonder if you'd think so if you could see it from the outside."

"I don't know." Her fingers tightened on his shoulders as he buried his other hand in her hair. "I never have."

As if his thoughts centered on it, Keane combed his fingers through her hair. Gradually, he pushed it back until only his hands framed her face. They stood in a pool of light that threw their shadows long behind them. "You are so lovely," he murmured.

Jo neither spoke nor moved. There was something different this time in the way he touched her. There was a gentleness and a hesitation she had not felt before. Though they looked directly into hers, she could not read his eyes. Their faces were close, and his breath fluttered against her mouth. Jo slid her arms around his neck and pressed her mouth to his.

Not until that moment had she realized how empty she had felt, how desperately she had needed to hold him. Her lips were hungry for his. She clung while all gentleness fled from his touch. His hands were greedy. The weeks that he had not touched her were forgotten as her skin warmed and hummed with quickening blood. Passion stripped her of inhibitions, and her tongue sought his, taking the kiss into wilder and darker depths. Their lips parted, only to meet again with sharp new demands. She understood that all needs and all desires were ultimately only one—Keane.

His mouth left hers, and for an instant he rested his cheek against her hair. For that moment Jo felt a contentment more complete than she had ever known. Abruptly, he drew away.

Puzzled, she watched as he drew out a cigar. She lifted a hand to run it through the hair he had just disturbed. He flicked on his lighter. "Keane?" She looked at him, knowing her eyes offered everything.

"You've had a long day," he began in an oddly polite tone. Jo winced as if he had struck her. "I'll walk you back to your trailer."

She stepped off the ring and away from him. Pain seared along her skin. "Why are you doing this?" To her humiliation, tears welled in her eyes and lodged in her throat. The tears acted as a prism, refracting the light and clouding her vision. She blinked them back. Keane's brows drew together at the gesture.

"I'll take you back," he said again. The detached tone of his voice accelerated all Jo's fury and grief.

"How dare you!" she demanded. "How dare you make me…" The word *love* nearly slipped through her lips, and she swallowed it. "How dare you make me want you, then turn away! I was right about you from the beginning. I thought I'd been wrong. You're cold and unfeeling." Her breath came quickly and unevenly, but she refused to retreat until she had said it all. Her face was pale with the passion of her emotions. "I don't know why I thought you'd ever understand what Frank had given you. You need a heart to see the intangible. I'll be glad when the season's over and you do whatever it is you're going to do. I'll be glad when I never have to see you again. I won't let you do this to me anymore!" Her voice wavered, but she made no attempt to steady it. "I don't want you to ever touch me again."

Keane studied her for a long moment, then took a careful drag on his cigar. "All right, Jo."

The very calmness of his answer tore a sob from her before she turned and ran from the Big Top.

Chapter 10

In July the troupe circled through Virginia, touched the tip of West Virginia on their way into Kentucky, then moved into Ohio. Audiences fanned themselves as the temperatures in the Big Top rose, but they still came.

Since the evening of the Fourth, Jo had avoided Keane. It was not as difficult as it might have been, as he spent half the month in Chicago dealing with his business. Jo functioned. She ate because eating was necessary in order to maintain her strength. She slept because rest was essential to remaining alert in the cage. She did not find any enjoyment in food nor was her sleep restful. Because so many in the troupe knew her well, Jo struggled to keep on a mask of normalcy. Above all, she needed to avoid any questions, any advice, any sympathy. It was necessary, because of her profession, to put her emotions on hold a great deal of the time. After some struggle and some failure, Jo achieved a reasonable success.

Her training of Gerry continued, as did his progress. The additional duty of working with him helped fill her small snatches of spare time. On afternoons when no matinee was scheduled, Jo took him into the big cage. As he grew more proficient, she brought other cats in to join Merlin. By the first week in August they were working together with her full complement of lions.

The only others who were rehearsing in the Big Top were the equestrian act. They ran through the Thread the Needle routine in the first ring. Hooves echoed dully on tanbark. Jo supervised while Gerry sent the cats into a pyramid. At his urging, Lazarus climbed up the wide, arched ladder that topped the grouping. Twice he balked, and twice Gerry was forced to reissue the command.

"Good," Jo commented when the pyramid was complete.

"He wouldn't go." Gerry began to complain, but she cut him off.

"Don't be in too much of a hurry. Bring them down." Her tone was brisk and professional. "Make certain they dismount and take their seats in the right order. It's important to stick to routine."

Hands resting on hips, Jo watched. In her opinion, Gerry had true potential. His nerves were good, he had a feeling for the animals, and he was slowly developing patience. Still she balked at the next step in his training: leaving him alone in the arena. Even with only Merlin, she felt it too risky. He was still too casual. Not yet did he possess enough respect for the lion's guile.

Jo moved around the arena, and the lions, used to her, were not disturbed. As the cats settled onto their pedestals, she once more moved to stand beside Gerry. "Now we'll walk down the line. You make each do a sit-up before we send them out."

One by one the cats rose on their haunches and pawed the air. Jo and Gerry moved down their ranks. The heat was becoming oppressive, and Jo shifted her shoulders, longing for a cool shower and a change of clothes. When they came to Hamlet, he ignored the command with a rebellious snarl.

Bad-tempered brute, thought Jo absently as she waited for Gerry to reissue the command. He did so but moved forward as if to emphasize the words.

"No, not so close!" Jo warned quickly. Even as she spoke, she saw the change in Hamlet's eyes.

Instinctively, she stepped over, nudging Gerry back and shielding his body with hers. Hamlet struck out, claws extended. There was a moment of blind heat in her shoulder as the skin ripped. Swiftly, she was facing the cat, holding tightly onto Gerry's arm as they stood just out of range.

"Don't run," she ordered, feeling his jerk of panic. Her arm was on fire as the blood began to flow freely. Keeping her movements quick but smooth, she took the whip from Gerry's nerveless hand and cracked it hard, using her left arm. She knew that if Hamlet continued his defiance and attacked, it was hopeless. The other cats were certain to join in a melee. It would be over before anything could be done. Already, Abra shifted restlessly and bared her teeth.

"Open the chute," Jo called out. Her voice was cool as ice. "Back toward the safety cage," she instructed Gerry as she gave the cats their signal to leave the arena. "I've got to get them out one at a time. Move slow, and if I tell you to stop, you stop dead. Understand?"

She heard him swallow as she watched the cats begin to leap off their pedestals and file into the chute. "He got you. Is it bad?" The words were barely a whisper and drenched in terror.

"I said go." Half the cats were gone, and still Hamlet's eyes were locked on hers. There was no time to waste. One part of her brain heard shouting outside the cage, but she blocked it out and focused all her concentration on the cat. "Go now," she repeated to Gerry. "Do as you're told."

He swallowed again and began to back away. Long seconds dragged until she heard the rattle of the safety cage door. When his turn came, Hamlet made no move to leave his seat. Jo was alone with him. She could smell the heat, the scent of the wild and the fragrance of her own blood. Her arm was alive with pain. Slowly, she tested him by backing up. The safety cage seemed hundreds of miles away. The cat tensed immediately, and she stopped. She knew he would not let her cross the arena. Outrunning him was impossible, as the distance between them could be covered in one spring. She had to outbluff him instead.

"Out," she ordered firmly. "Out, Hamlet." As he continued to watch her, Jo felt a trickle of sweat slide down between her shoulder blades. Her skin was clammy with it in contrast to the warmth of the blood that ran down her arm. There was a sudden, vivid picture inside her head of her father being dragged around the cage. Fear tripped inside her throat. There was a lightness fluttering in the top of her head, and she knew that a moment's terror would cause her to faint. She stiffened her spine and pushed it away.

Speed was important. The longer she allowed the cat to remain in the arena after his cue, the more defiant he would become. And the more dangerous. As yet he was unaware that he held her at such a sharp disadvantage. "Out, Hamlet." Jo repeated the command with a crack of the whip. He leaped from the pedestal. Jo's stomach trembled. She locked every muscle, and as the cat hesitated, she repeated the command. He was confused, and she knew this could work as an advantage or a curse. Confused, he might spring or retreat. Her fingers tightened on the stock of the whip and trembled. The cat paced nervously and watched her.

"Hamlet!" She raised her voice and bit off each syllable. "Go out." To the words she added the hand signal she had used before he was fully trained to voice command.

As if rebuffed, Hamlet relaxed his tail and padded into the chute. Before the door slid completely closed, Jo sank to her knees. Her body began to quake fiercely with the aftershock. No more than five minutes had passed since Hamlet had defied Gerry's command, but her muscles bore the strain of hours. For an instant her vision blurred. Even as she shook her head to clear it, Keane was on the ground beside her.

She heard him swear, ripping the tattered sleeve of her blouse from her arm. He fired questions at her, but she could do no more than shake her head and gulp in air. Focusing on him, she noticed his eyes were unusually dark against his face.

"What?" She followed his voice but not the words. He swore again, sharply enough to penetrate the first layer of her shock. He pulled her to her feet, then continuing the motion smoothly, lifted her into his arms. "Don't." Her mind struggled to break through the fog and function. "I'm all right."

"Shut up," he said harshly as he carried her from the cage. "Just shut up."

Because speaking cost her some effort, Jo obeyed. Closing her eyes, she let the mixture of excited voices whirl around her. Her arm screamed with pain, but the throbbing reassured her. Numbness would have terrified her. Still she kept her eyes shut, not yet having the courage to look at the damage. Being alive was enough.

When she opened her eyes again, Keane was carrying her into the administration wagon. At the sound of the chaos that followed them, Duffy strode through from his office. "What the…" he began, then stopped and paled beneath his freckles. He moved quickly forward as Keane set Jo in a chair. "How bad?"

"I don't know yet," Keane muttered. "Get a towel and the first-aid kit."

Buck had come in behind them and, already having secured the items, handed them to Keane. Then he moved to a cabinet and located a bottle of brandy.

"It's not too bad," Jo managed. Because her voice was tolerably steady, she screwed up her courage and looked down. Keane had fastened a rough bandage from the remains of her sleeve. Though the flow of blood had slowed, there were streaks of it down her arm, and too much spreading from the wound to be certain how extensive the cuts were. Nausea rocked in her stomach.

"How do you know?" Keane demanded between his teeth as he began to clean the wound. He wrung out the towel in the basin Buck set beside him.

"It's not bleeding that badly." Jo swallowed the queasiness. As her mind began to clear, she frowned at the tone of Keane's voice. Feeling her stare, he glanced up. In his eyes was such fury, she pulled away.

"Be still," he ordered roughly and gave his attention back to her arm.

The cat had delivered only a glancing blow, but even so, there were four long slices in her upper arm. Jo set her jaw as pain ripped through her. Keane's brusqueness brought more hurt, and she fought to show no reaction to either. The aftermath of fear was bubbling through her. She longed to be held, to be soothed by the hands that tended to her wound.

"She's going to need stitches," Keane said without looking at her.

"And an antitoxin shot," Buck added, handing Jo a generous glass of brandy. "Drink this, honey. It'll help settle you."

The gentleness in his voice nearly undid her. He laid his big hand against her cheek, and for a moment she pressed against it.

"Drink now," Buck ordered again. Obediently, Jo lifted the glass and swallowed. The room whirled, then snapped into focus. She made a small sound and pressed the glass to her forehead. "Tell me what happened in there." Buck crouched down beside her as Keane began to apply a temporary bandage.

Jo took a moment to draw air in and out of her lungs. She lowered the glass and spoke steadily. "Hamlet didn't respond, and Gerry repeated a command, but he stepped forward. Too close. I saw Hamlet's eyes, and I knew. I should have moved faster. I should have been watching him more carefully. It was a stupid mistake." She stared into the brandy as she berated herself.

"She stepped between the boy and the cat." Keane bit off the words as he completed the bandaging. Rising, he moved to the brandy and poured. Not once did he turn to look at Jo. Hurt, she stared at his back before looking back at Buck.

"How's Gerry?"

Buck urged the glass back to her lips. A faint tint of pink was creeping into her cheeks. "Pete's with him. Got his head between his knees. He'll be fine."

Jo nodded. "I guess I'll have to go to town and have this seen to." She handed the glass to Buck and wondered if she dare attempt to rise yet. With another deep breath, she glanced at Duffy. "Make sure he's ready to go in when I get back."

Keane turned from the window. "Go in where?" His face was set in hard lines.

In response, Jo's voice was chilled. "In the cage." She turned her eyes to Buck. "We should be able to have a short run-through before the evening show."

"No." Jo's head snapped up as Keane spoke. For a long moment they stared at each other with odd, unreasonable antagonism. "You're not going back in there today." His voice held curt authority.

"Of course I am," Jo countered, managing to keep the combination of pain and anger from her words. "And if Gerry wants to be a cat man, he's going in, too."

"Jo's right," Buck put in, trying to soothe what he sensed was an explosive situation. "It's like falling off a horse. You can't wait too long before you get back up, or you won't ride again."

Keane never took his eyes from Jo. He continued as if Buck hadn't spoken. "I won't permit it."

"You can't stop me." Indignation forced her to her feet. The brisk movement caused her arm to protest, and her struggle against it showed momentarily in her eyes.

"Yes, I can." Keane took a long swallow of brandy. "I own this circus."

Jo's fists tightened at his tone, at his careless use of his authority. Not once since he had knelt beside her in the cage had he given her any sign of comfort or reassurance. She had needed it from him. To masquerade its trembling, she kept her voice low. "But you don't own me, Mr. Prescott. And if you'll check your papers and the legalities, you'll see you don't own the lions or my equipment. I bought them, and I maintain them out of my salary. My contract doesn't give you the right to tell me when I can or can't rehearse my cats."

Keane's face was granite hard. "Neither does it give you the right to set up in the Big Top without my permission."

"Then I'll set up some place else," she tossed back. "But I *will* set up. That cat will be worked again today. I won't take the risk of losing months of training."

"But you will risk being killed," Keane shot back and slammed down his glass.

"What do you care?" Jo shouted. All control deserted

her. The cuts were deep on her emotions as well as her flesh. She had passed through a terror more acute than she had known since the night of her parents' death. More than anything else, she wanted to feel Keane's arms around her. She wanted to know the security she had felt when he had let her weep out her grief for Ari in his arms. "I'm nothing to you!" Her head shook quickly, tossing her hair. There was a bubble of hysteria in her voice, and Buck reached out to lay a hand on her shoulder.

"Jo," he warned in his soft, rumbling voice.

"No!" She shook her head and spoke rapidly. "He hasn't the right. You haven't the right to interfere with my life." She flared at Keane again with eyes vivid with emotion. "I know what I have to do. I know what I *will* do. Why should it matter to you? You aren't legally responsible if I get mauled. No one's going to sue you."

"Hold on, Jo." This time Buck spoke firmly. As he took her uninjured arm, he felt the tremors shooting through her. "She's too upset to know what she's saying," he told Keane.

There was a mask over Keane's face which concealed all emotion. "Oh, I think she knows what she's saying," he disagreed quietly. For a moment there was only the sound of Jo shuddering and the splash of brandy being poured into a glass. "You do what you have to do, Jo," he said after drinking again. "You're perfectly correct that I haven't any rights where you're concerned. Take her into town," he told Buck, then turned back to the window.

"Come on, Jo." Buck urged her to the door, slipping a supportive arm around her waist. Even as they stepped outside, Rose came running from the direction of the midway.

"Jo!" Her face was white with concern. "Jo, I just heard." She glanced at the bandage with wide, terrified eyes. "How bad is it?"

"Just scratches, really," Jo assured her. She added the best smile she could muster. "Buck's going to take me into town for a couple of stitches."

"Are you sure?" She looked up at the tall man for reassurance. "Buck?"

"Several stitches," he corrected but patted Rose's hand. "But it's not too bad."

"Do you want me to come with you?" She fell into step beside them as Buck began to lead Jo again.

"No. Thank you, Rose." Jo smiled with more feeling. "I'll be fine."

Because of the smile, Rose was able to relax. "I thought when I heard…well, I imagined all sorts of terrible things. I'm glad you're not badly hurt." They had reached Buck's truck, and Rose leaned over to kiss Jo's cheek. "We all love you so."

"I know." Squeezing her hand, Jo let Buck help her into the cab of his truck. As he maneuvered from the lot, Jo rested her head against the back of the seat and shut her eyes. Never could she remember feeling more spent, more battered.

"Hurt bad?" Buck asked as they switched to an asphalt road.

"Yes," she answered simply, thinking of her heart as much as her arm.

"You'll feel better when you're patched up."

Jo kept her eyes shut, knowing some wounds never heal. Or if they did, they left scars that ached at unexpected times.

"You shouldn't have gone off on him that way, Jo." There was light censure in Buck's voice.

"He shouldn't have interfered," Jo retorted. "It's none of his business. *I'm* none of his business."

"Jo, it's not like you to be so hard."

"Hard?" She opened her eyes and turned to Buck. "What about him? Couldn't he have been kinder, shown even the barest trace of compassion? Did he have to speak to me as if I were a criminal?"

"Jo, the man was terrified. You're only looking at this from one side." He scratched his beard and gave a gusty sigh. "You can't know what it's like to be outside that cage, helpless when someone you care about is facing down death. I had to all but knock him unconscious to keep him out of there until we got it through his head that he'd just get you killed for sure. He was scared, Jo. We were all scared."

Jo shook her head, certain Buck exaggerated because of his affection for her. Keane's voice had been hard, his eyes angry. "He doesn't care," she corrected quietly. "Not like the rest of you. You didn't swear at me. You weren't cold."

"Jo, people have different ways—" Buck began, but she interrupted.

"I know he wouldn't want to see me hurt, Buck. He's not heartless or cruel." She sighed as all the force of anger and fear washed out of her body and left her empty. "Please, I don't want to talk about him."

Buck heard the weariness in her voice and patted her hand. "Okay, honey, just relax. We'll have you all fixed up in no time."

Not all fixed up, Jo thought. Far from all fixed up.

Chapter 11

As the weeks passed, Jo's arm lost its stiffness. She healed cleanly. The only traces were thin scars that promised to fade but not disappear. She found, however, that some spark had gone out of her life. Constantly, she fought against a vague dissatisfaction. Nothing—not her work, not her friends, not her books—brought about the contentment she had grown up with. She had become a woman, and her needs had shifted. Jo knew the root of her problem was Keane, but the knowledge was not a solution. He had left the circus again on the very night of her accident. Nearly four weeks later he had not returned.

Three times Jo had sat down to write him, needing to assuage her guilt for the harsh things she had said to him. Three times she had torn up the paper in frustration. No matter how she rearranged the words, they were wrong. Instead, she clung to the hope that he would come back one last time. If, she felt, they could part as friends, without bitterness or hard words, she could accept the separation. Willing this to happen, she was able to return to her routine with some tranquility. She rehearsed, performed, joined in the daily duties of circus life. She waited. The caravan moved closer to Chicago.

Jo stood in the steaming Big Top on a late August afternoon. Dressed in a leotard, she worked on ground exercises with the Beirot Brothers. It was this daily regimentation that had aided in keeping her arm limber. She could now move into a back walk-over without feeling any protest in her injured arm.

"I feel good," Jo told Raoul as they worked out. "I feel really good." She did a quick series of pirouettes.

"You don't keep your shoulder in shape by dancing on your feet," Raoul challenged.

"My shoulder's fine," she tossed back, then proved her point by bending into a handstand. Slowly, she lowered her legs to a forty-five degree angle, bringing one foot to rest on the knee of the opposite leg. "It's perfect." She executed a forward roll and sprang to her feet. "I'm strong as an ox," she claimed and did a quick back handspring followed by a back flip.

She landed at Keane's feet.

The cascade of emotions that raced through her reflected briefly in her eyes before she regained her balance. "I didn't—I didn't know you were back." Instantly, she regretted the inanity of the words but could find no others. The longing was raw in her to hurl herself into his arms. She wondered that he could not feel her need through the pores of her skin.

"I just got in." His eyes continued to search her face after his hands dropped to his sides. "This is my mother," he added. "Rachael Loring, Jovilette Wilder."

At his words, Jo's gaze moved from his face. She saw the

woman beside him. If she had seen Rachael Loring in a crowd of two thousand, she would have known her for Keane's mother. The bone structure was the same, though hers was more elegant. Her brows were golden wings, flaring out at the end, as Keane's did. Her hair was smooth, brushed up and away from her face with no gray to mar its tawny perfection. But it was the eyes that sent a jolt through Jo. She had not thought to see them in anyone's face but Keane's. The woman was dressed simply in an unpretentiously tailored suit that bespoke taste and wealth. There was, however, none of the cool, distant polish that Jo had always attributed to the woman who had taken her son and left Frank. There was a charm to the smile that curved in greeting.

"Jovilette, such a lovely name. Keane's told me of you." She extended her hand, and Jo accepted, intending a quick, impersonal shake. Rachael Loring, however, laid her other hand atop their joined ones and added warmth. "Keane tells me you were very close to Frank. Perhaps we could talk."

The affection in her voice confused Jo into a stumbling reply. "I— Yes. I—if you'd like."

"I should like very much." She squeezed Jo's hand again before releasing it. "Perhaps you have time to show me around?" She smiled with the question, and Jo found it increasingly difficult to remain aloof. "I'm sure there've been some changes since I was here last. You must have some business to attend to," she said, looking up at Keane. "I'm sure Jovilette will take good care of me. Won't you, dear?" Without waiting for either to respond, Rachael tucked her arm through Jo's and began to walk. "I knew your parents," she said as Keane watched them move away. "Not terribly well, I'm afraid. They came here the same year I left. But I recall they were both thrilling performers. Keane tells me you've followed your father's profession."

"Yes, I…" She hesitated, feeling oddly at a disadvantage. "I did," she finished lamely.

"You're so young." Rachael gave her a gentle smile. "How terribly brave you must be."

"No…no, not really. It's my job."

"Yes, of course." Rachael laughed at some private memory. "I've heard that before."

They were outside now, and she paused to look thoughtfully around her. "I think perhaps I was wrong. It hasn't really changed, not in thirty years. It's a wonderful place, isn't it?"

"Why did you leave?" As soon as the words were spoken, Jo regretted them. "I'm sorry," she said quickly. "I shouldn't have asked."

"Of course you should." Rachael sighed and patted Jo's hand. "It's only natural. Duffy's still here, Keane tells me." At the change in subject, Jo imagined her question had been evaded.

"Yes, I suppose he always will be."

"Could we have some coffee, or some tea, perhaps?" Rachael smiled again. "It's such a long drive from town. Is your trailer nearby?"

"It's just over in the back yard."

"Oh, yes." Rachael laughed and began to walk again. "The neighborhood that never changes over thousands of miles. Do you know the story of the dog and the bones?" she asked. Though Jo knew it well, she said nothing. "One version is that a roustabout gave his dog a bone every night after dinner. The dog would bury the bone under the trailer, then the next day try to dig it back up. Of course, it was fifty miles behind in an empty lot. He never figured it out." Quietly, she laughed to herself.

Feeling awkward, Jo opened the door to her trailer. How could this woman be the one she had resented all of her life? How could this be the cold, heartless woman who had left Frank? Oddly, Rachael seemed totally at ease in the narrow confines of the trailer.

"How efficient these are." She looked around with interest and approval. "You must barely realize you're on wheels." Casually, she picked up the volume of Thoreau which lay on Jo's counter. "Keane told me you have an avid interest in literature. In language, too," she added, glancing up from the book. Her eyes were golden and direct like her son's. Jo was tossed back suddenly to the first morning of the season when she had looked down and found Keane's eyes on her.

It made her uncomfortable to learn Keane had discussed her with his mother. "I have some tea," Jo told her as she moved toward the kitchen. "It's a better gamble than my coffee."

"That's fine," Rachael said agreeably and followed her. "I'll just sit here while you fix it." She settled herself with apparent ease at the tiny table across from the kitchen.

"I'm afraid I haven't anything else to offer you." Jo kept her back turned as she routed through her cupboard.

"Tea and conversation," Rachael answered in mild tones, "will be fine."

Jo sighed and turned. "I'm sorry." She shook her head. "I'm being rude. I just don't know what to say to you, Mrs. Loring. I've resented you for as long as I can remember. Now you're here and not at all as I imagined." She managed to smile, albeit ruefully. "You're not cold and hateful, and you look so much like…" She stopped, horrified that she had nearly blurted out Keane's name. For a moment her eyes were utterly naked.

Rachael smoothed over the awkwardness. "I don't

wonder you resented me if you were as close to Frank as Keane tells me. Jovilette," she said softly, "did Frank resent me, too?"

Helpless, Jo responded to the hint of sadness. "No. Not while I knew him. I don't think Frank was capable of resentments."

"You understood him well, didn't you?" Rachael watched as Jo poured boiling water into mugs. "I understood him, too," she continued as Jo brought the mugs to the table. "He was a dreamer, a marvelous free spirit." Absently, she stirred her tea.

Consumed with curiosity, Jo sat across from her and waited for the story she sensed was coming.

"I was eighteen when I met him. I had come to the circus with a cousin. The Colossus was a bit smaller in those days," she added with a reminiscent smile, "but it was all the same. Oh, the magic!" She shook her head and sighed. "We tumbled into love so fast, married against all my family's objections and went on the road. It was exciting. I learned the web routine and helped out in wardrobe."

Jo's eyes widened. "You performed?"

"Oh, yes." Rachael's cheeks tinted a bit with pride. "I was quite good. Then I became pregnant. We were both like children waiting for Christmas. I wasn't quite nineteen when I had Keane, and I'd been with the circus for nearly a year. Things became difficult over the next season. I was young and a bit frightened of Keane. I panicked if he sneezed and was constantly dragging Frank into town to see doctors. How patient he was."

Rachael leaned forward and took Jo's hand. "Can you understand how hard this life is for one not meant for it? Can you see that through the magic of it, the excitement and wonder, there are hardships and fears and impossible demands? I was little more than a child myself, with an infant to care for, without the endurance or vocation of a trouper, without the experience or confidence of a mother. I lived on nerves for an entire season." She let out a little rush of breath. "When it was over, I went home to Chicago."

For the first time, Jo imagined the flight from Rachael's point of view. She could see a girl, younger than herself, in a strange, demanding world with a baby to care for. Over the years Jo had seen scores of people try the life she'd led and last only weeks. Still she shook her head in confusion.

"I think I understand how difficult it must have been for you. But if you and Frank loved each other, couldn't you have worked it out somehow?"

"How?" Rachael countered. "Should I have taken a house somewhere and lived with him half a year? I would have hated him. Should he have given up his life here and settled down with me and Keane? It would have destroyed everything I loved about him." Rachael shook her head, giving Jo a soft smile. "We did love each other, Jovilette, but not enough. Compromise isn't always possible, and neither of us were capable of adjusting to the needs of the other. I tried, and Frank would have tried had I asked him. But it was lost before it had really begun. We did the wisest thing under the circumstances." Looking into Jo's eyes, she saw youth and confidence. "It seems cold and hard to you, but it was no use dragging out a painful situation. He gave me Keane and two years I've always treasured. I gave him his freedom without bitterness. Ten years after Frank, I found happiness again." She smiled softly with the memory. "I loved Frank, and that love remains as young and sweet as the day I met him."

Jo swallowed. She searched for some way to apologize for a grudge held for a lifetime. "He—Frank kept a scrapbook on Keane. He followed the Chicago papers."

"Did he?" Rachael beamed, then leaned back in her chair and lifted her mug. "How like him. Was he happy, Jovilette? Did he have what he wanted?"

"Yes," Jo answered without hesitation. "Did you?"

Rachael's eyes came back to Jo's. For a moment the look was speculative, then it grew warm. "What a good heart you have, generous and understanding. Yes, I had what I wanted. And you, Jovilette, what do you want?"

At ease now, Jo shook her head and smiled. "More than I can have."

"You're too smart for that," Rachael observed, studying her. "I think you're a fighter, not a dreamer. When the time comes to make your choice, you won't settle for anything less than all." She smiled at Jo's intent look, then rose. "Will you show me your lions? I can't tell you how I'm looking forward to seeing you perform."

"Yes, of course." Jo stood, then hesitated. She held out her hand. "I'm glad you came."

Rachael accepted the gesture. "So am I."

Throughout the rest of the day Jo looked for Keane without success. After meeting and talking with his mother, it had become even more imperative that she speak with him. Her conscience would have no rest until she made amends. By showtime she had not yet found him.

Each act seemed to run on and on as she fretted for the finish. He would be with his mother in the audience, and undoubtedly she would find him after the show. She strained with impatience as the acts dragged.

After the finale she stood at the back door, unsure whether to wait or to go to his trailer. She was struck with both relief and alarm when she saw him approaching.

"Jovilette." Rachael spoke first, taking Jo's hands in hers.

"How marvelous you were, and how stunning. I see why Keane said you had an untamed beauty."

Surprised, Jo glanced up at Keane but met impassive amber eyes. "I'm glad you enjoyed it."

"Oh, I can't tell you how much. The day has brought me some very precious memories. Our talk this afternoon meant a great deal to me." To Jo's surprise, Rachael leaned over and kissed her. "I hope to see you again. I'm going to say goodbye to Duffy before you drive me back, Keane," she continued. "I'll meet you in the car. Goodbye, Jovilette."

"Goodbye, Mrs. Loring." Jo watched her go before she turned to Keane. "She's a wonderful person. She makes me ashamed."

"There's no need for that." He tucked his hands into his pockets and watched her. "We both had our reasons for resentments, and we were both wrong. How's your arm?"

"Oh." Jo's fingers traveled to the wound automatically. "It's fine. There's barely any scarring."

"Good." The word was short and followed by silence. For a moment Jo felt her courage fail her.

"Keane," she began, then forced herself to meet his eyes directly. "I want to apologize for the horrible way I behaved after the accident."

"I told you once before," he said coolly, "I don't care for apologies."

"Please." Jo swallowed her pride and touched his arm. "I've been saving this one for a very long time. I didn't mean those things I said," she added quickly. "I hope you'll forgive me." It wasn't the eloquent apology she had planned, but it was all she could manage. His expression never altered.

"There's nothing to forgive."

"Keane, please." Jo grabbed his arm again as he turned

to go. "Don't leave me feeling as if you don't forgive me. I know I said dreadful things. You have every right to be furious, but couldn't you—can't we be friends again?"

Something flickered over his face. Lifting his hand, he touched the back of it to her cheek. "You have a habit of disconcerting me, Jovilette." He dropped his hand, then thrust it into his pocket. "I've left something for you with Duffy. Be happy." He walked away from her while she dealt with the finality of his tone. He was walking out of her life. She watched him until he disappeared.

Jo had thought she would feel something, but there was nothing; no pain, no tears, no desperation. She had not known a human being could be so empty and still live.

"Jo." Duffy lumbered up to her, then held out a thick envelope. "Keane left this for you." Then he moved past her, anxious to see that all straggling towners were nudged on their way.

Jo felt all emotions had been stripped away. Absently, she glanced at the envelope as she walked to her trailer. Without enthusiasm, she stepped inside, then tore it open. She remained standing as she pulled out the contents. It took her several moments to decipher the legal jargon. She read the group of papers through twice before sitting down.

He's given it to me, she thought. Still she could not comprehend the magnitude of it. *He's given me the circus.*

Chapter 12

O'Hare Airport was an army of people and a cacophony of sound. Nearly losing herself in the chaos of it, Jo struggled through the masses and competed for a cab. At first she had merely gawked at the snow like a towner seeing his first sword swallower. Then, though she shivered inside the corduroy coat she had bought for the trip, she began to enjoy it. It was beautiful as it lay over the city, and it helped to turn her mind from the purpose of her journey. Never had she been north so late in the year. Chicago in November was a sensational sight.

She had learned, after the initial shock had worn off, that Keane had not only given her the circus but a responsibility as well. Almost immediately there had been contracts to negotiate. She had been tossed into a sea of paperwork, forced to rely heavily on Duffy's experience as she tried to regain her balance. As the season had come to a close, Jo had attempted a dozen times to call Chicago. Each time, she had hung up before Keane's number could be dialed. It would be, she had decided, more appropriate to see him in person. Her trip had been postponed a few weeks due to Jamie and Rose's wedding.

It was there, as she had stood as maid of honor, that Jo had realized what she must do. There was only one thing she truly wanted, and that was to be with Keane. Watching Rose's face as their vows had been exchanged, Jo had recalled her unflagging determination to win the man she loved.

And will I stay here? Jo had demanded of herself thousands of miles away from him. No. Her heart had begun to thud as she had mapped out a plan. She would go to Chicago to see him. She would not be turned away. He had wanted her once; she would make him want her again. She would not live out her life without at least some small portion of it being part of his. He didn't have to love her. It was enough that she loved him.

And so, shivering against the unfamiliar cold, Jo scrambled into a cab and headed across town. She brushed her hair free of snow with chilled fingers, thinking how idiotic she had been to forget to buy a hat and gloves. What if he isn't home? she thought suddenly. What if he's gone to Europe or Japan or California? Panic made her giddy, and she pushed it down. He has to be home. It's Sunday, and he's sitting at home reading or going over a brief—or entertaining a woman, she thought, appalled. I should stop and call. I should tell the driver to take me back to the airport. Closing her eyes, Jo fought to regain her calm. She took long, deep breaths and stared at the buildings and sidewalks. Gradually, she felt the tiny gurgle of hysteria dissipate.

I won't be afraid, she told herself and tried to believe it. I won't be afraid. But Jovilette, the woman who reclined on a living rug of lions, was very much afraid. What if he rejected her? I won't let him reject me, she told herself with a confident lift of her chin. *I'll seduce him.* She pressed her fingers to her temples. *I wouldn't know how to begin.* I've got to tell the driver to turn around.

But before she could form the words, the cab pulled up to a curb. With the precision of a robot, Jo paid the fare, over-tipping in her agitation, and climbed out.

Long after the cab had pulled away, she stood staring up at the massive glass-girdled building. Snow waltzed around her, sprinkling her hair and shoulders. A jostle from a rushing pedestrian broke the spell. She picked up her suit-cases and hurried through the front door of the apartment buildings.

The lobby was enormous, with smoked glass walls and a deep shag carpet. Not knowing she should give her name at the desk, Jo wandered toward the elevators, innocently avoiding detection by merging with a group of tenants. Once inside the car, Jo pushed the button for the penthouse with a nerveless forefinger. The chatter of those in the elevator with her registered only as a distant humming. She never noticed when the car stopped for their departure.

When it stopped a second time and the doors slid open, she stared at the empty space for ten full seconds. Only as the automatic doors began to close did she snap out of her daze. Pushing them open again, she stepped through and into the hall. Her legs were wobbly, but she forced them to move forward in the direction of the penthouse. Panic sped up and down her spine until she set down her bags and leaned her brow against Keane's door. She urged air in and out of her lungs. She remembered that Rachael Loring had called her a fighter. Jo swallowed, lifted her chin and knocked. The wait was mercifully brief before Keane opened the door. She saw surprise light his eyes as he stared at her.

Her hair was dusted with snow as it lay over the shoulders of her coat. Her face glowed with the cold, and her eyes were bright, nearly feverish with her struggle for calm. Only once did her mouth tremble before she spoke.

"Hello, Keane."

He only stared, his eyes running over her in disbelief. He was leaner, she thought as she studied his face. As she filled herself with the sight of him, she saw he wore a sweatshirt and jeans. His feet were bare. He hadn't shaved, and her hand itched to test the roughness of his beard.

"What are you doing here?" Jo felt a resurgence of panic. His tone was harsh, and he had not answered her smile. She strained for poise.

"May I come in?" she asked, her smile cracking.

"What?" He seemed distracted by the question. His brows lowered into a frown.

"May I come in?" she repeated, barely defeating the urge to turn tail and run.

"Oh, yes, of course. I'm sorry." Running a hand through his hair, Keane stepped back and gestured her inside.

Instantly, Jo's shoes sank into the luxurious pile of the buff-colored carpet. For a moment she allowed herself to gaze around the room, using the time for the additional purpose of regaining her composure. It was an open, sweeping room with sharp, contrasting colors. There was a deep brown sectional sofa with a chrome and glass coffee table. There were high-backed chairs in soft creams and vivid slashes of blue in chunky floor pillows. There were paintings, one she thought she recognized as a Picasso, and a sculpture she was certain was a Rodin.

On the far right of the room there was an elevation of two steps. Just beyond was a huge expanse of glass that featured a spreading view of Chicago. Jo moved toward it with un-disguised curiosity. Now, unexplicably, fear had lessened.

She found that once she had stepped over the threshold she had committed herself. She was no longer afraid.

"It's wonderful," she said, turning back to him. "How marvelous to have a whole city at your feet every day. You must feel like a king."

"I've never thought of it that way." With half the room between them, he studied her. She looked small and fragile with the bustling city at her back.

"I would," she said, and now her smile came easily. "I'd stand at the window and feel regal and pompous."

At last she saw his lips soften and curve. "Jovilette," he said quietly. "What are you doing in my world?"

"I needed to talk to you," she answered simply. "I had to come here to do it."

He moved to her then, but slowly, with his eyes on hers. "It must be important."

"I thought so."

His brow lifted, then he shrugged. "Well, then, we'll talk. But first, let's have your coat."

Jo's cold fingers fumbled with the buttons and caused Keane to frown again. "Good heavens, you're frozen." He captured her hands between his and swore. "Where are your gloves?" he demanded like an irate parent. "It must be all of twelve degrees outside."

"I forgot to buy any," Jo told him as she dealt with the heavenly feeling of his hands restoring warmth to hers.

"Idiot. Don't you know better than to come to Chicago in November without gloves?"

"No." Jo responded to his anger with a cheerful smile. "I've never been to Chicago in November before. It's wonderful."

His eyes lifted from her hands to her face. He watched her for a long moment, then she heard him sigh. "I'd nearly convinced myself I could be cured."

Jo's eyes clouded with concern. "Have you been ill?"

Keane laughed with a shake of his head, then he pushed away the question and became brisk again. "Here, let's have your coat. I'll get you some coffee."

"You needn't bother," she began as he undid the buttons on the coat himself and drew it from her shoulders.

"I'd feel better if I was certain your circulation was restored." He paused and looked down at her as he laid her coat over his arm. She wore a green angora sweater with pearl buttons and a gray skirt in thin wool. The soft fabric draped softly at her breasts and over her hips and thighs. Her shoes were dainty and impractical sling-back heels.

"Is something wrong?"

"I've never seen you wear anything but a costume or jeans."

"Oh." Jo laughed and combed her fingers through her damp hair. "I expect I look different."

"Yes, you do." His voice was low, and there was a frown in his eyes. "Right now you look as if you've come from college for the holidays." He touched the ends of her hair, then turned away. "Sit down. I'll get the coffee."

A bit puzzled by his mercurial moods, Jo wandered about the room, finally ignoring a chair to kneel beside one of the pillows near the picture window. Though the carpet swallowed Keane's footsteps, she sensed his return.

"How wonderful to have a real winter, if just for the snow." She turned a radiant face his way. "I've always wondered what Christmas is like with snow and icicles." Images of snowflakes danced in her eyes. Seeing he carried two mugs of coffee, she rose and took one. "Thank you."

"Are you warm enough?" he asked after a moment.

Jo nodded and sat in one of the two chairs opposite the sofa. The novelty of the city made her mission seem like a grand adventure. Keane sat beside her, and for a moment they drank in companionable silence.

"What did you want to talk to me about, Jo?"

Jo swallowed, ignoring the faint trembling in her chest. "A couple of things. The circus, for one." She shifted in her chair until she faced him. "I didn't write because I felt it too important. I didn't phone for the same reason. Keane…" All her carefully thought-out speeches deserted her. "You can't just give something like that away. I can't take it from you."

"Why not?" He shrugged and sipped his coffee. "We both know it's always been yours. A piece of paper doesn't change that one way or the other."

"Keane, Frank left it to you."

"And I gave it to you."

Jo made a small sound of frustration. "Perhaps if I could pay you for it…"

"Someone asked me once what was the value of a dream or the price of a human spirit." Jo shifted her eyes to his helplessly. "I didn't have an answer then. Do you have one now?"

She sighed and shook her head. "I don't know what to say to you. 'Thank you' is far from adequate."

"It's not necessary, either," Keane told her. "I simply gave back what was yours in any case. What else was there, Jo? You said there were a couple of things."

This was it, Jo's brain told her. Carefully, she set down the coffee and rose. Waiting for her stomach to settle, she walked a few feet out into the room, then turned. She allowed herself a deep breath before she met Keane's eyes.

"I want to be your mistress," she said with absolute calm.

"What?" Both Keane's face and voice registered utter shock.

Jo swallowed and repeated. "I want to be your mistress.

That's still the right term, isn't it, or is it antiquated? Is *lover* right? I've never done this before."

Slowly, Keane set his mug beside hers and rose. He did not move toward her but watched her with probing eyes. "Jo, you don't know what you're saying."

"Oh, yes, I do," she cut him off and nodded. "I might not have the terminology exactly right, but I do know what I mean, and I'm sure you do, too. I want to be with you," she continued and took a step toward him. "I want you to make love to me. I want to live with you if you'll let me, or at least close by."

"Jo, you're not talking sensibly." Sharply, Keane broke into her speech. Turning away, he thrust his hands into his pockets and balled them into fists. "You don't know what you're asking."

"Don't I appeal to you anymore?"

Keane whirled, infuriated with the trace of curiosity in her voice. "How can you ask me that?" he demanded. "Of course you appeal to me! I'm not dead or in the throes of senility!"

She moved closer to him. "Then if I want you, and you want me, why can't we be lovers?"

Keane swore violently and grabbed her shoulders. "Do you think I could have you for a winter and then blithely let you go? Do you think I could untangle myself at the start of the season and watch you stroll out of my life? Haven't you the sense to see what you do to me?" He shook her hard with the question, stealing any breath she might have used to answer him.

"You make me crazy!" Abruptly, he dragged her against him. His mouth bruised hers, his fingers dug into her flesh. Jo's head spun with confusion and pain and ecstasy. It seemed centuries since she had tasted his mouth on hers. She heard him groan as he tore himself away. He turned, leaving her to find her own balance as the room swayed. "What do I have to do to be rid of you?" His words came in furious undertones.

Jo blew out a breath. "I don't think kissing me like that is a very good start."

"I'm aware of that," he murmured. She watched the rise and fall of his shoulders. "I've been trying to avoid doing it since I opened the door."

Quietly, Jo walked to him and put a hand on his arm. "You're tense," she discovered and automatically sought to soothe the muscles. "I'm sorry if I'm going about this the wrong way. I thought telling you outright would be better than trying to seduce you. I don't think I'd be very good at that."

Keane made a sound somewhere between a laugh and a moan. "Jovilette," he murmured before he turned and gathered her into his arms. "How do I resist you? How many times must I pull away before I'm free of you? Even the thought of you drives me mad."

"Keane." She sighed and shut her eyes. "I've wanted you to hold me for so long. I want to belong to you, even for just a little while."

"No." He pulled away, then forced her chin up with his thumb and forefinger. "Don't you see that once would be too much and a lifetime wouldn't be enough? I love you too much to let you go and enough to know I have to." Shock robbed her of speech. She only stared as he continued. "It was different when I didn't know, when I thought I was— how did you put it? 'Dazzled.'" He smiled briefly at the word. "I was certain if I could make love to you, I could get you out of my system. Then, the night Ari died, I held you while you slept. I realized I was in love with you, had been in love with you right from the beginning."

"But you…" Jo shook her head as if to clear it. "You never told me, and you seemed so cold, so distant."

"I couldn't touch you without wanting more." He pulled her close again and for a moment buried his face in her hair. "But I couldn't stay away. I knew if I wanted to have you, to really have you, one of us had to give up what we did, what we were. I wondered if I could give up the law; it was really all I ever wanted to do. I discovered I wanted you more."

"Oh, Keane." She shook her head, but he put her from him suddenly.

"Then I found out that wouldn't work, either." Keane turned, paced to the window and stared out. The snow was falling heavily. "Every time you walked into that cage, I walked into hell. I thought perhaps I'd get used to it, but it only got worse. I tried leaving, coming back here, but I could never shake you loose. I kept coming back. The day you were hurt…" Keane paused. Jo heard him draw in his breath, and when he continued, his voice was deeper. "I watched you step in front of that boy and take the blow. I can't tell you what I felt at that moment; there aren't words for it. All I could think of was getting to you. I wonder if Pete ever told you that I decked him before Buck got to me. He took it very well, considering. Then I had to—to just stand there and watch while that cat stalked you. I've never known that kind of fear before. The kind that empties you out, body and soul."

He lapsed into silence. "Then it was over," he continued, "and I got to you. You were so white, and you were bleeding in my arms." He muttered an oath, then was silent again. He shook his head. "I wanted to burn the place down, get you away, strangle the cats with my bare hands. Anything. I wanted to hold you, but I couldn't get past the fear and the unreasonable anger at having been helpless. Before my hands stopped shaking, you were making plans to go back into that damnable cage. I wanted to kill you myself then and be done with it."

Slowly, Keane turned and walked back to her. "I saw it happen again every time I closed my eyes for weeks afterward. I can show you exactly where the scars are." He lifted a finger and traced four lines on her upper arm precisely where the claws had ripped her skin. He dropped his hand and shook his head. "I can't watch you go in the cage, Jo." He lifted his hand again and let it linger over her hair. "If I let you stay with me now, I wouldn't be able to let you go back to your own life. And I can't ask you to give it up."

"I wish you would." Solemn-eyed, Jo watched him. "I very much wish you would."

"Jo." Shaking his head, he turned away. "I know what it means to you."

"No more than the law means to you, I imagine," she said briskly. "But you said you were willing to give that up."

"Yes, but…"

"Oh, very well." She pushed back her hair. "If you won't ask me, I'll have to ask you. Will you marry me?"

Keane turned back, giving her his lowered brow frown. "Jo, you can't…"

"Of course I can. This is the twentieth century. If I want to ask you to marry me, then I will. I did," she pointed out.

"Jo, I don't…"

"Yes or no, please, counselor. This isn't an easy question." She stepped forward until they stood toe to toe. "I'm in love with you, and I want to marry you and have several babies. Is that agreeable?"

Keane's mouth opened and closed. He gave her an odd smile and lifted his hands to her shoulders. "This is rather sudden."

Jo felt a wild surge of joy. "Perhaps it is," she admitted. "I'll give you a minute to think about it. But I might as well tell you, I won't take no for an answer."

Keane's fingers traced the curve of her neck. "It seems I have little choice."

"None at all," she corrected. Boldly, she locked her arms around him and pulled his mouth down to hers. The kiss was instantly urgent, instantly searching. Joined, they lowered to the rug and clung. For a long, long moment, their lips were united in a language too complex for words. Then, as if to reassure himself she was real, Keane searched the familiar curves of her body, tasted the longed-for flavor of her skin.

"Why did I think I could live without you?" he whispered. His mouth came desperately back to hers. "Be sure, Jo, be sure." Roughened with emotion, his voice was low while the words were spoken against her lips. "I'll never be able to let you go. I'm asking you for everything."

"No. No, it's not like that. Hold me tighter. Kiss me again," she demanded as his lips roamed her face. "Kiss me." She wondered if the sound of pleasure she heard was his or her own. She had not known a kiss could be so intimate, so terrifyingly exciting. No, she thought as she soared with the knowledge that he loved her. He wasn't asking everything, he was giving it.

"I'm leaving something behind," she told him when their lips parted, "and replacing it with something infinitely more important." She buried her face in the curve of his neck. "When you realize how much I love you, you'll understand."

Keane drew away and stared down at her. At last he spoke, but it was only her name. It was a soft sigh of a sound. She smiled at it and lifted a hand to his cheek. "If there's a way to compromise…"

"No." She shook her head, remembering his mother's words. "Sometimes there can't be a compromise. We love each other enough not to need one. Please, don't think I'm making a sacrifice; I'm not." She smiled a little and rubbed her palm experimentally over the stubble of his neglected beard. "I don't regret one minute of my life in the circus, and I don't regret changing it. You've given me the circus, so I'll always be a part of it." Her smile faded, and her eyes grew serious. "Will you belong to me, Keane?"

He took her hand from his cheek and pressed it to his lips. "I already do. I love you, Jovilette. I'll spend a lifetime loving you."

"That's not long enough," she said as their lips met again. "I want more. I want forever."

With slow, building passion, his hands moved over her. Taking his time, he loosened the buttons on her sweater. "So beautiful," he murmured as his lips trailed down her throat and found the gentle swell. Jo's breath caught at the new intimacy. "You're trembling. I love knowing I can make your skin tremble under my hands." His lips roamed back to hers before he cradled her in his arms. "I've wanted to be with you, to hold you, just hold you, for so long. I can't remember not wanting it."

With a sigh washed with contentment, Jo snuggled against him. "Keane," she murmured.

"Hmm?"

"You never answered me."

"About what?" He kissed her closed lids, then tangled his fingers in her hair.

Jo opened her eyes. Her brows arched over them. "Are you going to marry me or not?"

Keane laughed, rolled her onto her back and planted a long, lingering kiss on her mouth. "Is tomorrow soon enough?"

* * * * *